THE

chosen

THE

chosen

VALKYRIE RISING

RAE Z RYANS

Published 2014 By Fictitious Publishing
www.fictitiouspublishing.com

The Chosen: Valkyrie Rising
Copyright © 2013 Rae Z. Ryans
ISBN 978-0-9916654-3-3 Paperback
ISBN 978-0-9916654-5-7 Hardback
ISBN 978-0-9916654-4-0 Electronic
www.raezryans.com

Cover and interior design: Raven Tree Design
www.raventreedesign.com

Editing: Jenny Carlsrud Sims
www.editing4indies.com

This book is for my grandmother, Velma Havard. May you rest among the stars, and may they offer you light among the darkness. It is also dedicated to those hiding within the darkness.

Contents

Dear Readers,

Thank you for purchasing Valkyrie Rising. This story is a complete work of fiction and not a simple retelling of Norse Mythology. A glossary is included for your reference, but detailed information can be found at raezryans.com

Mature audiences and those with an open mind will enjoy this chaotic tale of love and friendship best. In Valkyrie Rising, you'll find southern humor, action, magic, sexual scenes that involve heterosexual and homosexual couplings, and at least one scene involving light, playful spanking.

If any of the above subjects are offensive, I ask that you don't read past this point.

Ten percent of all proceeds from The Chosen: Valkyrie Rising will be donated to the Human Rights Campaign– fighting for lesbian, gay, bisexual, and transgender equality. I've long held a standing faith that love is love.

Thank you,
Rae Z. Ryans

NINE REALMS
GLOSSARY OF
TERMS, PLACES, AND
PEOPLE

The Nine Realms:
    Asgard, Alfheim, and Vanaheim make up the top tier, or upper realm.

    Midgard, Jotunheim, and Svartalfheim make up the middle tier, known as Middle Earth.

    Niflheim, Muspelheim, and Hel make up the Land of the Dead.

Midgard Languages of Magic:
    Old Norse, English, and Scottish Gaelic

LEADERS OF MIDGARD

The Order of the Nine:
    Council President: Merric Mc Douglas

    Faerie Liaison: Prince Duncan Graftfield

    Elven Liaison: Princess Maeve Graftfield

    Elementarist Liaison: Malinda Borne

    Giant Liaison: Queen Aegir Brekke

    Dwarven Liaison: King Norðri Goldsmith

Lycan Liaison: King Sköll Fenrir

Pooka Liaison: Grimmish Seedbearer

Vampire Liaison: Valentine De Luca

Hybrid Liaison: Prince Daniel Graftfield

Former Druid Liaison: Queen Morgana Graftfield

Army of the Void:

The Draugr order created by Lord Corentin, the Tempest. He's the original vampire and all vampires descend from him. However, the children of Valentine rule the AoV.

Gods, Demigods, and Mythical Creatures

Phoenix:

This is an aspect of the Goddess Freya. Children of the Phoenix inherit the power to invoke the Goddess, and strengthen their bond with the fiery elements of the Myst.

Loki:

A demi-god created by the Myst to bring balance among the gods.

Hugin and Munin:

Ravens that represent thought and memory.

Fenris Wolf:

The original Lycan created by Loki. The descendants are half-man and half-wolf and don't worship the Aesir.

Myst:

All life and magic originates with the Myst of the Nine Realms. It's a common reference for magic due to the misty glow it radiates. Mages and shamans harness it. The Myst can also manifest itself as an animal or person. It is the God of all Gods and is revered as such. He usually shows himself as Loki.

Norns:

Urðr ("What Once Was"), *Verðandi* ("What Is Coming into Being"), and *Skuld* ("What Shall Be")Weavers of fate and can change the past and future. They commonly use elementarists, with the gift of foresight, which to them are known as the norns or more commonly known as mages.

Ragnarok:
End of the world. It's also use to describe the unseating of the Gods.

Odin:
A complicated God, often considered being the All-father among his followers and himself. He's a member of the Aesir and associated with many aspects. Some of these include war, battle, victory and death, but also wisdom, Shamanism, magic, poetry, prophecy, and the hunt. However, there are many other Gods and Goddesses with the same attributes. He resides in Asgard.

Freya:
Goddess of love and fertility. In addition, she is the leader of the Valkyrie and receives half of the souls claimed in battle. Her hall is Sessrumnir, and her palace is Folkvang. She was originally a part of the Vanir.

Freyr:
King of Alfheim and God of sacral kingship, virility, and prosperity, with sunshine and fair weather. He is also the brother of Freya. He was originally a part of the Vanir.

Symbols

Brísingamen:
Talisman associated with the Goddess Freya and the Valkyrie. It's typically fashioned from rock or gemstone and etched with runes.

Valknut:
Symbol associated with Odin consisting of three interlocking triangles. It is said to represent the slain and unity.

Freya's Coat of Feathers:
A coat that can change the wearer into a falcon.

Runes:
> A language created by Odin consisting of the Elder Futhark has 24 runes.

Hybrid:
> The term can mean a mixture of races or classes. Also referred to as halfling, crossbreed, mutt, and other derogatory terms.

Lycan Codex:
> A set of honorable rules created by the original lycans for the safety of their people.

Races

Elementarist:
> These are supernaturals, with the ability to channel the elements. Each one typically specializes in one element, but they can draw from all four. They live an average life span of humans, but are immune to their diseases.

Faerie:
> A nation of supernaturals who gave magic to the nine realms. Pure Fae, born with various wings from butterfly to dragonfly shapes, tend to be in tune with magic more than nature. They are immortal, and their only weakness is solid iron mined in Alfheim.

Elf:
> Wingless Fae and often considered beneath the Fae. They tend to be in tune with nature more than magic. They are considered timeless, but their weakness is pure Alfheim iron.

Dwarf:
> Rarely found within Midgard, but are cousins to the Fae and Elves. While shorter than their kin, dwarves are much taller than the folk tales portray them. Males average sixty-five inches in height and females average sixty inches.

Lycan:
> Two-natured supernaturals that are half-human and half wolf, who can transform at any time into either form. However, during

a full moon they're known to cause mischief. Loki created the beings, and he gave them a place in Midgard. Lycans are typically born; however, there are ceremonies, which require the blessing of Loki to create these creatures. Pure *Alfheim* silver to the brain or heart will kill a Lycan. Other metals won't penetrate the skin.

Ethereal:

These ghosts of the supernatural remain in limbo on Midgard. In rare instances, a coma can cause the spirit to separate from the body.

Demons:

Also known as, the Dísir, are the original Valkyrie created by the Myst. Unlike the Norse legends, these Valkyrie can be male or female and they're born not chosen. They're fierce winged warriors of both magic and physical battle. But not all fight for the Light of the Nine Realms. There are legions that fight for the Darkness of Svartalfheim, which is the home of the former malevolent Unseelie Court of Alfheim, ruled by Queen Magda the Cruel.

Giants:

Unlike the name suggests this race is generally tall. Women and men alike reach heights close to seven and half feet. Most of the former Vanir pantheon was, in fact, of this race. Before Odin's rule, giants lived free primarily in the middle and lower realms. However, after coming into power he refused those without prestigious birth to the upper realms.

Dragons:

These neutral immortal beasts are rarely found on Midgard, but they do have the ability to shape shift into any creature or race. However, many of their lizard like attributes remain, such as their reptilian eyes, and their speech is often slithered. Their height typically gives them away as they tend to tower over the Fae and even some giants. The majority of the race lies under the protection of the God Freyr and the Seelie Court of Alfheim. Dragons also hold the ability to wield the Myst, but like the shamans and druids, they aren't limited like mages.

Classes

Valkyrie:

The Gods choose supernatural women of prominent heritage to assist the fallen warriors and heroes in Valhalla. As battles become scarce, and Ragnarok poses no threat, the women are unleashed upon Midgard with a new and unknown purpose.

Pooka:

Has the ability to turn into any living creature. Only faeries, elves, and hybrids have this ability. While dragons mimic the ability of the pooka, it was decided not to classify them as such. This class is also known as shape shifters.

Mage:

Elementarist, Faerie, Elf, Lycan, and some Vampires can harness the elements. However, like nature, a mage is unpredictable and dangerous. Elementarist mages tend to use one term to define themselves based on their elemental strength.

Phoenix:

They wield the power of the purest fire. Phoenix children are particularly vulnerable to sickness if the power is overused. Their eyes change color (golden) when the power fully manifests. They are also given the power of telepathy with their Guardian. Their goal is to protect the magical community and to protect the secret of magic from humankind.

Golem:

Much like the Phoenix except more common and they harness the earth. Golem children are in tune with nature and have exceptional patience. Eye color varies, but they gain the ability to shape shift into a rock golem. Their goal is to protect the magical community.

Maelstrom:

Like the Golem except they harness the power of air. Their walls of dust, fog, and tornados cause substantial damage. Their eyes are typically grey and they too help protect the magical community. Like the Phoenix, a maelstrom is a rarity, and they have the ability to become the storm if linked to a Dragon mage. Without the Dragon mage, they become a tornado.

Sea Dragon:

As rare as the Phoenix mage, the Sea Dragon wields the power of water and much like the Myst itself, its fluid and tranquility heals others. A Sea Dragon can self-heal in the body of fresh or salt water and it can shape shift into a sea dragon for underwater combat. They can also breathe underwater. They too protect the magical community.

Guardian:

Eyes are unnaturally green. Each has the ability to read minds of any super natural creature, but each individual becomes linked with a Phoenix. The prestige seems to be most common among the two-natured races; however, any supernatural race can become a Guardian of Magic and the Phoenix.

Draugr:

Similar to human mythology revolving around vampires. Creatures of the night but they can walk in daylight. They live off human or supernatural blood. They obtain immortality but a severed head or explosions can kill them. Humans and Elementarists can safely make the transition vampire. Elementarists carry any power they held before; however, threat of dementia is high. Elves and Faerie of Alfheim turn to dust. Lycans have shown little to no interest in becoming a vampire as they are already immortal.

The vampires are given protection by the Order of the Nine. They are rumored to have mutated from the Dark Elves of Svartalfheim, but it isn't certain. They are immune to theories such as sunlight, garlic, religious artifacts, but a stake to the heart can kill them. Vampires may only drink human blood and synthetic blood created by the Iron Legion. Animal blood sickens and weakens vampires leading to coma and eventual death.

Warden:

A created and born being that wields the power of submission. Through scientific discovery, the Nine found a way to combine all the magical essences into one being giving them incredible control over all magical creatures regardless of their family or previous condition. However, vampires are resistant and are, therefore, used to enforce them.

Druid:

A form of an elementarist that can utilize all forms of the Myst equally. Also known as a shaman. They're considered extinct on Midgard.

Bean Sidhe:

A Banshee that sees the future death of humans. Typically born as a human, and if not located by the supernatural world by their 16th birthday, they can cause great damage with their wails often resulting in death of those nearby.

The Hybrid:

A hybrid is much like a box of chocolates. One can never be sure which abilities will manifest and when. This includes high mages and Valkyries. Some view them as a threat, while others view them as the future of Midgard. The Nine enforces rules and conditions for hybrids, and those they cannot control are imprisoned.

chapter one

AURIEL GRAFTFIELD

New York City, NY 2014

Shades of death encircled my world. Tawny feathers floated from the sky. A gasp pinched my chest. Fire flashed on the horizon, bathing over the city, and then progressively swallowed the Nine Realms of the Myst. My eyes flew open, closed, then reopened, and I drew my dream journal from the nightstand drawer.

"How can I stop myself from burning the world into cindered ash if I don't understand this darkness tearing my light away?"

Each line and page was filled with my prophetic visions. More than one existed and like those journals, this one reflected the darkness of my secret. Every night another nightmare assaulted me as the light inched from of my soul; they grew bolder, and the death toll rose. White cleansing fire coated the world as if it were air. I blinked the weariness away.

The visions always came true, no matter how hard I tried to change the fate of those I loved. Auburn hair brushed the page and deft fingers swept it aside. Dry and wet golden splatters marred the white surface. I prayed for answers, guidance, and a ceasefire without the universe blowing up in my face.

"Gods, what have I done to anger you?" Why did I destroy when all I wanted was love?

As usual, the Gods offered no response. I sniffled and wiped my face. Blank lines taunted, daring me to write the mysterious secrets of my worlds. This journal would be different. I would alter the future or die trying.

Pages as bare as the future I ran away from four years ago awaited my thoughts. Downstairs bacon was frying; Momma whistled a tune. *Where did I go wrong?* My hand trembled, scribbling the words I didn't want to admit. Twenty-one years was a piss in the ocean, yet little ol' me managed to destroy the world. Daddy knocked on my bedroom door, and it creaked open.

"Mornin' Aurie," he said, stepping over the threshold carrying a mug of coffee. Timeless features chiseled his chin, elven ears pointed upward, and two blue eyes smiled as he set the cup on my nightstand. I forced my lips upward, returning the smile, and thanked him.

Not one to loiter, Daddy closed the door behind him. I waited as his footsteps pattered across the hardwood floor downstairs before I continued.

If someone asked me who would end the world, I would've said the humans. Before I ran, my job was protecting magic. All high mages enforced the Laws of the Myst. I was a Phoenix and master of elemental fire. At least I used to be before my family ventured into hiding.

The supernaturals I worked for turned on me. I tossed the pen down and refrained from chucking it across the bedroom. Knuckles cracked and my neck followed as I released the tension within my bones. The Council of the Nine despised my kind: hybrid. Hunted us down like rabid animals, all because we refused to live under their tyrannical control. I rolled from my bed, shuddering at the thought of living under the oppression of the Nine, and slipped into my favorite bunny slippers.

Hiding and fleeing were two things I learned at a young age, and it was possible that I didn't understand what normal meant, but I wanted it right alongside love. The doorbell chimed, and I glanced toward the bedroom door. Supernaturals were not normal. Shoulders slumped, I sipped my coffee and listened to the soft voices fluttering below. For one day, all I wanted was normality.

Truth settled in and chilled my bones. The warmth of the coffee penetrated my soul as I stared up at the white washed walls in our brownstone. Empty shelves lined my personal prison. Anything of importance fit into my duffel bag. Hot coffee, human television, and countless e-books filled my doldrum days. We rented the furniture and used delivery services for groceries. If I couldn't order it and have it delivered, I did not need it. The pages of my journal flipped closed as the chilly breeze swept through an open window.

My talisman warmed against my skin. I reached for my pillow, and the muffled cries died as the stone swung away from my skin. The Algiz, runic symbol for protection, glowed as the amulet increased in strength, and the stone flared with life.

Ribs and heart ticked like a bomb waiting to explode. Eyes whipped around, searching for anything or anyone to explain the sharp sear over my skin. I dropped my jaw, but nothing came out.

Shouts sounded in the distance, but the foreign words sounded muffled by the bustle of the Upper West Side. Voices rose from below as I tiptoed toward my closet and dragged my emergency bag from the shelf.

The Nine came for me; they had found me. Pain and thinking didn't mix. I paused, heart pounding within my ears, as the stairs creaked. My eyes flickered between the window and the door. Three sets of footsteps echoed their cadence.

The bag slung over my back, I wiggled my fat ass out the window, and I crept down the rickety fire escape adhered to my bedroom window. My stomach flipped with each sway or groan from the metal as my sweaty palms glided over the railing. *Did I stick to our plan, or fetch my parents first?* This marked the first time in four years that I'd had to move; the first time I'd ran as an adult.

The pendant scorched my skin as I descended the ladder that dropped into the alleyway. I winced and gnawed on the inside of my cheek as the tears built in my eyes. No supernatural was immune to pain.

Feet landed with a slight scuffle. The thumping of my heart vibrated through me, and my breath came in shortened gasps. Again, I gathered the talisman away from my skin. My gaze swept over the trash in the alleyway for signs of Momma or Daddy. Another shout drew my attention, and I struggled again to hear over the city noise. As the decibel grew stronger, I recognized the voice of my momma.

"We don't know where she is." Momma's tone borderlined on hysterical, shrieking as if she were a sidhe.

Another voice matching hers resonated inside my head. *"Run Auriel,"* the voice commanded, but I froze.

My legs weighed a million pounds, and my knees turned to jelly. They crashed to the glass littered ground, the shards rooting deep into my flesh and slicing through my skin. Tears flooded my vision, and my mouth opened to cry, but the sound refused to come. More shouts followed, as I fought to breathe and clutched at my chest.

Tears burned my eyes, and I choked on the piss and vinegar smells permeating through the alleyway. Pookas left an odor in their wake when they marked their territory. My back leaned against the brick wall, an ache spreading from my heart, but the hurt affecting me wasn't my own. I was an empath.

External wounds recovered as white Myst enveloped my body. Gashes mended, turning from red to pink to a faint white before they disappeared. A shriek ripped through the alley, and my eyes widened. Momma's emotions strengthened, and they ripped right through my shields. I fell under attack; my heart and soul struggled as the tears splashed, melding with my spilled blood on the ground.

Deep breaths recharged my nerves, and I asked the Myst to aid me. My hands grew warmer, and I envisioned the fiery white glow surrounding my body. It helped, but I still sensed her suffering.

"Aurie get out of here. Go, go now," Momma whimpered and pled with me. Her heart tore into shreds. My daddy remained silent, and I reckoned he shielded himself from me as he typically had before. Momma didn't have that luxury to offer.

"This is your last chance, Daniel. Where's Fainauriel?"

A deep breath filled my lungs, and my nose crinkled. Two-natured by her urine scent, but her green Myst read as a Guardian. At least she wasn't a Warden. Few knew me as Fainauriel; I often went by Aurie or Auriel. Wardens were like two-natured mages on steroids. Enforcers of the Nine and they had but one enemy.

Sure as heck wasn't little ol' me.

My parents said nothing. My lips lifted toward the sky and whispered a silent prayer to Freya and Freyr. The woman counted.

One … I crouched low and crawled toward the kitchen window. Two … Curiosity grabbed a hold of me, tangling its thick vines around me; my heart hammered and breathing burned my lungs. Three … My hand flew to my mouth as my leg slipped to the ground.

A shard of broken glass protruded from my left knee causing blood to ooze into my torn yoga pants. I reached down and grimaced; my stomach heaved at the crimson gash. Slippery fingers grasped the glass and yanked it free; my teeth clenched in hopes it softened the noise. Precious seconds passed, and the counting ended as I hobbled toward the brick wall.

Bang, Bang.

Gunpowder burned my nose as my eyes widened. I blinked; the view obscured by Momma's lacy curtains revealed nothing. Two shots fired. My breathing deepened.

Tears came, and they were my own. All senses, all feelings from my mother ceased. Lips quivered, blubbering in the air. Curses sounded from inside the townhouse. Teeth pressed into my lip, and I tore myself away from the window. Each step grew heavier, but not from the healed gash. A gaping hole existed inside my heart.

Momma and Daddy died; they were murdered because of my dang secrets. My head slammed against the brick wall, and I winced. Pain splintered my head, but it failed to distract my heart and soul. If there were an award for the worst daughter ever, I'd win.

The killer remained inside, but she'd find me if I stayed. *Move*, I moved. My teeth clenched against the sorrow building in my chest, and I ran. Thighs and lungs burned, screaming at my brain to stop. Faster than ever before, I ran as tears streamed down my face, blinding my vision. Ran, sniffled, ran, I turned and sniffled some more. My legs moved without real direction, as I weaved in and out of the Upper West Side.

"Stop, eun beag." A voice entered my mind. What the heck? He spoke partially in Scottish Gaelic, the magical language of mages. I tried to stop, heeding his advice pulsing through my head. The sidewalk had stayed wet throughout the morning, covered in spring dew, and I skidded into a lamppost. My rear hit the ground, and for once, I was thankful for the ample padding of my butt.

"Who is there?" I asked, staring down my legs at the fuzzy pink slippers. *No wonder I slid.* Thank goodness for the pole, or I would've ended up in the street.

The road crawled with humans. Their snickers reached my ears, but it allowed me some safety; the Nine wouldn't dare expose magic. Even as I talked to myself, no one paid me any attention. It was New York after all. I could have walked around naked, and no one would've cared. Maybe that was stretching the truth, but they sure didn't shock easily.

Supernaturals had lived everywhere on Earth amongst the unsuspecting humans. Scanning the length of the street, I didn't sense the familiar buzz of Myst, the life force and magic of all supernaturals. Just brownstones, shops, people, and the usual hustle and bustle of New York City revolved around me. Laughter escaped my lips, and a woman shot me a disapproving look. If she'd only known the reality of her little world, and that the truth was stranger than the imaginative fiction that paranormal lovers gobbled up. My eyes rolled as she passed without sparing a second glance.

Sometimes I wanted to scream at the top of my lungs and light up the sky. How many stern looks would that have garnered? I tossed the thought from my mind and concentrated on the voice from the street corner.

The inner voice was not my own, that much I believed. What I didn't understand was how or why it had spoken to me. Who could do this without my knowledge or a spell, let alone without my permission? Anything was possible.

I thought my momma did the same, and she was human. But the woman didn't use magic to dispatch my parents. My eyes widened, recalling the crime in the human world. Guns, knives, and bombs killed people. The supernatural world tended to enjoy barbaric methods. Decapitation, draining of blood or the Myst, and a silver knife through the heart were a few ways I knew would kill supernaturals. So why had she used a gun to murder my parents?

"You're just stressed," I sniffled, willing myself to stand. Each step became excruciating, with my heart breaking. Without my parents, I was lost. This was why they made me aware of the escape plan. Starting with my duffel bag and ending with a getaway vehicle.

They kept me sheltered for my own good. I was not human, and neither was Daddy. Walking shoulder to shoulder, packed against the morning commuters, I realized the importance of avoiding people. Each touch or brush threatened my shield, and without protection, I became a sitting duck.

With each street crossed, my head remained down. An occasional glance over my shoulder had revealed nothing out of the ordinary. Commuters chatted or texted. Cabs and cars honked. Every perfume or cologne ever created blended and the scents turned my stomach. But the humans and their side of our shared world could not bother my mind.

One thought repeated in my mind: I should've stopped her. My fist clenched, but the realization struck a chord. *Could I have stopped a bullet?*

"Please help me. Freya ..." I begged my patron Goddess through my sea of tears. Thunder rumbled in the distance as the rain started and assailed me from the sky. Umbrellas popped open but I didn't have one. Little notions like rain protection hadn't occurred to me.

The shield I'd constructed was heavy on my skin. My emotions flowed out of control as I jogged to the paid parking lot. As the morning progressed, more and more people joined the sidewalks, and the roads littered with exhaust spewing cabs. Too difficult to see if anyone followed me, everyone blended with everyone else.

One final glance over my shoulder and I ducked into the garage my parents used.

"Are you all right Miss? You look like ..." I stopped myself from glaring. The garage attendant, whose nametag read Jethro, showed genuine concern in his brown eyes. By the time I reached his booth, my chest heaved and burned for breath. I must've looked terrible if he'd left the confines of his plastic prison, but I doubted that was even his name. Who named their kid Jethro? I forced a smile and shook my head. *Humans, ugh, they're too nosy.* I passed him my ticket and identification. He studied it before repeating himself. My talisman no longer burned, but I remained cautious.

"Just trying to get out of the rain." His eyebrow rose, questioning my torn and bloodied yoga pants, slippers, and tank top I looked like something the tide had dragged in. And that was just my clothes. Knotted, rain soaked hair and make-up free face wasn't my usual look, and that probably didn't help matters either.

Cold outside this time of year, but the fire coursing through my veins allowed me to venture without heavy parkas, mittens, and those funny ear covers. Jethro's eyes narrowed, and he glanced over my shoulder. I followed his gaze as he said, "All right, I'll have this for you in a moment Miss Graftfield."

Heck … maybe I'd lost my mind. What if all this were some crazy dream? Nah, I wasn't that lucky, but I did wonder about my sanity. He reached in his booth and keys jingled. I shivered and rubbed my arms as he strolled from my view. A clock ticked over the sound of my heart. *No, I'm not a huge rush or anything, so take your time.* I kept those thoughts to myself. The thundering roar had settled into a gentle thump, but there was a long road ahead of me. I should've taken that time to develop a plan, but my mind refused to concentrate. This relentless, maddening idea of someone in my head bothered me. The fact that he knew danger stalked me … had he realized that I stayed forever in harm's way too? My existence mandated fleeing.

I leaned against the booth; even though I wasn't cold, the warmth of the plexiglass box had invited me in like a cozy blanket. This was all my fault. The running, no life, and now my parents' deaths too. Bloodied hands and they were mine.

If they hadn't had me, they would still be alive. I yearned for my journal, because I'd write the whole truth this time. The Norse Gods blessed me with powers beyond those of my peers, reaching beyond the Phoenix. I hadn't asked for them, and I didn't want them. They made me a threat in the eyes of the Nine who had tried to eradicate me more than once. The first time anyone saw, I was a day old. Another tear slid down my cheek. That was why we ran and why Momma and Daddy left the Nine before my birth. Somehow, they knew I'd be different.

"Miss Graftfield," said the valet, pulling up in a brand new truck. The leather interior wafted to where I stood. It was a welcome sight because the old Bronco was a good for nothing piece of junk.

"Just sign here and you can be on your way." A quick scribble and he handed me the keys. I mumbled thanks and climbed into the cab. My knees jammed into the steering wheel as a light curse left my lips. "Everything all right?" he asked.

The seat sat too close for my longer than average legs. "Yeah, how do I push the seat back? I can't find a lever."

He laughed as my hand fumbled underneath the seat.

"They ain't had them down yonder in years. O'ere on the side," Jethro said, pointing to the tiny levers. My cheeks heated as he pushed the lever up and down.

"This one here does lumbar support." He grinned, and my eyes widened at his protruding fangs. Draugr, I didn't care for them at all, but I wasn't afraid of them even though I hadn't met many before. Hollywood blew them out of proportion all of the time. According to my studies, they were relatively harmless, and there was a treaty keeping them in line. Granted, I guessed to a human, they were frightening.

"Thanks again," I muttered and wished to the Gods that there was a user manual. Situated and comfortable, I sat behind the wheel of the Ram truck, and realized I didn't have anywhere to go. Jethro eyed me, but said nothing more as my hands gripped the steering wheel. The truck was a beast, and I wasn't certain I could maneuver it. Well heck, I couldn't even figure out how to move the seat back for my five-foot-ten frame. Daddy usually drove even though I had a license.

My breath released in a steady stream, and I pulled onto the street. Here went nothing. A driver laid on his horn, and I slammed on the brakes. Hands white-knuckled the wheel. His fist shook at me, and his mouth moved releasing a string of curses. *Look before you pull out*, I chided and glanced around before easing onto the road.

"Now what?"

"*Head south, eun beag ... home.*" I leapt clear out of my skin. My head pounded against the roof as my foot gunned the gas pedal. By the grace of the Gods, I slammed the brakes again, barely missing a parked car.

What happened to me? *Think, Auriel, think ... South, what on the Gods' green earth laid south?* The Nine wanted me, dead or alive.

A storm brewed, and I stood at the center. The eye of the tempest whipped around me. It pushed and pulled against me like a maelstrom. Tears blinded my vision, and the ache shredded my tender heart. Home was South Carolina, but the Nine laid in wait there too.

"South," I whispered and wiped my eyes dry. I'd do this; I was stronger than this.

Checking my mirrors and tossing my blinker on, I waited for an opening. I couldn't just sit there and wallow. If the Nine caught me then my parents died for nothing. They sacrificed more than their lives for me. I must use their memory to press on and find their killer. Justice; I would take it come hell or high water.

Smoke poured from my palms at the thought of vengeance. Melted plastic surrounded my grip on the steering wheel, but it didn't burn me. Fire never burned my skin, but the same wasn't true for the remaining elements I wielded.

Silence within the truck took a toll on me. I used to love it— losing myself in a sort of serenity— but now it reminded me that I was alone.

At first, I tried to find something on the radio, but it led to one sad song after another. The news hadn't been much better, except to alert me of the gridlock I'd face until I crossed into New Jersey. Until I drove south of Washington DC, it wouldn't get any better.

"Why?" I asked myself, but I already knew the answer revolved around little ol' me. The gifts the Gods had bestowed upon me were a burden to anyone who dared to help. They'd done nothing but ruin my life. In order to stop hurting everyone I had once loved, I had to forget them.

The only memories that remained were the last four years on the run and of the small town of Six and Twenty in South Carolina from when I was just a little girl. Momma said I'd gone and done it to myself, but when I asked her why, she kept silent. Daddy just changed the subject. There was only one thing to do now—I had to press forward and stop dwelling in the past.

In Delaware, I stopped to rest my burning eyes. The headlights and passing cars were beginning to blend together. I watched the families and travelers with interest.

How'd they react if I kindled a fireball?

Sitting on the stone bench, I giggled at the idea and drew their stares. One law the majority of magical folk agreed with was to keep the secret.

After the Myst created humans, the Nine decreed they were not to wield our powers. The Gods blessed a few, but for the majority of humanity, they knew nothing of our world.

The Nine Council said humans were far too weak and corruptible to wield the Myst. I begged to differ. Supernaturals were just as guilty and corruptible. Were my dreams not proof enough?

Darkness dragged me down, wild lycans tore at my tender flesh, and Midgard burned and scorched in my cleansing fire. It was enough to scare anyone, and that included me. Dreams and visions cursed us all as they threatened Ragnarok.

I blew out my breath and sighed as a group of friends walked by. Their laughter and smiles warmed my soul even if I was the source of their amusement. None of it mattered now, I trusted no one, and friends didn't come easy to me. All I had left were my journals and an annoying voice inside my head. One of the girls giggled and pointed in my direction.

"At least I'm not six pounds of sugar in a five pound bag," I mumbled and lifted my chin higher. I was more than my dishelved appearance and fuzzy slippers.

Empathy just didn't mix with any society. I'd love to find others like me. No fear of exposing my divine side by some freak, hand-shaking, future seeing tragedy. *There's one place … Six and Twenty.*

"Go south the voice said," I mocked. My eyes rolled, and I wondered if I was going mad. Maybe everything took its toll, and insanity pulled ahead. Who the heck listened to the voices in their heads anyhow?

Oh right, I did.

I'd called it quits again in Virginia. Beyond exhausted, my body had nearly tuckered itself out. Even with the magic coursing through my veins, I couldn't keep going without rest and at least a few hours of sleep.

The vacancy sign flashed in a steady rhythm, and I pulled into the motel. A dive, but I couldn't leave a paper trail either. Places like

Value Sleep accepted cash, and they didn't ask too many questions. The Nine knew all about human technology and magic allowed them to avoid security barriers. They'd find me in a heartbeat if I swiped a credit card now.

The door jingled its beautiful song as it swung open. With haste, I paid for my room, ignoring the greasy man behind the desk as much as possible, and pushed my remaining Myst into another shield. The creepazoid's interest faded quickly, but I wouldn't let my guard down.

As I opened the hotel room door, the musty stench of skanky filth singed my nostrils. Eyes scanned over each object –there wasn't much –a chair and table, and the bed and nightstand. If the moaning from next door stood as any indication then the bed had touched tons of naked bodies … skin gross … doing who knew what … Their fluids mixing and sinking in, clinging to the mattress and sheets … I cringed at the mere thoughts and images flipping through my mind as the wall rattled.

I flicked on the light setting on the nightstand. My eyes blinked, adjusting to the brightness, when I saw a peculiar stain on the wall. It glistened as if still wet.

"No way," I said, leaning closer. My mouth dropped open, staring at the dark rusty stain. "Blood … well ain't that just peachy. What next, a dang body under the bed?"

I tossed my items on the tabletop, praying no one used it, and sat in the chair. Supernatural beings weren't naïve. I knew about sex and hormones, but my secrets kept me from both worlds. They didn't leave time for boyfriends or relationships.

My head fell into my hands, and I stared at the curtains. "So much has happened," I whispered to myself, half hoping the voice spoke again. My lips curled up, and I snorted when nothing happened. Maybe he'd direct me to a more sanitary hotel or the nut house. Funny how things worked like that; I wondered how many people found solace in their insanity. Desperate times called for desperate measures.

I tried sleeping, but sleep refused to come. Still sitting in the chair –I refused to touch the bed – my mind raced about in circles. My parents weren't ever far from my thoughts. Was it any worse than thinking about the nastiness crawling on my skin? No, not really, but I stood at an impasse.

What'd they think during those last moments? Did they feel any pain? Were they proud of me or did they regret having me?

This would get me nowhere. My breath hissed through my teeth, and I shook my head. All terrible thoughts aside, I concentrated on my parents' stories.

Generations were both American, but like most supernaturals, our ancestry hailed from Europe. The blood coursing through my veins consisted of Scottish, Viking, and English from the human side, and part frost giant and Unseelie elf from the supernatural tree.

The Nine separated everyone by blood and then again by their ability. They tiered off again depending upon secondary abilities. According to their laws, I was too powerful, and a cell waited with my name on it in Charlestown, South Carolina.

But I knew the truth. My great aunt tried to sacrifice me to Odin, and she sat of the Council of the Nine Realms. A tear fell, and I swiped it away. That was why we ran. Was the memory of a world that wanted me dead or locked away any better? Some parts of life were expendable, but not my parents.

Myst wouldn't bring them back, but I refused to let them go. Finally giving up on sleep, I decided to go through my bag. Idle hands and all that devilish crap. Besides, changing into some real clothes might cheer me up some. A shower too, but they couldn't pay me to get into the one here.

I dumped my black duffel bag; clothes, toiletries, a change of shoes–thank goodness–and a large, ordinary manila envelope poured out. Before then, I hadn't recalled seeing it. Cash, clothes, and sometimes new identities, but Daddy conjured those. My lip pulsed as I bit into my flesh. The weight grew heavy in my hand, and I tried to place it aside, but I couldn't.

Was it important? Why else would Momma or Dad put it in my bag? I tore into it. Two silver-scrolled envelopes were inside of it. But I wasn't ready to read the one addressed to me. The second was for a Paulo Skyland of Six and Twenty, South Carolina.

"That's where I was born," I whispered, clutching the letter to my chest.

I dozed off around three am. The nightmares returned, consuming my thoughts, as I lost the heavy-lidded battle.

"It is done, my lady," an unfamiliar voice said to me, but I couldn't reply or act. I remained nothing more than a bystander, as usual.

My head turned scanning the battle scene unfolding around me. Bodies scattered the earth, flocks of ravens flew over the corpses, and the only light shining came from the world set ablaze. My gaze dropped to my hands. Fingers gripped a silver metal shield and a jeweled sword, bloodied with the life force of others. Around my waist was a black leather belt with a rough sheath hanging from its rung. I dressed in dark brown leather that did little for the imagination.

"The secret will remain safe now." The words left my mouth. How I stayed composed was beyond me. Inside, the real me quivered as I sheathed my weapon. No. This bitter woman couldn't become the future me.

"They asked for it and were given fair warning. The Nine is pleased with our progress," I hissed at the dark-haired man whose mouth dripped with blood. Draugr ... gross. On the inside, I cringed.

He grasped my free hand and brought it to his heart. As our lips touched, the blood mingled in my hungry mouth. Hatred coursed through me at the idea. I wouldn't make such a stupid decision. Draugr weren't the worst of supernaturals, but the idea of slavery to blood disgusted me.

"Come, my love. Let us move on. We haven't much more time." The word love echoed in my mind. We parted; I noted the slight sheen of flame licking at his pale skin. The draugr held the Myst.

My nightmare flashed forward to a small town hall.

I stood before at least fifty shaking, wide-eyed people. The tall podium hid my body, but I wore more clothing this time. My shield rested upon my back, forcing my broad shoulders wider, the weighty sword dangling beneath my long, wine-colored cloak.

"You were warned time and again to follow the rules. How many warnings did you think we'd give before we took action?" I bellowed to the townsfolk, who murmured amongst themselves in the large hall. When they looked back upon me, their eyes—hollowed, endless, and nightmarish globes— judged me. I saw my startled expression within the blackened pools reflecting back to me. What were they? I'd never laid my eyes upon creatures such as these.

A tall young man entered the room; thick expansive shoulders sat atop his muscular body. He was different with his unkempt reddish hair, and he gazed at me as if searching for something. When he glanced away, the glowing green eyes appeared defeated, broken, and there were tears threatening to fall. A Guardian, but who was he charged with protecting?

My soul pulled toward him in both dream form and reality. His grief beckoned me. For some reason that I couldn't explain, the need to rush into his arms and hold him washed over me. Instead, my dream figure summoned white fire, the wall built and halted at my feet, and the ravens returned. The gut wrenching screams of people filled the air and mixed with the screeches; the smoke rose from the burning victims.

They didn't fight back.

"You must pay the price for your defiance," I said, sickened by my actions in both states. There remained a tiny amount of solace; I didn't enjoy the carnage I created. The stranger held his ground, as the flames licked at his body, but his eyes did not leave mine. A whisper reached my ears. The draugr beckoned me to kill him. I couldn't do it. Green, smoky Myst swirled around my visitor, and in a flash, he disappeared.

I woke up with a start, shooting up off the grime-covered bed. Eww, how did I get over here? Drenched in sticky sweat, my shirt was plastered to my body. My heart pounded, resonating and rattling in my head. I attempted to shake away the haziness, maneuvering through my strange surroundings, seeking my journal. Once I found it, I scrambled to write my new and unsettling dream down.

The wickedness I'd done sent involuntary shivers running down my spine. How could I have slaughtered innocent people, people just trying to survive?

The book dropped to the floor and opened to the previous entry. Stapled to the page was his photograph. No, I'd remember a gorgeous man with glowing green eyes and rusty sunset hair. Yet as I flipped the pages, he reappeared in my writing as both human and lycan.

I stared at the photograph. He appeared younger, a teenager maybe, but it was the man from my dreams. New purpose burned within me. I must find him and the meaning behind his existence within my visions. Six and Twenty came first. I redressed, slipping out of the sweat-drenched tank top and into clothing from my bag. I swam in the larger clothing, but it was better than smelling as if I hadn't showered. After gathering up my meager belongings, I closed the door and dropped off the key in the night box.

My eyes scanned the parking lot as a prickle rolled over my skin. That wasn't unusual when another mage was nearby. Parked next to my truck sat a dark sedan. I blinked, noticing the hum vibrating from inside. Glass crashed and drew my attention away. *"Go eun beag,"* he said.

I'd do whatever it took to stop these dreams and the voices. My head nodded, and a lump formed in my throat. A lycans walked around the hotel dumpster. Something about his blue eyes spoke to me. He nodded, as if reading my thoughts, and my heart rate increased.

My hand hit the unlock button on the key fob, and I walked toward the truck. Our eyes didn't falter as we assessed each other. Like a stray dog, it was foolish to approach a shifted lycans. My eyebrow rose, and the massive beast lowered his head. His eyes darted to the dark sedan and then back to me. Was he protecting me? The lycan nodded again, and my eyes widened.

"You are in my head ..."

"Aye, south eun beag, and no more stopping."

"No rest for the wicked," I muttered, and I shut the truck door. One simple churning motion and the engine roared to life. I headed home.

chapter two

LIAM SKYLAND

A Guardian's job never ceased even if they didn't have a charge. That was me, but I still read the Myst and watched for her. She would come one day, but that was all I had understood from the Oracle's prophecy.

Heaviness washed through the evening air and coated my skin. This disturbance wasn't human. Not quite magical either. Whatever headed to Six and Twenty held pieces from both worlds, and I was drawn to it like flies to honey.

My hand ran over my face. "The Oracle."

Yes, she always knew more. Keelan Graftfield remained our resident psychic mage. A powerful ice –water and air – mage, nothing got past the old woman. The crazy, eccentric bat saw into the future. I'd waited four years already, but the Oracle refused to tell me when. She'd said I'd feel *it* when I met her. I didn't know what she meant but guessed I'd know somehow. My eyes lifted toward the starry sky. Until then, I dreamed.

With a weighty sigh and crackling stretch, I undressed, not wanting to shred my favorite jeans. The transformation from man to beast took years of daily practice to master. The noise of all my bones cracking, the skin dissolving under layers of thick, glossy fur that replaced it, and of course there was the act of watching the torso twist and contort. Gruesome came to mind, but I eventually got used to it.

A pelt replaced my tan, tattooed skin, and I shook my new coat violently, as I relished the muggy breeze rushing through it. My muzzle aimed into the purple sky, and my call rippled over the cricket chirps and tree frog songs; it alerted my team that I'd shifted.

"Thought you were on vacation?" Nick asked telepathically.

Like the rest of Six and Twenty, I too was a supernatural. As an earth mage-lycan hybrid and a Guardian of the Dísir, it made me a sought after combination. Sought meaning they'd rather kill me than lock my furry ass up in their fancy prison. The Nine despised me for it as they did most supernaturals refusing their control, but being born as the King's bastard son equated death.

"Yep. Make sure to double check all the boundaries, something's ... off," I said, replying in the same manner.

Nickolas Kerr was a massive pureblooded lycan and my best friend. Beast might've been a better word, biggest I'd ever laid eyes on. Nick was closer to four feet tall shifted at the head, and nearer to seven feet as a human. He enjoyed reminding me of those facts, since we were also pack cousins but not blood related.. I laughed; he had a good three inches on me in both forms.

"I sense it too, but don't fear it, Liam." His laughter resonated through my head.

Our colorings, however, were an irregular pattern of salt and pepper grey. All that remained of my previous features were my green eyes, and three birthmarks located on my biceps. The raised marks mirrored the moon phases, with a valknut below – two marks combined. Guardian mark of triple horns and the Fenrir mark of the triple moon – in the center, but the opposite bicep resembled an ash tree; Yggdrasill: the tree of life from which all nine realms stemmed from.

"You're keeping secrets, Nick." It wasn't the first time; I'd always suspected there was more to him and his sister than either led on.

"I'll let Reggie know about the borders," Nick said, ignoring my comment, and I shook my furry head.

His secrets didn't bother me as much as having Regin all alone. We shouldn't both take off work; we were the best defense this town had against the Nine. She wasn't adept in magic since she was just a lycan. Nick was a Phoenix too, which meant he'd the ability to cast spells like a mage.

"Any special plans?" I gave my coat another vigorous shake as I ran toward Mrs. Graftfield's house, stopping only to catch any off scents, but I found nothing. At least I could relax a bit easier. The Nine hadn't breached the community's defenses.

"Out of town," Nick channeled into my mind. *"What are you up to?"*

"Seeing the Oracle, besides you know shifting is the new green." I laughed back at him, and if I'd seen his face, I'd bet he rolled his eyes. We weren't pooka, but both races used the term shifting or changed. Pooka chose different animals, and I envied the choice.

Years had passed since the Nine had last attempted to penetrate our defenses. Because of it, I feared the town council had grown slack. Little stopped the Nine from waltzing in and capturing us all. The town remained shielded, but that was put in place for humans. I pleaded with my dad to find alternatives, but the response remained no.

"Why do we need more defenses? It's been years since they last tried to break through." He'd always refuted my attempts.

Sure, Dad was correct, but if they tried now we'd have a real hard time holding them off. Loki help us, if they'd ever came in with a mighty force, we'd lose. I shivered at the thought of my family and friends in captivity—forced to rot in magical prisons – and betray their kind. There was always death, if we were lucky. My momma had been lucky.

A war was coming, brewing and melding outside our shields, but this community was not prepared.

When I arrived, Mrs. Graftfield waited on her front porch, rocking without a care in the world. Her walker sat in front of her, teetering as if she'd just stepped out. She knew I'd come; I always did when the Myst shifted.

"You feel it too, Liam?" Her voice croaked, and I padded up the short stairs. My tongue lolled out and panted. She patted my head, scratching in the right spot behind my ears, and a soft whimper left my maw.

"She is coming, but there is danger. Another seeks her too, and they are closing in." She spoke in gentle tones, keeping me calm. Keelan Graftfield seldom talked with deep fondness for anyone but my soul mate. I'd asked her about it before, but she'd shrugged and never told me.

A scowl fell across her wrinkled face. "The one who follows has yet to decide. He is torn between his mission and what is right." Her eyes rolled back into her head. My heart rate increased, beating faster with each second.

"Fiery tears will fall and purify the waters. Wings of peaked mountains will cleanse the air. Blood will cover the world of Midgard." The Oracle's voice deepened, and it sounded like two speaking as one. I shook my head; that wasn't possible. The Oracle's eyes and voice returned to normal as soon as the thought crossed my mind.

"You must prepare yourself. It's a long road ahead of us, and Liam, she will need your protection."

After returning from Mrs. Graftfield's house, I tried settling down. *She* came, and the Nine was not far behind. I didn't know which unnerved me more; battle, or the one who was prophesized as my soul mate. I shut my eyes, stretching out on my wraparound front porch, and pictured her. My imagination ran away, showing me long blond hair, a slender body, and beautiful blue eyes. I prayed: Gods, please let her look just like I imagined.

From the histories, there weren't many fair-haired Phoenixes. Instead, they all tended to have hints of red or auburn, like my older brother, but a man could dream.

"Yeah man, keep on dreaming." Nick laughed at me. He was lucky I wasn't near him.

"Is he brooding about the girl again?" Regin piped in, and my cheeks warmed. They'd both heard me talk at lengths about the prophecy and the woman. Madness and laughter resulted every time. I loved a good jibe, but talk of my mysterious woman embarrassed me.

What if she didn't like me? The question was not far from my mind. Fated didn't promise an easy outcome. I still remembered sitting around the campfire and listening to the Oracle talk about the day my destiny began. The words were simple enough to recall, though I couldn't remember how old I was, when she first told the story:

"Many centuries ago, there remained a secret society of druids, who called upon the spirit of the Phoenix. They'd sought answers on how to restore the balance between good and evil before humanity destroyed itself. The humans called it the great flood, but it served as a cleansing during Ragnarok. The Phoenix listened as the druids spoke about magic falling into the hands of those who'd use it to destroy Midgard. However, the Phoenix reminded them darkness always existed as long as there was light in the Nine Realms. In the beginning, there'd been the Myst, and it created the light and darkness. When each race came to be, the Myst bore each supernatural with both in their hearts. The Phoenix vowed to come back to give her answer after seven days, and if needed, a solution. After seven days, she returned as promised, but refused to intervene. Instead, she offered this prophecy.

"Today I grant each of you with an extraordinary power, each one will be unique. You will become resistant to disease, sickness, and non-lethal injuries. When you die, your power will be absorbed into the spirit, which will be reborn into another.

"When all of the powers granted reunite, a child will be born with my whole essence, holding power greater than any other being. This bloodline will become the defenders of all that lives. She or he will restore the balance and bring peace to mankind."

"But how can the spirit be reborn if we never die?" one of the druids asked.

"Ah, but that is where each of you will have to make the decision. Decide whether your life is greater than the restoration of balance," she replied, but then added a warning, "Keep the secret of magic safe, but most of all keep the Phoenix out of mortal hands. I will imbue them with great power. They are dangerous weapons in the wrong hands. Failure will bring not lone destruction, but the end of goodness in this plane for all." And with her final warning delivered, the Phoenix burst into a ball of golden flame.

A lot of myth and fairy tales painted into her tale. Odd how I saw it now, but as a kid, I hadn't questioned any of her legends.

There were different versions families passed down to their children and our multitude of races allowed such variations to develop. Still the Phoenix, Golem, Maelstrom, and Dragon mages making up the Dísir, and their Guardians were real. For my brother and I were walking proof. Families, the immortal races were present that day and they were alive and kicking.

While she'd fibbed parts of this prophecy to small children, she wasn't lying about my soul mate. A spark within me burned for her to return. It lay in wait for my soul mate, as if on some strange level, it knew her more than the conscious me did. If that wasn't confirmation, than I didn't know what was. My spirit called her home, home to my heart, and into my life. She was mine.

CHAPTER THREE

JAMISON MC DOUGLASS-SKYLAND

I remained calm and lingered far enough away from Fainauriel. She wouldn't recognize my car, or me, not after she forgot. My hand flicked the turn signal, and I pulled onto the exit ramp. I'd tried approaching her over the past four years, but either she didn't have a clue or her parents intervened.

They hadn't forgotten me, but sent me packing nonetheless. Aurie spooked easier than I remembered. She hadn't seemed to ever leave her house in New York either. I turned left at the light and searched for her truck. Now was not the time to reveal myself. She'd been weary of strangers, humans above other supes, because she didn't understand them. We'd learned their history along with our own growing up, but Aurie couldn't wrap her mind around the hatred and destruction they'd caused. I sighed, missing those days when we'd hang out and talk.

One day she'd up and left us, so I left home to find her. The best chance I'd found meant joining the Nine. They'd searched for her too but failed. People disappeared all the time, but Aurie's fading proved far too mysterious to ignore. How often did a girl wipe herself away, including the memories of those who loved her? Some of us remembered; the Phoenixes who shared her fire element didn't forget.

What surprised me most was when Liam failed to remember her too. After all, he was her Guardian and according to the damned Oracle, they were soul mates. I wasn't perfect, but neither was my half-brother. On the outside, Liam appeared faultless, and he got everything he wanted.

My life yielded the opposite, but I worked hard. At twenty-three, and after three and half years, I had finally closed in on Aurie. She'd not belong to me, Nick and Keelan had said. There's a bit of truth there, but that part of my heart died. I sighed recalling the salty scent as if it were yesterday. The Gods took my love away from me, but I alone took responsibility for his death. My heart still ached and called for him. After he'd died and Aurie ran away, I'd filled the void with finding her. She remained the one piece in the puzzle I held the power to change.

I loved her; we all loved Aurie in our own ways. But love and friendship were only half the reasons I'd sought her. "Damn it." I slammed my fist into the steering wheel, wincing as my bone radiated in pain.

No, the Oracle hated me. She'd not stand for my polluted blood, and the old bat even found a way to rob me of my Phoenix. As a slap in the face, she imbued Liam with my power, my birthright. The names she'd called me that night rang through my head. I shook it, removing the horrid words. He'd promised to protect me from her, but Nick hadn't rescued me. He died. I'd fallen in love all right, but not with her precious Aurie. My eyes burned, but I swallowed the pain. It was my badge of shame, and I'd bear it. My heart belonged to Nick, and I'd killed him. If that made me tainted, so be it.

Up ahead, I recognized her red truck at a hotel that looked straight out of a horror movie. The place gave new meaning to the creeps. My head shook; she deserved better. I considered the cracked and peeling blue paint, sidewalks littered with trash, and a rust-colored stain bleeding into a suspicious spot outside the first unit.

Yeah, she deserved better than this.

The office door swung wide, and she waltzed out, anger and revulsion etched across her soft features. My heart hammered, aching at the sight of my lost friend. By Nine decree, it had become my responsibility to capture the Dísir, but I struggled with the decision. The Nine allowed some to remain free, like Liam, but what made her so special? We'd grown up together, and I guaranteed she would not harm a bee trying to sting her. I hissed a breath through my teeth. From the sidelines, I watched as the community went crazy and forgot everything, forgot about her. How, I didn't know, but I supposed potent magic. Just like the potent magic that was required to remove another mage's power, but this wasn't like the Oracle. I remembered, and if she'd wanted anyone to forget, it would've been me.

"You're still a mage," Merric and Paulo both reminded me. I told them both where they could stick their notions of fatherhood. My fingers whitened as I clenched the wheel. Vengeance; someday I'd have it on the Nine. They murdered my mother. Passed unfair laws sanctioning whom we'd love. My head leaned on the wheel as Aurie walked into her room. They'd dared to call humans barbaric, but at least they hadn't condemned each other to death over love. Sure, there'd always be the hate groups and religious zealots in the world no matter what laws existed, but the Nine ruled over the supernaturals, and they seldom changed laws. Nick and I had hid even within the so-called free community, but it hadn't mattered.

In the end, I'd killed him and all chances for true love. This void threatened to swallow me in darkness. I needed to love her, to love someone again, and let the light in. *Get your crap together, man.*

I worked my nerve up and stepped from my car. My hand dragged through my unmanageable hair. Damn, I couldn't recall the last time I was nervous. *Right before I kissed him*, I shook my head at the memory, stepped toward her door, and let out my breath in a jagged blow.

"Reòta," a familiar Scotsman said behind me. I froze in place as his Myst caressed me. My eyes closed; his hot breath danced over my neck. Nick … my eyes opened, widening with a combination of joy and shock. He'd survived … Sköll said he killed them all. It'd drain my magic reserves to break free of his spell, even if it was to kiss him.

My eyes darted around as footsteps drew closer. "There tis ken chance in Hel I'm gonna let ye near her, Jamie," he said, standing behind me. His breath brushed against my neck again, and I swallowed hard.

"Why if it isn't Nikolas … Fenrir, does your uncle know you're still alive?" Goading a lycan Phoenix probably wasn't the best idea, but I pushed his buttons. Anything to see his face again. The fact that Nikolas hadn't killed me on the spot meant he cared. The last time we'd parted, I'd run away again to the Nine, and he was supposedly dead.

He snorted in my ear. "She is no' yers and ne'er was."

I chuckled. Even if I found a way to win her over, she'd not be him. But we'd make a solid match, a front for the Nine, and one they'd never see coming. We held similar goals if she would remember them. In my heart, Aurie wouldn't replace him. No one did, and I had tried. They didn't make my blood simmer or gasp for air like Nicky.

"Ye lost the right to call me that, dearie," Nick replied, reading my mind. I had always called him Nicky when I was younger. I blinked, as my heart ached. He grabbed my arms but didn't touch my palms. Smart doggy; mages absorbed power through our hands. Nick tossed me into my backseat; my head smacked into the door, and I winced.

I was too tall to actually fit but nowhere near his size. Gods, I hated lycans. My eyes narrowed on his cold blue gaze. I hated lycan Phoenixes' even more. Crazy hybrid, he'd pay.

"She's not yours either, flea bag," I muttered. He crawled on top of me, shoving his knee between my thighs. Nikolas punched me in the stomach as a grimace pulled my lips back, and a groan escaped. I puckered my lips in a mocked kiss refusing to give him the satisfaction. Although he had every right to hate me. "Yeah, love you too mutt."

The truth at last. Gods, I loved my Nicky, but he hadn't forgiven me yet, and he might never find a way to let the past go. I sighed as he shoved my knees into my chest and slammed the door. Stupid mistakes had a way of haunting me.

Nick stayed close as the night progressed, and I held in my emotions. My thoughts tampered down too. The Dísir's minds connected, but our bond weaved deeper. I was Nicky's mate until the day I died, and I wanted him more than revenge.

CHAPTER FOUR

AURIEL

Somewhere on I-85, Virginia

A yawn left my mouth, and I shook it away. I rolled onto the asphalt highway as the sun lightened the sky. The pinkish hue awakened serenity, and the stars were fast asleep. A calming effect smoothed over my mind, as I drove down I-85. Tall, swaying sugar maples lined the road, mixing with lofty pines. Wildflowers grew untamed over the median strip, tinting the green grass lavender and burnt orange. It lay before me like picturesque spring, unlike the chilly northern April. The closest I'd witnessed were those few times I'd ventured into the park to reconnect with nature.

My truck swerved and rattled over the rumble strip. My eyes jarred forward, and my heart raced in tune with the shuddering madness the ribbon created as my tires thudded along it. With a squelched shriek, my hands jerked the wheel left. Mages were not immune to death by driver stupidity.

Before long, my mind wandered again, but back to the dream this time. The images I recalled twisted and churned my stomach. A draugr ... ew, ew, ew. I didn't understand why anyone chose slavery over freedom. Cold, dead, and the inability to love were three reasons why I would not want to date a draugr. The thought alone gave me a spine-chasing willy, leaving me dancing and antsy in my seat.

The destruction and execution were far worse than the idea of a bloodsucker boyfriend, but I didn't want to contemplate that. At the same time, I could not ignore it. *Were my hands capable of murder?* Yes, I thought as much. High mages hunted and captured or killed anyone disobeying the laws of magic, but the memory loss wiped out most of my training. Every person, supernatural or human, was able to kill. The realism factor laid enrooted in our survival tactics, all but ingrained into our DNA, but to deny the truth made us nothing more than a bunch of liars. When push came to shove, and all that jazz, we fight for what we held in our hearts.

So why did I run away like a frightened sissy child instead of facing my parent's murderer? My rights as their child allowed me vengeance, true. Instead, I ran away like a panicky snot-faced kid. Scared, yes I was, and confused too. The voice hadn't helped either, but I should've taken a stand against their murderer. I learned something though; I didn't want to repeat my actions again. Auriel Graftfield ran away with her tail tucked between her legs no longer. The woman in the dream made the supernaturals, or supes, tremble and beg. The influence of her presence scorched into my veins. My left foot stomped and my hands ached from gripping the wheel. Past or present, the woman remained me. While I didn't want to hurt anyone, I refused to become helpless and weak again. The hiding and running stopped now.

Satisfied, I chuckled. Either I'd lost my dang mind, or I'd changed. The town remained hours away, but I'd made decent time. My mind drifted onto another memory. I hoped it proved beneficial to my sanity. If not I'd overanalyze the dream until I was more confused than a chameleon in a packet of Skittles.

Speculation was a game I often played when bored. I didn't recall my life all that much before we ran and I cast the memory spell, but I retained a working idea of life in the communities. There was but one speculative question now... Was it the same Six and Twenty I remembered from my childhood? Such a strange name, so I doubted there was more than one.

I'd ask Paulo about it. My eyes rolled with little effort as I listened to myself. He was going to hate me, and I'd sound like a nagging child. There were more questions than I could count. Did he know me? What were my parents like before we ran? Were they always that uptight? Could Six and Twenty stand against the Nine now?

Freedom, it tasted like the morning dew. In a community, I remained free to unleash years of energy. What was it like to use magic freely? If we'd stayed in a community then I would've been able to use my Myst. Daddy told me about Six and Twenty, and how it differed from the Nine's Charlestown. Both allowed magic, but the community encouraged learning and spiritual growth, where the Nine's laws oppressed its citizens. Each of those laws carried a stiff sentence too.

Imprisonment and death. I chewed my lip thinking about their cells. There were stories I'd overheard Momma and Daddy talking about. One of our relatives found herself locked up in Charlestown, but I didn't know if they were there now. If the Nine caught me, would they bother, or would they just kill me? *Was it terrible to wish for the latter?* I pushed the thought aside knowing there remained plenty to live for.

"Huh," I said, leaning forward into the steering wheel. "The more I think about it, the more I've lost to that stupid spell." My mouth opened wide and released a yawn. I needed some coffee stat, but the voice said no stopping.

At least I trained in some areas of magic, but I also lost the majority of my instruction due to the spell. I had cast some minor spells and conjured fire. Other elements, however, and casting the Myst under pressure remained difficult.

There were rules with magic, more than the Nine imposed on its followers. For starters, no one commanded the elements. A mage could control all the power in the universe, but it was up to the element if it wanted to acknowledge the requests. If it did, then it did, or if it didn't want to, it didn't.

Perhaps that was why the supernaturals seldom embarked upon wars. In the past, all battles fought used hand-to-hand combat. Magic healed wounds and created food, water, clothing, and shelter. Conjuring wasn't my strongest suit. My mind tended to mimic wildfire, and it grew harder to clear my mind. On the other hand, forgetting the languages of magic hadn't helped either. I recognized the letters, but the words and their meanings eluded me.

"Thank goodness I wasn't responsible for packing," I mumbled, peeking down at my sneaker clad feet.

Gentle motion lowered my lids, and I didn't want to reopen them. The truck swerved, and the squealing tires jolted my head back onto the seat. Maneuvering the truck to the shoulder, I slammed on the brakes. A loud, thundering noise filled the gap of the cab, and I searched for the source, but found nothing other than the pounding of my own heart. Fuzziness and a tingling sensation traveled down my spine. I rested my forehead on the steering wheel and chided myself. There was no time for mistakes, and no time for sleep.

Maybe I was crazy, my brain protested. But I knew better. No one mistook a lycans for another animal. The books didn't lie. Supes called them beasts for a reason, their massive height and bulk being one of them.

A creation of the Myst, the same Myst shielding my body and channeled into spells. Momma and Daddy hadn't left me alone often, but I practiced some minor spells when they ventured out into the city. Their forbidding of magic was stifling, and for me, it was like starving for air. The Myst spiraled inside of me, calling and pushing me for release.

I am a time bomb.

My mother couldn't understand the frustrations. She was a human who fell in love with a hybrid mage. That was what she'd said, but sometimes I wondered if she lied to me. Little things I hadn't paid attention to before would make more sense if she wasn't human. She always knew when I lied, even tiny fibs. Momma was also quite strong and larger than female humans in height and build just like me.

"Lettie Graftfield was strong willed too," I reminded myself. Momma put up with Daddy's thirst for magic and mine too. I glued my eyes to the road and watched the cars whiz by. More vehicles graced the roads, and I awaited an opening. She wasn't supposed to know about the Myst or supernaturals, but Daddy believed in absolute honesty. That was a trait I admired, but also struggled with the notion. I think Momma was why he left the Nine, so they could share their lives together. My hand flicked the turn signal, and I rejoined the highway traffic.

"Wait a doggone second…" My mouth fell open. How'd Momma ever live there? Dad left Charlestown, the Nine Headquarters of the United States and home of the Council. I shook my head. No, either she wasn't human or she didn't live there.

They were gone, and it didn't matter anymore. Tears pooled in my eyes. But I didn't know how to let them go. My heart ached, but I felt them inside. Their memory wouldn't die and even in death, I doubted a stronger bond existed anywhere in this realm. With a bit of luck, they'd find each other in death as they had in life.

I reached over for a tissue to wipe my leaking eyes, and the truck drifted again. Another vehicle honked back at me, the driver shaking a fist. My lips mumbled an apologetic sorry, but they neither saw nor heard me.

Lights flashed in my review mirror as a blurt of sirens rang out. "Dang it."

I let my breath out in a tantrum and pulled over. The new truck smell burned my nose like acrid smoke. Then again, I'd melted the steering wheel. I reached into the glove box for my documents and pulled my driver's license from my back pocket. My mind reeled, recalling how they'd done it on the television; for a fleeting moment, I considered outrunning the officer, but that never ended well. Attention, nope I didn't need any more interest drawn to me.

My hand fussed with the buttons until I hit the one that lowered the window. The officer sat in his car, and I eyed him from the side mirror. When he decided to grace me with his presence, my finger drummed on my leg.

"You're a long way from home ma'am …" he twanged, peering at me suspiciously through his navigator sunglasses perched on his button nose. "You were going close to ninety MPH. Do you realize it's a sixty-five zone?"

Wait, the sign had said seventy-five MPH, and I'd barely gotten up to speed. "Sorry sir, I didn't realize I was going that fast."

I swallowed hard, and my palms dampened. *You were only speeding*, I chanted to myself even though I didn't believe it. If a random lycans read my thoughts, who said the Nine didn't have the capability too? The officer leaned closer to the window, and I held my breath.

"Alright give me your license, registration, and ... proof of insurance." He bent close enough that I could smell his minty fresh breath and oranges; the combination nauseated me. After handing over the documents, the officer walked back to his silver unmarked car. I released my breath.

My reflection caught my attention in the mirror instead of observing him. Golden eyes tuckered out. The telltale signs of puffy, purple circles lay beneath. The once luxurious, dark auburn tresses matted in a sweaty pile atop my head. The pale skin, typically aglow, appeared sallower than a rotten egg yolk. All of it matched my mood as the bile reared up my throat. I looked how I felt: rode hard and put up wet.

Six and Twenty, not a stupid speeding ticket, concerned me more. I tapped my fingers on the steering wheel. But each minute that passed added to my time wasted. I'd hoped to roll in before sundown. I didn't want to wait till tomorrow to see Mr. Skyland.

The officer took his dear old time, and panic set in over my documents. My eyes widened; I had no idea which names —even last names – were on any of them. Every time we moved, I'd assumed a new identity. My first name remained the same, but my parents insisted the last name change.

Fainauriel Graftfield didn't exist anymore. But A. Carmen Kerr and Auriel N. O'Nally did.

I was sweating like a whore in church on Sunday by the time the officer returned. The closer he came to my door the more an odd, stinging sensation ran over my skin. My amulet hadn't responded, though I rested my hand over it just in case.

"Alright ma'am, if you promise to slow down I'll let you off with a warning. It looks like you're all set." He passed my documents back. A bright yellow warning slip sat on top.

I blinked, and then stuttered out a "Thank you." The officer returned a smile, albeit a little lopsided, and winked. The familiarity shifted like the energy in the air.

"Be safe and slow down, please." His voice shook. Why would he be as nervous as me?

"Thank goodness for SPGPS," I said, pulling off the highway, and onto some bumpy back road. A yawn threatened, and I fought it, gently smacking my face.

The truck shook my body from head to toe. Okay maybe not so terrible, but it was no New York City that was for sure. SPGPS was impressive for navigating hidden communities, but it also meant no hiding from the Nine. Shield Probing Global Positioning Service detected enchantments and the Myst. My version also used standard, human GPS, but it pinged for large doses of magic when activated and overlaid the normal map with yellow tones.

"I sure hope you don't drive me off of a cliff," I mumbled at the machine that kept telling me to turn left. According to humans, the road ended up ahead, but the SPGPS picked up a large area to the west. Without a doubt, the road continued, and I followed straight, ignoring the warnings.

Overall, the scenery painted a beautiful picture with its rolling, vibrant blooming hillsides and mountain peaks far off in the distance. Like a Monet watercolor scene. I rendered myself speechless and blinked.

Spectacular in the fall, I was certain, when the leaves transformed into energetic earthy hues. In the springtime though, the trees were alive, radiating the power of nature. Flowering trees, with fragrant peachy blossoms, lined the road. The trees, grasses, bushes, and flowers were singing a song of serenity that blanketed this section of the world.

A rickety bridge lay ahead, and I stopped to check its safety. The graying wood didn't look like it would hold me up let alone the truck. Walking the length, I noted that it was sturdier than it appeared. The boards hadn't even squeaked or groaned.

A babbling brook ran on either side. But the real draw was the Myst. The thickness of the air reached an almost unbreathable level, and my lungs screamed in protest. I stepped back to the truck and took a round of breaths to clear my airway.

Maybe it used to be bigger, I noticed boulders on the banks. They sat off from the water's edge. I hopped in the truck and said a silent prayer to the Gods. My foot tapped the gas, and the vehicle crawled over the bridge; I braced myself for the shield I couldn't see, but was there.

My breath sucked in, and I gave the truck another tap of gas. Every inch of my body crawled with the shield's essence, as it decided whether to admit me into the town. I tried keeping my eyes open but instinct screamed for me to shut them tight. The shield fought to suffocate me, but I was stronger, and pushed against the intrusion with my defensive shields. Ha, I thought, this wasn't my day, and no shield was going to end me. With my eyes closed, I gunned the truck, and the shield spat me out on the other side.

I located a weathered wooden sign that read: Welcome to Six and Twenty. There was more, but it was in two different languages, which reminded me of Gaelic and Norse Runes. Both were languages of magic and represented the Aesir and the Vanir on Midgard. I followed the road and kept my pace slower than the posted signs. Eyes peered into the thick woods as I passed through them to the center of town. Six and Twenty utilized the natural barrier; it funneled me into the town's square. The Nine did the same just in case the shields failed and humans discovered us.

There were no flashy chain stores or hopping fast food joints anywhere in sight. Every shop had a mom and pop feel, and the thought made me smile. What a peculiar and quaint place they had here. Eerie and quiet in contrast to the city life for sure.

Past the deserted town square, I gawked at the houses. They weren't mansions by any means, but they were larger than I'd seen in the city. More like smaller versions of plantation houses. My family had chosen to rent apartments and townhouses in New York. They said it was easier to rent than own with all our fudged documents.

The house number matching the envelope caught my attention. The Skyland residence sat a ways off the road surrounded by a seven-foot wrought iron fence. By far, it appeared the largest house I'd passed. Nestled inside the fence lay another identical house, but it didn't sit behind it.

Maybe it is a guesthouse?

My palms dampened, and dizziness washed over me. The gate creaked open, and I pulled onto the driveway. Perhaps pushing myself wasn't a brilliant idea. Too late now.

A blur of movement caught my eye in the rearview mirror, but when I looked, I saw nothing there. Copious amounts of caffeine and my sheer willpower had brought me this far. I shook it off and crept my way up the winding driveway. At the end of the drive, I stopped the truck and waited for several breaths. I wasn't going to let anything stop me now.

"You can do this," I said and opened my door. My vision blinked out, and darkness surrounded me. The humid breeze whisked past my face, and my nose wrinkled at a campfire burning in the distance. The cold ground I'd expected to smash into didn't come. Instead, a cocoon of warmth rolled over me, caressing my aching skin. The rough palms brushed against me, sending a shiver down my spine. No one had touched me before. My parents avoided contact too. Touch made the empathic bond stronger.

I opened my eyes, blinking moisture away, and found a pair of mysterious, green eyes. Unsettling, glowing, and more emerald than the spring median meadow. They stared right back into mine as they narrowed. My mouth opened to speak, but nothing came out. Set on a rugged face and framed with shaggy sunset hair, stood a face I recognized.

"You all right ma'am?" he asked in a husky voice that pricked at my skin. Blinking, I could hardly think, as I stared back at the stranger who'd haunted my dreams and nightmares. "Well shut my mouth ..."

The twisted response wasn't what I'd expected. His scowl deepened, and his face reddened like a wet hen. I winced, fighting hard to maintain my shield. He fought against it, and I poured more Myst, enveloping myself in the white fire until he stopped. I willed myself to stand, but the stranger didn't let me go, and held my elbows. His eyes bore into me, and I looked down expecting scorch marks.

"Yes, thank you," I whispered. My heart beat fast, too fast, and I started to lose my balance again. *Gods leave it to me to make a complete ass of myself.* Stars clouded my vision, and I tried shaking the mental shinnies away.

"You need to sit, darlin'. You're not well." His funny accent sang a harmony, and it penetrated my soul after the past few hellish days. An odd combination of southern, and British maybe, but I wasn't certain.

I said, "Thanks." My voice remained small and apologetic, and my mouth dried like a cotton field during a long drought.

He glanced to my truck. "New York, huh … That's a long drive to make by yourself."

I nodded, wondering if he was making small talk, or if it all meant something. This was the first contact I'd had with any supernaturals since my father. Unless you counted the lycan at the hotel that might or might not have also had telepathy.

My eyes soaked in his Myst. Oh yes, this one was two-natured. The two souls quarreled, one human and one animal. For a moment, I almost saw a third, but it wasn't possible. Anything was possible, I reminded myself and ignored this man's piercing stare.

"She's something else …" Whoa, what now? My eyes widened, and I cursed myself. The last thing I needed right now was another ability. *"I waited and waited …"*

His head cocked, and his eyes narrowed again. I wished he'd shut-up and stop analyzing me. To think, I'd wanted to find him. "Are you Paulo, Paulo Skyland by any chance?"

The words came out in a whoosh. I kneeled down; my breath slowed and grew shallow. He didn't answer me though. Peeking up, I couldn't deny the evidence. Lycan-mage with three Myst-born signatures; a hybrid just like me, but the stranger from my dream loathed my presence in his town.

chapter five

JAMIE

Oh my Gods, he had lived. No wonder I hadn't died all those years ago. My head ached, stomach too, all aftereffects of Nick. Other parts of my body panged too, courtesy of our lycans bond. I needed the reprieve, but I would not admit it to the mangy mutt. How she'd ever become friends with him still baffled me. I shook my head and laughed. We would've not crossed paths otherwise, but he'd belonged with our ragtag of misfits. My brows rose. Even if he was five hundred years my senior, guess I liked them older, hairy men. Nah, those baby blues pierced me and held me captive.

My hand rested over my raging heart. On the inside though, he remained loving and kind. I'd been a stupid fool to shove him aside, and it hadn't solved a damn thing. I loved him. Every inch of my darkened soul loved both man and beast. But that was unimportant. I cursed. He'd taken my keys. He'd been here.

I groaned and smacked my head on the steering column. Stranger events had unfolded than I'd cared to admit. A Fenrir tracked Aurie ... nope, hadn't expected that, but Nick's interference allowed me to think. My heart soared, but his being alive changed my plans. I would not let him go again even if I had to beg and grovel at his feet.

Part of it might've been from the lycan bond. When I was eighteen, I'd tried placing all the blame on it. A spark ignited between us, and I'd tried like hell to fight it, but lycans mated for life. Nicky chose me, as he put it, not by choice. One day the feelings between us exploded, and for months, we couldn't keep our hands off each other. Aurie caught us making out one night and realization fell like a ton of bricks. I loved them both, but only loving her made sense. Years later, I understood why I'd done it. Fear and stupidity –bond or not, I loved him, and that was all that mattered in life.

I wished someone had told my eighteen-year-old self that. We'd broken up, but it wasn't enough. He haunted me even though he'd respected my requests to stay away. I shook my head; I kept running back into his large arms. The draw to him overpowered every sense I'd had then and now.

My hand grabbed my cell phone, and I punched in the number I dreaded calling.

"I found her," I informed Merric –my birth father. "I let her go for now but placed that charm you gave me on her documents."

"Good work, son." My brows knitted together, and I stared at the phone.

He didn't sound like my father. No yelling or degrading bull, just normal conversation came from his mouth. If I were a smarter man, I'd learn the game he was playing at. With Merric, there was always an angle. But all I cared about was my heart and keeping my head in the process of figuring it out.

I hated him, as much as I despised the Nine. Merric didn't deserve the title of father. Perhaps sperm donor suited him better. After all, he'd abandoned me in order to pursue his political career. He called it revenge, but I was just a little boy when he tossed me aside. On the outside, I hadn't shunned him or his connections. Instead, I snatched a page from his book and kept him closer. My eyes narrowed; always keep your enemies closer.

Merric rose quicker than anyone thought possible. It took a few years; I grew wiser but wished him best. We were the same now, and in many ways that I didn't like to admit. He taught me the finer points in being selfish, acting as if he gave a damn, when it fitted his needs. Now it only suited him because of my connection to Auriel. My hands clenched the steering wheel and my jaw popped. The Nine wanted her, Merric wanted her, but Aurie wasn't theirs to claim.

"Anyone wanting what Merric did is insane." My eyes rolled, remembering the day Paulo told me my father became a draugr hybrid. I was six at the time, and I stared up at Paulo with my big fiery Phoenix eyes. There wasn't a way to understand what he meant, but I recalled being confused. I still loved Merric back then, and I loved Paulo.

Both were draugr, so what was wrong with that?

"I need her," I reassured myself, although I didn't believe my own words. But letting her reach Six and Twenty killed my dreams. Nil, zilch, zero ... the language didn't change the definition. But the same would result if I called in the Wardens and stole her away by force. At least there was a slim chance of keeping her in my life; if I made sure she arrived. "Damned if I do and damned if I don't."

My fingers drummed on the wheel, and my vision flashed back to Nicky. He remained the one man who drove me crazy. Between his thick Scottish brogue and his muscled body, he transformed into my personal heaven.

Those blue eyes enthralled me and dried my mouth. I laughed, recalling the first time I realized it, and leaned my head against the headrest. All five of us were hanging out, but he'd arrived late. When he walked through the door, my heart raced, and the wind was knocked out of my lungs. Nick stopped dead in his tracks, and his pale cheeks flushed. Neither of us stood a chance then. Why would we now?

Sweat beaded on my brow, as the energy of the Myst dissipated. My reserves ran low; I needed a recharge before I attempted another spell. Those weren't favorable odds when it came to the lion's den. Paulo and Liam made it quite clear I wasn't welcome home anymore. That didn't bode well, but I shrugged it off.

A knock sounded on my window, and I jumped. "Ye best let me in." I unlocked the door, and Nicky slid into the passenger seat. My gaze averted when I saw him naked, and my cheeks blazed. "Yer prittier than I remembered."

I chewed my lip to stop myself from reacting. His nearness ... the nakedness. "Mind tellin' me what's going on?"

He jingled my keys. "Aye dae traitor."

I reached for them, but he pulled them out of my reach. Traitor, yes I betrayed him, but did he mean the Nine or before? "I'm going ta skelp yer wee behind."

The Nine. He'd want to murder me where I sat otherwise. I deserved it, but if he never learned the truth of my idiocy then I held a chance. The bond gave me his soul and heart, but I wanted his trust. There was a song about love not being enough, and I swore they wrote it with us in mind.

His scent filled the car, and it alone made my cock stiffen. He knew it too. "Give 'em over."

Nick grasped my hand, but I refused to look at him. All sense flew right out the window when we made eye contact. I hadn't ever come close to the lycans's control. Five hundred years of life offered him a massive advantage. My hand dragged down my face slowly, and the building sigh escaped. His hand slid down my arm, and he might as well have been stroking my skin with a feather.

He tugged me over the console and grasped my chin. "Am I making' ye squirm, laddie?" I held my breath as my eyes met his. Hot hands ran down my back to my ass and squeezed through the uniform I wore. The submissive Nick I knew left, and the beast rose. Those baby blues tinged with yellow. He dragged my pants down. Moist air bit at my exposed flesh as he kneaded it in his large palms. My cock grew rigid, and my balls ached for attention.

Whom did I think I was kidding?

My back arched as his fingers pinched my ass. "Aye, that's it." His hand slapped my cheek in quick succession. I winced and moaned as my cock strained against the fabric. My ass stung, and I bit my lip. Nick breathed harder and smacked me again. Each time he hit me, he cupped and rubbed his rough palm over my ass.

"Please Nicky." He reclined the passenger seat and wrapped his arms around me. My face plastered against his furry chest, and he removed my shoes and pants. I kissed his nipples, swirling my tongue over the hardened nubs, and enjoying his cock jerking against my belly. His finger slowly assaulted my asshole as I begged. We'd never gone this far before, but I'd experimented and was accustomed to toys. My fingers dug into his shoulders, and I pushed my ass toward his hand.

He popped the center console and removed a condom. I'd kept them on hand for emergencies, even though we hadn't ventured this far before, but how had he known they were in there? Nick tore into the package with his teeth and slid it over his erect cock. His fingers slid out, and he ran them over the lubricated condom, before placing them back in my ass. I groaned and rocked my hips as he rotated his wrist. But all too soon, he removed them and slapped my ass. The force flattened me against his chest. Our cocks rubbed together, and it took every clenched muscle to stop myself. "Turn round."

I blinked, unsure of what he meant. His large hands grasped my hips and spun me around. Dizziness settled over my mind, and he pressed his head against my slick opening. I gritted my teeth as my fingernails scraped the dashboard. Inch by ripping inch, Nick guided me down his thick shaft. My body trembled, and he whispered, "Breathe, dearie."

Dearie? What happened to hen? None of the physical mattered. My head rested on my hands, and as the cars whipped by, I no longer cared about anything else in the world. My lips thinned; he'd no decency, no care for my heart. Everything happened too fast and now it sunk in like a freight train. He'd forced me to turn; Nick hated me.

His hands smoothed over my spine, tracing the line of my muscles. The tingling caresses helped me relax and take those final inches. But my mind and heart weren't fooled. They screamed for me to retreat, run, and curl around myself. My eyes burned, not from his cock buried in my ass and not from his spanking. No, my insides tore because this moment of raw lust felt empty of the tenderness and love I knew him capable of; I sighed. My mind grew heavier, tampering and locking it away. I swallowed the gnawing sensation as it feasted on my insides, but its tendrils shot from my mouth.

"Stop."

Nick said nothing and pulled out. My face hit the windshield as I grabbed for my clothing on the floor. Thank the Gods I was the short one. I flung the passenger door open and stared into the woods lining the highway. I wanted to run and hide. A tear rolled down my cheek, and Merric's voice sounded off in my head. Gods what was I doing? I shook my head and tossed my pants on. The voice didn't relent as it repeated those words. "Stop crying and man-up. No one gives a shit." I was four; I'd just watched a draugr suck the life from my mother. The thanks I got was a hand across my face. I hadn't cried again since then without a damn good reason.

Nick's hand fell to my shoulder. "Don't."

The grip tightened, and I pulled away. He treated me like dirt and then tried to turn into my boyfriend again. *No.* Nick held every right under the sun to be pissed off, but he could shove the kindness up his ass. The Oracle was right. *Tainted blood ran through my veins.*

I sat behind the wheel and scooped the keys up, trying to empty my thoughts and determine my next move. Nick slid into the passenger seat. "Ye going to say something?"

My eyes shot to him. "Put some damn clothes on."

The engine roared, and I sped away rejoining the cars gracing the interstate. We were all heading to the same place.

He mumbled under his breath as his Myst shifted. Clothing formed, threads weaving in his hand. The sooner the better, although I knew better than to think clothes stopped the lusty thoughts or Merric's hateful words. My foot slammed harder on the gas; I weaved in and out of the cars rolling between me and Six and Twenty. No distance in the world stopped the menacing voice sounding off in my head again.

Nick snorted and turned to me. "Merric's a wee scunner."

"Stay out of my head," I said, gritting my teeth. "Gods, you know I hate that." Laughter shook me and my brow rose. "Scunner?"

Scotts Gaelic I understood, but there were times I swore Nicky pulled words out of his ass. Most I followed, understanding the context, but when every curse word in the book described my birth father …

"Whiny." His hand caressed my cheek, and I fought to keep my eyes on the road. "Did ye mean what ye said last night?"

"Before or after you froze me and stuffed me in a car?" I shifted in my seat and leaned toward the dashboard.

Nick whispered, "Afterward," and stared out the window.

"Depends …" I fiddled with the radio much preferring to hear bad country songs to admitting I loved him. Every time I had, the voice had grown louder. He laughed and grasped my hand resting on the center console. Our fingers folded together, and he lifted my knuckles to his lips. My eyes fought to remain open instead of falling into the stirred bliss.

Nick kissed each fingertip; his tongue flickered over each tip. "Does it depend?"

My mouth opened to answer, but nothing came out. I bit my lip, rolling it between my teeth.

"Why'd you let me believe you were dead?" He made a noise, and I jerked the car onto the shoulder. My hand tore free, and I slammed it into park. "Almost four years, babe ..."

I glanced away, the tears rearing again. The blood coated the houses; the bodies ripped to shreds. We couldn't identify them all. Gods why did I make that call?

His fingers grasped my chin and forced my gaze. Our lips hovered close, and I longed to taste them.

"Ach, twas ye then." I flinched expecting him to punch me again. Oh, I'd more than warranted it, but he didn't hurt me. "Tis a pitty yer mine; I cannae kill ye." Nick blew out a breath. "Look I wasn't trying to hurt ye earlier; as ye said it's been almost four years."

He flashed me a grin that made my head spin. "I—" Saying I was sorry wasn't good enough, and I shut my mouth. I truly hadn't known his uncle's plans or what Merric planned with the information. I'd hoped my dad would help me break the bond back then. Hindsight was a bitch.

"No." He released my chin and dragged his hand through his cropped blond hair. He hadn't trusted me. The truth twisted inside of me, but in his shoes, I wouldn't have trusted me either.

"No, tis a lie; Aurie warned us ye know, but M'athair refused to leave. Others followed him; Reggie, Liam, and I fled with a few pups."

Aurie thank the Gods for her visions. I thought back to the day before the attack. Paulo sent both Liam and me away; we'd gone to the beach and joked about leaving the state when our feet entered the water. Just us brothers enjoying a little normality and talking about plans for the future. Silence fell between us as the cars whizzed by. Liam planned to propose to Auriel as soon as school ended. He'd already bought a ring. Weeks later and the world as we all knew it ended. For me, my soul mate lay dead in a nameless pit, and Liam's memory altered to where he didn't remember why he'd bought a ring or who Fainauriel Graftfield was.

Nick grasped my hand again and squeezed it. The first time I walked away from him, it was the hardest decision of my life. Would he give me a second chance? Would I mess it up again?

"Aye, but yer no' going to like it." I swallowed hard and glanced away. "The Norns poked their heeds into eun beag's business again. Ye need to proceed as if no'things changed." He released a steady breath. "We hate each other, even yer thoughts unless ye alone." His fingers stroked my rough cheek. "How'd ye get more handsome ... c'mere."

Handsome? My eyes rolled at the thought. I didn't have a chance to ask what he meant. His hands pulled me across the console and into his lap again. Nicky kissed me, holding me hostage with his mouth as my hands held his face. Anything, I'd do anything to win his love and trust back.

"We'll figure it out, Jamie, but fer now keep the secret. Auriel's too important. Ye'll see fer yerself, but I canna tell ye more."

"Shut your mouth." The notion had us both laughing. There wasn't an actual name for the mind connection. The Dísir shared it, but the Guardians read all supernaturals, like the Valkyries read emotions. The Myst created us to work together, but without my Phoenix, I'd thought I'd lost the ability. Had Nicky blocked me all these years?

He didn't answer my thoughts as he nipped my lips apart. My hands ran through his hair, grasping fistfuls of blond tufts and dragging him closer. Every inch of my body burned inside, my skin dimpled where his expert fingers dipped under my shirt and ran over my chest. The light within him filled me and chased the darkness away. Nick trailed his nails, scraping down my abs, and followed the trail of dark hair to my pants. I moaned against his mouth; he teased me, dipping his fingers between my aching skin and the fabric.

Sirens blared and I shot back, slamming my head against the roof. I cursed, but the smile refused to leave my face. "Busted."

Anderson, SC

"'Tis a good thing I found ye." I sighed; my eyes rolled over the span of his tight t-shirt. Even clothed he distracted me. I shot him a glance and forced a smile. He saw through it and squeezed my thigh.

"Watch it." Eyes fell on us as we sat in my car outside Anderson's only diner. We'd arrived right as the sun peeked from behind the trees, but the people inside eyed us with suspicion. After he'd spelled the cops into thinking we'd had a flat tire, we hadn't wasted any more time necking on the side of the road.

Some areas were more accepting of our kind, whatever we were. I didn't consider myself gay; women turned me on and during the past years, I'd slept with my fair share. But none of them came close to comparing to Nicky.

Nick not so much, although he'd bred with women out of duty. "Stop worrying, hen."

My heart fluttered at his use of my old pet name. But not worrying was easier said than done. Old problems arose in my mind and made my stomach ache.

He claimed my soul that fateful day, and I'd ripped his heart out over a stupid law. A two-fold issue lay before us. Part of it revolved around the Nine and the other with the immortality I lacked. Unlike my friends, I was a mortal –Mage. I'd age and die. There were two ways for my kind to obtain immortal life. One was draugr blood and death. The second took Loki's permission and blessing to become a created lycans.

I glanced over my shoulder, and Nick leaned over the console. His brows rose. "Yer a fidgety wee thing."

"Shut your mouth." He crossed his arms over his chest. My eyes followed every movement, every twitch or flex, and I knew. "Do you have any idea how many laws I broke today?"

My face grew hotter even with the air conditioning on full blast. If I'd done my damn job, the council promised to change me. Paulo refused when I begged him. After I'd thought Nick died, again trying to save my ass from his bond, I had forged the plan. His hand brushed against my unshaven face, and I closed my eyes. All my emotions bubbled to the surface.

"Ye think I'd let them touch ye?"

I shrugged; he'd always promised to protect me, but failed when the Oracle stole my Phoenix. Where was he when Aurie decided to erase herself? Where was he when I made the call? I stared into his eyes and sought answers. The blame and guilt were mine to shoulder, and I took full responsibility. But I'd put my faith in him before, just as I'd done countless times with Merric over the years. Disappointing moments filled my life; I both understood and accepted that, but I didn't make promises I wouldn't keep.

"What we waitin' for?" I asked and shoved a stick of gum in my mouth. My goal hadn't been to make him guilty. I trusted him to do what he felt was right whether it benefitted me or not. That meant allowing the Nine to lock me up, beat me up, or execute me.

Nick opened the door and stepped from the car without a word. I guessed he'd listened to my thoughts. My eyes closed, and I rested my chin on the steering wheel. His lanky large frame walked around the front of the car. It amazed me how lean he appeared, but he was solid muscle. He hadn't changed, and I doubted he'd even changed in the last five hundred years. Nick knocked on my window, and I opened the door.

He grabbed my arm, but I dragged it away. "Not in public," I mumbled under my breath wondering if he'd forgotten his earlier warning. Nicky didn't listen and grabbed my arm again. No one paid much attention as he pulled me toward the side of the diner. My face flared to life, burning and twisting. I bit my lip and stared at my feet.

"I'm going to say this once. Look at me." His fist curled into my shirt, and he shook me. "Jamison Hamilton Mc Douglass." My gaze snapped up at the use of my birth name. No one ever dared to use it, but the way he said the name tugged at my heart. My hands rested on his chest, but I didn't know what he wanted me to do.

I cocked my head and grinned. "Nikolai Ulf Fenrir … that works two ways you know." He chuckled but didn't release my shirt. Nick's head moved closer, and his lips hovered. The electricity grew with each evasion; my stomach pulled and the butterflies danced. I leaned forward, but he backed away. "Kiss me already or get the hell out of—"

Nick smashed my back against the brick wall of the diner. I cried out from the impact, and stars littering my vision. His hands twisted my shirt and pushed against my chest. Nick mumbled something about being sorry. My hands grasped his face and dragged his mouth to mine; I rose onto my toes to shorten the reach. A smile spread, as his nose rubbed against mine, and he slanted his lips over mine. When was the last time I'd smiled and felt its power radiate through me?

"Aye." Nick pulled away and rubbed the back of my hand. "Tis time I go."

My mouth dropped, and I gaped at him. He grinned, and shrugged, but walked away. No good-bye, no nothing, before he vanished into the woods. His scent filled my lungs and stood as one reminder that he'd touched me.

"Love you too, mutt," I said into the palm of my hand as my fingers caressed my swollen lips.

I slid down the wall and rested my chin on my knees. The cold darkness came for me; it ate away at my heart and soul. Shivers dimpled my flesh as the shadows rose from the earth. Gods did it ache; the emptiness I'd felt for years thinking he was dead. Darkness swirled at my feet and readied their assault. The tears I held inside, the lovers I had buried my guilt in, and the copious amounts of alcohol hadn't done nothing to erase the misery or pain.

I itched for a drink now and, lucky for me, the diner had a bar. That wasn't a normal occurrence in Anderson. My hand rested on my heart, and I closed my eyes. Hell, it used to be a dry town, but life moved forward. People changed; I changed too. The muggy air assaulted me, but it didn't wipe Nick's scent from my skin. Seascape ocean waves of his Highland birthplace clung to him, and now it washed over me like a salty tide. For anyone else, it'd curl their nose, but to me it reminded me of a home I'd not known. Orkney Island, where my bloodline started and pieces survived today. Hundreds of years prior to my birth, Nickolas grew up there. Kismet. He'd known my family long before I took my first breath. My hand slid back to my lips, no longer raw from his scruffy shadow, and I frowned.

"Here goes nothing." I shrugged, climbing the steps, and entering the diner.

The blond waitress eyed me, disgust written over her face. My features remained impassive, but the slap stung like Nick's love taps on my sore ass. I shouldn't care what the stranger thought, but it tore at my insides like a plague, and the voice whispered again. My finger pointed toward the bar, and she nodded. I sat my weary ass on the swivel seat and placed my order. Scotch Whiskey, just another reminder of the man who stole my soul and bound it to his.

I prayed for Auriel, as she stayed in Six and Twenty, and sipped my finger o' whiskey. Nicky kept me apprised of Liam's conversations, but spoke of nothing else as the hours ticked by and the sun began its descent. I chuckled, amused and disappointed. My brother the fool; I drew the waitress's stare. The voice grew louder, reminding me how tainted and evil I'd become. The cheap booze burned the words away and tasted of burnt plastic as it slid down my throat. Shaky hands set the glass down, and I wiped my mouth on my sleeve. Old habits died hard, but I'd kill for something stronger. Graftfield Scotch Whiskey flittered through my mind, like a strong body with rich smoky flavor as opposed to sipping on battery acid. Human made spirits didn't add up.

"Clear yer pritty heed. No' looking so good here."

Liam let her go? After all, it was her home. Aurie belonged there. I sighed and rested my head on clenched fists. How many rules would I have to break in one day? *"A lot, hen."*

Much changed though, and I wondered how warm of a welcome Auriel had received. Paulo wouldn't have turned her away. That remained his thing, like a calling card, he took in strays and runaways. I covered my mouth and shook my head.

Liam always played the big tough enforcer, dreamed of it ever since he was a kid. Gods, he was such an idiot. Aurie would roll her eyes at him. I tapped my chin recalling what she used to say.

"Six and Twenty's but a spat in the ocean. Expend your energy fighting for those you love or die trying."

The words whispered on the wind, rattling against the glass, but it hadn't been Nick's voice. There lay a hidden meaning in the message, but I wasn't certain. Toward the end, she became philosophical and handed out advice for the future. She told me to follow my heart and not care what others thought. Aurie didn't judge Nick or me for that matter, and she kept our secret.

None of it mattered now. The waitress handed me another drink, and the diner door swung open. Nicky smiled and winked at me in the mirror. My cheeks warmed, but he turned his attention to the blond waitress approaching him. She looked familiar, but I couldn't place where I'd seen her before. He handed her an envelope, and she touched her neck. Her hand held onto the edge of the bar, and she shook her head as he walked away.

chapter six

AURIEL

"You know where I can find h.m?" I asked all the while wondering if coming here had been such a hot idea after all. That little voice in the back of my head screamed caution. Something was off, more than his two-natured, err, three-natured existence. Maybe it was the uneasiness of his eyes, but when he smiled, it disappeared. When he smirked, I wanted to melt away into nothingness, but he didn't have the same reaction to my presence. The nearness made my heart erratic, and my head swam in a pool of dizziness.

All of it confused me and following his Myst became downright exhausting. I tilted my head, soaking and surveying the situation. Every moment in his presence worsened the effects. Was it just me? Yeah, I was the problem all right. None of it should've mattered; I hadn't trekked down the East Coast on no sleep to impress a man. Yet the notion of his rejection ate at my stomach and twisted my senses. The dreams perhaps were also to blame, because they had painted this picture in my head. Things were rarely as they seemed, Daddy used to say that often. I blinked and pushed past the tears threatening to rise.

"He's not lived here for a while. Why you looking for him?" Liam raised his arms in a lofty swinging motion, and his t-shirt lifted enough to reveal tribal tattooed flesh. Dang he rippled like a chiseled sculpture, and I bit my lip to keep from gasping. My eyes followed every minuscule movement and undulation of flesh. On the inside, I fanned myself like a crazed teenager, and it wasn't the eighty-degree heat boiling my blood. He leaned forward, lifting his rusty head a fraction. The longer tendrils fell into his face, and my breath hissed out as those eyes met mine.

The man righted himself, face tight as if frozen, and placed large hands on his hips; he had yet to ease himself in my presence. My hands trembled, and I hid the weakness behind my back. Six and Twenty wasn't what I'd expected; a near ghost town with a crazed lycans draining me dry might've been the highlight of my life.

"What business do you have with him?"

His attitude remained defensive, but I wouldn't let him intimidate me. Big strong man or not, I'd find another way if he didn't want to help me. I'd come this far on my own, and I wasn't ready to throw in the cards just yet.

"I have a letter." I stumbled toward my truck and wobbled a bit. Liam grabbed my arm, but I waved him off, as a stream of stars twinkled over my vision. Strange how his touch worsened my vertigo but space made it better.

Unsteadily I made it to the truck and retrieved the letter. My hands still trembling, I stroked its smooth surface. Momma's angelic face popped into my head. Liam asked if I was all right, but I ignored his question. It broke the memory apart, and my heart ached; I doubted he'd understand or even care. "My parents wrote it. They wanted him to have it."

I pretended to search through my bag. Fingers touched the envelope, latching on to the one possession of Momma's I had. His gaze burned through my back, damp hairs drying on my neck despite my cheeks growing hotter than Hades on a summer day. The setting sun perhaps, as it beat down on my skin. I wiped the sweat from my brow, but the sensations didn't falter. He was up to no good, but I'd risk total exposure, leaving my secrets, open wide like a whore on Sunday. . I chewed my lip and thought over the consequences. Death made the top of the list, but there was little fear there.

With the letter in my unstable hand, I faced Liam. The invisible bubble that I held melted away as the white Myst retracted into my skin. I'd get a clearer read on the situation now.

I winced, regretting the decision at once; his thoughts crowded into my mind and overpowered his emotions. Why'd I hear his thoughts anyhow? They plucked at my flesh, carving deep divots as I flinched.

"Not the one, too plain, not beautiful, not blond, not skinny, freaky eyes ... No, you're wrong ... mine ...precious, strong, warm ... No!"

Liam's mind continued listing every defect his eyes saw as another part conflicted inside of him. But it was easy to guess which one held the control ... the one holding disgust in his eyes. Once the voices dulled to a whisper, his emotions intensified, and I wrestled against the burn of my eyes and swelling of my throat. Hatred, distrust, annoyance, and repulsion rolled off him with every tick of his jaw and flew through me to the point of breaking, tearing at my soul. Quivering, my lips couldn't form the words to scream at him to shut up. Heck, I wasn't perfect; Liam wasn't perfect either, but dang it. Why did I care what he thought?

"Eun Beag, run, ye must leave now." The Scottish voice rose over Liam's thoughts and feelings. I lifted my eyes, seeking the large beast I'd seen at the hotel. My head ached as the voices rumbled through my brain.

The situation grew hopeless with each second. I tried denying the signs, and every moment the danger intensified. Liam's body twitched, and his eyes altered from green to yellow. My head tilted, and those eyes held me frozen to the ground. I stayed when I needed to go. My brain relayed the same thoughts, but my body refused to obey.

"No, I have to stay. They can help me. I need ...help. Please, someone help me ... " Liam shook, and his body bent on the verge of losing control. His eyes dilated, and surprise flickered across his face. He'd heard me but why hadn't he before? His mouth opened to speak, but he clamped it shut. My heart raced. Liam's pretty-boy face contorted; those thick lips curled up into a silent snarl and flashed his teeth. His nostrils flared, and his body shuddered under my gaze. The letter in my hand moved in time with my bottom lip, but I tightened my grip, crumpling the letter in my sweaty palm. His eyes followed mine to the envelope. He waved his hand, but the anger remained.

His mouth opened, and he barked, "Give it to me."

His knuckles turned whiter than snow. I glanced around, but there wasn't anyone else except us. My heart sunk. There was no one to help me or hear my screams. My shield might hold, but I didn't want to hurt him either. My soul had witnessed its fair share of death and destruction, and it had seen enough to last a lifetime. I backed into my truck, scrambling to close the door as he lunged forward. A yip left my mouth as his fully changed yellow eyes bore down on me through the glass. The voice was right, and I'd find another way to Paulo. It wasn't worth killing him … his head cocked.

Liam placed his hand on the glass. "No hurt you."

No. I would hurt you. To my toes, I knew it as truth. One day I would harm the man and maybe the beast too.

My heart thundered. "Sorry … to bother … you," I said through my window, my voice rocking like my hands. Precious seconds ticked away as I grabbed at the key dangling from the ignition. My hand turned it; I spared one last glance at the strange, three-natured beast. Liam was gone; all that remained were torn clothes.

"That was …" bizarre, strange, crazy and then some other words I … I couldn't even describe what'd happened. The beast's words replayed. I found myself at a standstill with finding Paulo Skyland, and figuring out why my parents died, but I found the mystery man from my dreams. Too bad appearances were deceiving. Maybe the draugr was the good one after all, or in my loneliness, the idea of a friend got the better of me, and I had imagined something that could never be.

"Well a crap load of good coming south did for me," I yelled at the empty space of the truck cab and looked for anything to throw. My stomach growled in response, and a growing ache in my head reared out of nowhere. I hadn't eaten since leaving New York. Coffee didn't quite count as a food group. I bet the stress of having a hot, three-natured lycans glare at me as if I were nothing hadn't helped. No, he'd treated me worse than nothing, if such a notion existed. Shivers ransacked my spine at the thought of Liam, all six-foot-seven of him—give or take an inch. Gods, he unnerved me with his ... everything, but it didn't matter. He had more interest in getting me to leave than staying.

Liam allowed the beast control. That made him young or stupid. Or both. Lycans required control or the beast would rise and dominate the man.

I felt every ounce of his emotions and tried my best not to respond. No one needed to know I was an empath. My head rested on the steering wheel, and I waited for the traffic light. Liam's thoughts were worse than his emotions. Now, I knew I wasn't runway-model perfect, but I was comfortable with my curves. Dang, all giantesses were curvy and tall. He... Gods he'd tortured my ... A car horn broke my thoughts, and I glanced up to see the green arrow. I gunned the gas; screw him and his perfection.

Why'd I even care what some asinine crazed lycans thought about me? I pulled over into a restaurant parking lot to gather my wits.

"How'd I get to this place in my life and will it ever end?"

I'd already given up on the notion of a white picket fence and all that jazz. Like some women, I wanted that vision, but I didn't have a strong understanding of love, relationships, or men. I couldn't fathom any man–human or not–wanting any part of my hectic life. The truth remained factual. No matter how far I ran, I'd never find safety on Midgard. The Nine held a cell for me, but I'd created my own.

"Maybe I'd be better off turning myself in," I said as a breath pushed past my lips. At least then, the running would end, and I would not have to glance over my shoulder every other second. My lips pressed together as I fought against the realization of my words. If I'd done that years ago, my parents would still be alive. My head turned, and I buried it within my hands. "No."

Either way my destiny sucked. My thoughts trailed, and I caught my likeness again. The woman reflecting back at me wasn't me, not even close.

"It's not like I'll ever see him again." And if I did, I'd be sure to look like myself just so I could rub it in. With an effort to look presentable, I finger combed out the knots in my hair. I gave up and threw it back up into a messy bun. It looked better, but I couldn't do anything for the raccoon eyes or the discoloring of my skin. Not all the makeup in the world could help me fake it either. The Myst tied into our blood and bodies. The more we used, the worse off we appeared. If a mage used too much too soon they'd kill themselves.

Jellied legs hopped from the cab, and I grasped the mirror for support. At least everything else seemed back to normal, now that I'd left Liam behind. But I still refused to shake his judgment of me. He acted nothing like in my dreams, where we'd appeared as kindred spirits or even close friends. But perhaps it was what it was, and it was just a dream. I dropped all thoughts of him. He couldn't even fall from his high and mighty horse to lend me a hand. I'd risk his insanity again when I visited tomorrow, but for tonight, I was done.

Lips curled into a smile and reflected from the mirror. Oh yes, I'd go back one way or another. Shoulders pushed back and I lifted my chin. "You ain't seen the last of me, Liam."

My stomach growled as I entered the quaint diner. Did they even call them that in the South? The variety of foods infiltrated my nose. Fried chicken, baked sweets, and gravy mixed with various other scents from the patrons' dishes. My mouth watered. I smiled at the young server, who held a hand up and signaled me to wait. There wasn't a huge rush, so I nodded my head and offered a small smile. My gaze wandered around as she finished with her customer, and my eyes landed on the back of a tall man seated at the bar, swirling a glass of amber liquid. I sniffed lightly, honing in on the bar and separating the smells. Scotch, a drink I'd known all too well, and I smelled its pungent odor mixed with orange oil from the alcove. It wasn't Graftfield Scotch Whiskey; my family's money came from distilling the spirit.

The man's reflection drew my attention, but I tried not to stare. The hawk-like features intrigued me, though his nose didn't quite match his face. A little small, but somehow still fitting as it curved upward. Adorable nonetheless … Something about him I recognized.

A finger tapped my chin, but when I chased the memory, it burned away. He looked about my age, maybe a little older. Clothing was messy like his dark brown hair and unshaven face. He glanced in my direction, and I averted my gaze. As soon as he turned back around, I stole another peek. A smirk tugged at the corner of his mouth, and grey eyes met mine in the mirror. *Busted.* Thank goodness the server arrived and saved me from further embarrassment. She seated me in a booth and handed over a menu.

"Take a moment to glance over the menu. What'd you like to drink, sugar?"

I smiled and replied, "Coffee, please, and a glass of water —"

"Make those two coffees." The man from the bar leaned against the separator. A blush spread over my cheeks. His lips widened into a grin. "Sorry, but I figured who wants to eat alone?"

Swallowing hard, I nodded and glanced away. Silvery eyes drew me back in and consumed my curiosity. *Where'd I know him from?* The warmth of his smile affected me, and I found myself grinning back. When was the last time I'd smiled? My eyes shifted, unsure of what to say or do. I failed to recall my mother's stern warnings over interacting with humans and public places.

"Sure, that'd be great."

Just a meal, don't tell him anything and nothing terrible will come of this.

"I saw you ride up. You don't talk like a Yankee." He plastered a goofy grin on his face, crooked but quite charming.

I blinked as the words registered. "Wait, how'd you see from at the bar?" Hidden from view my fingers danced in my lap. I held his gaze; years of training steadied my composure as my parents' voices shouted the rules. The first was easy, until I knew for sure; everyone I encountered worked for the Nine. Trust no one, as Agent Mulder from *The X-files* would've said.

"Ah, so you were checking me out." Crap. He chuckled and glanced over his shoulder. The door jingled, and my eyes followed his. An older man came in, and he turned his attention back to me. "Saw your plates walking over."

My face burned all the way to the tips of my ears. Dang it, this was what happened when my parents sheltered me. I told them it'd backfire, and here I was, making an ass of myself.

"Sorry, I was just—" I started but stopped, shaking my head. No more distractions allowed. Heck, I needed food and sleep, and to figure out where to go from here. My parents always had a plan, but mine ended with finding Paulo.

"S'alright, nothing to be embarrassed about." He reached out and touched my hand. The caress startled me, and I pulled away. "So what brings you into Anderson?"

Is that where I was? Looking around again, I had a strange sense I'd been here before, but it wasn't possible. Still if I'd any logic left, I'd go, run far away and not look back. I lacked the energy, at least tonight, to run anymore.

"Just passing through." His gaze darkened, and he leaned closer, resting his elbows on the table. I swallowed the lump forming in my throat and tore into the breadbasket.

Between bites I asked, "You from 'round here?"

"Yes and no, I'm from Charleston originally, but I used to live around here." He gazed at me. "I'm just down this way checking colleges out. What about you?"

"I grew up in New York." I blinked, hoping he'd bought the lie.

He tilted his head. "Planning on going to school?"

"Me?" My eyes widened. "No, no plans." I took a long sip before replying. "What'll you study?"

"Veterinary medicine. I've a soft spot for animals." I loved animals too, but I had never owned any.

The server approached us as we talked about our furry connection. Life on the run didn't allow for much of a career, but I liked the idea of helping and saving. *If I were human or remotely normal, I'd …* The server interrupted my thought. "What can I get y'all?"

A pad appeared from her stained apron. My eyes did a double take as it jumped from the pocket into her hand. She smiled and repeated her question. I hadn't glanced at the menu and had her recommend a dish. At that point, I didn't care. As long as it was food and edible, I'd devour it.

My dinner guest was another story. Here I was, living on no sleep and loads of caffeine. I refused to buy into anything he slung at me; the light touches, the smoldering gaze. I shoved it all off and reinforced my shield to block him. For once in my life, I honestly didn't want to know the truth. I wanted my entire body to numb itself and strung the notion around me like a security blanket. No thinking, no words, no nothing but the quiet darkness to envelop my broken soul.

Was it normal for a person you just met to be so touchy-feely? I'd watched human television, but my experience ended there. Liam, he touched me too, but not like this. *Because I repulsed him.* White pain clouded my vision. My head pounded from everything in the now, and all the events that led me here lingered. Uncertainty arose at every smile, laugh, or gleam of everyone's eyes.

There were similarities too, between the stranger and the supernaturals, more than I cared to admit. Maybe I grasped at straws ... the edges of my insanity contracting. Confusion jumbled with sitcom cliché until I couldn't see where the real world melded with mine. My head shook and reached for a sugar packet. The sweet tea never seemed sweet enough anymore. The bread tasted off, too, and had turned to ash in my mouth.

He breathed in, and those grey eyes trailed out the window. Pain flashed for a brief moment but disappeared. This man was confused too.

I wanted to know why he resembled Liam. They weren't twins or anything. Eyes and hair both differed between the men, but they were almost the same height. I mean it wasn't rare to see two tall men in one day, but with our server's magic tricks tossed into the mix along with her pretty face and model legs ... she screamed supernatural.

Usually I'd glance and read their Myst, but neither the man nor server seemed to have any. Had I drained myself that much? After Liam, I didn't believe anyone wanted to help me. Were they reaching out in their own way or was I a fool to think anyone could put their opinions aside and care? Humans, according to the news I read, had a tough time with that too. They always judged one another on the silliest notions, but supernaturals were just as superficial and a tad more vain.

Yeah, I understood I looked like a cross between a drowned sewer rat and someone kicked by a stubborn mule, but it didn't make me one. Wasn't that normal, bruised egos and rejection going hand in hand, right?

My chin lifted higher, and I decided I was through with even thinking of what's-his-face. My brow rose. How had I ended up dwelling on him again? Well he could screw himself for all I cared, and with an attitude like that, I bet he did it often.

Call me mad, crazy, and even absurd, but I would not allow a man's thoughts or feelings to pull me down again. I was my own woman now, on my own, and trying to survive in a new world. *If that meant being alone, oh well, here was to becoming the next crazy cat lady.*

"You know, I never caught your name." Our eyes locked again, and my heart stuttered against my rib cage. The grey in his eyes, I swore it stirred. My amulet remained cold, but there was a mage nearby. The server maybe. She'd conjured the pad, I was certain. I sensed the Mysts' fiery depth in the air; faint, but it was there.

"I'm Jamie Mc Douglass." He extended his hand. Why did everyone give full names? My shield faltered as I held his smooth fingers. Heat radiated off them, but not strong enough to burn. Dang it, he was the mage. The Myst lay faint, but it was there. Jamie's eyes continued to hold mine. Sparks ignited in the silver swirls, and specks of gold appeared too.

Fire and Air, now there was an intriguing combination.

"Beautiful, like a precious gem ... " His thoughts raced through my mind, and I cursed the Gods for this new power. I didn't want it, not now, not ever. Being empathic was hard enough.

"I'm Aurie," I said, withdrawing my hand in record speed. "You think I look ..."

His brow rose, and I let the words die out. To ask Jamie meant exposing me. Twice in one day was pushing my luck. I wasn't wrong most of the time. He might not realize what I was. I wasn't familiar with how or why I could read another supernatural. Like everything else unanswered, I just did it.

Jamie grasped my hand, and before I could react, he brought it to his lips. He trailed kisses over each knuckle. I froze as the heat rose in my cheeks. His voice lowered as he said, "I think you look like what?"

The lopsided grin returned. As if to challenge me further, his eyes swam rapidly, forming and then collapsing, as if filled with liquid smoke. When his tongue licked across his full bottom lip, I took a deep, cleansing breath to clear my mind of all thoughts. What in Freya's fire was he trying to do? He acted like a raging lunatic high on firewater. I'd half the mind to ask him how much he'd drunk but held my tongue.

"Hell?" I shrugged, returning his smile and ignoring whatever the heck that was all about. Jamie distracted me with his mouth, the corners turning up into a devilish grin, and flashing perfect, pearly whites. If the food didn't come soon, I'd be in trouble. All the same regrettable trouble with a capital T, because I'd had it up to my neck, and his crap made me madder than a wet hen.

"I promise you, you don't look like hell, Aurie ... Maybe well traveled is a better description?" He laughed, and I rolled my eyes at his jest. My cheeks cooled, and we fell into a calmer silence. As if he'd read my mind, the odd behavior ended. I tried to keep myself distracted by watching traffic through the window, but all I saw was Jamie's reflection in the dark glass. He winked at something he watched too, but not me. My eyes searched for whoever it was, but there wasn't anyone outside. I jumped out of my seat as a clatter of plates crashed to the floor.

"Sorry, y'all," our server said. "Wasn't your food, I promise." She scurried by with a tray of steaming, intoxicating food. Her blond ponytail whipped to and fro with the sway of her hips.

Grace and poise were two abilities I lacked. She returned with two plates that were more oval than round and set them in front of us. I was starving, but now regarded my food as poison.

Vertigo rose again, and my head rested in the palm of my hand. I peered out the window, seeking anything to explain the dizzying sensation that numbed my skull. The signs of life in this town died down, and I checked my watch for the time. It was eight o'clock, where was everyone?

Anderson didn't seem like a small town on the map. A speck compared to the city, but why'd the quaint town seem to shut down? I sighed, capturing the sound in my palm. The streets fell into complete darkness as the moon slowly rose. Here I was, stuck with a mage, who might or might not be with the Nine, and who might or might not be messing with my head. The same sensation happened with Liam. Had he followed me? I hoped not. There was more than enough crap filling my plate. My breath fogged the large window. If my parents could see me now, they'd blow their tops.

"Something wrong with the food?" Jamie whispered, concern lacing his tone. I spared him a glance and saw the same emotion in his creased face. Why'd he care if I ate? My shoulders shrugged.

Gods I didn't know what anything in this world meant. Maybe I'd overreacted, and this was normal for supes. Didn't humans go all gaga when someone paid them attention? At least they did on the TV and in books. Aimlessly, I pushed at the food, trying not to scrape my plate.

"Like not hungry at all, or would you rather have something else?" he asked, looking down at his plate.

I didn't answer, not knowing what else to do, and returned my gaze out the window. The truth was crude, and I didn't think I could allow the words to flow from my lips. "I don't trust you, don't know you, and I spent my entire life away from ... away from reality." Those seemed like the wrong words to say.

That was it, major headdesk moment. I'd have smacked my forehead if the notion wouldn't have posed more questions. No friends, and never boyfriends, dang I seldom left my house out of dread. I realized how sheltered I truly was right then. Survival alone had allowed me the courage to fuel my soul and this feeling that if I didn't come south then somehow I'd fail. My parents, their death wasn't in vain.

"It's strange ... this ... I don't know how," I lowered my voice, "to be normal." Jamie's brow rose as he cut his sandwich into halves and then into quarters. "My parents were ..." Smirking, he tossed two pieces onto my plate and swiped my baked potato. I raised an eyebrow in response. "What're you doing?"

"You need to eat, nibble on those, and drink your water," Jamie said in a mock-maternal tone, and before I could argue, he stole my coffee mug too. Gods, he was an odd one, but ... he was strange just like me.

"Okay Momma," I murmured and rolled my eyes.

Pain wrinkled his brow. "You have a good mother."

She was a terrific mother. Blinking my tears away, I eyed the window. The memory of her seeped back in, ripping layers off one at a time. Her laugh, I'd never hear it again. My dad's kindness, that was gone too. It hit me hard like a punch to the stomach, a knife through my bleeding heart.

My parents were dead, and they'd never come back.

"Hey, are you alright?" Jamie's hand touched my shoulder as he slid in next me. Our thighs touched, the heat radiated up and down the length, sparks igniting a surge of energy between us. Not in a sexual way, these sparks were the Myst. He glanced down, but I couldn't cast my eyes away. The light danced across his skin as it flickered.

Was I supplying power to him, or was he siphoning it from me?

"What's wrong Aurie?" he whispered, and his soft fingertips stroked against my cheek. I held my breath as the smooth pads whisked a stray hair behind my ear. Coolness followed the wake of his touch.

I needed to be one hundred percent sure that Jamie was not with the Nine. I'd rather learn the truth now as opposed to later. The risk was more substantial this time with so many people; I stared into his eyes and willed my shield down. My head flipped to the window as I winced into my shoulder. Emotions trickled in, no thoughts, and I dissected each one, pushing past the fickle patrons to zero in on Jamie.

I was wrong again. No, I saw … My lips pressed together, and I pressed myself further as the essence reached out to him. The gentle white light, invisible to human eyes, spread over his body. Daddy's books said it was supposed to stimulate supernaturals. Jamie sat stoically, as if there was nothing going on. I blinked, and my mouth dropped open. The Myst encircled him, the waitress, and a patron I hadn't seen. My hand trembled as their energies rolled over my skin. Our server's emotions contradicted my theory as two signatures billowed out. Same went for the hidden patron remaining out of view. My fingers curled. They were both lycans. Was Six and Twenty a refuge? I turned my depleting white energy toward Jamie. A faint hum of Myst pulsed against my dampened skin.

My breath blew out as I dragged the Myst back into me. My skin turned clammy, and my fuzziness returned. Jamie said my name and shook my shoulder. "It's just been an awfully long day, err days actually. I have, I am just tired is all. My parents passed away and … I should go."

I tried to stand, but he blocked my exit.

"We all get like that sometimes." Jamie leaned away and rested his arms out to the sides. "Grief, eh, it is different for everyone." He stared at his knuckles, and my eyes followed. They were bone white. Ah, Jamie wasn't so stoic after all. I was right, but why'd his power read low? He shook his head and the light blinked from his eyes. Jamie lowered his head. "I lost my parents too. I was just a kid."

My brow furrowed as he spoke about his parents. The brightness in his grey eyes dulled even more. In his darkness, my heart soared. He'd understood and lost someone dear to him too. My hand clamped over his and squeezed. "It still hurts doesn't it?"

"Every day. Every day I think of them." Jamie's gaze faltered; eyes welled for a moment and then cleared. He changed the subject to mundane topics after that, but my mind never drifted far from my parents. I half listened, gazing off into space and slipping glances out the window.

Movement caught my eye. "Did you see that?"

At some point, he brought his plate over, yet I didn't remember him moving it. Jamie nodded his head to my spoken question, while shoveling his potato, err, my potato into his mouth. My appetite remained obsolete as I watched him eat.

"What?" he mumbled with his mouthful, and I swallowed the bile. Momma would've slapped me for that. "You need to eat," Jamie added.

I forced a smile and lifted my sandwich. "What'd you think that was? Looked like a wolf to me."

Jamie froze and his mouth gaped. Slowly his eyes panned the window. Howls cut through the glass, and I glanced over my shoulder. Green and blue eyes glowed in my peripheral; those eyes belonged to two lycans.

CHAPTER SEVEN

LIAM

My mind replayed the events with Auriel as I ran toward the Oracle's house. I knelt by her side on the front porch as she sat there, fiddling with her fingers as I eyed her. Pushed, shoved, and touched, but none of it mattered. Her mind remained behind the towering barriers she'd constructed. For as long as I could remember there was one person who held the power to knock me out. Instead of mind reading, I'd fallen back on old senses and tried figuring all this out. Her truck settled in the driveway. Cherry red, yet it seemed like an odd choice for how she dressed. All in all, she didn't peg me as the type to drive a flashy new truck.

The clothes on her back appeared outdated, worn but not ruined. But what did I know about fashion? Jamie's expertise was fashion, although my brother slacked over the past few years. She lifted her face and followed a noise. I hadn't bothered glancing; it was Regin. Auriel's Myst read more powerful than I'd expected, hell, it was more than I'd ever seen. Hybrids tended to pack a punch, but this bordered ridiculous even for a supposed high mage.

No matter how hard I'd pushed at her mind though, I'd heard nothing but static. Only the Oracle did that. I sighed inward, not allowing weakness to shine through in my body language. Holding my emotions in wasn't something I maintained well long term. Lycans held short tempers, and I hadn't the best grip over the beast yet. But I tried at first. The internal battle began, as the beast's voice shouted through my head; it screamed to hold on. On to what, I didn't know.

No, this couldn't be her, right? Those were my thoughts as my eyes glanced to the clear sky. The Oracle was wrong, Gods she had to be wrong. Yet my intuitions kicked into gear, screaming for me to guard and keep her near me. That voice belonged to my Guardian Myst and was not all that shouted. Warmth washed over my body when I'd touched her supple skin. I hadn't wanted to stop touching, but I forced myself to drop her. Guardian or not, there was something strange going on there, and I aimed to figure it out.

She'd blinked and asked, "Sorry. What'd you say?"

"Have we met before?" I'd blurted out again and messed with a potted plant, righting it on the porch. I couldn't shake the déjà vu whenever I'd gazed into her amber eyes or studied her cherub cheeks. Her Myst swam in them like small molten pools of lava, and her face reminded me of someone I couldn't place.

Phoenixes tended to have golden eyes like the Guardians had green eyes, but that wasn't always the case. Her head cocked, rocking back and forth, and her brow scrunched. Sweaty sheen beaded on her temple. Lycans, by nature, tended to make others uncomfortable, but I hadn't bothered her. *Holding no fear could make a person dangerous.*

"I don't think so." She'd shrugged her broad shoulders. "Name's Auriel."

"Ariel? Like that fish woman?"

"Naw." She'd chuckled softly. "Sounds like the bird oriole but spelled different is all." Tendrils plastered to her neck and disappeared beneath her collar. Dark lines hinted from below the neckline. Tattoos. Like humans, we supes never had enough ink, and we tended to start young. By fourteen, I'd already had more than a handful. Even prim and proper Jamie had them. But tattoos hadn't eased my mind either.

Her accent mirrored a southern belle, and her sweet tone warmed me. I swallowed hard. Auriel's laughter made me want to smile and laugh along with her. But I couldn't and stuck to my gut. My hands shoved into my pockets, and I'd rocked onto my heels before setting myself on the stoop. She'd tucked a stray strand of auburn hair behind her ear but refrained from making eye contact.

Her scent encompassed me with notes of lime, earth, and motor oil. Well shut my mouth, I hadn't a clue what to do with this woman. Auriel was the complete opposite of girls I'd dated –not that I'd dated much. Six and Twenty wasn't exactly crawling with eligible ladies.

I preferred blondes like Regin, but not her specifically, seeing as she was my cousin. We weren't into inbreeding although it happened from time to time with distant cousins. Loki's original lycans weren't blood related even though they'd referred to each other as cousin, brother, or sister.

My inner voice –the beast – disagreed with my assumptions over Auriel. He'd growled deep, reverberating a request that etched and seared into my mind.

Mine.

"I'm Liam Skyland," I'd said and offered my hand. She'd scoffed at the gesture and stood up, brushing her hands over baggy jeans. Auriel's legs wobbled, but she'd regained her balance as she latched onto the porch railing. Her eyes widened into saucers and the Myst circling her form shifted before it too had righted itself. The long list of oddities grew with each moment I'd spent in her company.

"I take it you're related to Paulo?"

A smirk formed on my face. "Not really, but we share a last name."

My relation to the elder draugr stayed ceremonious at best. I owed him for life. He saved me, and I loved him as a father. In turn, he loved Jamie and me as his sons. Letting out a frustrated breath, Auriel glanced around. Her eyes never settled one place for long, before they'd zoomed onto something else. She'd noticed sounds too, sounds a mage –even a Phoenix – shouldn't hear. No...everything about this curious creature sounded warning bells through my head.

Keelan's words from last night repeated. Sure she'd hinted at the woman holding incredible power, I'd give her that much. But I had a tough time accepting that this woman was my one true love. Where were the intense emotions? I'd examined her, but my own superficial opinions built a wall around me. She wasn't ugly, but ... I couldn't place my finger on it.

A groan left my lips as I'd risen from the porch, but she hadn't garnished a glance in my direction. I'd tapped into her thoughts again, hoping before was a fluke. White noise, an endless stretch of dotted highway, a lycan by a dumpster that appeared much too large, and then a reflection of my brother Jamie breezed through her mind. My face reddened, and my fists clenched. *Damn it Jamison.* Was I too late? Hell, we're all doomed if he had Auriel working for the Nine. She needed to leave, and there was one way I'd know how. My Myst retracted, and I'd pulled all my barriers down. We'd see how far her fearlessness reached when the beast uncaged and ran free.

Paulo's voice already resounded in my head the entire time I pushed Auriel. Dad wouldn't think of turning down a supernatural in need or tossing what he didn't understand aside. Panting hard, I scratched at the Oracle's weathered door.

"Liam, where's the woman?" she asked, poking her head out the entrance. A frown dropped over her wrinkled face, and she slammed the door on my muzzle. I yelped, as a whisker tore free. Moments later, she tossed out a change of clothes. I gathered them in my mouth and trotted to the side of her small house to change.

"Where's she at, boy?" the Oracle asked through her gritted teeth, as I rounded the corner. Her eyes flashed between black and blue. On instinct alone, I moved backward to allow space between us.

"There is no—" I started, raking my hand through my hair, avoiding her odd eyes. My heart thrummed in my chest, and no amount of air helped calm it down. I couldn't find words to explain my actions, and nothing I said made it all better, or changed the hard lines painted over the Oracle's face.

"Gods, have I taught you nothing? I ain't ever took you to be shallow."

I averted my gaze, staring off into her flowerbed. My cheeks burned. She stepped toward me, stabbing her bony finger into my chest with more effort than expected. Was I that easy to read?

"You look at me when I'm talking to you, boy." My eyes rose to meet her gaze. "That poor lost girl … just spent days on the road runnin' for her life." How'd she know she came from far away? "Did you think she'd show up all perty and perfect?"

Yes, but looking at it from that perspective, she was right.

"I'll fix it," I whispered, biting back the void growing inside the pit of my stomach. The butterflies had caressed my skin in delicious warmth but had disappeared with her, and I wanted them back.

"It won't be easy." Her voice softened with the lines around her blue again eyes. "Search deep inside, how you feelin' now?"

I swallowed hard and palmed my neck. "I won't fail, I …" Mrs. Graftfield placed her hand on my shoulder.

"Auriel's quite gifted; she's an empath." I mouthed the words. The only empathic creatures were the Valkyrie, and only the born held the ability, but they were extinct. "Whatever you felt she knows."

An odd burning sensation stung my eyes. I'd thought some awful words. The Oracle sighed. "It gits worse. Fainauriel is a Phoenix like I warned you." Her finger wagged at me, but I blinked at the name. I knew that name and tilted my head as if it would fall free. All that dropped was the fact that I hadn't told the Oracle her name, or that she called herself Auriel.

"What'd I gone and told you about them?"

My fingers twitched, and I cracked my neck. High mages had full access to a Guardian, or another high mage's thoughts if unshielded, and as an empath, Auriel read my emotions too.

But how did she block me?

No words defended what I'd done or thought. Even if Auriel wasn't what I expected, I had no right to behave that way. I'd judged her, when she came here for help. She'd cried that she needed help, and I had driven her off. Dad would kill me when he found out, and Keelan would tell him.

The Oracle paced; gravel and grass crunched beneath her walker. "Your brother … you'll have to fight Jamie now that she's left Six and Twenty."

Jamison … A hand cupped my chin. My thoughts trailed to her words last night. She'd spoken of someone making a decision. I hadn't expected Jamie to be the one.

"The girl will walk … the Nine …" Had he already tried and failed? Was that why I saw him in her mind? I should've listened to the wolf. My eyes closed, and his claws rose again.

"You should trust me, mate."

"Gods, Liam I thought Paulo raised you better than this … I would've never bothered … what you waitin' for? You standin' there

with your mouth open waitin' for rain? Git out of 'ere, and don't
you dare come back till you find her."

Eyes flung open as the Oracle shoved me.

*"Always trust me; we know Auriel and she knows us ... somehow,
we must all remember."* I gave a curt nod and stepped to the side of
the house before shifting again.

She yelled after me, "Mind your feelings and keep 'em in check
while you're at it too ..."

She mumbled something else, but even I couldn't make it out.

My wolf form made it easier to track Auriel's smell. Night vision
helped too, and there were fewer distractions. From my driveway, I
caught any reminisce of Auriel. Too distracted to notice the subtle
floral and fruity notes before, it affected me now. Like a siren's song
on the wild sea, the scent became my beacon. I trailed the odd
combined scent of patchouli, peach blossoms, and lime to the old
truck stop right outside of town. Pained hazel eyes stared through
the window and off into the distance.

"You caused that ache," the beast spoke inside my head. Her gaze
flickered but never connected with mine.

I let out a gut wrenching howl, making myself known. Nick
trotted up beside me and sat on his haunches. Why was he here? Pink
tongue slid from his mouth and he panted. Blue eyes trained on me.
For me, he had come to help me and this was our combined show of
power. Yet I couldn't ignore my brother's influence over the elements
either. I heard them speaking to him, but they'd sided with me. Too
bad their opinion mattered little and the one that did sat beside Jamie.

"Let her go, Jamie. Her greatness isn't meant for you, but for us all."

"No, brother I can't. I'm sorry, Liam," Jamie replied.

Shock ran over me for a moment, my eyes met with his, but
Auriel did not acknowledge me as she stared out the window.

I turned to Nick. *"Is she shielding him?"*

"Aye she tis, but I daena thinks she realizes," Nick said, although I
didn't understand why his accent changed. Not quite a thick brogue
but not his usual accent either. My head tilted, but he didn't com-
municate further.

We watched, listened, and waited. I was helpless; there was
nothing else to do but wait, and I relayed that to Reggie who'd

covered the back door. Aurie's eyes connected with mine after my brother whispered something. My ears strained and twitched. She turned and spoke to Jamie, but I heard nothing through the glass. When Aurie faced me again, her hand clutched her chest, and her face contorted as if pained. An ache swelled within me, and I fought the urge to lift my muzzle to the sky.

Jamie nodded and then appeared deep in thought, his eyes not leaving mine. He rose and left her. I had a chance. He'd parted without a kiss or even a hug. Hope flared and pumped through my pounding heart. Jamie hadn't sunk his claws into her yet.

I wouldn't hurt her. Never again would I hurt her, but I didn't think my message penetrated her shield. Auriel waved to a server, without looking away, until the woman approached her table.

A door slammed and Regin yelped; Jamie ran.

"Go after him. I'll make sure she's safe." Nick darted after his sister. I slinked through the cars, hiding from Auriel's view.

I didn't want her to fear me and hated that she already did. Another fault to add to my growing list, but this time it was mine.

I asked Nick, *"Any luck?"* but there was no response.

After she left the restaurant, I kept my distance. If I had to guess, I'd say she made sure we were gone. A giant ass, yes, but I wasn't her enemy. At least we'd managed to chase Jamie away from her.

"Now to find a way to keep him away," the beast spoke up. Six and Twenty was the only way. My traitor brother couldn't come and go as he pleased anymore.

Auriel climbed into her truck, and I jumped on a beater parked in the lot for a better view. She pulled her hair down and shook it out. *"Far prettier when it's down,"* the beast spoke, and I agreed. Something ignited within me, a primal instinct exploded as she drove away.

I was on her trail, and my heart resonated throughout my whole body as it tried catching up. Tongue lopping in a heavy pant, I growled and nipped at the air. No, she couldn't leave me. The truck slowed down. Confusion settled in as my head whipped around. Auriel didn't leave, and instead she parked at the adjoining hotel that shared a general lot.

I halted ten feet away. Our eyes connected in her rearview mirror. My breath hitched, burning my lungs, and I coughed.

"Liam, we need ye now," Nick cried over the stilling night.

"I told the waitress I wasn't crazy," Auriel thought. *"I know what I saw, and I saw wolves. Where'd the other go?"* Tilting my head to the sky, I cried out my answer.

Auriel knew what I was. She froze, wide amber eyes holding my gaze in her rearview mirror. *"It has green eyes like Liam, not blue like the other one."*

A mage's vision shouldn't have differed from that of a human. How'd she see our eyes? Auriel's thoughts ceased, but she didn't move. My paws were heavy and planted, as I awaited her next move.

My head lowered. Ache pulled, swelling within my chest. Her scent filled my nostrils, and saliva drooled from my muzzle. *"We told you,"* the beast rose again, *"she is the one."*

Why now? Why didn't this happen when she'd first come to me?

"We are under a spell. I told you as much. She was ours, and we knew her." I began to think my beast was crazy. Perhaps even crazier than I was for stalking a Phoenix mage. Unless I was her Guardian, the power coursing off her shield was enough to end me. Unless …

"Yes" … the beast hissed. I cocked my head.

Was I her Guardian?

Auriel couldn't leave and neither could I. The Guardian bond was when souls united. History said that if they were ever apart the hurt built to agonizing proportions. When a Guardian bonded with a high mage or immortal, it was for a lifetime. But a lycan bond was similar, affecting both partners. Since I was both, would separation hurt even more? Would I die when she died?

"Aye," Nick said with an accent again.

Lycans loved hard; lycans loved to the death. The tug in my chest, was that love? I wasn't sure, and I lay on the gravel lot, panting as my tongue lobbed. We watched one another, but she remained cautious. Auriel's shield faltered again.

"Stop being a wuss. It's just a lycan, and you're a Phoenix," she berated herself. Giving in to my presence, she killed the engine. My tail kicked up gravel dust. Moments passed before she slowly opened her door and inched around to the truck bed. Auriel's eyes refused to leave mine.

"Don't even think about it, rover." I snorted and refrained from barking. "Pretty eyes," she whispered, and a low growl rose in my throat. *I am anything but pretty.*

She pulled a bag from the truck bed and peeled off her baggy t-shirt, revealing a tiny tank top that hugged her body. My breath staggered, as I observed what I was blind to just hours before.

The Oracle was right … about everything. Why hadn't I noticed it before? Smooth and creamy skin marred with tribal wing designs spanned her shoulders. Ebony ink embraced the sultry curve of her hips, as they swayed back and forth. Whimpers left my lips, and I backed into a hedge. The beast rose, and I shut my eyes. My body trembled, as a voice screamed inside my head.

Auriel whipped around and peered into the night. Gods, I was a fool. Those full lips lay parted as if to speak, and I longed to hear her voice even if it was to scream. *"You deserve it … She's a Goddess in both beauty and power. Let us have her, Liam."*

I shook my head. Yes, I wanted her, but not like this. To just take her was wrong. Her eyes searched for me even as she walked into the office. When she departed with a key, her gaze floated over the parking lot, seeking me out. One day soon, our paths would cross again, but not tonight. For tonight Auriel was safe. Despite the ache it caused, I helped her better by taking Jamie down.

By the time I hooked up with the team, they'd chased my brother into the next county where we couldn't cross. The human population was too dense and three wolves running around Pickens might have risen more than a few eyebrows.

"He's a mage and powerful. He came a hair close to killing Reggie. But she'll recover." Nick doubled forward, catching his breath. "We're sorry we couldn't catch him, man. Did the girl get away too?" he added, but I shook my head.

I didn't want to tell him too much. I trusted him and Reggie with my life, but this was personal. I'd involved them because I couldn't be in two places at once, and right now, I'd left Auriel unguarded longer than I liked.

He grimaced and straightened. My eyes followed his movements. Nick clutched his chest, but there was no sign of injury.

"We're being asked to protect her from the Nine. I don't know why she was with Jamie, but come hell or high water, I'll find out." Until I figured it out, I wasn't about to trust anyone but Paulo and the Oracle. Nick was next, but the accent changes, and the way he looked at Auriel … as if he knew her.

"Saw her driving through town earlier and assumed, sorry man." He finished dressing and pulled a t-shirt over his head. The downfall to shifting was the nakedness afterward. He tossed me a set of clothes too. I called them staples; we dressed alike in jeans and pocket tees. Anything else itched against my skin.

"She made me feel the same way, nervous and anxious, but then I caught a glimpse of Jamie and lost it." I enlightened him further on the events. Bizarre and asinine were two words I used a lot. This time I didn't leave out the part where I'd made an ass of myself.

"Ouch, so what do you think Jamie wants with her?"

"I haven't a clue, but from the way he's all over her, I'd bet you it's nothing we want to discover." My eyes glanced toward the moon and then back to him. "I just can't determine if we're dealing with my brother or an agent of the Nine."

Nick grimaced again and swallowed hard. I let it slide and didn't press him about it. Neither made it easier, but my brother I could handle. The latter meant more interference; we weren't ready for an invasion.

"So, you think she is the one?" More than curiosity piqued in his voice. "The one the Oracle told you 'bout," he added.

I shrugged and let my breath release. I hadn't known what to think. Before … her warm smile floated into my mind. As hard as I tried, I couldn't shake it. Her patchouli and lime hit me like a sucker punch to the nose, but we were miles from the hotel. All control dissipated, and I burst into my wolf again, running as fast as I could.

"You do love her, and you've got the moon madness."

Nick chuckled after me, as I raced back to the hotel, telling myself that I'd check on her, just one last time, before heading home. It was a lie; I had to see her again. But there was nothing to see when I arrived. Auriel had closed her blinds. I lay down at her door anyway. Her scent assaulted me through the door. The draw, the pull increased, and nothing in my world combated it.

"You have moon madness," Nick said again, enjoying his good laugh at my expense. A two-natured thing that most supes didn't understand, but we'd smell where a female was at with her cycle. Moon madness occurred when a female we liked was fertile and a lycan would do insane things to win her attention. I didn't grasp Nick's meaning. Auriel wasn't fertile.

I whined my frustration at the door standing between us. She ached; it nipped at my own heart, as her mind struggled, laden with increasing pain over the death of someone near to her heart. Her mind opened to me, and I didn't know why now. If I saw this before ... I'd ... who knew what my idiot self would've done. I waited, pleading for her to hear me, and released a low whimper.

Auriel failed to come outside and investigate.

Giving up, my eyes scanned the parking lot. Part of me hoped Jamie would show while I took watch. Pent up energy needed releasing. A growl left my muzzle at the thought of ripping him to pieces. I didn't know where the hatred stemmed from. He was my brother. Nothing changed that fact. I reminded myself the threat he posed with Auriel, and another snarl rippled from within. The beast wanted blood, but it wouldn't stop the Nine. They'd send another, and another, and then another, until they sent an army. We were all doomed if it got that far.

"Go home, Liam," Reggie scolded. I glanced at the door. By the snoring, Auriel was deep asleep. *"I've got this."*

"You know the drill if he shows. Howl, the shield will stop –"

She snorted and pushed me aside. *"Yeah, yeah, I've got it lover boy."*

chapter eight

JAMIE

Nick's plan went to hell in a handbasket before it'd even begun. Unless he'd wanted to teach me a lesson. The mere fact that Liam thought I'd harm Auriel proved he'd lost his damn mind. By a whisker, I escaped those mangy mutts. Thank goodness, she hadn't notice I'd siphoned her power back at the diner. For a moment, I thought she caught me. If she found out, and I prayed she didn't, I didn't want her thinking that was the reason I couldn't keep my hands off her. The thought of using Aurie left a bitter taste in my mouth, but I had no other choice. Still, it wasn't the worst crime I'd ever committed, and I silently promised to make it up to her.

Without it, Nick would've caught me. I smiled at the thought, but his ferocious attitude sent me reeling. Hell—he nipped at me. My hand rested over my beating heart. Sweat cascaded down my face, and I fought to catch my breath. The car felt like a ploy now. He'd meant none of it and used me.

I closed my eyes and pinched the bridge of my nose. His seascape scent penetrated me, and I lulled my head against the sharp tree bark. The feelings weren't alien to me, even if they were all wrong.

Punishment for all my misdeeds. The Nine managed to penalize me still. I grasped and pulled at my hair.

Murdering my mother wasn't enough. The Nine passed laws against homosexuality even though the Gods themselves often partook in such relationships. Humans weren't much better, especially in the South.

My ringer blared into the woods. "Crap." Merric's number flashed across the screen, and I answered it.

"Do you have her yet?" My brow rose at the English-Alfheimian accent. Duncan Graftfield never called me before, and why'd he call from Dad's phone? As the ancient Prince of the Unseelie Faeries, he co-chaired on the Council with his Elven twin sister, since they too were technically Fae.

I pled my case, leaving out a few details. Like letting her go into Six and Twenty and running into Nicky. "No, she's guarded tonight by a pack of pooka. I can't—" Okay, so I left out most of the truth.

"Do you value your life at all? Shifters should ne'er be a problem for you, *Jamie of the Phoenix*." Duncan said nothing else, hanging up on me before I had a chance to rebut. My eyes narrowed on the screen. Two were Fenrir lycans, and that alone made all the difference. Loki himself protected his ilk. That was what I got for lying, though I needed to cover my own ass.

My fists clenched, threatening to crush the phone. I couldn't ignore Duncan's bullying. My breath huffed, and I glanced around. He didn't know the half of it, and I doubted he'd ever gone so far to lose everything he cherished for love. As far as the Nine and the damned council was concerned, there were hiccups. They didn't need to know many things.

For starters, they didn't need to know that Nick was alive or that I loved him. Neither truth would bring happiness. With the Fae's threat on my head, I'd reach out to Paulo and tell him, no warn him, about Auriel. I didn't like it one bit, but there wasn't a choice if the Nine sent the Wardens out. They're the created army, imbued with unnatural power stolen from the shamans, mages, and druids. The one race that didn't fear them were the draugr, and for reasons unknown, they were immune.

However, I did hold doubts that a Warden could subdue Auriel. She always wielded power stronger than my own and Merric's combined. I laughed. That was saying something. Merric was one of the strongest mages alive, and a vamp hybrid now. That remained his strength over my Aurie.

Howls in the distance broke through my thoughts eluding that the coast was clear. A small reprieve, but I'd take the opportunity. I had to find Aurie too and apologize for disappearing; Paulo was but a call away. He'd know what to do and the best way to get her where she belonged. The draugr, for all his faults, wouldn't turn either of us down. He loved charity cases about as much as he hated the Nine. If I obtained his blessing then my brother couldn't touch me and neither could Nick.

I stepped from the woods and headed toward the diner. Glances swung with each noise. I didn't know what Aurie's plans were or where she'd go. Instinct told me not far. The path thinned out, and I could see the lights from the highway. The air grew cooler, and I shivered from the sudden drop in the spring night. Liam was probably watching her now. Unlike him, I couldn't trace her by scent. My feet hit the dead pavement. Anderson wasn't known for its nightlife. A large town, but half of it spread out into farm and woods. Our homes bordered the latter, separated by the streams and rivers of Hartwell Lake. I glanced to the diner; it was empty. My car sat in the parking lot, but her truck was gone.

Did Liam have the slightest inkling of what she once meant to the both of us? Somewhere, locked away deep in the recesses of his mind, Liam had to remember Auriel. A broken bond wasn't a good sign, and like white on rice, those two just belonged together. The five of us were a posse, chosen by the Myst and the Norns, and Aurie remained our common ground. But she disappeared, and we all tore apart.

"Ye tore us apart," the wind whispered, but it was Nick's voice trickling into my ears. Sweat broke on my forehead, and I pushed him away. *"Traitor."* His words sliced at me. But those words held truth.

Blue eyes flashed in the bushes, and soft steps followed; he stalked me. "Aye."

I blinked, as he stepped from the trees and underbrush. My heart pounded into my ears, and a smirk painted over his strong jaw. "Nicky … I …" Words caught in my throat, as he closed the distance between us.

His large hand wrapped around my throat, and he pinned me to the tree.

"I told ye to mind yer thoughts, hen." A low rumble rose in his throat and vibrated against me. He loosened his grip and trailed his finger down to my chin. The heat of him penetrated me and dragged me under a spell. I stared into his icy blue eyes tinting with yellow. My lips parted, and Nick dipped down. His mouth stole away my breath, and the butterflies pounced around seeking more. Rough hands cupped my face, and my fingers grasped his shirt. The solid ridges of the Scotsman teased my fingertips. He hadn't changed at all. Nick groaned as his tongue pressed into my mouth.

I sucked in a sharp breath. Electricity shocked every nerve in my body as his hands ran down my chest. Unlike before, I'd filled out. No longer was I a scraggly mage. Nick drew away, and rested his forehead against mine. My lungs burned for air; his nose rubbed along mine.

"Go and find our eun beag." My body froze; it didn't want to leave, but my mind screamed. I couldn't … I wasn't … My brows furrowed, as the grin spread over Nick's thick lips. "Jamie, go before I do something rash."

His hand brushed down my side; I shivered, wanting more.

"Rùn feum," I said, and he blinked.

Where the words came from, I didn't understand. My mouth opened, and they spilled out. How much longer could I fight the impulses? *I need him.* His lips grazed my forehead, and I closed my eyes, savoring his heat. I loved him, but those words I didn't say.

When I opened them again, he was gone. Cold emptiness encircled me like the other night when I awoke alone in the car, and then again at the diner when he left. My hand touched my lips, swollen and burning with his kiss. Had I imagined the kiss? Was I so far gone that I imagined his tenderness? Too much darkness existed in my life, much of it my own doing, but to love someone to the point of madness and then have them flee … I shook my head. No, Nicky wasn't cruel and ruthless. At least not with me.

I wanted to throw my head back and scream. What he did to me wasn't right. My eyes burned knowing what my fathers would say. The dreams … my career … revenge was over and for Nick, I'd tossed it all away. A tear dribbled down my cheek. Since my mother died, I'd shed them for him. Confusion clouded my vision at every turn, but I couldn't have him. I picked up a stone and tossed it into the trees.

Where did I go from here? I laughed; he was right to call me a traitor. Yet every time we parted, a piece of me died inside.

Last time I didn't think I'd make it. Between searching for Aurie and putting my time in at the Nine, I'd scraped through. My hands though were empty, and my heart remained shattered into bits. The guilt swallowed me, and training with the Wardens kept me alive. Their camaraderie and two-natured fury reminded me of Nick, and I made it my goal to help them. The Myst wasn't easy to use, and I guided them better than Merric. Guess now I turned on them too.

"Maybe that's just my destiny." The tear dried on my cheek. "No matter what I do, I hurt someone." And myself too.

I wasn't the only one who twisted on those he loved. The Oracle was powerful; she'd knocked me on my ass at full Phoenix. But the old bag didn't have the Myst to erase a whole town. Liam was a mage hybrid, and even with the Phoenix, he wasn't powerful enough either. Duncan or Danny could … maybe, but that made no sense. Danny's spell would've broken on death, and Duncan wanted to find her.

"Why'd everyone forget?"

That left Aurie. I grabbed a handful of stones and tossed them at the trees. There weren't enough of them. Out of all the hybrids I'd met, Auriel showed the greatest control and potential.

But tonight she'd lost control of her own emotions, and it showed. I shook my head. If she didn't remember soon, we'd all be in a heap of trouble. Her power though … if she were the one, war came for us all. We weren't prepared; none of us would survive unless she remembered.

I stayed across the street and strolled up the road a ways. Part of me searched for Nick. My heart hammered just remembering the kiss and the shock to my body. When I kissed women … that didn't happen. I walked back to the woods and around, returning to the rear of the diner. Every touch or kiss we shared, I ran away.

Damn the Gods. The confusion swam in my head. Darkness fell and blanketed the area. The diner closed, but the hotel stayed open. The dim parking lights and flashing vacancy sign offered a subtle glow. My eyes scanned the road and parking lot seeking out whichever mutt was on guard. At first, I couldn't find anyone and my heart plummeted, but then I saw her. It was the wolf I hit, the scent of burning fur lingered. The eyes of the beast flashed a frosty blue and speared a chill into my spine. Regin, Nick's baby sister by about five hundred years. Her eyes mirrored his.

My shield held up, and I decided what the best plan of action was here. Auriel's truck sat outside at the hotel, but I couldn't just show up now. I chewed my lip, thinking over the options available. However, I could move closer. All I needed was a distraction.

"Damn it, this better work," I muttered to myself and tapped further into my reserves than I was comfortable with. Hindsight, I could've borrowed energy from Nick; he was a Phoenix too. One of the many things we shared in common besides our friendship with Aurie.

The Myst dragged into me; I melded a ball of energy between my palms. If I slowed the motion down, it'd be like watching an artisan pull taffy, stretching the molecules and mixing the energy until perfection was achieved. In reality, the process took precious milliseconds to accomplish the act, and all that remained was to aim and discharge the Myst.

I let it float out of my fingers. The wolf barked at it, and I gave the sphere another thrust with my mind. The ball raced toward my car outside the diner. Already I was halfway to the building when the car alarm blared through my head. She never saw me … With a smile, I entered the office and sealed the door with my last ounce of energy.

My brow dampened, and my t-shirt clung to my body. "Can I help you?"

"Yes …" My lip quirked, and I dug into my wallet. A mind-manipulation charm was illegal, but desperate times … I waved it over the credit card I'd swiped from Merric, before handing it over to the clerk.

The man's eyes glazed, and he nodded when I asked for a room beside the redhead. My eyes scanned over the register, and the last entry signed in as Betony O'Nally. I pointed to the signature. "Her."

He rang me up and handed over my room key. I glanced over my shoulder. The lycans had come back; she wasn't alone. My chest panged, but I shook it away. My legs grew weighty, as the door clanged opened. I had enough energy to make it to my room. A small shield would have to do. It'd take only a smidgen of time, but the exposure was risky. My essence wouldn't recharge until I slept or drew Myst from another mage. Each step proved more difficult, but I had no other choice.

Aurie's energy wrapped around me before I reached my door. It brushed against my skin, caressing my darkest places, and reawakening my need. She was pure, unadulterated Myst, and for the first time I recognized the source. *Valkyrie ... the highest of the Dísir ...* outlawed by Odin himself. No wonder the Nine wanted me to bring her into the headquarters. They tortured and killed the born Valkyrie. Red, boiling blood replaced everything, as I sprinted the last few feet to my door.

Valkyries, the choosers of the slain. The poetic and prose Eddas spoke highly of the virgin warrior women who ushered the souls of the battle slain. Freya marked her, and it made sense why. Her love and acceptance alone mirrored our shared matron.

But she wasn't a fighter. Like Frigg, Auriel was a lover, and not in the sexual sense, but more like a mother. My brows rose and fell. Frigg was Odin's wife.

Part of me wanted to apologize and explain my actions tonight. Instead, I opened and closed the hotel room door as fast as I could. Calming my thrumming heart, I huffed and puffed my shortened breaths. My head tilted against the door, as I added up everything I knew of Fainauriel.

Even growing up with her ... I didn't know about her lineage except for relation to the Council. Both her grandfather and great aunt sat on the Council of Nine but even that was a rumor based on the shared last name. A paw scratched at the door, and I glanced out the curtain half expecting to see Liam's green eyes peering at me. *"Let me explain."* I shook my head even though he couldn't see. Nick's comfort came too easy. *"Aye promise no' touching. My hands are honorable, hen."*

A sigh tickled my throat as shoulders slumped forward. Saying no wasn't an option. Nicky was my mate; to be this close and not touch was like piercing my heart with needles. Like a dart through my heart, spreading poison along my limb. I strained to breath and groaned. Always within reach, Nick was, until my fingers reached for him. But this time he was real.

My hand removed the chain, and I opened the door. The massive grey wolf barged in and shifted before the door had shut. I cringed, as his bones crunched. A salty scent burned my nose like none other. Nick pressed my body against the door. Hot lips brushed against the back of my neck, and sharp teeth grazed my skin.

"You … you … promised." Large hands grasped my hips and drew me toward him. Was this the beast or Nick? Did it matter? I gulped, swallowing the saliva flooding my mouth. His name whispered from my lips. Nick's tongue swirled behind my ear, and I shuddered against him.

"Dae ye want me to stop?" Nick's hands brushed forward and over my thighs, feathered caresses, and he squeezed my hardened cock. I ground into his large palm and moaned. Nick flipped me around and warm hands cupped my face, forcing my gaze. "Aurie tis special to us all. She's the chosen one, Jamie, and we all have our parts to play too."

My eyes drifted over the span of his solid chest, blond hairs lining him like a pelt. They tapered off into a single trail, and disappeared into his groin. Hard to ignore the massive monster, as it rubbed against my stomach. I licked my lips in a slow and lazy circle.

"Touch me," he said, moving to my zipper. My gaze shot up, and I backed into the door. "Stop fighting it." Nick's eyes softened, but he trapped me against the exit. Lips roamed over my neck, nipping and teasing my flesh. My shirt ripped in two, and he chuckled in my ear. His words hummed against my skin, vibrating and surging into my depths. Nick dropped to his knees and glanced up with his big blue eyes. His hot lips kissed the outline of my cock.

"Please," I begged, knowing I'd return the favor.

My zipper dropped slowly, and his mouth followed the lazy dark trail over my stomach. I wasn't as hairy, or as big, in any sense.

"Ye perfect," he whispered, as he reached my head.

I glanced down as his wet tongue swirled over my tip and groaned. Nick shimmied my jeans down and tossed them out of the way. My fingers combed through his hair and pulled him closer as he grabbed my ass, drawing me nearer. Neither action seemed to connect our flesh enough. Four years apart felt like eternity but could I be enough for him? Nick, not the beast, would I be enough for the insatiable man as I was for the creature within?

Nicky answered my thoughts and kissed my tip. "Babe," I said as those thick lips covered the head. Desire thickened the air as he hummed and took me further into his mouth. Stars painted my vision, and my head tossed back, hitting the heavy door. I bit my lip as he sucked faster.

"Nicky," I breathed his name. My balls tingled and tightened; I wouldn't last long, not after his earlier teasing. As his tongue wiggled about, Nick's hand massaged my balls, brushing his fingers underneath. I quaked and tensed. "Nick," I warned him again, but he growled, vibrating his intention from my tip to my base. "Nicky babe ..."

I arched, head smacking into the door again as my body shot hard, clenching and releasing, as I'd never experienced before. I cried out his name, as his hot mouth devoured every drop of my sanity.

Knees gave out, as I heaved for breath, and toppled forward. Large arms swooped me up and steadied me. Nick's lips found mine and engulfed me. Dizziness swept over my head, and I swam in his bliss. His hand grasped mine and moved it to his hard cock. My fingers wrapped around the hot steel, and he groaned into my mouth. His arms shifted, a cool breeze calming my hot cheeks.

"Bed," he grumbled, tossing me onto the soft surface. He rose and smacked the A/C unit until it rattled on. "Yer killing me."

His hand ran through his hair, as I watched him from the bed. Thick, corded muscles tensed in his back and rippled from neck to toes. A sniffle followed. Nick braced himself against the unit and his blond hair bounced back and forth. Why didn't he let me in?

I swallowed and stared at my hands. My whole body tingled and trembled. The bed groaned, and my feet padded to his side. Arms slid around his trim waist, and my cheek rested on his shoulder blades. All I wanted for the past four years was to do this, to just be with the man I loved and not worry about anything else. "Nicky," I whispered. "Talk to me, babe. Please ... don't shut me out."

"Ye gonna run *again*. I daena ken if I canna take it *again*." He faced me, and I stroked his cheek. Nick turned into my touch and said, "I no' saying ye need to decide tonight, but one day ye gonna 'ave to. Yer mine and I yers."

The words tickled my skin, and rushed my blood.

"I was a dumb kid." Nick snorted. My forehead tightened. So much was left unsaid between us, and I didn't know where to begin. "I'm sorry."

Sorry would never be good enough. I released him and strolled to the bed. My body melded with the surface, and I sighed. Would he leave me again? Would I think this too a façade or dream?

Nick made a sound and sauntered to my side. He towered over me looking more like a giant than a lycan prince. My finger crooked, and a grin tugged over his jaw. Still, he didn't move. A hammering sounded through my ears, but I swallowed my tension, shifted, and knelt before him. Nick sucked in a sharp breath, as my hand cupped his heavy balls. Rough hands caressed my back, and I parted my dry lips.

Shiny moisture beaded on his head, and I licked it away, savoring his salty essence. His cock jerked, and his legs tensed. It wasn't easy to surprise him, and I smiled at the thought. My tongue swirled over his head, as he murmured my name. All he'd done to me, I did in return to the best of my ability. A hand jerked up and down his length, while my mouth busied itself with suckling his tip. Nick wrenched himself away and pressed me to the bed. His mouth dropped to mine, and his hand stroked my cock hard.

"Claim me," he said against my mouth. "Make me yers."

He reached down, pulled a condom from my jeans, ripped it open with his teeth, and rolled it over my dick. Nick spat on his hand and rubbed my cock. Before I could object, he lowered his ass, taking every inch of me in a steady stroke as my body arched.

Nicky rode me slow, kissing me with no abandon. Gods this was a dream, a fantasy come true. My body surged and tingled, as I thrust myself into him. Hands slid to trim hips, grasping and rocking Nick faster. I couldn't fight this, this perfection between us. *Us,* I sighed at the thought. We connected from birth to death and only the reaper could take us away.

"Hen," Nick moaned against my lips and cursed. Our sweaty bodies milked his cock and spread his sticky seed over our skin. As his hips rocked, and I plunged, our fate was sealed. Nick righted himself and sat up, strong thighs straddling my groin. His spent cock remained in a semi-hardened state and bobbed with his quick movements. Breathing ached as I gasped for breath and matched his inhuman speed. Rough fingers flicked my nipples and I knew I was a goner.

"Babe ... I'm gonna ..." My body stiffened and teeth clenched. Nick ground down, swirling around my base, as I exploded. My body trembled hard from the release. I jerked again, spasming harder than earlier. Nick leaned forward; he kissed me, smiled, and pulled away.

Muscles clenched my cock. "Dae I look like a wee bairn?"

I laughed, rubbing his thick, furry thigh. Nick cocked his brow, and rubbed his hands over my chest. *How would I explain this to my dad?* Nick sighed and glanced to the door. Dad relied on my affection toward Aurie. But little did he realize that my heart belonged to another.

"We all have parts to play, hen. Play yer part, but remember ye are mine."

"So you're saying to keep this up?" Nick leaned forward and kissed me again.

My legs wrapped around him, and I rolled him over. Nick never answered me and changed the subject. After a few more hours of rekindled romance, I fell asleep curled against his chest. Little did I realize my confusion was just beginning.

The next morning I awoke to the sound of an alarm clock. I didn't recall setting it, and groggy eyed, I fumbled with smacking the nightstand until my hand struck the cold plastic. My hand patted the cold mattress.

Alone. Nicky had left, and I sighed, staring up at the mirrored ceiling. Too engrossed in Nick, I had failed to notice it.

Physically unmarked, emotional trauma was still out. Secret lovers in an archaic world. My hand rested over my heart. Would he still want me when I aged?

I glanced at the clock again. A few more days and I'd grow closer to death. Draugr life looked sweeter every day. What did I care if I needed blood to survive? My arm rested behind my head, and I rested in my thoughts.

The fate awaiting me wasn't sweet. Death for both of us if they had caught us. The Nine enforced their asinine rules, ruling with iron fists. Draugr held their own rules above the Nine and so had the lycans courtesy of the Codex. In layman's terms, it stated the beast itself was asexual and therefore homosexual impulses couldn't be controlled or punished. I wondered if Poroflr wrote in the clause for his son.

I swear we'd find a way. One day I wanted to wake up in his arms and fear no reprimand or repercussions. Did Nicky even feel the same way? I blew out a frustrated groan and tugged at my hair. Before, I thought I had lost him, and I wouldn't risk him again. The Nine already stole my mother and in effect my father too. He wasn't enough or didn't love her enough. In the end, she had an affair, and then died because of it. Father lost his marbles, and Paulo swept Liam and me away to Six and Twenty. Nick was worth more than that, and I didn't want to give up without fighting for him. Too bad my younger self didn't realize that.

"Love you, mutt." I cherished our reunion and wished I hadn't been an idiot kid before. What would've happened if I hadn't made that call? It's not like our relationship would've stayed a secret forever. Aurie knew but had anyone else? "I can't change the past, but maybe we can change the future."

I rolled from the bed. After a quick shower and shave, I conjured new clothing. I changed the colors too even though I was a black on black sort of guy. Blue on grey, a blend of Nick and me. With Auriel close, I had her Myst to use freely. Besides, conjuring was easier than glamouring.

most of the morning came and passed by the time I'd finished my yoga and meditation sessions and re-showered. Peeking out the window, I searched for signs of the wolves or Auriel as I sipped my complimentary coffee. Black and murky, like my soul, but I wasn't risking my life for cream and sugar.

Few things and even fewer people that I'd risk my life for; one of them was Nickolas, followed by Aurie, and the other was my brother. Paulo too, and even though we didn't see eye-to-eye, Merric. My family, yeah, I'd die for them, and aside from my birth father, they'd die for me too.

My eyes scanned the lot again. Those fleabags –and I meant that in the most endearing way – were out there somewhere, but my mage eyes failed me. Two options and both turned my stomach. I could stay here and brood all day, or make a run for it.

"Here goes nothing." My head shook, and I shoved the room's keycard into my denim pocket. I swallowed the fear building its walls around me.

The door creaked open, and I immediately sensed eyes watching as the noon sun blinded me. The hair on my neck stood at attention. I squinted but couldn't focus. The door slammed behind me and a dog barked, or maybe it was the wolves. I dashed into a sprint. Lungs and legs burned, neither used to physical exertion. The soreness from last night returned with a vengeance. My heart pounded into my ears, as I darted across the parking lot. Sweat covered my face and stung my eyes.

Exposed.

My car sat a few paces ahead. Gravel crunched behind me, but I didn't dare look. I fumbled for my key fob to unlock the doors. A car honked, and an alarm blared in the distance. The animals howled. My hand gripped the heated metal, searing my skin. I glanced over my shoulder, and caught the grey blur slinking through the parked cars next door. A smirk spread over my face, as I slid into the driver's seat.

The thud in my chest subsided, but the scorching vinyl seared my skin through my t-shirt. I turned the key, and cranked the A/C on before the stench and heat fried me. After locking myself in, I allowed myself to relax.

Neither Liam nor Regin would attack with this many people. Nick would keep his distance too, and his words repeated in my head. I remained on his mission for Loki, and I must continue pretending to pursue Aurie. All around me, patrons passed. Most didn't pay me a glance, but the tension remained. Aurie hadn't returned.

Noon settled into afternoon. The air inside my car grew heavy with my growing despair. Where the hell was she? The stifling heat didn't help either, but I didn't dare risk a run-in with Liam. Not until Aurie was with me. My head dropped to the steering wheel; I didn't think I was powerful enough to take them on.

Dark auburn waves flittered out the door of Aurie's hotel room, and I craned my neck to stare. Whatever I was sexually, I wasn't blind. The wind whipped around the tresses, and the sun gleamed off the wine-stained strands. My breath hitched, as the sway of her full hips brought her closer. Why did the Gods create such a vessel and then deny the world of her touch? Such a shame that we allowed the laws to bind our hearts.

Auriel wasn't built like today's waifs that blew over in a stiff breeze. Her curves accentuated every inch of her, as it assaulted every aspect that made me a man. How Liam let her slip away was beyond me. What a stupid prick; the mere thought made my smile widen. It became easier to pretend, the closer she got.

Our gazes locked, and I stepped from the car. Her cheeks blushed, as I leaned against my door and let out a long sigh. Not for her, no, Nicky's salty scent reached out to me. He distracted me, and I was thankful for the dark sunglasses hiding my wandering eyes.

"Hey you're still here." At least she didn't slap me. My head tilted up to meet her gaze. Auriel grabbed a clip and wound her hair up on top of her head. The frown tugged at my lips. I wished she'd leave it down. The way the tendrils spilled down her back and those exposed, freckled shoulders were sexy. She needed to wow Liam's socks off already.

"Yeah, sorry about last night ..." She raised an eyebrow. Lying to her was suicide, but I didn't think to prepare myself. Thinking went out the window when she was near.

Molten eyes narrowed, and her hand curved those delicate fingers into a point. "The part where you left without a word," she said stepping closer. "Or how you stole my Myst last night and then again this morning?"

Well damn me ... shit. My hand flew to my mouth, and I closed my eyes. Why didn't she tell me until now? I scratched my head and glanced around. Here I thought I'd been crafty.

"Both. I didn't think you realized. I'm sorry Aurie. If it's any conciliation it saved my ass." She smiled, but it didn't reach her eyes. My heart pounded; she glanced over her shoulder. Regin snarled at me. A car door slammed, and the wolf disappeared. Auriel turned, shook her head, and placed her hand on my arm.

"Your magic is reading stronger this morning ... my fire and your air. That's an intriguing mixture." She reached for my hand, and it took all my strength not to drag her into my arms. Love and warmth radiated from her being. The strange pull rekindled inside of me and drew me in. Auriel studied my palm and leaned closer. Heat spread over me, as her fingers traced the lines. I reached out and touched her face. She didn't flinch away. My eyes closed; I breathed deeply, calming the surge building at my center. But it wasn't her face I saw.

Innocent blue eyes blinked at me. A sigh escaped my lips, sucking me back to the present reality. "Passion is strong with this one."

I peeked at her for only a moment. Auriel's half-lidded eyes locked onto mine. She stepped closer, intertwining her fingers into mine. The contact ignited my whole body in an inferno, as she fed me her Myst. The practice stirred my cock to life. When she dropped my hand, the temperature remained, beading moisture on my brow.

"You didn't have to do that," I said staggering, drunk on her power. The need to stroke flesh grew stronger. She flirted right out of my path.

"I know, but that's what friends are for, right? Though I'm more interested in why you're drained."

Friends, I didn't want her friendship at all right then. My hormones surged, ramped up and pooling right into my balls. Though, I'd be all over that friendship thing, if it brought Nicky back.

"It's a long story," I mumbled, finally succeeding in grabbing her hand before she walked away. A tug of her arm was all it took to have her lips inches from mine. I shouldn't, but I couldn't resist brushing against her full lips. It backfired as she shoved me away. The stabbing in my chest increased, and her shocked face reddened. *Gods, please I beg you*, I prayed.

Auriel whipped around and pinned me to the car. Anger and fire glinted across her swirling eyes I'd awoken something primal, a side of Aurie I'd never met, and I liked it.

Her parted lips were close. I swallowed hard, tasting her citrus scent in the air. Nick growled behind me. Auriel's presence made me not care. Her heat radiated on my skin as if it were sunshine. I leaned into her, but Aurie held me down, nails digging into my arms. "Tell me over lunch," she whispered and turned away; I fought to breathe.

CHAPTER NINE

LIAM

"Why won't he give up already?" I growled. My fury heightened as my head lowered. I put too much faith in Regin, too much. Not only had she failed to notify me, but she'd also lost sight of Jamie. A year younger than me, but at least I wasn't fooled by the Myst. My paws stomped over the gravel.

My brother wasn't hard to find. I'd snickered, skirting the edge of his town car. His heartbeat had increased. Anything to make him paranoid.

Auriel wouldn't become his, even if I had to drag her ass off to Six and Twenty; I'd do it too. She could kick and scream all she wanted. Mine … I'd make her mine, and I'd kill my brother along with anyone else if they so much looked at her wrong. The beast cried out, and I agreed. Jamie was my brother, and I loved him, but there were boundaries. Kill was a strong word, but this was a no second chances situation.

Auriel was the one; I was her Guardian.

The breeze shifted and with it came her scent. I halted; my body alerted and teetered on the edge. Hinges creaked. Her hotel door lay open.

Backing away, I blinked, unsure if I'd stumbled into a dream. Gods, I'd been dead wrong. Auriel stepped out into the sun, her hazel eyes squinting in the midmorning sun. My jaws fell open. I'd resisted the urge to bark even as my tail wagged. The ache itched over my fur, digging claws deep into my flesh.

There weren't words for the luminescent skin, tinged peach, or the copper hair swirling in the heavy breeze as if the strands were falling leaves. Fire in her eyes sparked into molten rage as her long legs clicked across the parking lot. Her knee length skirt hugged her svelte body. Each step she'd taken with conviction and demanding my attention. I'd spied her as she'd bee lined across the adjoining parking lot, and right toward a parked black town car. It belonged to Jamie; I scowled, a low snarl curling my gums. Moments passed as they talked. My ears twitched, but the words fell on deaf ears. The beast screamed blood.

Auriel shifted, glancing over her shoulder. Her smile widened. My head lifted, ears alert, and I attempted a wolfy smile. With just a glimpse, she'd cooled the fiend's anger.

"Ma tha gaol agad air rud, leig mar sgaoil e; ma thilleas e, tha e leat-sa gu siorruidh, mur a till, cha robh e riamh an dàn dhut."

The old Gaelic phrase echoed through my mind, a memory perhaps, but I'd not set her free. Besides, I hadn't even begun to win her heart. Auriel turned back to Jamie, grabbing his palm. My head spun, scenting Nick nearby. He'd stand watch while I shifted and made myself more presentable.

"Liam you going to let him paw her like that?" Nick's eye twitched, and I turned to investigate. He stepped forward and growled, flashing his teeth at my brother. Auriel's wide eyes dropped to Nick. *"He kissed her."*

Pain radiated in his voice, and I shook it off. The bile rose in my stomach, twisting and churning my insides thinking about his lips kissing her. Concentrate Liam. My head swam with the image, and I tore it away. I'd held her likeness in my mind, narrowing in on those large eyes.

Instead of Jamie, she'd touched me and caressed my hand. What'd that feel like now? I'd not allowed a woman to affect me before. Dates hadn't counted. No girlfriends either. The Oracle said Auriel would come, and I'd waited, saving everything for her.

My teeth gritted, and my skin stretched, threatening to tear me open. I'd shouted, releasing the fury fighting against me. Shifting wasn't always this hard, but my mind fought back. My body writhed, twisting on the gravel ground. With an audible gasp, I lay there, twitching and sweating. Deep breaths cleared the fog away. I stood and conjured clothing, creating two additional pairs for Regin and Nick.

I strolled toward my secluded spot among the trucks and kneeled, pretending to tie my shoe. Nick came up beside me, and I scratched his head. Two humans passed by, and he ducked under a rig. He was too large to squeeze under anything else and too large to ignore. Unlike shifters, we didn't choose our forms. My eyes scanned the windows. The auburn hair gave her away as she lifted a mug to her lips. Seated in a booth, both smiling and laughing, as if they didn't have a care in the world. My hand rested over my heart and settled the stress she created. How hard was it to make her smile?

I thought to yesterday; she hadn't smiled once. Jamie always had charm. He must've gotten it from Merric because that gene eluded me. I had plenty of my father's wrath and suspicion though.

"Jealousy's natural, but don't let it rule you," Nick reminded me, but his strained tone sounded as if he was speaking to himself too. I brushed it off because if it wasn't for my cousin, this lycan gene would've driven me crazy.

We'd kept it between the three of us for a long time. Jamie figured it out on his own, but Paulo, my adopted father, didn't know. Lycans and magic rarely mixed. Nick and I were unique, but our friendship ran deeper than the Myst and my tainted blood. My head shook, and I clenched my chest. It sickened me every time Jamie touched her, every time she laughed at him, or touched him. This was my fault. I chased her off and right into his willing arms. Now I'd have to play this game Jamie's way: dirty.

"Give me something I can work with. I need a way into her heart," I prayed to the Gods. The sky remained calm and blue, but lightning struck the ground near my feet. The impact sent me flying backward into a parked car. I shook the stars from my eyes.

"What was that?" someone shouted.

"Liam?"

"I'm … fine. I'll live. Tell you later."

My rear planted on the ground, and I tried to stand. Instead, I stumbled and landed face down. Concrete shredded the side of my face, and I bit into my cheek. My blood trickled into my mouth, and I spat it on the ground. Maybe not quite fine after all, and my eyes rolled, recalling something about kicking a gift horse in the mouth. Thor couldn't have found another way to help?

"Damn," I mumbled, and I attempted to sit up. Stars danced around my eyes again. Opening and closing my eyes, my focus returned as my injuries healed. The ache was nothing but a dull throb now, but I'd taken a few more deep breaths before I attempted to stand again. I failed, nothing like a little lightning and thunder to knock me on my ass.

My brow furrowed, and my shoulders shrugged. I glanced back to the ground. By my left hand, right next to my fingertips, lay a necklace. Shiny silver glinted in the sun, and the design wasn't unknown to me. A common valknut with an emerald-eyed raven, but not something you expected to find in the "bible belt" either. Odin ...Thor ... thank you. The talisman dangled from my hand. I smiled wide and approached the diner. The Gods were on my side.

His gaze met mine, and his head cocked. I nodded. "Time's up."

chapter
ten

AURIEL

My skin came alive with a mind of its own. Burning pain seared my veins from the inside out. The blood rushed out of my head, and rainbow spots littered my vision. My hands grasped the table. Sharp breaths centered my thoughts, but it didn't help much. Similar to yesterday except this time everything moved slower, and was more antagonizing than anything I'd ever felt before. Gods, why'd this happen to me?

"Crap," I mumbled and lowered my gaze. The bell on the door jingled, and without looking up, I sensed Liam. The blazing red anger rolled out to my shield. His scent of campfire, autumn leaves, and pine added to the fuzziness of my brain. Somehow, it comforted and bothered me at the same time.

"What's the matter?" Jamie's voice stayed quiet and gentle as he clasped my hand. His smooth thumbs stroked my skin. The comfort was minimal, but I didn't pull away.

"My shield's down," I lied and pinched the bridge of my nose. Liam's voice remained low, and I couldn't make out his words. Without turning around, I became aware, as his three natured emotions grew stronger. The thickness increased with each thud of his boots. Blinking, I eyed Jamie who clenched his jaw tight; his steely gaze pierced Liam. They both foamed with bitter rage and envy. My heart pounded hard, and the vibrations reached my toes. The power pulsated around me, and I glanced between the two men. Neither said a word, but it wasn't needed. Their body language spoke for them. I refused to get in the middle of this pissing match. My head shook and I tried standing when, with a loud plop, my ass hit the cushioned bench with a rattling thud.

"Hey, sorry to bother you folks. Miss –"

My eyebrow shot up. *Really, he's actually going to try that line?* He stood there for two minutes before uttering a single word. Liam turned his body fully and spoke to me. His eyes burned through mine. Everything hit me at once, and I didn't know if a shield could've made a difference.

Rage, jealousy, and lust? The last two I hadn't expected and didn't understand what it meant. The onslaught within my mind continued as he hounded me with the combined emotions. I grasped my talisman, hoping it would center me. Nothing I tried seemed to protect me from him.

Magically, I'd never felt this helpless, this exposed.

A rainbow of colors glittered my vision, and it tunneled in and out. I shut my eyes. "Go," my voice weakened and the only words I mustered as darkness closed in; I faded out.

m y head swam frantically, and the voices assaulted my ears. Thick accents reminded me of Old Norse. I couldn't understand what they said. Frustration overwhelmed me, and I screamed out for them to stop.

"Hush," I heard someone say in English with a heady Nordic accent and silence followed.

"Where am I?" I asked the shadows. Fire filled the hall. Soft light danced in gilded sconces and candelabras. It bounced off golden walls, tables made of dark, exotic wood, and dark crimson velvet cascaded from the windows.

My mouth dropped as a scantily clad, curvy giantess approached me. Freya, I recognized her from my books. She nodded at my realization. Her curly golden locks swayed in time with her white dress. Pale skin and ruby lips centered her rounded face. My mouth dropped open. In her presence, I humbled into silence.

"Daughter, welcome to Asgard," Freya said. Her amber eyes drew me in. No, this was a dream, right?

I shut my eyes tight against her. No, this was a dream, I repeated, only a beautiful dream. She caressed my face and brushed my hair back like my mother used to do. I almost fainted from the sheer excitement as I forced my eyes open. I was in Asgard, and I knelt in the presence of the Gods and Goddesses of the Nine Realms.

My heart raced as Freya took my hand. I'd expected her touch to feel different but warmth radiated from the Goddess. She tugged lightly to pick me up from the floor, and I followed her, trying not to trip over myself. It proved difficult to move as she led me to Odin's side. Even with his graying hair, outdated velvet robes, and eye patch, he made my pulse quicken and my breath catch.

I knelt before him, for he was the all father. He'd birthed the idea of Nine Realms and the humans who survived on Midgard.

"You did not lie of her beauty, Freya. She looks much like her ancestor."

My eyes shifted between them.

"All except the hair." Freya laughed. "And she is a bit on the small side for a giant." She tapped her chin and turned away. "Wouldn't you agree, Loki?"

I glanced over my shoulder and saw a robed figure lurking to the side.

"She is faultless. Long legs and broad shoulders." His robes swished against the marble floor as he neared the step where I waited.

"Please, my daughter, come join us," Odin spoke again. Why'd he call me that? And what ancestors? Without thinking, I shied away. My head shook the absurdity of his words … of this place away… it was a dream.

"I think she is frightened." Odin laughed as my cheeks burned.

Loki placed his hand on my shoulder. His grip tore into my skin, spilling blood. I screamed as his voice burned inside my head. *Daughter of Freya, born Valkyrie, you have lost your way. Find your … "* But my body pulled me away before Loki finished. All I remembered was that I must find … something … and … Valkyrie. Yes, that was once my secret. I was a born Valkyrie.

chapter eleven

LIAM

I wondered if my presence caused her dizzy spells. But that time she outright fainted, and she stopped breathing. I'd tried to catch Auriel, but her eyes lulled back, and she'd toppled over before I could react. At least she hadn't gone headfirst into the steaming coffee. Nothing made any sense to me, and Jamie's bewilderment stunned me too. His head shook, and his eyes were wider than the saucer his mug rested upon. Neither of us said a word. What was there to say?

I ran my fingers along her neck. The pulse stayed strong, but her skin chilled to the touch. Clammy, too, with a flickering glimmer I didn't recall seeing yesterday. There remained quite a bit I'd missed. My hand dragged over my face, and I'd shaken my head. I'd ask Jamie if she'd done this around him, but the answer was painted over his paled face.

"How can her heart beat but lungs not breathe?"

Nick didn't reply.

The server peered over my shoulder. "Hey is she alright?"

Auriel's cat-like eyes fluttered open, and she gasped for air, taking in a giant gulp. "Asgard." Relief flooded my mind, but it was short lived. "What … Odin … Wait … Freya …Loki … Find … no, did I?" Auriel's large golden eyes stared at me. Her lips moved, speaking more and more gibberish.

"Sorry, darlin'," I whispered as I leaned close. My hand rested on the booth and table. I kneeled down, keeping my tone as gentle as possible. "You passed out."

Her eyes shot back and forth between Jamie and me; she blinked. "Why are you here?" Auriel's tone was sharp, and her eyes peered with growing apprehension of my presence. After the way I'd treated her, I deserved it.

I rubbed the back of my neck but didn't look away. "Why is he here?" she asked again. Her raging gaze snapped to Jamie.

"I found a necklace in the parking lot. Thought someone may've dropped it." Auriel sat up slowly. I offered her my hand for support, but she slapped me away.

"I don't wear jewelry." Her voice stayed low, sultry, and harsh, but she lied. Her neck sported a silver chain. Those auburn brows rose and twisted. "Why would you think it's mine anyway?" Auriel added.

I groaned, running my hand over my face. Was she kidding me? Yes, I was an asshole, but she hadn't even given me a chance to apologize. My teeth gritted, and the Oracle's warnings sounded off in my head. Taking a deep breath, I concentrated on what hid behind the mask of loathing she wore for my benefit.

"Well, *princess*, it could've belonged to anyone, but it's a talisman. Last I checked you're the new supe on the block 'round here, darlin'." Her eyes softened a tad as she nodded. Jamie remained silent and broody. My brow rose at him, but that was how my brother always acted these days. Glad I could make him squirm; bet he didn't expect me to show my face.

My eyes shot back to her. Those molten eyes studied me. They undressed me, moving up and down my body. I was naked in her presence as the butterflies caressed my skin. She'd stripped my defensive layers. I didn't stop her; I wanted her trust. Ache spread, a glorious tingling pain as her gaze deepened. Images flashed before my vision, but they disappeared before I made sense of them. A kiss here, a touch there, laughter of youth, and a boulder by the stream; did she see them too?

"What is a talisman doing out in the parking lot?" Jamie crossed his arms and grunted. The connection severed, but the effect of her eyes didn't falter. I was the boy in those visions. I wanted them … I needed them like I desired her.

Breathtaking, I resisted the urge to clutch my chest, but I did let the grin spread across my lips. "I'm sorry." She turned in her seat to face me, her lips pressing together as if she'd heard my silent plea.

"That's what I'm trying to figure out." I placed a hand on her bare shoulder, but she tossed it off, moving her body away. I should have taken the hint, but didn't, and planted my ass down next to hers.

"Don't recall asking you to join," Jamie mumbled while Auriel fiddled with a sugar packet.

"Can I see it?" she whispered, ignoring my brother. I retrieved the valknut from my pocket.

She moved fast. The instant it freed from my jeans, Auriel swiped it away. Her face contorted as fury settled and twisted over her face. Those eyes deepened, and the waterworks welled. Her lips tugged down, quivering for a millisecond as she fought to control the emotions. Tossing her head, she whispered one word.

"Màthair," Auriel said in perfect Scottish Gaelic. Mother ... In an instant, tears spilled over onto her pink cheeks. Glittering, golden streams poured down. My mouth dropped, and no words came.

What was she; the Phoenixes didn't cry rivers of gold? Freya did that.

"You recognize it?" Jamie asked her, and he reached for her hands. His eyes kept glancing out the window. I leaned my arms on the table and pretended to fiddle with a napkin. Good, he realized we surrounded him.

"Yes." Auriel sniffled, squeaking the word like a mouse. I chewed my lip as she accepted his touch.

My arms crossed tightly across my chest, and Jamie smirked. A fight would come one way or another. A brawl within me warred on; it turned into a struggle not to tear his head off. *Mine,* the beast screamed in agonizing intensity. I wanted to push back into his head and divulge all his secrets to Auriel. She'd run; scream in terror knowing what he'd done to his own kind. *Traitor.* What Jamie wanted, Jamie got. He wanted the Nine, and he got it.

Gods, why'd he have to want her too? As I attempted to shove into his mind, Jamie snapped his head in my direction. He held something back; his mischievous smile spread wider. But his shield knocked me out with every attempt. I let out a sigh of frustration when Auriel turned to me again.

Her fingers stroked the raven and the inscription. "Where'd you find it again?"

Sniffles ceased, and her tone softened. Emotion swirled in her eyes like magma, but her expression crossed between surprise and regret. I wanted to wipe it away. Pain wasn't new to me. I'd walked around my whole life with a gaping hole in my chest. That cavernous darkness promised to disappear when the one walked into my life. The Oracle foresaw her. Was it the real reason I'd pushed Auriel away?

My forehead crinkled. "Outside on the ground, in the parking lot."

Her eyes clenched tight, and she swallowed hard. She tapped on the glass window and said, "This was my momma's necklace. There ain't no way magical or human it dropped in that there parking lot."

Auriel didn't call me a liar, not directly, but she implied it with her accusing tone. Before I could retort her claim, she stood up. A growl left her clenching lips as her hands gripped the table. With a huff, she slammed the slab to a screeching clatter and pushed her way past me. My poor brother barely moved in time, before the Formica table teetered into his lap, spilling its contents all over the floor. Aurie stormed off toward the bathroom. I turned to follow, but Jamie stood, drenched in coffee, and blocked my way.

The diner grew silent. The patrons and staff stared in speechless bewilderment. I had smiled, shrugging my shoulders, before reaching to correct the scene of destruction the firecracker created. Afterwards everyone murmured, but their attention and thoughts remained on us.

"Haven't you caused enough damage here?" he scowled and pressed his palm into my chest, shoving me backwards. Jamie knew better than to openly use his power on me. He'd bend the rules if needed, but we all understood the repercussions of exposing magic.

"I don't know what your problem is bro, but I'm the one trying to help her. She needs protection from the likes of you," I snarled, coming nose to nose with him, before shoving him aside and sending him tumbling back down into the booth. Shock fell over his face as a smirk played on mine. Did he think he'd overpower me physically? I shook my head. No time for any of this, I had to find Auriel and explain. I'd explain everything if she'd let me.

chapter twelve

AURIEL

My mind raced with scenarios as I stared down at the Valknut. The water ran, drowning out the diner chatter slamming against my brain. I splashed the icy water on my face and washed the tearstains away.

"One day …" One day, the pain would lessen. I'd stop this endless crying and have my justice. The raven mocked me. Neither a blessing nor a curse, but how did Liam get it off my mother's dead body? I sighed, stuffing it into my jeans pocket. He was a douchebag, but that didn't make him a murderer.

"I didn't mean to upset you." His muffled voice called through the bathroom door.

"Darlin' I promise you, I found it outside." He banged on the door. "You absolutely sure it's your momma's?"

Yes, it was. The piece had been in my family for centuries. "I'm coming in if you don't answer me." A groan left my mouth before I could stop it. *Go away; leave me alone, damn it, would everyone just leave me alone.* My eyes shut tight as a wave of vertigo slammed into me. The door creaked, and the intensity of his body surrounded me. The air shifted, and I grasped onto the sink to keep myself steady.

"I'm sorry," he whispered in my ear, and dizziness threatened further as his hand caressed my cheek. I kept my eyes closed tight and swallowed hard. Control, I fought for control. The internal struggle hastened, and something inside of me attempted to climb up. I pushed it back down with every ounce of energy I had.

"When'd you visit New York?" I asked him through my clenched teeth.

He stroked my cheek as my lungs burned. *Breathe Auriel*, but air wasn't what I needed.

"I've barely gone out of state." The words tickled across my skin. The three-natured man spoke the truth. It'd be easier if he lied. Then I would have killed him without remorse. My heart hammered at the thought. Whoa, where'd that thought come from?

"What's the deal with necklace, darlin'? Valknut's not your symbol?" Liam'shands moved to my shoulders, and I grew tense under his touch. Was it the three natures affecting me? His hands caressed my neck and then moved down my spine. Soft, delicate touches, but still bizarre. Were all supernaturals like this? I couldn't recall my parents caressing often, but I didn't pay attention much either. Maybe I should've.

Shocks spread through my body and breathing became harder. His warm hands continued their contact, brushing against my skin. I didn't want it to end; it was right and wrong at the same time. My mind screamed he should stop, but my body bent like bamboo into his capable hands. As if sensing the change, Liam turned me around. His arms wrapped around me like a cocoon of constant warmth. I shivered, and the ache inside pulsed deeper.

"I think you're alright now. Everything will be fine, darlin'." Liam stroked my hair and kissed my head. Green eyes was right. My world steadied, but for how long? It seemed to ebb and flow like the tide … like his moods did.

My head shook as the tears reared their head. "Momma never took the necklace off." I couldn't stop the sobs. "She … she died … with it on." Daddy had given it to her, a gift from his father, when I was born.

He'd engraved our names. Over the years, it'd worn down in places, but I didn't tell Liam this. His fingers caressed my cheek. "When did this happen?" he asked, but I'd lost track of the days.

I opened my eyes. "What day is it?" My hands came up to touch his chest. The hard muscles contracted, and his heart beat faster.

Liam nibbled his thick bottom lip. I wanted to taste it. All thoughts and feelings I didn't understand, and yet I couldn't shake them off. There was something about Liam.

"Tuesday."

"Oh, Saturday morning." Large arms crushed me, and I thumped his chest. He whispered a string of apologies.

Liam's eyebrow rose, but he smirked. "You assumed it was me because of the necklace?"

My gaze dropped, and my fingers danced over his broad chest. Not an actual question, but the guilt washed over me, and twisted my empty stomach. The shame was mine; green eyes remained innocent on this account. But I hadn't forgotten yesterday.

My tears dried, and I sniffled. "Naw ..."

The evidence didn't add up. I risked touching his skin and cupped his rough cheek. The longer we touched the less vertigo I felt. A smile forced over my lips. Liam cleared his throat.

"Not unless you secretly work for the Nine. That's all I know. We'd run long enough; I knew not to stick around." Part of that was true, but I left out the guiding voice, and crazy draw the letter created. As if the moment I touched the letter, an urge swept over me, and charged me with driving south.

"Daughter of Freya." I blinked at his words and dropped my hand. The Gods spoke those same words. I pulled back slightly and stared into his green eyes.

"They called me that too. I think my spirit went to Asgard." I shook my head. Even I didn't believe the words leaving my mouth, but Liam did. His eyes sparked and flashed blue for a second.

"The Oracle said Phoenix."

My brow cocked, and I nodded. But who was this Oracle? "Phoenix, yes I'm marked."

I lifted my shirt a bit, showing him the flame on my side in the mirror. His breath sucked in, and Liam ran his finger over the birthmark. My teeth sunk into my cheek to keep me from giggling, but the warmth of him made my insides quiver.

"Why didn't ya tell me yesterday? Well damn darlin'."

Liam hissed out a breath, and his fingers traced the outline again. I'd received the mark the day I came into my powers like everyone else did. According to my daddy, it'd been within moments of birth. In the history of mages, no one grew into their Myst before the age of six. No, there was another too, but every time I'd pictured the person, the image disappeared.

"I was frightened," I lied and stared down at my twitching fingers. Only toward the end, I was a bit scared. "And well you were angry ... with me."

For no legitimate reason, I wanted to add, and don't even get me started on the jerk part. Liam gnawed on his bottom lip.

"Is it possible that I am both? Why'd Odin call to me, when I'm marked as a Phoenix?"

Technically, we were both Dísir. It was a rank given to the highest classes, like high mages, Guardians, norns with a little n, seers, and so forth. After Odin's purge, they reserved the name for the born Valkyrie.

I wasn't ready to announce, hey I'm a born too. A great prejudice against born Valkyrie remained within the Nine, more so than hybrids. Six and Twenty wasn't the Nine, but better to err with caution.

"Yes. You've one of Freya's runes. Not the Fehu, but the Algiz is Vanir." He pulled away and paced the length of the ladies' room. I fingered the talisman, rolling the stone over my fingertips. The forked Y wasn't visible to human eyes, but it wasn't glowing either.

No one told me it belonged to the Goddess. "The piece is in our history books. It's not a replica either."

Liam's mood shifted, and I leaned against the sink for support, watching him from the mirror. The cold porcelain wasn't enough to center my nerves, and the pacing did nothing for Liam. One truth remained, and I didn't want to accept it yet. All these years on the run, whatever I'd chosen to forget, I needed to remember.

"I've always had it."

Brows mashed together and he halted. Liam shook his head and started pacing again. "Freya gave it to Eir when she retired from service."

Eir became a Goddess and attended Frigg, Odin's wife. His feet squeaked over the tile as I turned the cold water on. None of this made sense. My hands shook under the flow as the liquid ran over my skin. The Myst and the mind were much like the element. Hard to control and mold without the proper tools. I must've been quite powerful to manipulate and navigate the depths of mine. The cloud blocking my path wouldn't reveal all the truth. The Nine, the Gods, and maybe this town too; everyone had their own agendas.

"About yesterday ..." he said but didn't look me in the eye. "It's a long story, but I wasn't angry at you." *Liar. Here we go*, I thought and faced him. "I wanted to help you, but ..." It wasn't just the anger.

Emotions were easier to forgive. They came and went fast like passing thoughts, or sometimes they stayed for days, months, and years at a time, but I expected others to feel. The words and his actions, that was what Liam should apologize for, not trivial notions, anger, and ... I couldn't even remember what else ran through that crazy head of his.

"But?"

He ran a hand through his unruly hair. "The company you keep isn't helping your cause."

I fought the urge to roll my eyes, but the chuckle escaped. Just my luck that I found a friend and no one approved of him. "Jamie is harmless." Wasn't he? My amulet stayed calm in his presence. Then again, the talisman had remained icy with Liam too. He grabbed my forearms and shook me.

My heart startled and leapt into my throat.

"I think you should get some rest. Go back to your hotel. I'll come for you soon. My friends will keep you safe until then." His face showed no emotions. Liam had shut himself down.

I winced at his attitude. "Where are you going?" I whispered as he reached the door.

He sighed, and I wondered was it me who sent Liam running. Was I that repulsive? I wanted to ask him, make him explain it to me. But the squeak of leather and the slamming door meant he was gone. The bitter truth nipped at me as Liam left me with emptiness shivering down my spine where his warmth had radiated moments before.

"Figures," I mumbled, not knowing what the heck was going on anymore. My attention turned back to the water. Not my element, yet it called to me on some level. All the elements were like that for me.

The air, water, earth, fire, and the wilds spoke to me. But the druids and shamans of the world were gone. The Nine hunted and murdered them for their power. Those who survived fled Midgard or hid themselves away until they died. No, I wasn't one of them. Collecting myself, I walked out of the restroom and back to my table but found Jamie gone too. Everyone left me in the end just like in the dreams. Maybe it was all for the best.

"He paid the check, sweetie," the blond server said, but I sat back down anyway. What else was I to do? How else would I find Paulo Skyland? I sighed, picking at the sugar packets. When did my life become this complicated?

chapter thirteen

JAMIE

I waved off the server, picked up the table, and set everything right again. For a split second, the old Aurie I once knew shined through when her anger rose. She'd never taken crap from Liam, Nick, or me. Reggie was another story, but they rarely fought. Those two used to be stuck together with glue. Laughter shook me as the absurdity slapped me in the face. She'd forgotten us all.

Of all the harebrained notions … the server brought me a cup of coffee. No one uttered a word over the scene that had played out minutes before, but I assumed southern hospitality had more to do with it than anything else.

The common misconception about the supernatural was that we were just another version of humans. The truth lay farther than anyone imagined. We breathed, ate, drank, and eliminated like human beings, but our similarities ended there. Our upbringings varied, but I wasn't childish and superficial with friendships. At least I wasn't back then except when it came to Nicky. I'd watch it all the time on television, those afterschool special type shows where everyone stabbed each other in the back. We weren't perfect, but each episode was few and far between. My call to the Nine about

Nick's father, after the aftermath, marked the last time we'd fought. She'd known; hell, she'd foreseen it, but Aurie hadn't stopped me. The reason, the only reason, I didn't want her to remember was because of that night.

Liam and I had returned from the beach and stopped in the town square. The car hadn't stopped yet before my brother flung open the door. I stepped from the still running vehicle; flip flop clad feet squished beneath me. My eyes went wide as I soaked in the carnage of our hometown.

The bricks, roads, grass … there were bodies burning and blood coated surfaces. Aurie stood at the center; the gleam in her eye had made me shake and shiver. Golden streams shone in the smoky haze. I'd rubbed my arms as Liam ran to her side. "Nick," I yelled; my body trembled from head to toe. The burning scent of fur, bodies, flesh … "Nick," I screamed, the well of my heart jerking into my throat. She shook her head, her eyes bore into me. I'd rubbed my chest and whispered, "Nicky? No, not my …" *Mate. Boyfriend. Future husband.* I said none of those things aloud, but the man I loved was all of them. My eyes ached, but I held the tears back. Legs refused to move, glued with the blood of the Fenrir clan. His family accepted me … us. They brought me in and showered me with love and kindness. I betrayed them and shared their secrets with Merric.

"We can't tell, Jamie." Her face disappeared into Liam's chest as my eyes closed. Aurie knew what I had done. Her fists balled at my brother's back. *"Poroflr's gone. Sköll kill- … murdered them all."*

Those last three words knocked my knees out from underneath my body. Murdered them all. I murdered them all. Not Sköll – but me, myself, and I – was responsible for the bloody visage painting the town red, and for murdering the one I loved. My heart died that day in the town square. I'd known, she'd known; the blame fell to me. She'd let go of Liam and knelt by my side. Her warmth encompassing me as it always had a million times before.

My fingers rested in her dainty palms, and the temperature rose slowly at first. Heat seared through my veins as she connected to me through her Myst. The white flicker rolled over my balmy skin as the vision replayed.

I'd hung up the phone and plopped down into an armchair. My eyes stared off into the crackling fire. Liam came in, laughing and smiling as he'd done a hundred times before. His happiness cut through me and reminded me of what would never come. A man wasn't supposed to love another man.

That was what Merric said when I'd asked about the laws, skirting through the dangerous waters of truth. When I first inquired, I was just fourteen. Sure, I could have blamed confusion or curiosity if my father had bothered to ask. He hadn't and as always, I bothered him. His sharp replies to my questions ended in a swift click of the phone. Merric hadn't bothered to say good-bye anytime I called him, but those times stung. I needed a father, needed someone to tell me that love was love.

My eighteen-year-old self believed all the lies he told himself. It was the bond. I hadn't loved him until my birthday. All of it sounded absurd, but I'd believed it. Just as I believed I could bury my guilt and anguish in women or scotch. No. None of those rang the truth. Pieces of my heart and soul, if not all of it, always loved the Scottish brute.

The whole notion made Nick appear as a giant perve, and maybe that was why I denied it until I became of age. Maybe he hadn't looked upon me all those years as I did him. None of it mattered anymore. That was what I told myself as I stared into the orange flames. I'd ended it, drove a wedge between the evil that spread through our lust.

Nicky hadn't known I'd called him then either. Countless times, I'd picked up the receiver and dialed Merric and as many times I'd tried talking to Paulo. Merric brushed me off while Paulo fell back on an equally archaic notion. The draugr had been a devout catholic human before learning of our world. After five hundred years, give or take a hundred as he'd say, he still fell back on Christian theology.

Fourteen years old and he'd told me homosexuals burned in Hell. I'd blinked, holding in the tears, until safely in my room. The notions of being in love compounded and weighed me down as the years progressed. Love, it was always love for me. For as long as I could remember, I'd loved Nikolas Fenrir. In the beginning, his hearty laugh drew me in and dazzled me. It didn't take much to win me over.

My infatuation blossomed and grew over the years until the day he returned my gaze. The same day we gathered to celebrate my eighteenth birthday. The beginning of the end, I'd called it, and perhaps I was right.

He'd walked with me into the woods. Neither of us said much, and I'd assumed the feelings were new to him. Nick stopped when we reached the water's edge and folded his hand in mine. My heart fluttered, and dizziness swept over me. I stumbled back onto a boulder, and he'd chuckled. His large body loomed over me, but he sat by my side and pulled me to his chest. Those large hands ran through my hair and he spoke, apologizing at first. I said nothing and closed my eyes, basking in his salty scent.

His lips grazed my forehead, but he didn't pressure me. I became the guide; if I wanted something, I had to ask him for it. Laughter shook me as I recalled the week it'd taken to build up the nerve. I wanted to kiss him that first night but had chickened out. As usual, I turned into a broody hen and rightfully so earned my nickname: hen or hinny.

We'd stood holding hands on my back porch a week later. "Ye want me to kiss ye? That's what all tis 'bout?" Nick dragged his hand over his mouth, trying to hide his laugh. "Yer like a wee wet hen."

I swallowed, and my mouth had gone dry. "Yes," I'd whispered. "Well hen, ye ken stop worrying." Nick lifted my chin and dipped his head. His lips brushed against mine, and the surge jolted my body. My toes curled under as they tingled. The heat of his mouth deepened; he groaned, vibrating words tickling my lips open. His tongue pressed against mine, and my eyes flew open.

His Myst rolled along my skin, or maybe it was his exploring hands, but it stroked and touched me in places only I had traveled. I grasped his shirt and tugged him closer, pressing my tongue slowly against his, and relishing in his sweet taste. Nick's legs gave out, and he toppled backwards. I followed, not relenting on my belated birthday kiss. Each time we'd kissed since then, it'd gotten better, less awkward too, but the strands that bound us have strengthened.

Nicky gave me full control, responsibility for every aspect of us. Granted, we didn't last long. The time between my eighteenth birthday and the phone call was only six months, and half the time I'd freaked out and ran away. Part of it was fear, and part of it was him.

Nick blamed the bond from day one as I nestled content in his arms. The truth was I'd loved him before, and those words stung when he mentioned the lycan bond. It was as if he'd never have loved me or wanted me otherwise. Back then, it fed the darkness of a boy no one wanted. Even with Paulo, I remained an afterthought. He hadn't planned to steal two boys that fateful day the Nine killed my mother, yet there I was, discarded again.

And here I was now, pushed aside. I gulped the steamy coffee and relished in the burn scorching my throat. My nose ran and I wiped it on a napkin. I didn't deserve a second chance; murders didn't walk free.

I blinked, sitting back in the diner. Alone. Maybe Merric had the right idea all along. He'd rather be alone than lose his heart to love. Hearts stood in the way and blinded the darkness, he'd said. For years I believed him. After Nicky, I'd let myself go but never forgave. My clothes, hair, and pastimes no longer mattered. I replaced it with training and bulking up with the Wardens or chasing after the elusive Aurie.

I went back to that day at the square, and the words she'd said to me. She'd held my hands, squeezing them in her tiny palms. Aurie saw through my darkness. She saw the distraught and confused boy but never judged me. I'd thought Sköll would arrest them. My forehead dropped to hers and she'd spoken. "One day you'll reap the damage of today. The darkness is your burden to bear."

Darkness had ruled my heart since that day. If there were a way to take it all back, I would. The world became a darker place for lycans; it became a prison for Nick. I'd rather hide in the shadows and have him in my life than what has become of us. In my mind, he died, but my heart and soul must have known he lived. There were only so many ways a man could say, "I'm sorry."

But I hadn't lied, cheated, or stolen. With one phone call, I'd almost eradicated an entire family. I murdered his mother and father, and countless other family members who refused Aurie's warning. There was some solace; Nick, Regin and Liam heeded her counsel, but why didn't she stop me?

Granted, I never expected forgiveness for the sins, nor did I blame her for my actions. I stared at the empty coffee cup.

Even so, if by some miracle I managed to earn it, would Nicky ever love me again? Or would he spend the rest of my short miserable life tormenting me for my shortcomings? Did I deserve any less?

He'd used me last night. In many ways, I was still the broken boy torn between three paths: revenge, confusion, and love.

Back at the restaurant, I paid the tab. There lay a small foyer toward the rear for emergencies and deliveries. I'd used it last night, and countless times before, to escape while I thought my brother was busy with Aurie. Luck wasn't on my side though then or now. As I reached for the handle, Liam knocked my hand away. He pressed me backward into the cleaning station.

Dirty water sloshed out onto my clothes, and it smelled worse than wet dog. Damn my stubborn, pig-headed brother; he had gone and ruined a perfectly decent outfit. My hands wrung out the filth.

"Jamison …" He rolled his eyes, and it made me want to punch his pretty boy face. There were two ways to get under my skin, and he'd managed both in a span of ten seconds.

I released a breath and ignored his jab. "You know her. Why are y'all acting like you've never met?"

How did the whole town forget about her? I always suspected a spell. My brow scrunched. But it didn't make sense. She was the only one capable, and that had a reason. Aurie had believed in love conquering all. If someone forced her to leave … The wheels clicked into place. That was it, wasn't it? She'd loved us enough to leave and hadn't planned on returning. Nothing else made a lick of sense.

"Auriel …" His eyes flickered over my shoulder, but I sensed him. "No, bro." He rubbed his neck. "I think I'd remember a woman like that." Liam winked.

Brackish water tickled my nose. "A woman like that comes 'round once in a million years." Nickolas spoke up, missing his accent, from behind me. I realized Liam's plan a moment too late. They closed in around me.

Nick's hands rested over my shoulders, and my heart rate sped up. At the same time, it shattered. Liam's eyes bore into me, glowing deeper. His brows tensed as he pressed against my mind. The dull ache grew, but I knocked against his attempt.

Regin announced nonchalantly, before walking out the back door. "I don't see the big deal." My mouth gaped; she was our waitress last night.

"Maybe I'm not alone." I let the thoughts race through my mind. If for nothing else, I'd enjoy the reaction on Liam's face. I loved it when he panicked, but he smirked in return. After all the years, Liam still hadn't learned I remained a step ahead.

"Riojey," I whispered the words, and I grabbed both Liam and Nickolas, freezing them in place.

Time was of the essence, and I had to restore Aurie's memory fast, before she decided to run again. With her pure heart and soul, she would try. I didn't have time for playing Nick's games ... I'd be done with those too, no matter how much it hurt.

With a magicless Reggie standing guard at the back, I turned on my heels and headed for the front door. Aurie had left, her red head blazing across the lot. I grinned and shook my head before jogging after her.

"You following me?" I asked Auriel in jest as I walked up to the room neighboring her own.

She shook her bowed head. "You left me again." Her tone turned cold and her eyes red. I didn't need to be an empath to feel her pain. Everyone left me too. "You know if I didn't know any better, I'd think y'all were trying to get away from me." A half-sheepish smile crossed her lips.

I asked, "So you're in a big hurry to get back here?" She shrugged. I looked at her eyes again, and they were heavy and dark. Aurie gave a little sniff. What the hell did Liam say to her this time? This wasn't a good sign at all; what if I was too late and she left now?

"If you need anything, even just to talk ... I'm here for whatever you need, Aurie." She could run to the end of the Earth, and I'd follow. Friends to the end even if I remained invisible. This love crap was overrated and friendship wasn't too far behind.

"Thanks. I ... I just want to be ... alone."

Auriel shut the door behind her. Four years ago, she did the same, and I thought I'd never see her again. But this time it was not my fault. My fists clenched, and I bit my lip. I should've stopped him. How dare he hurt her? What game were they playing?

My mind ached with questions. But I was wrong; I played my part in this façade too. Like Aurie, anything Nicky wanted, I gave. Years ago, I wasn't so gullible, but I'd do anything to win him back.

"See ya round," I whispered and closed my door.

This had to end; all of it, I was through with hurting her. I raked my hand through my hair and tugged the roots hard enough that

I winced. It was all going to hell, and I needed a grip fast. On the inside, my thoughts screamed out, and my heart punctured like daggers piercing the flesh. A never-ending circle of groveling and slaving at his feet forced to hurt my friends.

I splashed water on my face, and thought about meditating to cleanse my mind. The water had barely begun to run when the door slammed shut. For a fleeting moment, I wished that it were Nick or Aurie. I knew better. Looking up in the mirror reflected the green eyes of my own blood, my enemy.

"That didn't take you long," I said to Liam. Green fire burned in his hand; the light shimmered an eerie, sickening glow over us both. Helfire, Auriel had once called it Helfire.

"You love her," Liam replied, extinguishing the flame.

I blinked. "We all do."

Everyone who crossed her good graces loved her. In return, she loved back. Aurie never pushed me aside, even after I'd screwed up, and I had done that all the time. The sister or mother I never had, that was our love.

Lycans though … damn it they knew nothing of real love. Even Nick hadn't learned after five hundred years that true love broke past all bonds.

"Oracle- " My maniacal laughter cut him off.

I caught my reflection in the mirror but didn't recognize the man anymore. He appeared old and twisted. His dark hair stuck out all over the place. This man no longer cared. Cold and calculating grey eyes stared back at me … *Merric's eyes.* The thought of him sickened me; I didn't want any part of his life, and I wanted Liam out of mine.

"I don't give a shit what that crazy bitch told you." *You're tainted.* "Auriel was your girlfriend, your first kiss, your first love, and damn it she belongs to you, Liam." He didn't flinch at my words, but his eyes swam with rage. Lycans had short tempers, and it didn't matter that we shared blood. At least it wasn't the same blood as Nicky.

"If that were true, wouldn't I remember her?" Liam crossed his arms over his chest. Gods, I wanted to grab his collar and scream. His breathing steadied, and his eyes calmed to their usual green. In some ways, I was proud at the control he managed to hold.

"Man, I've been telling you that for years. Someone messed with your h …" The choking sensation constricted my throat. I could say no more, think no more; the curse was far too strong.

His boots thudded over the tile as he watched. Reaching out for him, Liam ignored me. I grasped my neck and collapsed to the floor. I my chest heaved, struggling to breathe. Aurie called for me, but I was helpless. The last image I saw was his backside before the darkness claimed me.

chapter fourteen

AURIEL

"Jamie?" I called out his name at the hotel door. For ten minutes, I pounded on it until my knuckles ached and reddened. But I sensed his Myst inside. My brows creased, and my stomach churned when he didn't respond. The coast remained clear; a quick spell on the doorknob should do the trick. Nope, it just sizzled and melted the knob.

"Crap." I sighed as my head rested on the door.

This was crazy. What was I doing? My fist clenched, and my teeth ground. I shouldn't have been a bitch to him. I berated myself and turned toward my room.

Out of the corner of my eye, I saw movement. The curtain swayed as if someone was there, and I halted in my tracks. Someone was in there.

"Jamie, I'm sorry. Please let me in." I placed my hand on the large pane of glass. No response came, and I saw no more movement. My ears strained, but there were no sounds either. "If you don't let me in I'll … I'll kick the door down."

One, two … ten seconds passed. I invoked the Myst as my foot contacted with the door. Failed, not even a dent, and I cursed up an unladylike storm in response.

My spells should not fall short.

Something went wrong. My body shivered in the noon heat and shook off the doubt. The Myst surrounded me again, and I dragged it inside my body, sending it to my leg. I swung my foot back again. With every ounce of strength, I willed my foot forward and called upon my talisman.

A loud crack curled my spine. Pain ripped through my left leg. My mouth dropped, and a scream ripped from my throat. When I opened my eyes, the limb laid on a awkward angle, the bone jutting out to the side. I screamed again. The skin broke, and my blood flowed faster than my tears. The white bone pierced through the veins and tendons.

"Oh my Gods," Jamie said, opening the door. Oh my Gods was an understatement. His eyes widened with fright, his breath panicky, and a sheen of moisture covered his face. Yet my attention darted back to his eyes. They weren't the usual smoky grey. There was a slight tinge of mossy green, and they appeared to glow. Somehow, I'd noticed all of this, and I centered my attention on him instead of the bone sticking out of my pulsating leg.

The white Myst lay around me, dormant. "Feàrr," I chanted under my breath, willing the skin, bone, nerves, and tendons to knit back together. Thank goodness, Momma and Daddy had me memorize the spell for severe injuries.

He knelt by my side and grasped my hands. "What … wait you can heal?"

I said nothing and stared deeply into his eyes, gritting my teeth through the pain. Now there was another understatement. Repair always hurt worse than the damage that caused the injury. Momma always claimed it was the Faerie blood. Their immortality healed my wounds and kept sickness at bay, but she liked to tell stories. I always relied on the simple spell Dad taught me. Fate, bloodlines, and all that jazz made great tales, but in reality, this offered me piece of mind.

"Why aren't you talking to me?" Jamie snapped fingers in front of my face. In response, I snatched his hand and crushed it. The skin didn't feel the same as Jamie's. No, it was much too rough. My eyes searched for more clues, darting about his body, but I saw nothing else. Wait, he called me Auriel … I didn't give Jamie that name.

"Help me up damn it. I've been out here for half an hour," I muttered my frustration and confusion. My eyes grew heavy, and I fought the yawn. This wasn't abnormal. Mages died if they used too much Myst. But this felt different, yet I couldn't place my finger on it. Every second that passed was like a muddy uphill battle during a rainstorm.

I needed to know Jamie was safe though, and this wasn't him. Who wanted to impersonate him? Was it the reason why his essence read minuscule? Did he run from the Nine too?

"Sorry." He closed his eyes and muttered something Gaelic. I didn't understand. It sounded like *seean ewhe*, and I made a mental note to look it up later.

"I heard you call for help," I lied, hobbling along the stone wall linking our rooms. A throbbing ache built bone-deep, and when I stood upon it, the leg screamed under the pressure. It'd eventually heal if I stayed off it, but what concerned me more was the unsteadiness surrounding me.

"Auriel, I didn't." Liam, it had to be Liam. He ran his hand through his hair and glanced over his shoulder. "Call for help. I was in the shower, and thought I'd heard a noise." My eyes narrowed. Fully dressed, hair was not wet ... His energy swayed in response, giving me a flicker of the truth behind the mask. Three distinct lines of Myst. Liam ... damn him, what had he gone and done with Jamie. More so why'd he gone and done something with him in the first place?

"I heard something alright." Pushing the imposter away from me, I barely made it to my door and slammed it in his fake face. The barrier between us wasn't much, and I'd weakened more than anticipated. I was too drained to create a shield and block him from me. I took a breath, cleansing my mind, and called out to the Myst again. Sweat formed on my brow as my concentration increased.

Hands trembled, and my arms shook. "No," I whispered through my dry lips. My power proved useless against him, but it wasn't before. What changed?

A string of curses left his mouth. My heart pounded away in my chest. I prayed to the Gods he'd leave. Sweat streamed down my forehead, and my hands balled at my sides. Run, I grew tired of the infinite cycle. My dreams wouldn't happen if I took a stand. Not the nightmares, but the aspirations I held in my heart. The air spun as his Myst reached out to me. All signs pointed toward one undeniable sign.

Maybe it was time to face the choir; at least he wasn't with the Nine. My parents never told me to fear anyone but them. Liam was neither a human, nor a card-carrying follower of the elitist Nine Realms Council. I lifted my trembling hands. Did it make me any less frightened of the hybrid standing outside my door?

No.

The truth, he had terrified me from the top of my head to my toes. I feared him; I feared how my body came alive … he made my heart stop, and I didn't know what any of it meant.

He didn't leave. Those feuding emotions rolled at me like a freight train. Underneath it all lay something I hadn't noticed before that moment. Pain, Liam hurt inside, but it wasn't physical.

"Guardian of the Dísir, eun beag."

Guardian, I'd been right in my assumptions.

My eyes blinked. Using the doorknob to hoist myself up, I unlocked the door. With great effort, I hobbled toward the little table and sat down before I changed my mind. The click of the entry caused every muscle in my body to tense. My body twisted and faced the door; he still held the disguise of Jamie. I frowned, I didn't like it one bit. The uneasiness churned the bile in my stomach. Already, I missed those sparkling green eyes, thick pink lips, but most of all I wanted his smile.

Green glowing eyes. Why hadn't I noticed it before? Wait, I had, but I never thought he'd be *my* Guardian. He'd said Phoenix too back at the diner. Only a Guardian would've looked out for a Phoenix. Blinded by myself; my head dropped to the table. I whispered, "You're a dang Guardian."

Etched in my mind and burned into my soul. If I were to close my eyes, I saw it again. But why on Midgard did he walk around like that? He was way hotter than Jamie. I chewed my lip. He needed to learn a thing or two about how to treat people. A little bit of kindness and dignity went a long way.

Liam smirked as if he'd heard every word I'd thought, and leaned against the door, clicking it closed under his weight. My cheeks fired, and the warmth spread its tingling feelers over my sensitive skin. Guardians were telepathic. Gods that was just the icing on the cake, wasn't it?

He must get off on hideous women checking out his assets and drooling over him. Well when I was done, I'd make Mr. Lycan Mutt wish he'd never met me. He might be immune to the Myst, but he wasn't immune to a scorned woman's fury. Liam opened his mouth to speak, but I cut him off.

"Shut your mouth; I've 'bout had it with being pushed around." I stood up and stepped closer; my balled hands smoked. He stared at his twiddling thumbs. My legs bowed and shook, but I pressed on. "Y'all want to dictate my life, yet no one wants to help me." I crossed the distance. More like dragged, because my leg refused to support the weight. "Jamie's my friend, and so far, he's the only one who accepts me for who I am. Now you're going to tell me who you are, or," I conjured a pure white fire into my palm, "or I'll burn the truth out of you."

My Myst might not harm him, but who said he realized that fact? A rusty brow rose as if daring me.

"My name is Liam. I told you already." I snorted. *That was all he had to say to me?* I should've set him on fire anyway just for that lame excuse. "It's common courtesy to give your name when introductions are taking place." Liam shoved his hands in his pockets and stared at his bare feet. My eyes followed for a moment, noticing the red dirt staining the tops. Carolina clay became a staple color for those living there. I blinked; how'd I know that?

My eyes narrowed as they met his gaze. "That's not what I meant, and you dang well know it."

His eyes sparked, head cocking to the side. For a millisecond, Liam shined through, eyes widening and stretching to hide the man beneath.

"You knew it was me all along?" he whispered as I stumbled away, and grabbed a drink. He might've resembled Jamie, but Liam still parched my throat. The cool glass rolled over my brow.

I shrugged and refrained from calling him an idiot. "Where's Jamie?" I asked calmer than I expected and leaned against the table for support.

His fingers tapped on the door, the tapping cut through the silence, but the air in the room changed. Electricity charged through the Myst and my hairs stood up on my arms. His Myst trickled around his frame. It wasn't possession; he didn't steal Jamie's body.

"No one's noticed before, darlin'."

He blushed as his eyes met mine. I'd never made a man do that …ever. I closed the space between us, neither forgetting nor forgiving what he'd done to me, and cocked Liam square in the jaw. A growl escaped his lips in response, and I managed to conceal the shooting sting radiating through my hand.

"Nice swing." His eyes rolled, and it infuriated me more. "You hit like a girl."

My fist lifted again. "Where is Jamie?" I asked, shoving a finger into his hard, muscular chest.

"He is sleeping," Liam whispered, glancing toward the wall that separated the rooms. I stepped back, but he grabbed my wrists, tugging me into his body.

My face pressed up against his chest, and his heart raced as fast as mine did. The scent, his scent, reminded me of the woods as I breathed him in, like burning timber and dampening decay, with a touch of musk. In his Jamie suit, Liam had still managed to smell like himself.

A Guardian all right but was he truly mine? The thought comforted me even though it shouldn't, not while he wore the disguise of another. Our Mysts shot forth, filling the space around us. Watching his tricolored Myst merge with mine sealed our fate.

I became the proud owner a Hybrid Guardian … and three-natured to boot. Whoopty-do-da-day, we were stuck with each other.

His finger hooked my chin. "I'm not that bad, darlin'."

Liam lowered his face, which still looked like Jamie. He hovered mere inches from my lips. The heat between us grew as our Mysts merged again.

One moment he burned for me, but the ice would come. I waited for the other shoe to drop. The memory of his thoughts, the blistering cold cut me, and my insides bled raw. Yet I craved the misery for the passing minutes of this tender ache, blossoming inside of me.

"Darlin', I said sorry."

"What'd you call me?" My hand shoved into his chest, trying to push away. *Such a weak gesture.* I didn't have the strength to fight him. A wave of vertigo imploded as Liam's mouth brushed against mine. My vision exploded and blinded me.

"What the hell?" That was all I heard before my legs wobbled, and the world shadowed over my mind.

Knock, knock ...

My conscious mind filled with wandering thoughts as I feathered my eyes open. The cold floor cradled my back. Desperately I processed the events. Liam .... I rose up too fast and slammed into the wall. *Thud ... clunk ... bang.*

"Ow," I whispered. "Dang it." My hand rubbed my elbow, where it collided with the wall.

Knock, Knock, Knock...

"Just a moment," I called out and shook my head from the sleepy daze. No reply came. Looking through the peephole, I saw a hunched, elderly woman wearing an outdated seersucker muumuu and pushing a walker. I was sweating up a storm and wondered how the heck she stayed cool in that get-up.

The air was cranked up on high, and I wore nothing more than a spaghetti tank top and a knee-length lace skirt. Wait – when did I change? I had on a jean skirt earlier. Shrugging it off, I took a final glance around the room. There wasn't a single sign of Liam. Maybe it had been a dream?

"Hello?" I asked and opened the door. My eyes adjusted to the late afternoon sun. I didn't bother with the safety chain. How much damage could a little old lady have done, right?

"Don't—" Jamie shouted, but the woman was quick. She held up her hand and flicked her wrist. A wave of blue Myst shot from her palm tossing him clear across the parking lot. *Ice.* My heart pounded a little faster, and I rested my hand on my throat. Her eyes smiled, but a scowl held on her aging face. *Well shut my mouth.* Whoa, talk about Yoda syndrome.

"There ain't time, child. Git your things." But I just stood there and crossed my arms. Who the heck did she think she was? Hey, and what the heck happened to Liam? I peeked out around her, expecting to see him, but there was no one else. Rubbing my arms, the chill, that icy pain rolled over me again.

"That man will be your downfall; he'll hurt you again. He," she pointed to an unconscious Jamie, "works for the Nine."

I shook my head in disbelief; no, she was wrong. Liam warned me too, but I refused to believe Jamie would harm me. He hadn't yet, and I'd given him plenty of opportunity.

"Jamie's harmless." I ran my hand through my hair and glanced to where he lay on the sidewalk; at least, now he was harmless since she'd knocked him out cold. Jamie's chest rose and fell in a steady rhythm. My brows knitted together, and I rubbed my arms. Why'd he bother without a shield? My Myst should have provided plenty.

Slap. I rubbed my stinging cheek and widened my eyes. Mother never struck me.

"What the hell was that for?" Only a crazy woman slapped a stranger.

"Come I'll take you straight to Mr. Skyland, you have something for him? Yes, course you do. Your parents ..." The elderly woman jabbered on, and I eyed her closer. How'd she know? Her blue eyes flashed warmth, and then they flittered to a hazy black, like in the dream with the town and Liam. "He told me everything," she continued. "Hurry ain't got a moment to spare."

I barely had a word in before she started up again. She tugged at my arm, but I refused to move. Besides, who in their right mind answered themselves aloud while having a conversation with someone else?

"Liam wouldn't let me see him." *Liam where were you?* Out of the corner of my eye, a blur of grey moved through the shrubs separating the two parking lots. My talisman warmed against my sticky skin, or maybe I was just hot. I stepped backward; she pulled me.

"Thick-headed kids," the woman muttered under her breath. "Come, we'll go see him. Where's the letter?"

She yanked my lanky, barefooted frame out the door; I let out a squeal. The crazy mage made a beeline right for my truck. Nervously I glanced around. Had Liam told her everything about me?

Jamie stirred, and I made for his side. At the very least to make sure he was all right. That was what friends did, right? "You got rocks for brains?"

My mouth opened to protest, but I'd be fighting a losing battle. Momma always said, "You can't reason with crazy." The hope of meeting Paulo and seeing Liam again started outweighing Jamie's well-being. All this happened for a reason. I hated it, and I'm sure he did too, but Liam was my Guardian.

"Time is of the essence, child." The woman tapped her foot and placed her hands on her hips. As soon as my back turned, my eyes rolled, which in turn caused me to stumble over my own feet. The pavement broke my fall and scratched against my bare feet.

My body plastered to the ground, and I glanced up. Liam – I sensed Liam; my heart hammered, and my brow dampened. My eyes scanned the area. Where was he? My skin prickled, and I picked myself up, staggering forward. He wanted me to go, but I didn't know how Liam relayed the message. My hand shook as I retrieved my keys from her hand. My brow rose, but I didn't want to know how she had them. The locks clicked and I leaned in, putting them in the ignition.

"It's bugged child," the woman said. "Grab that there letter and we'll take mine." I stared at her, still not understanding her rant. "It's how Jamie's been tracking you." She pointed toward him, and I shook my head. No way. "Are you simple, child? Leave it."

She stormed over – well not quite; a snail moved faster, and she grabbed my arm. With a swift tug, she led me to a beat-up truck that looked like it was as old as the woman was.

"Eun beag, caution."

The voice returned, but this time it did nothing to guide me. I glanced around, seeking out my lycan friend, and taking one last look at Jamie.

Instinct moved my hand to the talisman; the stone remained somewhat warm. Caution against what though; the old woman, Jamie, or seeing Paulo? I asked the questions within my mind, but no reply came.

"Who are you?" I asked, tugging myself free of her titan grip.

The woman sighed as if I were an annoyance. "For now call me the Oracle. Everyone else calls me that." If she started foaming at the mouth or rocking, I was out of there. Jamie stirred and the compulsion to check on him arose again.

"Fainauriel." My mouth dropped at the use of my full name. "Lolly about all day, or we can see Paulo now. He's been waitin' for you. Of course, there's always 'morrow or the next day, but the Nine knows where you're at. How long do you think they'll wait?"

I studied her for a long moment. As tall as me, with piercing blue eyes and a sea dragon tattooed on her wrinkled, chubby bicep. Her sky colored gaze reminded me of my father until she scowled and mumbled to herself. That was all I needed to glance away. Daddy hadn't ever scowled, had he?

She made several valid points, and I couldn't argue with any of them. Something scratched at the gravel. I glanced toward the bushes. A wolf waited. The eyes of the lycan were crystal blue. He, I was certain, spoke inside my head. The beast had followed me.

"Go with her, but ye heed caution, eun beag," he said.

With a nod in his direction, I climbed into the ancient rust-colored F-150. We drove for what felt like an eternity, weaving in and out of more deserted streets. Of course, the Oracle drove about as fast as she walked.

Peering over, I saw the speedometer barely registered fifteen MPH. I found it odd that the town outside of Six and Twenty lay empty too. Last night, I admitted that there weren't many patrons, but there were people. Human and supernatural alike, yet now there were neither. "Where's everybody?"

The Oracle chewed on her lip and didn't answer right away. "We're a town within a town close to the perimeter."

My brow rose at the cryptic answer, but she didn't elaborate. The scenery didn't interest me, lycans did. What was their interest in me?

The wolf trotted behind the truck. Maybe that was why she drove so dang slow. If that were the case, why not pull over and let him in? I eyed the mirror as the beast sped up, his legs moving in fluid rhythm. My mouth dropped, watching in awe as he leapt into the truck bed. The vehicle wobbled and the metal groaned under his weight. I grasped the idiot bar and held on tight until the truck settled itself from the maneuver.

My eyes wandered, refusing to connect with its cold stare. All the bordering houses held that eerie ghost town feel. The roads were bare, and we didn't pass another car. The bridge loomed up ahead, and I braced myself. I sucked in a breath, holding it until we were over it. This time I was ready for it, and it wasn't as suffocating. When we reached the town square, it too laid empty. Bizarre, as the marker said the town held over a hundred people.

In silence, we pulled into a parking spot. The red brick building reminded me of an old but updated plantation house. I had passed this building on my way to Liam's house yesterday. There were multiple stories and sleek whitewashed pillars. There was even a double wraparound porch, with white rocking chairs gracing the front lawn. They sat empty, but they moved, rocking back and forth. I shivered audibly, and the Oracle gave me a blank look.

"It's not ghosts, child." Her voice screeched, but she gave me a confused glare. "We do what we do here to keep the community safe."

I shrugged and nodded though I didn't understand at all. Couldn't she have just lied and blamed it on the wind?

We walked through the double doors, and my damp skin dimpled from the blast of icy air. My hair stuck to my face, and I smoothed it back, tucking the sweaty strands behind my ears. That truck was hotter and stuffier than Hel.

A chest high fae poked into the foyer. "Miss Graftfield, how delightful to meet you. Name's Pam and I'm Paul – err Mr. Skyland's assistant." The bubbly woman extended her hand. I reached out to grasp it when I glanced down, my fingers stiffened, and my body froze.

"It's alright now, sweetie," she said. My eyes rimmed with tears. "You're safe now, so you stop that." Pam smiled wide.

Warmth reached her tinged lavender eyes. Not surprising since she was a Faerie mage, but I gauged that from Pam's iridescent wings and pointy ears. The mage was a guess. All Faeries and Elves had magic at their disposal. After all, they'd spread the Myst to the Nine Realms

"He's ready to see you," Pam said. I iced up again as every muscle screamed to run. Unsure of what to do, I glanced at the Oracle. She beckoned me to follow with her wrinkled hand. The old hag even smiled too. "Well bless my heart; we'll get you right as rain."

We strolled down a long, empty corridor until we reached a door with a name plaque. It read Paulo Skyland, Mayor in a standard font, and the plate was encased in brass. Pam's long fingers curled and knocked rapidly on the door.

"Come in," a male voice bellowed. This was it; the chance I'd waited for. So why'd my stomach flip? My legs, they begged to flee. The door opened, and I paused before stepping over the threshold. Thump, thump, thump filled my ears as my heart stuttered. "Please sit ladies."

I swallowed hard. The Oracle barreled past me, dragging me to a chair in front of his cherrywood desk. Frames lined the outer edge but none faced me. His walls were bare of awards or those funny certificates, but his book collection widened my eyes. I'd always loved books. Their scent filled the room as oil and leather calmed me.

"Thank you for seeing me," I said. My voice trembled. I raised my gaze to the man himself. My lips parted and closed. Not a man in the sense I had pictured, but not a child either … Paulo wasn't much older than I was.

Long, jet-colored hair framed his pale face, falling past his crisp white shirt. Thick blood-stained lips smiled. Two extended fangs jutted from his gums. I cocked my head. Hazel eyes appeared wiser than his young visage. None of this ruffled my feathers. Never in a million years would I have pegged him as draugr.

The Oracle shoved my arm, and I glanced at her, my mouth parting again. "Show some respect girl," she scolded.

"I'm sorry. I … um …" Yeah, what was I supposed to say? I turned to her and raised my brows.

"Auriel, please forgive my lack of hospitality. I've had a small lapse in memory. I recall your parents, but not you." Paulo cut right to the chase. I liked him already. My attention snapped to him as his odd accent reached my ears. It wasn't American; Spanish maybe but it wasn't anything I'd encountered before. Thankfully, he spoke slow and enunciated his words enough for me to follow.

My parents had confided enough in him to leave a letter. I nodded slowly. I'd afforded him the same reciprocal trust, but how far I'd stretch it depended on his answers.

"I don't remember you either. No hard feelings." I offered a saccharine smile as he brought a goblet to his lips. The tinge of red remained until he licked it away, and I repressed my shudder. Draugr required blood, human or supernatural, to survive. They didn't sparkle or eat animals unless they were feasting on a lycan or pooka.

Paulo seemed misplaced by a few hundred centuries. The clothes he wore were modern, but not all of his adornments were from this century. He faced the window and placed the goblet down. A slender ornate sword and pistol hung from his belt, but the two katanas gracing his back gave me pause.

A mixture of history graced him ranging from oriental to the Wild West. The navy coat hanging from his chair looked right out of a pirate's movie, right down to the fancy brass buckles. Neither matched the pinstripe suit pants nor patterned power tie hanging from his scarred neck.

Draugr, vampire, vamps, bloodsuckers, the devil's children; all were names representing the greatest of the supernatural creatures. Living for long periods, I assumed one picked up these items and habits. My legs shifted as my eyes wandered over the artifacts. This bordered on overkill unless Paulo was eccentric or into cosplay, but I wasn't judging him.

"You're not afraid?" he asked, and his eyes skated over me as if summing up an enemy. My curiosity ran on overdrive and plum knocked out my fear switch altogether.

"Nope. I was raised to fear the Nine." I grinned. My voice filled with courage registering the fearless fact.

Blood stained teeth glinted the fluorescent light, but Paulo's tone stayed cold. "Your parents were smart in that aspect."

My brow rose. For such an eccentric man he sure had a stick up his ass.

"I found a letter addressed to you," I said pulling the folded envelope from my pocket.

"So my son said."

I blinked and cocked my head. Had I heard him right? How was Liam's father a draugr? Heck, Paulo could've passed for his brother, not in looks but age.

"You met him the other day." I nodded as he continued, swallowing the need to question him further. "I'm sorry for how he treated you, Auriel." Yes, he was an odd one. But how much had my green-eyed Guardian told him?

"It's the least of my concerns," I lied knowing it no longer mattered. The memory ached, but we'd bonded. Whether we liked it or not, we were stuck together until one of us died. "I just want answers. Maybe I can find some closure or an understanding of what happened."

My shoulders slumped and doubt crept in. His black brows furrowed for a split second, cracking his stoic surface.

He approached me, walking with feline grace. "Can I see the letter?" The Oracle squeezed my knee, and I stared over at her smiling blue eyes.

"S'all right, show it to him."

Paulo reached out his bone white hand. "I'll try and answer any questions you have." His mouth opened wide into a toothy grin. I handed the folded envelope over.

"Thank you," he said. As he stepped to the window, I noticed Paulo was short, at least for a man, and his body emaciated. Through his white shirt, I counted his ribs. Starvation, famine; what century was he born to? The odd clothing came to mind, and my brain attempted to add it all up. Was Paulo Skyland a pirate?

chapter
fifteen

PAULO SKYLAND

Opening the envelope hit me with water lilies after a fresh spring rain. It reminded me of her deep green eyes, and how Lettuce Graftfield had always smiled as if there wasn't a care in the world. I never would have survived those early years of parenthood without Lettie's help.

"Dearest Paulo,

If this letter has reached you, then you may assume that Danny and I are gone from the world. Before we left Six and Twenty, Auriel released a pandemonium of sorts. We repaired what we could, but until she is ready, there is nothing anyone can do.

The pain of leaving proved greater than our Aurie could handle. With the help of her father, she removed her memories of our little town. I tried my best to talk her out of it, but you know kids. No matter what, Paulo, we need you to protect her with your life. Auriel is a Phoenix, but if left on her own, I fear she will spiral out of control. Remember the history I told you and Ragnarok. There is more, but I do not dare write it down. Everything you need to know you will find in our family safe.

The Nine must never learn of her existence, but if you are reading this, then I guess they found out. Merric knows some, but not the total truth. It will not be long before he does. They would use her as a weapon against the demons. Please, Paulo, please keep her protected!

With all my heart,
Lettuce Graftfield

Safe; what safe? Try as I might, I couldn't recall a safe in their home. My hand stroked my chin as I recalled the layout of the house. First chance I had, I'd run over there and see, but the house layout mirrored mine.

The young woman's gaze darted between the windows and the door. Keelan reached for her, but Auriel shied away. More fear reflected in her eyes, but it wasn't for me. The Nine as she claimed … finger danced along my thigh.

Her name rolled over in my mind. The Graftfield's attracted trouble. I folded the letter and met the young woman's gaze. Odd referring to her as such, as I didn't appear much older, but I was.

Something about Auriel bothered me. Nothing Liam spoke of but she appeared skittish. Like a mouse afraid of its own shadow, with a tongue as brutal as a viper. The latter I hadn't witnessed for myself, but Liam had warned me.

Everyone showed their true colors sooner or later.

Keelan asked, "What'd you think?"

I shook my head. Right now, there remained too many unanswered questions despite the Oracle's track record. The house though, I hadn't visited since the day they'd left. I guessed it was Auriel's home now, but I didn't want her on her own. Not yet. Until I assessed who— if anyone – was seriously after her. Liam could hate me later, but he was the one person I trusted to watch over her.

Auriel cleared her throat. Beautiful creature but I believed my original assumptions. My dear friends were gone from our world. Leaving the Nine always posed the risk, if they were responsible for the murder.

"How did they die?" Auriel's eyes snapped up; lips parted. Words flowed as she spoke rapidly jumping between that morning's events and ending with meeting Liam. I nodded along as her hands flailed and allowed her to finish. By them my eyes widened, more with awe over her bravery. Memories or not, she was a Graftfield and both Danny and Lettie would've been proud.

Auriel studied me with that same intense gaze of her mother. Her eyes open, soaking in her surroundings like Danny. I leaned on my desk and pressed the intercom button.

"Please Miss Pam, get Liam in here."

The speaker crackled. "He's already here. Should I send him in?"

Auriel gripped the edge of her chair. Her knuckles turned white, and a frown fell over her lips. But her eyes, they searched and scanned the room.

Liam poked his head into the room. "You wanted to see me, Dad?"

"Excuse me a moment ladies." I shooed him out the door, but not before I witnessed the embers that flowed between my son and the young woman. It'd been a long while since I saw Liam's face light up.

We stepped into the hallway, and I motioned for him to walk toward the staircase. It led up into my small apartment. Lettie was a Pooka and that would make her daughter a hybrid. I didn't want to risk her overhearing even if we whispered.

"Can you read her?" Liam shook his head and cracked his knuckles. I hated when he did that and sighed. Bad enough I had to hear him shift, knowing the pain it caused. That wasn't a good sign. His telepathy had never failed before. I wondered if Auriel or something else interfered.

Both were frightening thoughts.

"I just get like static. Sometimes I get through. Oh and I forgot …" Liam told me about Jamison's involvement. I didn't want to believe he would stoop so low. No. Dark hair shook free of the leather thong holding it back.

I whispered, "Jamie's … Jamie, but he isn't evil." Liam nodded. "Shit." I paced the hallway. "All right … I need to know how much she knows."

"What aren't you telling me, Dad?" Liam's eyes peered down at me, but my thoughts were safe from him. I wasn't a mage, but I'd witnessed the power of the Myst. When memories distorted, one had to be careful. Telling wasn't the same as remembering. "Jamie told me she doesn't remember anything."

I halted and faced him. "Wait, *your brother* is involved in that too?"

Liam scratched his head and shot me a confused look. "Yeah that's what I just said."

Right … a parent never wants to think of their kids … I waved Liam on but my mind reverted to Jamison. Jamie, I loved him, but he caused a storm every time he returned home from the Nine. Merric sent him to spy on us, because I refused to turn my friends out on the streets.

"He followed Auriel from New York." Liam filled me in, using air quotes too often. He even spoke faster than normal, and his foot tapped until I threatened to break it if he didn't stop.

"You should probably read this." I handed him Lettie's letter. "I'm concerned about, well, all of it. According to this, Auriel's released something in Six and Twenty."

His knuckles flexed. The last thing I wanted to do was upset him and send him over the edge, but he had a right to know too. So did Auriel, and I'd let her read it too and damn the consequences. I sighed as he stared at me. He crossed his leg and leaned his chin down to his closed fist.

"I knew her parents, Danny and Lettie, but I can't remember the woman sitting in that room." I pointed toward the door, and Liam's eyes shifted. "Lettie helped me raise you and Jamie. I'd have recalled a child." A sigh released and he nodded. "What do you think of the letter, Liam?"

He closed his eyes. "I don't understand, Dad. How can she be this powerful? The history books don't speak of it, just of the Phoenixes like Jamie." Liam pinched the bridge of his nose and let out a long, harsh breath. "I sensed something else altogether. Auriel is more than just a Phoenix. I think it's why we clash." His eyes squinted before he'd closed them again.

That was his tell. He understood, but Liam buried the reason away. But draugr smelled the lies of others, but we kept that ability a secret.

"You clash? What is that some sort of new slang?" I asked, and Liam snickered.

A sigh followed as his hand rested over his heart. Love was an emotion I didn't understand. Draugr could and often did fall in love but not me. My heart belonged to my boys, and my life was too hectic. I barely deserved their love let alone a blossom in its purest form. Liam interrupted my thoughts. "She faints a lot when I'm around. It's almost like I'm ... I don't know. I repel her?"

I shrugged and knelt to the floor. Magic was nowhere in my expertise, but the Oracle might shine some light on this predicament.

"I should remember Lettie having a daughter." My thoughts swayed, struggling with the memory. Lettie's been gone for four years. "Aurie looks to be your age, son. We need to speak with—"

"Dad, we can't trust him," Liam pled. My pacing resumed.

"Do we honestly have a choice? Maybe your brother can fill in all the gaps."

I said, "I've spent the last twenty-four hours hounding Keelan Graftfield for answers, and she is not saying a word. They even share the same last name."

But every time I think I've pieced it together, the memory escapes me, and a wall builds around my mind.

"He asked me why I couldn't remember her," Liam whispered like the small child he once was. "What if someone messed with our memories?" He ran his hand through his hair. "I'd remember a girl like her otherwise."

"I'm immune to spells, son. All draugr are immune to magic," I said, shaking my head. "What does Nick say?"

He shrugged. The look on his face said enough.

"What if you're wrong?" I halted again and stared at Liam. If I'd learned anything in my five hundred years, it was that anything was possible with the Myst. My thoughts raced as he walked back into the room. "Gods help us all if we're wrong."

I dragged out my phone and voice dialed.

"Call Duncan ... Graftfield." The phone rang but went to voice-mail. "It's Paulo. I'm sorry for your loss." The urge to tell him about Auriel rose.

chapter sixteen

LIAM

Guardian; I was Auriel's Guardian. Why I'd kept it from Dad, I didn't know, but with all the confusion .... My sigh rose in my throat, and I forced it aside as I entered Dad's office. Our eyes met; I gulped and forced my gaze away.

She stared at me but held no readable expression. Her lime scent reached down into the depths of my soul. There was some familiarity this time where there was none before. I leaned against the wall, fighting the instinct screaming through my head.

"Sorry about that, Auriel." Paulo smiled at Auriel, but her eyes locked with mine again. Her chin tilted as she took me in, pinning me down by her innocence. My heart pounded hard enough to ache. I wished I could explain it, understand it, and then maybe we'd figure this out together.

Together, I liked the sound of that and flashed her a grin. "It's all right, so what's the verdict?" Auriel asked without breaking her gaze. Her teeth nibbled at her bottom lip. Had I made her nervous or was it my dad?

Auriel's eyes fell to her lap. *"I don't understand his thoughts. Either of their thoughts, I didn't make this up. Gods I wish I had. Miss them so much. Why now?"* Her thoughts continued as my eyes burned. We were making everything worse for Auriel, but I didn't have a choice. We had to protect her from the Nine.

"I want you to stay in Six and Twenty." She opened her mouth, eyes lifting to meet him, but Dad raised a hand. "Now when did you say you left here?"

He sat on his desk and crossed his legs. I had wanted to know too, though if a spell was involved it might not matter what she said. She glanced down at her fidgeting hands again. "I'm pretty sure Momma said it was when I was six."

Six, I think I'd still recall her. That would've made me seven and Jamie eight. My head tilted to the left as I searched my memory for the millionth time.

"There's a problem," I interrupted, refraining from calling her darlin'. Whether she liked it or not, Auriel was a darlin'. In time, she'd come around. She shifted in her seat, crossing her long bare legs. I envied her skirt. The fabric teased me with its eyelet lace, flashing bits of creamy, soft skin.

"What'd ya mean?" Her eyes swirled into a fiery storm. Those delicate hands moved and dug into the armrests too. My brow rose, and I smirked. Looked like I'd found a button to push, the little darlin' didn't like a challenge.

"Well," Paulo continued on my behalf, "Your parents and I were close …"

"Oh gee y'all cowards … They don't remember you." The Oracle waved her hand in my direction, and my cheeks heated. I was not a coward, and I did not fear Auriel. Her spells faltered, and I'd realized why. A charge couldn't harm their Guardian with the Myst. On the contrary, she'd drawn me in until I'd cared about nothing else. That was how bonds worked.

My hand touched my chest. It hurt there when we were apart. I hated to admit my brother was right, but it was the only way this all made sense. She held the power whether she realized it or not. Phoenix mages wielded insane amounts of fire. Same went for the marked high mages of the other three elements. Dragon, Maelstrom, Golem mages were rarities, but the fire was the rarest of them all. All received Guardians too.

"I think it's a spell." But I couldn't say the words while looking Auriel in the eye and glanced to Dad instead.

"Draugr are immune, Liam," the Oracle snapped.

"Anything's possible," Auriel mumbled under her breath and shrugged her shoulders. I studied her, smiling, but she stared down at her bare feet. Where were her shoes?

The Oracle chewed Auriel out; I gaped at how she treated her. "Anything's feasible with enough magic," Dad said.

"I believe her," I clasped my hands together and met Auriel's blinking molten eyes, "Dad wants to talk to Jamie."

Auriel slowly nodded. She hadn't expected me to side with her. I did because she wasn't like anyone else I'd ever met. We finally agreed on something. That was a start.

Her mouth dropped, and she glanced to me. "Wait. What does Jamie have to do with any of this?"

My lip tugged up. Jamie didn't tell her; oh well played big brother. Her wide molten eyes appealed to me. I couldn't blame her, not after what I'd done to him at the hotel. That wasn't including the Oracle throwing him across the parking lot, which Nick had filled me in on. *Ouch, that had to have hurt.* Her eyes swung to my dad, and her auburn brow rose.

"And who said draugr are immune to all magic?" she asked.

I blinked, noting a slight change in Auriel's voice. She cleared her throat and said nothing more. Auburn hair shook and a tendril fell across her peach tinted cheek, but she stared at the floor. Did empaths feed off other people's emotions? Did she feel the agony coursing through my body or the need welling inside my chest?

"I don't see what good that will do us." The Oracle spoke, placing a hand on Auriel's knee. She recoiled from the touch, and my smirk widened. Nothing got past her; her glare alone could've set me on fire. "Child, in the history of mages, no one's held the ability or level of power to destroy a draugr. Even Wardens fear them. It's like the Myst itself protects them."

Auriel's eyes rolled, and I covered my mouth in order to hide my laughter. Defiant to the end, she crossed her arms over her chest and released a huff. Damn, her fury was intoxicating. Fire sparked in her palm, and she stood. "Care to test y'all's theory?"

My eyes squinted as her white fire burned bright as the sun. White fire? I shook my head and sucked in a breath. She stepped toward Dad. Worry creased his brow as he glanced to me.

We believed her, and I inched to her side. My hand closed over hers, and I noticed the fire didn't burn my skin. As if I needed more proof. I was her Guardian; her magic couldn't hurt me. Her eyes blinked, rising to meet mine; soft lips parted, and my heart surged. Auriel drew me in. Someone coughed as I leaned forward, closer as if we were magnetic. Our hands sizzled. Sparks of Myst ignited where we touched. I pushed the stray lock, brushing the wisp behind her slightly pointed ear.

My tongue slid against my bottom lip; it twitched, wanting to kiss her regardless of our murmuring audience. She staggered into me or maybe I pulled. Did it matter who moved first? The beating heart thumped harder as she rested against my chest. Auriel whispered sorry, and I squeezed her body, never wanting to let her go.

"No harm done," Dad said. "Send Nick to fetch Jamie and remind him he's not to harm him." Dad's hands gripped the desk, a splinter clattered to the floor. Auriel hopped away but held on to my hand. The loss followed by rushing cold air. Dad drew my attention as his eyes turned dark red.

"Maybe you can clear this up right here, right now," he said to the Oracle. His jaw clenched, grinding his fanged teeth in a steady rhythm to the Oracle's heartbeat. I held onto Auriel's sweaty palm. His impatience spread as he drummed his fingers on the dark wood.

I wasn't a draugr, nor did I ever want to become one, but you didn't live with one and not pick up on their cues. Auriel's eyes danced between the two, and her hands smoked. Gods how I wished I could peek into her mind. The tension grew thicker than molasses; how'd she stand it?

"Excuse me," Auriel said and slipped from my grasp. Before anyone uttered a word, she rushed out the door like a turpentine-covered cat. I started after her, but the Oracle stopped me, grabbing my shirt to pull me back. My mouth dropped at the force she possessed.

"She can't know yet, Paulo," Mrs. Graftfield hissed. Couldn't know what? Why'd I feel like everyone but me knew what was going on?

"Why the hell not?" Dad shouted, his pale face darkening. I shrunk back into the wall, my heart thundering as I gauged the scene unfolding. I'd never seen Dad this upset with anyone, not even Merric. Hell, it was like another side of him.

"Because she has to realize the truth for herself." The Oracle tossed her hands up in mock defeat, but I was still lost as to what they were arguing about. "She can't be told the past; it must be relearned."

"When did she leave, Keelan?" Paulo pressed her and glanced to me for help. My concern was for Auriel, but I crossed my arms and squinted my eyes. "Surely you can tell me that much."

"When she was sixteen." Mrs. Graftfield sighed and leaned against her walker. Her eyes locked with mine, and I no longer pretended, as my blood boiled and fists tightened. "You all just forgot 'bout her. Liam surprised me the most, but you say Jamie remembers?" She sat down, brows mashing together and whispered, "Perhaps I was wrong all along."

"How'd I forget? Why didn't you tell me the truth about her?" I got right in her face. Gods, Jamie was right. I tried to see into her mind, but she blocked me. Her Myst contorted, blackening into thick smoke at every attempt.

Her eyes welled, but she held my gaze. "For the same reasons I can't tell Fainauriel, and I've already told you too much, my dear." She wagged her finger at me.

"What the hell are you playing at?" Paulo roared, drawing my attention away and pointing his finger toward her. I blinked, amazed at his control, but stunned at my own.

"Nothing, I didn't do this," she scoffed. "Someone should go see what's keeping my granddaughter." Granddaughter ... Graftfield ... Dad said they shared a last name ... damn it why hadn't I pieced it together before. Because I was too busy trying to make her leave, and then occupied with trying to win her back. Dad pointed to the door and snapped his fingers. Yep, that was his way of telling me to shift. Torn, my gaze shifted toward the door, between finding Auriel and staying to catch the old woman off guard.

I had to know the truth, all of it, even if it ripped me apart at the seams. Hell, it couldn't get any worse. My hand ran through my hair. Intended to love a virgin; the white ones remained pure forever. Laughter caught in my throat. Had Jamie realized it yet?

"Liam, go find her, now!" I hung my head and scanned the building. Auriel's brain broadcasted different from the others. My eyes closed, and I reached out with my other senses. The trail was there, but it grew fainter with each passing moment. White Myst flowed out the front door of Town Hall. Wait, Valkyries didn't have white Myst. They didn't have any Myst.

"She isn't here, Dad, she's gone," I whispered, jogging up the second story, to shift in private.

Upstairs in Dad's apartment I stripped in record speed. Before I took two steps back out the door, my body contorted. Four paws hit the hardwood floor, and I barreled down the steps ruffling my silver coat.

Pam opened the door for me and barely skirted herself out of my way. Auriel's faint scent blended with the outdoors. Putting my head to the sky, I belted out a warning to the shifters and lycans living among us. More so, I alerted Nick and Regin to be on the lookout. She was the only visitor, so it made it easy to spot or smell her. I'd worry about my brother later and needed the lycan siblings on this alone.

No one here would harm her, but I couldn't say the same for Jamie, or if she crossed outside the shield. Without the protection it gave us, anyone could waltz right in. She was fair game on the exterior and vulnerable to the Nine.

Shit, that was why it didn't set off warning bells. If she lived here at some point, Auriel's Myst rested in the shield. It wouldn't see her as an enemy. Jamie was right. I had to find him, but not until my Auriel was safe.

chapter
seventeen

AURIEL

Running away seemed like a good idea at the time. That was life, right? Now here I was in the middle of a forest, with no sign of the little town or houses. The wind whipped the hot humid air, but it offered no relief from the sweat beading on my forehead.

My life compounded and crushed me from all four corners of the world. Thick tension, faulty magic, more questions instead of answers, and the list dragged on and on with no end in sight. Why'd I leave his side? I'd wanted to stay, but I'd wanted to go. Wasn't there an old human song about that? His protective rough hold became nothing more than a memory.

I'd grown dead tired of everyone making decisions for me and treating me as if I was a helpless child. My parents had done it, and now these folks were too. I might not remember this town or the people in it, but that hadn't given them the right to act like I didn't exist.

My fists balled up as I continued my stampeding march through the woods. The whole notion made me madder than a wet hen. Everything around me was beautiful and free. That was what I'd always wanted, so why couldn't I be free too?

The whole town covered its necks in mystery. Sure, everyone had secrets, and no, I wasn't an exception. Where was the obscurity in life if everyone knows your business? Daddy would've disagreed but look where his honesty got him.

"Dead, with a big fat capital D."

The difference, though, was I'd take responsibility. My back rested against a large maple tree as I caught my breath. The new ability drove me crazy. I'd overheard Paulo and Liam in the hallway. In addition, I had learned Jamie was Liam's older brother. By the time they'd returned … Were they right? Had I done in their memories like mine? No, he'd said Jamie remembered, and I'd known them both even though Liam didn't remember me. My head shook, and my hair tumbled from its clip.

No, they're lying, they had to be lying. I groaned; they didn't have the right. Neither of them accused me outright, but they believed whatever they wanted. My hand snatched a twig from the ground.

How hard and long could I bend it before it broke into pieces? That was what this felt like. Momma said I erased my memories, but she had never said anything about anyone else. But draugr or not, Paulo wasn't immune to me, if I cast the spell. Somehow, I knew this as truth even though I had no proof.

His accusing tone and hazed eyes were more than enough for a novice empath. I'd even heard all their thoughts except the Oracle woman. I chewed on my lip and tried following all the conversations. It was harder than anything I'd done before. Heck, I couldn't even blink without the fear I'd give myself away.

I rested against a tree for a moment and wiped the sweat away. "Are Valkyrie's that powerful?" My brows scrunched.

Paulo's hunch, there was more truth to that than I had wanted to admit. I'd not fault him too much, seeing as the letter from Momma ratted me out. I scoffed, kicking the sandy earth. The Myst worked in mysterious ways, but only blood canceled blood. That meant a spell broke when the caster removed it or died. Who else in the town benefited from everyone forgetting other than me? Me – that was the answer.

How in Odin's feathers had I managed to erase my Guardian's memory? That would've meant I controlled the Myst, but that notion went against the laws of magic. No one controlled it. One asked, and if deemed worthy, the Myst flowed forth and granted the caster their wish.

Guardians and charges held similar laws. I recalled the books my parents had hidden from me. An unbreakable bond formed except for when the job ended, if the position was temporary, or death occurred. My mouth dropped; I'd ruined a Guardian bond.

"Gods what does it all mean?" I shouted into the woods. Birds clattered to the cloudless sky and chirped violently in reply.

The mental release changed nothing, and it decided nothing. Odin's words echoed in my mind. Child of Freya, he'd called me. Dísir, but he'd despised her born Valkyrie. I shook my head. The more I thought about it the more confused I became.

My legs collapsed to the ground. Images flashed through my mind. Wings, swords, shields, and eternal battle and glory whipped through my memories, but it hadn't connected as if it were my past. But Liam was there standing at my feet, and another passed where he fought by my side against the people with blackened eyes.

"I should have insisted upon reading the letter." My head dropped into my hands. Something told me it held the secrets or answers I'd desperately sought. Like what was behind these visions and the memory loss beyond the fact that I'd gone and done it. I wanted to know why. My hands brushed the dirt from my skirt as I stood.

"Great," I said turning about in a circle. I laughed; I was lost, and the sun was setting. What time was it? I could not have been gone that long. Nothing made any sense since it wasn't even three o'clock when we'd arrived. I would not find my way back under the cloak of darkness.

The woods enticed me, but the rushing water drew my attention more. I recalled crossing a bridge, but that had crossed a tiny creek. The water roared in my ears. I stepped closer to the whooshing. Up ahead, I saw nothing but dimness as the sun finally set behind the lofty maples. I couldn't fathom how I'd lost time, but I gave a slight shrug and pressed on. That was unimportant. Fire conjured into my palm. The white light would guide me.

"Foolish, I'm such a fool. Why did I ever believe her lies? It's all a lie." Who was lying? His sultry voice was far too distinct.

"Liam ...?" I thought, hoping it worked, but my thoughts churned away in response. I'd been combating Liam left and right,

and perhaps it affected me. My brow rose, and I snapped my fingers. What would happen if I stopped pushing against his attempts?

Howls echoed in the distance, and my head whipped around to find the source. Fear – nope it wasn't there. I'd chuckled thinking to how the lycan hitched a ride into town. How could I fear that? Besides, Liam said the wolves protected me; he would keep me safe. As my Guardian, I believed in him. As the man who thought those rotten things, not so much. My bare feet pressed on until I reached the water. Let the wolves come; I'd handle myself.

An immense boulder perched on the bank. The rock seemed out of place, as there were no others nearby. But there were ones by the bridge. I didn't see it there in the approaching darkness.

The fire lit my way, and I moved closer to the water's edge. With my luck, I'd end up in the creek if I extinguished it. My hands ran over the worn surface of the waist-high boulder. Warmer than I expected and smooth as silk on top. I leaned in further, studying the stone, when my light caught an inscription on the side.

"Aurie and Jamie Friends 4 ever." I read it aloud, and I shook my head. A heart surrounded the words. Oddly enough, it'd been crossed out with a big X through it, but it was still readable. More writing etched below it. Like a lot things in this town, the language was Gaelic. I didn't read anything other than English, but I did recall a few words from my lessons. The fire and earth mages used it for magic. Ice and air tended to use Old Norse, and so did the Fenrir lycans. Loki created them in what was now present day Norway.

I sat back on my heels, allowing the dots to reconnect within my mind. A grin spread tight and wide over my face at the thought. Fenrir, and here I'd thought Liam was my first face-to-face lycan encounter. No, I was certain of it as the triple moon flashed before my eyes. I'd met the elder clan before, and the leader had two names. A wolf name that eluded me, but his other name was Ulf. The second name meant wolf.

Cracking and rustling drew my attention away from the boulder. I whisked my head around; I saw nothing out of the ordinary, but the sounds grew louder with each crunching step. My heart revved into overdrive now that the beasts closed in on my location.

Easy to push fear aside when it was not bounding toward you. My hand trembled, and a twin flame sparked in my damp palm.

What if it were a bear or some other wild animal? My breath stopped as the sounds slowed. Two wolves approached me from the rear. They crouched low to the ground, snarls and yips leaving their grey muzzles. Their heads investigated our surroundings. These weren't wild wolves; they were lycans. Their size alone gave them away, but the pale Myst surrounding them told me the truth.

But were they *my* lycans?

My vision flashed back to the nightmares. There was nowhere to run. My body froze. The boulder, intimidation … I had a plan. My legs slid up, and I stood, pressing my shoulders back. I opened my palms, pouring white Myst into each palm, and willed the balls of white fire to float.

"Bring it on," I whispered, staring into the cold blue eyes of the beasts. *"Do no' attack, eun beag. We were sent to find ye."*

I snorted and shook my head. Why'd he snarl and show teeth? It was akin to saying, "No, he won't bite," as a rabid dog foamed at the mouth and readied for blood.

My eyes widened as they came closer. I scrambled backward until I was as far away as possible. The edge of the rock overlooked the water. My heels teetered off the drop.

"If y'all bite me, I'll hunt you down and kill you," I grumbled aloud to the Scottish voice echoing in my head. The wolves stopped a few feet away and sat on their haunches. Moments passed as we stared and sized each other up.

Both wolves flashed baby blue eyes and grey speckled coats. They were large, like the ones from the diner and the one from both hotels, with massive paws. They were both equally beautiful and frightening at the same time. The larger of the two held my gaze, and the pressure built in my mind. My fire combined into a massive ball, and I willed it to float closer. The lycans whined, but I shook my head. My goal was to investigate their markings not injure them.

"I won't hurt you," I whispered. As my fire moved in, I saw the birthmarks and Myst-born tattoos. Theirs transferred to the beast.

A triple moon: "Fenrir …" I swore they nodded as the whisper left my astonished lips. Both spun and walked away.

"No, don't go," I added, and the wolves turned around. I didn't want them gone. The larger of the two wolves turned its head. Something flashed in his eyes and nodded toward me again.

My fire died out, and I enjoyed the darkness with my new companions. The crickets and frogs chirped their songs as the water added a dull percussion. The breathing of the furry beasts soothed me. What we waited for, I didn't know. No, that was a whoppin' lie. I waited for Liam and prayed he came soon. The damp air chilled my skin, leaving behind dimpled flesh.

If I'd known I'd go traipsing through the woods, I would have worn suitable clothes. Shoes too, I always forgot my shoes.

As if it realized my discomfort, the larger wolf approached me. He–I thought it was a he – moved slowly, as I patted the stone I'd perched upon. Without any effort, the lycan hopped onto the boulder and lay across my lap.

"Sure, make yourself at home." I giggled. The warmth radiated into my bones. As a thank you, I cautiously put my hand out for him to sniff.

The wolf licked it, and I laughed from the sensation.

"Can I pet you?" I asked him, and the lycan lowered his head down to his paws in response. Moving little by little, I allowed my hand to bury into the soft coat. Crushed velvet ran over my palm as I swept my hands up and down. A gurgling groan left his mouth, and I stopped, unsure of what that meant.

The lycan let out a soft whine, and he wagged his tail. "You like it, don't you?" I asked in a childlike voice, and he cocked his head in that heart sighing way. The gesture was adorable and melted my aching heart. When I stopped, he sat up for a second.

My heart pounded away into my ears. The movement was all too sudden. He yipped and nuzzled my hand. My laughter bubbled as my lips pulled up at the simplicity of this ferocious beast. Beginning again, I didn't hold back, and I gave him a proper rub down. My cheeks warmed to inferno temperatures as I tried not to think about this beast as a man.

Movement and sounds pulled my attention again, and my hands grabbed hold of the fur, pulling the beast closer. Faint noise but someone approached. The animal in my lap whined again but showed no outward sign of aggression. He was calm then I'd stay relaxed too, but I wasn't a fool. "Hush," I said. But my palms sweated, trailing wetness in the lycans fur. Up ahead I saw a glow of orange light. Far too low to the ground for anyone to carry, yet there it was floating through the forest. My hands tightened into balls, and I removed them from the animal before I accidentally burned him.

What I didn't expect was another wolf, and I didn't anticipate one whose coat danced with fiery Myst. Bright enough I squinted in the darkness. Three natured and something else, I'd recalled my original impression of Liam.

I gasped as his head lifted and green eyes blazed before me. With each step he took, the blood rushed from my head. I fought to keep my star-littered eyes fixated, breathing deeply until he halted at my feet. Liam lowered his head, resting it on the boulder.

"Well ain't you a sight for sore eyes." No question about it like when he wore Jamie's visage. He whined and wagged his tail. Furry cuteness melted my aching heart.

He wolf growled. The vibration rumbled low and steady reminding me of the New York City subway minus the god-awful squealing. Green eyes moved between the beast on my lap and me.

Anger and jealousy rippled off his fiery fur. I feared he'd start a showdown of lycan proportions. That wasn't something I wanted to see. On impulse, I laid my free hand down for Liam to sniff. He threw his muzzle into the gesture and forced me to pet him too.

I laughed, raising my brow at him. Jealous little bugger. I laughed harder at the thought. Yesterday I disgusted him. Today he wanted lovin'.

One of the wolves let out a threatening snarl. My heart stammered, and I snapped my hands back. When it didn't stop, I turned to look behind me.

Glowing sapphire Myst flew toward my head. Too fast for me to duck and I froze. The wolves pushed and pulled me, but not soon enough.

The icy force penetrated and spread over my back and side. Burning and charring my flesh, cutting right through my low shield. My talisman flared to life a little too late as I fell onto the lycans.

Voices screamed through my head, but words refused to roll from my tongue. One rang through the loudest, but it wasn't Liam, Jamie, or the mysterious Scottish brogue.

"C'mon Aurie luv, hang in there, ducky."

CHAPTER EIGHTEEN

JAMIE

I crossed into Six and Twenty to find my adopted father Paulo. He'd called me and invited me in, but I was already here looking for Nick. As I arrived, Keelan sneaked from the back of his offices. I'd followed her into the woods. How she'd managed to get away with her old lady act baffled me. Appearances were deceiving; I chuckled into my palm.

She maintained a good distance, and I'd turned northwest, staying close but not close enough that she'd see me. Nick sat across the stream with Reggie and Aurie. My throat swelled and ache ran over my skin. He'd refused to acknowledge my presence, but he'd known I was there.

Liam came up, but my widened eyes refused to leave Nick. I dragged my hand over my face and shook my head. My feet inched back when a glowing ball zoomed across the creek. All eyes flew to me, and I stared downstream, but the Oracle left.

My heart pounded as I turned and ran. Regin and Nick were on my heels right away. He issued no warning, no comfort as I barreled through the woods. Regin flanked right, but it hadn't mattered. They were both faster than me.

I skidded to a halt and he pounced, knocking me to the ground. Our eyes locked, and he lunged for my throat. Hot saliva and sharp teeth grazed my flesh but didn't pierce the skin. I closed my eyes. The pressure on my chest changed, and the fuzzy maw replaced itself with rough lips.

Nicky whispered, "Ye ken I canna dae it, hen."

"But you want to." I kept my eyes closed, too afraid to see the truth reflected in his eyes. Rustling and crunching took off in the distance, and I assumed he sent Regin away.

His hand stroked my face. "No, therra times I dae, but no why ye think; I ken, dagda ken twas only a matter of time."

"I made the—" My eyes flew open.

He kissed my rough cheek. "Aye, ye picked up a telly, but ye din come and slit the throats, hen."

Truth didn't stop me from feeling the guilt, but his forgiveness warmed me. "Why—"

"Why chase down eun beag? Why act like I hate ye?" I nodded as his hand ran underneath my shirt. A shiver erupted and burned through my skin. He tugged it up and kissed my chest. "Dae ye wanna?"

My cock stirred with each inch his lips covered. "Nick."

He sighed and rested his head over my stomach. My fingers brushed through his hair. A time would come when the sight of him didn't simmer my blood and dry my throat. I feared the day even if it was the bond driving us to lustful madness. At least I knew my feelings developed long before then.

"She left keys. I was the first. Ye were the second. Liam tis the third, but we dinna expect him to turn into a selfish prick." I laughed; yeah he'd changed all right. "Before she came I ken he'd send 'er away."

Loki again, I wondered how much he communed with the demi-god. He refused me, which went without saying since I was nothing more than a mate to own of his creations. Like Aurie, I was a child of Freya. It hadn't seemed to matter that our Gods were on the same side. We lay there in the forest for a few moments as my brain tied everything together. I stroked Nick's hair and listened to the wild songs overpower his heartbeat. From the past to the present, we'd all become puppets. He'd turned me into a pawn.

"You made me make him jealous." Lips trailed up my stomach, and his body shimmied along mine. Through my clothes, I became aware of his body. He hadn't answered me, but I'd understood even if I didn't agree.

Liam would've eventually come around once the bond rewove. My hands pulled his face to mine. I stared into those blue eyes, lined with blond lashes. If my younger self could see me now, I wonder what he'd have done differently. He shushed me and flashed a charming grin. "Ach, ye'll be the death of me yet."

"Does Regin remember?" He shook his head. I gulped. "Does she know about us?"

Nicky groaned and rolled back. I leaned up on my elbows and ate up the sight of his large naked frame. Nick sat there for a few moments, staring off into the woods. His chin rested on his fist. "Auriel's spell tis the next step, hen. Ye need to help her undo it."

He'd ignored my question. Every time I brought up us, he swept it under the rug. Whether we wanted it or not, our bond strengthened as we spent more time together. The surge running through my body, the need to kiss and touch him, none of it would go away.

"Anything for you … and her. Will she be all right?" My hoarse words trembled the truth of my soul. The same went for my brother even if he hated me. Gone was the selfish boy.

He muttered words under his breath and clothing manifested from the Myst. I frowned as he covered his flesh. Still, he'd make any clothing look better. Low slung jeans on his narrow taut waist were my favorite. "I'll come to ye tonight, hen; we've much to discuss. There's one weapon that can kill eun beag, and the Oracle daena have it."

Nick offered his hand, and I grasped it. He hefted me up and held me for a moment. The gentle sound of his heart overpowered the night denizens. My arms snaked around his neck. "We need a word."

His laughter shook my head, and I winced. "Trust that I love ye; no harm will come from me or Regin. She kens 'bout ye. Daena like ye since yer with the Nine, but kens yer mine."

"Walk me home?" His eyes brightened, and his fingers folded around mine.

I told him I wanted to tell Liam and Paulo that I was … whatever I was. The idea made my head spin, but I didn't want to hide. All of my problems began out of fear, but together, we'd tackle it. "If he kicks ye out, yer welcome to stay with me."

We kept walking, but I didn't respond to his offer. I chewed the words over as my cheek ached. The thought of living with Nick hadn't crossed my mind.

I glanced over my shoulder. Hell, two days ago I thought him dead. Could we get along long enough not to kill each other? Metaphorical killing of course because neither of us was capable of harming the other in a physical sense. Mentally and emotionally, though, yeah we'd done that before.

"Ferget it, hen." The disappointment in his voice cut against my skin. I halted and pressed Nick against the nearest tree. He opened his mouth to protest, and I pressed a finger to his lips. Nick's nostrils flared as my chest leaned into him. Wanton hands ran down his smooth neck, dragging his head closer.

I nipped at his bottom lip and ran my tongue over the surface. He always managed to taste delicious, like a blend of sweet hay and salt. I fought the urge to climb into his arms as they cupped my ass. Nick dragged me closer until his heat blanketed me.

The outline of his erect cock pressed against my stomach as we kissed. Hips thrust forward as Nick's tongue slipped into my mouth. The surge jolted my body, and my fingers dug into Nick's neck. Last night wasn't enough. *Would I ever have enough?*

Nicky groaned an agreement, and I chuckled against his lips. One day he wouldn't be able to hide behind his shield any more. I'd know all his secrets and how he felt. Out of everything, I'd missed the mind connection the most.

Even if he turned me down, it wasn't possible to love him less. I leaned away and cupped his face. He was right last night when he said I had to stop running away. But was he ready for me to embrace us? Had he meant it when he offered his home? Did he love me beyond the lycan bond?

"Race you," I said and darted away.

The back lawn lay a few feet away. Gods, he was on my heels faster than I could blink. I wanted him in my arms and in a bed that belonged to one of us.

My feet skidded into the door as Nick's weight smashed me against the glass. I laughed and turned around. His hands cupped my face, and his lips crushed mine. Fingers curled into his waistband and dragged him closer.

Spinning around, I fumbled with keys as my hands trembled. Nicky's hands slid into my pockets as he pressed against my backside. My heart pounded, but I refused to let the fear and darkness rule over my thoughts. The door opened, and I scampered for the steps. Nick stayed on my toes until we'd made it to my old bedroom.

He shut the door and hungry eyes gazed me up and down. Ocean tide filled the space, and my mouth watered. Nick whispered my name and cocked his finger. My shaky legs closed the distance, and I tore his shirt over his head. A grin spread over his face as I kissed his chest, moving to his nipple, and flicking my tongue over the hardened nub.

Nick groaned and ran his fingers through my hair. He grabbed a fistful and tore my head away, dipping down, and kissing me to a point of pure stupor. I staggered backward, falling onto the bed and having it moan in protest of our combined weight.

Another shirt ruined as he ripped it free. He dropped his hands to my jeans, rubbing over my straining cock. I tried to pull him away, but it was no use. His name rolled off my lips as he tore my pants down in a single swoop. Warmth and wetness swallowed my nerves, and I arched my back.

Nick wasn't being soft or sweet as his mouth devoured me. He drew away, yellow eyes bearing into me. Large rough hands spread my thighs wide. My hands ran through his hair as he trailed kisses along my skin. Gods he was a tease. He smirked, hearing my thoughts.

Good because if he didn't take me soon, I'd go crazy. Nicky stood, his cock straining and tenting in his jeans. My hand ran over the stiff surface and tugged him toward me. He kissed me, sliding his tongue against mine as my hands made quick work of his jeans. My hands wrapped around his thick cock, loving the heat and hardness in my palm.

My free hand stumbled, smacking for the nightstand drawer. I wrapped my hand around the cold bottle of lube and flipped the cap. Nicky moaned and attempted to grab the bottle, but I slapped his hand away. My pulse quickened, and I prepared myself for the coming pain.

The slick lube dribbled onto my belly. He studied me through his heavy lidded gaze as I scooped it up, and rubbed it over his dick. His head fell back with a throaty moan. I jerked him with slow twisting strokes until I'd worked the lube over his entire shaft. My hips rose off the bed, and I lifted my legs onto his shoulders.

Nick's head snapped forward, and he blinked. "Ye sure, hen?"

My ass rocked against him as I nodded. With a promise to take it slow, he inched closer. Nick bit his lip, and his brows mashed together, but I wanted him … My heart ached as he took his time. Since he'd popped back into my life, my heart refused to calm down. I held my breath as his tip pressed into me. He wrapped his hand around my cock and stroked me. My hips bucked easing the adjustment until he was in.

The three and a half years of toys were no replacement for Nick. The sensation was fullness as opposed to painful, but nothing like the car. Nick moved my legs down, wrapping them around his waist, and he bent forward, flattening his body over mine. As he kissed me, he withdrew and thrust himself forward. A cry ripped through my mouth, but his beautiful lips muffled it.

The bed squeaked, and his salty scent filled the stuffy bedroom. Pressure built deep in my balls with each stroke, but I held on. My arms grasped his neck and kept him close. Nicky whispered harsh words my mind failed to comprehend in the moment. The primal beast laid claim to my body.

My eyes rolled back, and my body arched into him as a soft moan brushed against his mouth. The speed increased as my heart and breathing hammered out of control. Hands ran over his wide shoulders and down his thick biceps. His lips trailed down my neck, nipping at my skin.

I moaned and grabbed his hips, pulling him against me faster. He was close, and I wanted all of him inside me. Out of all the pain and loss I'd endured, I prayed the Gods would give me him. I loved him more than life itself. He belonged to me and me to him.

Nick growled and nipped my ear. His lips paved down my neck again. He whispered, "Aye."

His hot breath grunted against my skin. Teeth tore through my shoulder, and I screamed. My hands grabbed his ass, but he caught them and pinned them above my head.

Nick held me down as he filled me with his seed, and feasted on my neck. My heart swelled knowing I'd done that to him. Gods, nothing had ever turned me on more.

"Tis official hen." Blood covered his lips … my blood. Nicky released my hands. My neck throbbed; I tried touching it, but he pulled my hands away. "It's a wee bite, but not fatal."

I had a feeling I'd disagree over the small bite notion and raised my brows.

Nick chuckled and grabbed my cock, tugging my hardened length. "Yer turn."

He rocked back and settled onto all fours. My cock jerked, and I'd thought I'd blow right then and there. Gods I loved his perfect bubble ass and thought of little else these past years. I kissed his cheeks and kneaded his flesh through my palms.

The past years apart, I'd relied on memories. My hands spread him wide, and I ran my tongue along his crack, pausing at the rosebud. Nick groaned and pressed against me. I circled his bud with my tongue allowing his sounds of pleasure to caress me. Each noise stirred my balls; I had to stop myself a few times. He begged, whimpering into the fisted sheets.

"Babe, I'm not going to last if you keep that racket up." He was hard again, and I fondled the length.

I pulled away, stroking my cock. Nick moved fast, pinning me down and tearing my hands from their task. He flipped me onto my belly and entered me from behind. The sensation changed and I bit the pillow as a scream escaped.

"Aye, hen." His rough hands dragged my hips back. Nick slapped my cheek, and the sting rolled over my skin. My breathing grew harsh, and I slammed my ass against his groin. Toes ached as they curled into themselves. "Tell me ..."

"Babe ... Gods ... there ..." I cried out as my cock spurt all over the bedding. I hadn't even touched myself. Nick slowed, deepening each thrust until my moans echoed from the walls. Another sensation ripped through me as he brushed against my prostate. I raised back, and his arms held me hostage against his chest.

Nicky's heat encompassed me and rolled over my tender skin. I never wanted to leave his embrace. Hell, the thought alone burned my eyes. Gods is this what he felt every time I ran? Nick growled in my ear, and I quieted my thoughts. The pace of his thrusts built within me again. He rolled backward but didn't let go. Every time I tried to move or speak, Nick growled or nipped at my ear.

He pounded against me hard and fast. "C'mon wifey, yer so damned sexy and tight."

His breath staggered, my heart echoed as our bodies clenched. Those hot words were all I needed to hear. Shouts deafened my ears as we came together.

I rolled onto my stomach. We were both spent and relishing in post orgasmic bliss. His hands stroked through my sweaty hair as my breath caught. It was official; I'd given him every inch of my heart, soul, and body just as he'd once given me the same.

Rough lips kissed my cheek. "Daenna tell Liam yet." He rolled off me and fetched his clothes. I didn't understand why he fled. All of his actions seemed to contradict his words. "I want him to remember, hen. He ken more 'bout us than ye thought."

I sighed as his jeans covered his ass. He smirked over his shoulder and bent down to retrieve my clothes. Nick tossed them to me and made for the door. My poor heart ached enough, but every time he left, the pain sliced through my chest.

My legs swung over the side, and I balled up the soiled comforter. The quilt remained one of the few reminders of my mother. Floorboards creaked, and I turned to find Nicky standing behind me. His hand cupped my face as he dragged me into his arms. "Thought you were leaving?"

"I ne'er said good-bye." *Oh, so he'd still leave me.* "I ne'er said I twas leavin' either, wifey."

Laughter brewed and shook my body. "Sure thing, babe."

"I'm not a wee bairn."

"And I'm not a woman."

"No, but yer mine now."

I glanced up into his eyes. "I was always yours." He blinked as my words sunk in. Nick cocked his head, and I chewed on my cheek. "I loved you long before the bond."

The darkness rose up inside my mind and shouted. His blond brows furrowed, and I awaited the stab of his words. The front door slammed, and I jumped away. Nick grasped my arm; pain seared from the pressure. Keys clattered and stairs groaned. Liam and Aurie were home.

Removing his hand, I turned off the light; thankful my room lay at the end of the hall and faced the backyard. I tiptoed to my bathroom and cleaned myself off, before redressing. Nick waited but said nothing aloud or inside my mind.

Easy to understand that I had been right all along and even though the Fenrir was gay, without the bond, he had never loved me. Not as I loved him. The Mc Douglass curse struck once more.

I'd expected my darkness to rear up and torment me with the thought, but it lay silent. Heavy steps walked back and forth; sounded like Liam had transformed into an elephant. I wasn't about to hide out in my room forever and stepped toward the door. Nick didn't stop me.

L iam stood there like a raving lunatic and accused me of trying to steal Aurie. I'd just slept with his best friend and laughed in his face. Darkness raged and screamed.

"It's not like that." I shook my head and bit my cheek to stop my chuckling. The calm, whatever existed, had been sucked from the room. I'd nowhere to run or hide, from my brother or Nicky. The longer I stood there, telling the lies, the more confused I became.

"What does tell the lie mean then?" he asked, picking through my thoughts.

"I know what the prophecy says, baby bro. I'm not taking her from you." My stomach turned; Nick, I loved him. The words wanted to rip free, but they refused to budge. "If her choice of punishment is my death so be it." My legs wobbled, and I clenched my stomach as I rose. My throat constricted as I forced the words out. My hand hit the doorframe, and I grasped it for support. The darkness shot forth and reached for him. "Besides, I'd never hurt her."

The whole scenario felt like another set-up. Like all the ones Nick orchestrated before. He set me up. He lied to me. He had not forgiven me. He had not loved me. I chewed my lip, realizing the truth. All of this … He knew Liam would defend Auriel, and he'd see me as a threat on his mate.

"I'm tired of your lies, Jamie." Liam yanked at his already disheveled hair and plopped down on the bed. "I've already decided the Prophecy is full of shit, but it doesn't change the fact that I love every inch of that woman." I got it, I honestly did. He'd always loved Auriel. My lip burned as I bit into the flesh.

"Look into my eyes, Liam. Tear me apart; I'll let you have at me if it makes you believe." He turned his attention to Auriel. I stepped forward and knelt at the edge of the bed. "I've always loved her, Liam and so have you." I swallowed hard. "She loves us both too." She loved him or did before she left. I loved her enough to help them both remember, even if that meant revealing my dark secret.

His sea green eyes squinted as the crimson and blue veins bulged across his face. "It doesn't matter; neither of us can have her." Liam stood, knocking me over, and charged for the wall. His white knuckles splintered through the sheetrock, clouding the air with twenty-year-old dust. When it cleared, the patches of fur sprouted over his skin. Blood covered his hairy knuckles. He knew she was Valkyrie.

"Look anyway," I said. Liam shook his head and faced me. "Then believe me; I love you both, and believe it, or not, I'm here to help."

"I believe you even though I shouldn't."

"I'm not after her, really bro I'm not." Liam snorted, and I sighed inside. Now or never, I swallowed hard. My gaze rose to his and my mouth opened. I clasped his cheek and closed my eyes. "I'm in love with someone else."

"Who?"

"I made them a promise and can't tell you." I stood and walked toward the hole he'd punched in the wall. "I broke a lot of laws making sure she arrived, and I break even more by staying. What's one more?"

chapter NINETEEN

LIAM

Jamie had ducked as my fist slammed through the plaster again. I hadn't aimed for him, but he skirted to the side. If not him, then who attacked her? My head leaned above the new hole I'd created as a cough rattled my chest. I must've possessed a damned soul, or the Gods laughed at this misfortune. My body flustered with amusement at the mere idea of loving someone I couldn't have. Tears sprung in my eyes as I hefted forward and clenched my belly. My head swayed back and forth.

"What's so funny?" Jamie asked, placing a hand on my shoulder. I pivoted to face him, and I resisted the urge to crash my head into the wall. Anything to stop me from thinking of Auriel, but that was an impossible notion. Every breath, the slightest movement, or sound – I was hyperaware. *Guardian, damn me now.* My fists clenched, and I swallowed hard. Jamie cocked his brow and slapped my back again.

"Nothing …" Even his begging. All of it was absurd, but nothing overpowered her. "Well at least one of us is getting laid." Jamie's face reddened.

"Dude, go shower or something.' He coughed, choking on his tongue. Did he think I wouldn't notice? I hadn't at first, not with everything that went down. But he reeked of sex, and his mind kept … "You're gay."

The words blurted from my lips. I grasped his collar and tugged it down to reveal a nasty purple bruise. "Marked … what the hell Jamie?"

He stared at his feet. "Yes to the second question." I recognized the scent, but why would they keep it from me? "I find women attractive, but—" He shrugged his shoulders and glanced away. "Dad doesn't know."

He'd know in an instant if he didn't shower, but I kept that to myself. I wrapped my arm around his shoulder and patted his back.

"I like this secret better than you trying to steal my girl." A breath whooshed from my lungs. "You're my brother and I love you, but I'll beat your ass if you change your mind."

Jamie chuckled.

"How long you been together with your boyfriend?" Jamie left out names and descriptions, but he went on to tell me the story. He'd stayed with the Nine because of Auriel and tried to live a normal life. The rhythm of her heart, a crowded room wouldn't matter, I'd find her by the gentle beat. Or her scent, my mouth watered at the citrus notes hitting my tongue. That was how it was for lycan mates too. "We have something in common now." I rubbed my neck.

"I mean the adult us. We both have mates who don't seem to realize we exist."

"Yours loved you before though."

My affection, my love grew sprouting seeds that entangled this rapid, hybrid heart the longer she remained in my presence. I walked across the room to her side; I wondered if a day without her nearby was possible now. A day without her songbird twang, even if to berate me, was a day in Hel. "The letter to Paulo says something about a spell," I said, keeping my voice low and touched Auriel's hand. We were due for a subject change, as Jamie grew fidgety and broody. I swore his mate was Nickolas, which confused me even more.

"We met her a long time ago, hell Liam we grew up with her. That empty house next door? That's the Graftfield home, where Auriel was born. You even shared a birthday right down to the exact minute just a year apart."

Auriel stirred every time his voice rose. There remained a giant hole when it came to the house next door. I'd passed it every day for the span of my life, and not once did I question why it stood empty, why Paulo had me mow the lawn or feed the stray cats.

"Let me help. I can't tell you, but allow me to show you," he whispered. He grasped my shoulder. Darkness fluttered over Jamie's mind as I began my painstaking task. The tendrils reached out again like a smoky Myst, but Auriel's white Myst surrounded me. The warmth penetrated my bones. The darkness shrunk away, hissing. Her hand pressed into my back, shooting her Myst into my body. I grimaced as it sliced through my flesh. We were connected, the three of us. Always ... the three of us.

"Five," Nick said. *"Five of us."*

Images flashed and strobed through his mind and mine. My body screamed as they burned into me. Aurie, Nick, Jamie, Reggie, and me together ... We played, trained, and laughed together.

Jamie's thoughts shifted, and I followed the path. He filled to the brim with resentment toward the people of Six and Twenty, the Nine, and Merric. That last part I understood. If our mother wasn't executed, it was possible that our life would've been different for us both.

One last image played out as the beast roared. Our town painted red as furry bodies burned on a pyre. My brother knelt at my feet and mumbled his apologies during the mass funeral of my extended family. I blinked, recalling the reason behind my hatred. Jamie was involved with the Fenrir massacre.

"It wasn't me." I sensed a partial lie as the memory replayed in his mind. Jamie saw whoever threw the Myst just like he'd been involved that fateful day.

"Let it go, Liam."

"Ice ... You saw it," I snapped at him.

My eye twitched. I grew tired of these games. It was all fun and games until ... someone did get hurt.

My hand squeezed Auriel's, and I winced recalling the soul tearing pain that gripped me when her heart stopped beating.

"Since when could I wield the power of ice?" Air and Fire were his most powerful connections with the Myst. "Liam, surely you haven't forgotten."

"Tell me who," I growled. Standing, I pressed my brother further. My hand came to his chest as a sheen broke across Jamie's forehead. What if he lied?

"I would never—"

I pushed him. "Tell me damn it."

"I love …" He smiled. "It wasn't supposed to be this way." His voice rose and fell. Jamie backed himself against the wall, hands wringing and fidgeting. My brother feared me. I tried not to chuckle.

"Don't tempt me. You stay away until I sort this out. Stay away from me, and I'll let you live." Jamie's head cocked, and he bit his lip as I thought the words. Could he hear me too? Did it matter? No, it didn't matter to me. My brother's next words might be his last if he didn't stop pushing me.

"Yes," Jamie whispered, "I heard you."

I sighed and rubbed the back of my neck. Not the answer I wanted, but at least he didn't say anything stupid. Gods knew I wanted nothing more than to stop this hatred rushing through my veins. Rage bloomed like a volatile poison.

Jamie was blood; he was my brother, and I loved him. This wasn't about anything other than Auriel. He should remember how easy it was for me to lose control of the beast. Other than the lycans and Paulo, he was the only one who knew my secret.

"Does Auriel love me? I mean did she before," I asked, though I almost choked on the words as they left my mouth.

"Yes …" Good, but I still didn't feel any better.

My brow rose, and I leaned against my desk. "So you've returned to try and what, win her friendship back?"

"Get in my way, and I'll make it the last thing you ever do," the beast added telepathically.

Jamie gulped and nodded his head. Sheets shifted, and the bed creaked. Every nerve fired in my body, but I didn't glance. I forced a smile and crossed my arms over my chest. This might end. Jamie, he'd dig his own damned hole, and bury himself with the lies.

"No," Jamie said. "She needs to remember. You need to remember." His words jumbled together. "We need to unfold the puzzle, the mystery that shrouds the mind." His eyes widened as he spoke. For a fleeting second, I wondered if he was under the effects of magic too.

"And you expect me to just take your word for it?" My arms tightened over my bare chest, and I peered down at my older brother. I believed him, but I didn't want to lose the upper hand. And with Auriel awake, I wanted her to hear this straight from his mouth.

"Nope. I can prove it to you just give me some time," Jamie's bottom lips quivered like his hands. "I can prove it to everyone in Six and Twenty. The Oracle cannot be trusted, and –" He always blamed her. My eyes rolled without effort even if I recalled the dirt and leaves in her hair.

"Stop." I lifted my hand. "I'm tired of this. I know your real plans."

My eyes narrowed as we stared each other down. "I want to know where Auriel plays into them."

I shuddered inside, recalling the rumors. I had no real problem with draugr, but there was a reason that there were few hybrids. Supernaturals almost never survived the process. The thought of anyone wanting it made no sense. Plus, he was my brother and no matter what, I'd hate to lose him to something trivial. If he wanted immortality, he only needed to ask Nick or even Regin. Lycans were just as hard to kill.

"She doesn't." He glanced down at his hands, before lifting his steely gaze. "I'm in love with someone else. You smell him on me." I nodded, and he cocked a brow. "Even if he kicked me to the curb tomorrow, I'd not make a move on Aurie. Your beast is out of control, bro."

I took a deep breath, noting those familiar scents. Everything I'd heard about my brother contradicted what he told me tonight, but the smells were on his side. Nick would set the story straight one way or another.

CHAPTER TWENTY

AURIEL

y head pounded. Their bickering tones sliced through my temples. My thoughts hammered around in my achy head. Escape was what I sought, but I wasn't ready to face them. I pushed my Myst harder until the voices ceased. A rush of warmth ran over my skin. The calmness rippled as if pebbles plunged into the depths of a calm lake. My mind floated away as if it was nothing more than debris bobbling on the tranquil surface.

"Who attacked me?" I asked the water. *"Why has this happened to me?"* I asked the earth beneath me. The fire, the air, and my spirit responded with a tepid, muggy breeze that swept against my damp, sensitive skin.

It whispered, *"You know the answer, Valkyrie."*

"What is my purpose then?" I asked the elements, but only the spirit heeded my call.

"You hold the answers you seek within your heart. Fear alone stops you from your purpose." Fear, yes, I didn't deny the truth was rather frightening. My fingers trembled, and my breathing struggled at the mere thought. I swiped at my forehead, the cold sweat coursed over my whole body. The more I thought about unwinding the intricate web I cast, the more I dreaded tearing the barrier down.

I didn't want that life. The Gods only blessed powers of this level to their vessels, and that meant plenty of danger, loss, and pain. But no one asked me what I desired.

Perhaps, if I continued to deny what I was, then there remained a chance at a normal life. Maybe the world would forget I existed. No, I couldn't do that. As much as I wanted to, the outcome of my visions stopped me.

"Heed my messenger, Daughter of Freya. Do not fear him no matter what your mind leads you to believe." The spirit spoke before fading away into the Myst.

My utopia vanished and reality returned.

Someone touched my hand using short, soft strokes, and I flung up from the bed searching for the source in the darkness. A male voice, soft and silky, spoke to me in Gaelic with a thick, husky Scottish accent, but the words, I didn't comprehend.

"Eun beag, lass ye must fix this mess. Only ye can dae it before it's too late to claim yer destiny. Daughter of Freya."

The light clicked on by the bed. I squinted as my eyes adjusted. My heart pounded as they scanned the room. The confusion blinked away; Jamie stood against the wall with Liam close by. My eyes fell to the chair and the large blond man. Almost identical to Liam except his eyes were a sparkling blue, and his hair was both blond and short. My eyes shifted between them as he stared at me. A lycan all right and the exact one who protected me, followed me, and guided me south.

"It's you," I whispered. The one who'd laid upon my lap tonight. My eyes rolled over his large arms, marked with ink and birthmarks. His salted scent curled my nose. "You brought me here."

Fenrir ... "Lass, ye are safe, fer now."

My eyes widened and then narrowed at the flame rising near his neck. "Fenrir and a Phoenix?"

"I am as ye are but far older and no' but a humble warrior of Freya and Loki."

Shield bearers weren't Valkyrie, but they often assisted in battle. He smiled, reaching into his unlined eyes. Being a Lycan Phoenix gave him access to the Myst, but he still paid homage to Loki. Both were of the Vanir and giants. Had I known him too? Fenrir didn't appear a day over twenty-five. How old was he?

I crossed my legs. "What's your name?"

"There tis much ye forgot, and no' much time. I will keep in touch until tis the moment of no' return." I opened my mouth to speak again; he put a finger to my lips and tapped his head. *"Direct yer thoughts to me, and only me, but inside yer head."*

He guided my hand, and our fingers interlaced. Our Mysts joined as one, creating a link.

I asked, *"Why must we speak this way?"*

"I'm an old friend, lass, and one who has sworn an allegiance to serve ye till the verra end. I'm a lycan and a Phoenix, but ye already ken that." He winked and rubbed my hand. *"We speak this way because we must. I daena trust Jamie, even if he tis my mate. His father, no, I've already said too much, eun beag."*

Mate? Jamie mated with a Fenrir? I almost laughed but stopped myself. Father? As I contemplated his words, flashes ran through my mind, flashes of him and me running through the woods. Hugs, laughter, and pain surrounded us as the tears ran down our faces.

A clearing lay beyond the stream, houses nestled into the wooded hillsides, and blood painted the water, earth, and greenery crimson. Massacre occurred. Two words whispered over the breeze: darkness and Fenrir.

The image haunted my thoughts, and I'd dreamt it before. A chill raced down my spine. The massacre meant to end the line but some survived. Before me sat one of the survivors, but he was not the only one. As sure as the sun shined ... Liam had to be one too. The resemblance alone ... My eyes darted between them.

"Aye, lass ye remember some, but alas naught all came to pass. There were three of us and a few halflings that survived, and I left ye to seek more friendly to our cause."

His eyes flittered to Liam and back to mine. More, yes there were more. I saw both the death and day of their redemption once, but one of them must fall. Which one, I didn't know, but I vowed I'd change it ... that was what I'd promised them all.

"Ye know why ye see as no other can?" he asked me, breaking through my remembrance of a past dream and shifting his legs.

"No, not really, it doesn't make sense." Chooser of the slain ... how much did I do or interfere with the slaughter of the Fenrir clan?

His leg crossed over his thigh. *"There were prophecies about yer kind, eun beag. They say that Odin vowed to end the Dísir altogether, and thus created a deeper gap between our two worlds."*

"I've heard the tales." Valkyries protected Midgard and the humans. My kind – he said it as if there were more like me in the world. The thought both frightened and comforted me, to know my struggles were not my own.

"But another intervened, wanting them to survive." He shifted closer. Born Valkyries were a disgrace according to Odin. The God went as far as to create new ones in their likeness. The born ones, the white ones, eventually he had called us demons. Even the humans heard our tales, but they too were twisted. There wasn't Satan or Lucifer; the Myst ruled the born Valkyrie. The Myst ruled us all.

The Dísir remained a broad term but the tone used implied whether it was an insult. The single term covered the protectors of the Myst, and it included Guardians. We protected of the Nine Realms. Only the born Valkyrie ignored the tyrant's commands to kill the innocent and wreak havoc on the worlds.

Instead, they sought peace and divine vengeance when warranted by the Myst or Norns. I glanced away, hiding my uneasiness over the topic in the folds of the blanket. As Dísir … if they learned the truth would they still help me?

"That tis how the Gods first tried to bridge the gap, but they realized it failed. The floods only sent the Dísir into hiding, and as time went on, they rebuilt themselves into a new Legion," he said.

I am Legion was what the High Valkyrie said. The story claimed that Odin created him, and then he fell from grace. The whole of the born Dísir followed him.

Over time, his story spread hatred and lies. I read the stories in Momma's books. They said his hair was as pale as the sunshine, and eyes were bluer than the seven seas, but his visage twisted from the evil corrupting his soul.

"Where do I fit into this?" I was neither evil nor vindictive. We all held faults and made mistakes, but I didn't believe in all evil or all pure either.

"Born, my eun beag, ye are the Valkyrie of another God. But how are we to ken the true intentions of others?"

My brow twisted as I followed his words. His message was cryptic. What other God? Freya? His eyes widened, and his brows lifted. Ah, the Fenrir was trying to invoke memories. But I didn't need them to answer his question. *"The General. The Norns choose a Valkyrie General. The Gods bless ..."* No. No. No freaking way was I the General.

He nodded his head, and I shook mine hard enough my hair fell free. *"Aye wee one; Loki, Freya, and Freyr chose ye. The Myst chose ye, and the Norns weaved yer fate."*

My mouth dropped but words refused to leave. What did I know about leading people? I couldn't keep my own life on track. No, there was a mistake; I was sure of it. The General encompassed eight virtues: magic, chastity, temperance, charity, diligence, patience, kindness, and humility. What of those did I have aside from magic?

The lycan chuckled. *"Ye do have those lass, but yer team makes up fer what ye lack."*

My team? His brow rose as his eyes scanned over Jamie and Liam. Oh, I saw what he meant. Those who fought with me would make up for anything I lacked.

"Fenrir, I can't do this." His shoulders shifted into a shrug. *"I'm not courageous."* Always running and hiding from everything, I was a coward.

"When ye remember, ye'll see the amount of bravery ye possess. Ye were born to do this, eun beag. There tis no other. But there tis more to it than that."

"Tell me, please," I begged. *"Tell me how to remember."* He shook his head in response, but his eyes sparkled, as they fell on the frozen Jamie.

"Eun beag, ye can't be told." He leaned in close, speaking aloud now. "I'm only ye messenger here to tell ye that unless ye fix the mess ye began that the Gods will intervene." Well that didn't sound too terrible, so what were they waiting for? "Auriel this tis serious," Fenrir hissed. "The Gods daena walk among us without breaking the laws of the Myst. Ye must remember, or ye risk Ragnarok. It will undo all the Nine Realms."

"Yeah, so no pressure, right?" I pushed a breath through my clenched teeth and plopped backward on the bed. A man's bed as there weren't enough pillows. "I don't want to remember." My hands tightened on the blanket and I lifted it. "Where is my choice in all of this? Because let me tell you something, Fenrir." I leaned close,

close enough that the heat of his body radiated onto my skin. "I didn't ask for this life. This shitty existence where I've felt endless pain. It's deep enough to bury the realms forever."

Tears trickled. Lights flickered inside the house, and the earth rumbled. Lightning crashed through the sky. Anger and ache fell hand in hand; the storm, my storm, was just beginning. My eyes ran over Liam and Jamie. I remembered the cause of their pain and mine too.

This mess was all my fault. I jumped from the bed, blood blinding my vision, and paced to the window seat. Their bickering, my parents' death … if the Gods had chosen another, anyone else then all would be right as rain. But they chose me, and I'd let everyone I cared about down. More than that, people died because I ran from my destiny. The fault was mine because I was born.

The rain pelted, flowing and sinking into the earth as a crack of lightning flashed through the sky. Four years ago, I did the same from my own darkened window next door. I forced Liam to forget me. He deserved a life free of my memory. Liam didn't move on though as I once hoped.

I loved him, and that was why I took it away; I removed myself. Out of love, I cast the spell, and the Myst complied with my reasoning. I knew that we could never … Gods, but that was years ago. My eyes trailed back to Liam; I broke the bond, but fate gave us a second chance. Could he love me again without ever learning the truth? Could I keep such a secret? I shook my head. No, not for long.

Gone was the awkward boy with dimples and eyes that gleamed. He'd hardened his body, and his persona was colder now, but he still called me darlin'. My eyes stung recalling the moments, the precious seconds until I said good-bye. How the sight of him used to raise the butterflies hiding under my skin. Liam still did that in dream and reality.

I didn't deserve his affection, love, or protection. What I'd done to him turned my stomach, and bile burned a course up my throat. I wanted to go to my grave, knowing Liam would move on with his life. Yet here he was, four years later, and he was waiting for … I didn't know. Was it wishful thinking, hoping that he'd waited for me?

The bile churned harder as my teeth gritted. Fists clenched as I pummeled them into the pillow; it was all for nothing. Valkyrie, Gods how did I forget, that was what it meant. A freaking daughter of Freya meant Born Valkyrie. Another God, Fenrir said ... *I was Vanir.*

Laughter caught in my throat, and Fenrir leaned away, smiling as bits of old memories knitted back together. At least they made sense unlike the fragments from earlier. Freya made me her vessel, and the Nine tried to snuff it out. They –my family on the council – meant to sacrifice me, and I was prepared to die, but something changed. My head tilted as I forced the memory forward. The old book someone delivered. My parents didn't let me have it, but after that we ran away; that was when I chose to forget too.

"Aye, lass ye are remembering. But why give Liam the power of the Phoenix? I knew ye erased yerself fer love, but the magic I daeno understand."

I glared at him. "I didn't do that, Nickolas."

His eyes widened, and a grin spread across his timeless face. Nickolas Ulf Fenrir; my best friend, my protector, and confidant. He left after the massacre vision, but he was there when I needed him most.

For being well over five hundred years old, I would think he would have had better things to do with his time instead of chasing after me and cleaning up my messes. My breath released slowly, and I glanced at the crumpled bedding.

"Eun beag."

Little bird, Nick called me that for forever because I flew and had wings. Only born Valkyrie received them.

The window seat groaned as his weight eased beside me. Rough fingers flipped my chin upward. "I've always been with ye, and until ye scurry me off, I always will."

His eyes closed for a moment. "I may no' love ye as Liam once did, as he might one day love ye again, but I dae love ye all the same." The words tilted my lips into a teary smile. I loved him too; loved him like a large furry brother.

"Will he forgive me?" Nick grunted. My lip trembled, and the waves continued coating my cheeks. The world around me rotated, around him too, yet we wouldn't age or die. Guilt ate and stole residence in the pit of my stomach. For eternity it festered and remained.

"Aye, I believe he already has, lass." Nick patted my hand, and I sniffled. "Tis best ye get some rest fer now, and I must visit with

Loki … to see if he can help us fix all this." He glanced to Jamie and then back to me. "One more thing, eun beag," he whispered in my ear and spun me around into a suffocating bear hug. "Yer mum's alive too."

I blinked. "What?" He winked, shifted, and disappeared. Momma was alive. "Nick," I said. "Nickolas you get your ass back here right now and explain."

Loki was more important than my question. Not a God but made into a demi-god by those who worshiped him and creator of the lycan. But this was not what I thought about as Momma filled my mind and heart.

Eyes grew heavy, the rain and utter exhaustion lulling my mind. I returned to the bed, halted for a moment, and grinned. Momma was alive. Liam loved me. Two impossible notions came true.

chapter
twenty-one

LIAM

"What's wrong, Liam?" Jamie's head cocked to the side.

I noticed the subtle change in Auriel's breathing. She stirred just a second ago but then fell into a deep, snoring sleep. I found it peculiar that she flip flopped so quickly until a clock chimed. I counted the chimes as I held my breath. One, two, three, four, five, six, seven, eight … I began to release my breath, when the ninth chime shot an icy chill skirting down my spine.

My heart pounded when I turned to check on her. She wasn't in the bed, but there were stains on the cover and sheets. Movement caught my eye, and I found her in the reading nook I built. I walked to her side. Kneeling, I clasped her hand, and checked for any damage that explained the pinkish brown stains on the sheets.

There wasn't any, and I let out a strong breath, before leaning to kiss her forehead. Her head tilted up into me, and I resisted the temptation of her mouth. My brows knitted together. This did not make sense.

"What time did you arrive?" I asked and sniffed the air. Lycan, but it was faint. My feet moved on their own, pacing the room. I tried gauging when it left. My hand stroked my chin, deciding a course of action. No harm came to Auriel, but how did the beast manipulate time?

"Nick, Regin where are you?"

A murmur escaped Auriel's lips.

My brother shrugged. "I was already here when you came in, why?"

"Because I haven't been back an hour." I pointed to the clock and watched Jamie's eyes widen. "Someone was here, someone who ... I don't know." He disappeared into the hallway. Nick, the seascape scent reminded me of my friend. Jamie thrashed around the house, kicking up a ruckus.

He ran back in breathless, buckling over. "They're gone." His watery eyes said more. Nick must've been here when he'd come in the room.

"Well I could have told you that." My eyes rolled, and I tapped my nose.

"She's safe now, right?" I nodded to Jamie and kneeled by her side again. My head dropped into my hands, and I ran them through my hair, tugging the long strands. What if I couldn't protect her and something happened? My throat constricted at the thought.

My arms lifted her from the nook, and I asked, "Jamie, why did she do this?" I deserved the truth.

"I don't know why."

A sigh left my lips, and Auriel stirred in my bed. One golden eye peeked up at me from under heavy lids. She closed it quickly, and my teeth clenched stopping the smirk.

"I'm not going anywhere; I want to make that clear now," Jamie said as I lay down beside her and shielded my eyes with my arm. Hard to admit, but I had needed him to stay too. Two were better than one, although I'd feel better with Nick and Regin nearby too. No one would touch her with four capable guards.

"Fine, but remember where you are and that there is more at stake with your presence among us." Saying the words and believing them were two different things. I lifted my arm and peeked through the opening. Jamie offered a slight nod, but his tight set jaw didn't relax. His being here was akin to waving an enormous flag, flashing lights, and blaring a damn siren all at once? I hoped he understood the danger his presence brought for the rest of us in Six and Twenty.

"I'll be in my room. Get me when she wakes up or if anyone comes in."

Jamie's eyes ignited as he drew the Myst from me. Dizziness and sweat beaded on my forehead as the blood rushed from my head. I cursed as he drained me. He shrugged and left me there. Part of me expected him to fight me; I was vulnerable. Not that it mattered; even with my hybrid status, Jamie was always the strongest between us. Leaving me weakened wasn't the best way to protect Auriel.

"He's gone now." I turned over. She'd fallen asleep again, and I cursed under my breath. My hand curled around her soft body and dragged her against me. Warmth stirred beneath my surface in ways I hadn't experienced before. Fingers combed through her tresses, catching on bloodied knots.

She fit perfectly in my arms, and her sweet skin eased the tension of the day into nothingness. Her lips parted and closed, but the words were lower than a whisper. I stared at her sleeping form and listened to her deep breathing. Lost in Auriel's mesmerizing trance of peacefulness, the world ceased.

Reaching with my Myst, I penetrated her dreams. All I saw was darkness, but then the white fire exploded, spreading everywhere. People screamed and animals fled. The world grew into an inferno of madness. A ball of flickering light soared down like a meteor, crashing into the burnt ground at my feet. Wings flexed, buffering the wind around my face.

"You should not be here," Auriel said, sheathing her sword. The soot and bloody grime dusted her body. Her eyes gleamed golden fire before, but they retreated to icy blue, rimmed within a gilded circle. Falcon feathers flexed. "Ragnarok threatens us Liam."

Auriel spoke again, but she wasn't the same woman I lay next to in the safety of Six and Twenty. Her long hair swept into a braid, and it knotted away from her face. I reached out to touch it, but she shied away and tugged the massive auburn tendrils free.

"I have to be here," I said, swallowing hard; I allowed my eyes to flow downward. She wore leather scraps scarcely covering her full breasts and a tattered, blackened dress, which clung by mere threads. The urge to rip her free thundered inside my shaking core.

"You can't save them, Liam." Her swollen eyes threatened to leak. "I love you, William, but you can't save me either."

Auriel bent down and cradled the burnt earth; a golden tear dropped. A shield and sword swayed from her side. Sparks ignited from her hands, spreading out and charring her flesh. Auriel's ashes crumbled into a pile as I fell to my knees, heart ripping inside my chest.

I dislodged from her mind and shifted closer to her. Skin brushed against hers, but it wasn't enough. I glanced at her. She might hate me later, but I dragged her body flush along my bare chest. Dry lips grazed her damp brow, and I resisted the urge to kiss her. So much darkness, so much destruction. The room spun when I attempted to decipher this mess. Yet as I closed my eyes, flashes of auburn waves and golden eyes greeted me.

Mine, my mind roared, awakening the beast inside. Yes, she was ours. I calmed the animal; my veins surged with the raw need. No, I fought back, not now, not ever. *Mine won't hurt ... need her ...*

I bit my tongue and sucked in a harsh breath. Auriel squirmed, her hands wrapped tight around my neck. A gurgle emitted from my chest as it struggled for air.

"Darlin'," I croaked. "Auriel ... please ... can't ... breathe." The effects were immediate as my limbs thrashed about, but her grip failed to loosen. Multicolored lights obscured my vision, and my arm connected with her torso. With a grunt, she released my neck.

Her frowning lips came into focus, and she straddled my waist. Heat surged to my groin, and I bit the inside of my cheek. "Liam ... come back to me."

Auriel followed the line of muscle from my chest, but I fixated on her eyes. The gold and blue melded together like they did in the vision. She stared at me, unblinking as her hands rested palm down on my chest.

"I'm right here, darlin'," I murmured even though it felt like a thousand shards of glass sliced my throat.

"My love." Tender hands stroked my face. "William, I haven't lost you after all."

Auriel slunk forward and rested her head on my throbbing chest. Wetness pooled on my skin, and my words wouldn't hold back any longer.

"Auriel, I've waited, and I'll keep waiting till the end of time." Repeatedly she mumbled for me to forgive her as I caressed her tangled locks. I sure as hell couldn't walk away from her. Whatever happened in the past was the past; I loved her. It took less than two days to realize it, even if I wasn't ready to say those words to her. The Oracle was right; Auriel was my soul mate. My insides smiled, and the beast calmed. She belonged to us, and we belonged to her.

chapter
twenty-two

AURIEL

Sixteen years old again and my heart had torn into two. On one hand, there was my destiny, and on the other, there was Liam. I ran to save him; erased me to keep him. Fainauriel Graftfield should not have existed anymore, but here I was, wrapped in his inviting arms once again. Everything changed … my eyes reopened to the truth. I'd escaped my prophesized death and found out the Norns bore me to lead a dying, incarcerated, hated race.

Dísir … the time would come soon enough. We'd all need to band together, not just the born Valkyrie, but also all the protector races of the Nine Realms. I took a deep breath and centered on my Guardian's warmth and gentle breaths. *Who would follow me?* Heck, even I wouldn't follow me.

Non-stop I had trained for years in secret. They taught me defense. Born to die and save the world; that was what the Nine had told my parents. My great aunt even held the sacrificial knife. No creature in all the Nine Realms could permanently escape death. "It doesn't make the decisions any easier, does it darlin'?" Liam said, stroking my hair. Piece by piece my memories of my former life returned, but there were gaps and holes. I didn't know when I would remember.

I lifted my head up, but his eyes stayed closed. "Nothing is ever simple. You taught me that."

His smile was bleak. We both understood the repercussions. Purity, I'd been a fool to love him. Even without death, I still had a job to do, and so did my Guardian. Yet I loved him anyway.

"I know what you are, and … we'll find a way." Liam might know what ran through my veins, but he didn't have the whole picture. There wasn't a rush of memories flooding his judgment. *Four years ago … four years apart.* The mere thought of what I had done to us was unbearable. And none of it changed what I was, what I'd become.

Chooser of the Slain they called me. Ceremonial and pain-less, the Council of the Nine had promised. But prior to that, I believed— we all believed—the lies. My own family prepared to slaughter me, and for what? Was that why they killed my father? Were they baiting me with my momma? That was a decision I didn't want to make. My destiny …

I swallowed hard. I was worth more than her life, even more than my daddy's life too. But if there were a way, I'd find it and rescue her. Sorry didn't cut it. Everything changed now, thanks to me. Somehow, the Myst allowed me to adjust my destiny. The punishment became clear now that I remembered. Liam met me with disgust, and I was thankful that I didn't have the memory of our love. Still, a thousand daggers pierced my heart; what changed his mind. Was it Jamie or Nick? Was this some odd jealousy thing?

I stared out the window. The moon sat heavy and high in the sky. A bird cawed in the distance, but its song spoke to me. The animals of this world always did. With its cry, another memory resurfaced, long ago forgotten. Four years ago, I stared out my own window. The house next door bathed in darkness now.

"Will you do the same for Jamie?" Momma had asked me in regards to the memory spell. My eyes narrowed on her. Jamie didn't deserve my sympathy after what he did.

All of us were friends back then despite Nick being older. Over time, we drifted apart and branched off as we grew up, but we cared for one another. Regin, Nicky, Liam, and Paulo at times too remained close but then there was Jamie and Nick. I'd caught them kissing, and they both freaked out. I remember telling them how stupid it was to hide in a free community, but both insisted I keep it secret until they were ready.

That time didn't come, but I told no one, not even Liam. The vision of the massacre came, and I warned the Fenrir clan. Nick took his sister, and Paulo sent Liam away, but Jamie didn't know about Nicky.

I should've done more to protect my friends. When Nick and Reggie returned, I couldn't hide the truth from either of them. Jamie's betrayal cut too deep. Our family was never the same. I fled. The hardest part was all choice. An exchange even if they didn't realize the sacrifice. My freedom died so that the residents of Six and Twenty remained safe.

"Auriel," Liam whispered my name. I murmured a response with a half sniffle. "I want to remember, all of it too." His hands tangled in my hair. "But you need to let the past go."

My chest shook, tinged with amusement. "I forgot the spell."

"No rush. As long as you stay with me now." He sighed, and I inched my head closer to his. Liam was quiet, as I memorized the curve of his jaw, coarse from his stubble. Thick lips curved into a smile as my fingers stroked his cheek. His arms came up, grabbing my waist. Liam's eyes opened. My heart pounded, and he sucked in a sharp breath. "You drive me crazy."

Those were some of the last words he'd said to me four years ago, when he'd pinned me against the tree. I'd tried saying good-bye, but the words refused to come. Liam kissed me long and hard as if a part of him knew.

"No more good-byes."

His hands ran up my sides, brushing against the sides of my breasts. I held my breath as warmth rushed to my center. His fingers walked up, tracing the curve, before settling between them. One hand slid down my back, cupping my ass as the other trailed down my chest. Liam stopped at my navel and inhaled a deep breath. His eyes blinked, yellow replacing the green.

They raked over my body as he trembled beneath me. "Darlin' … ducky." Liam's voice grew harsh and distorted. I inched away, but his grip tightened. "No." He sat up and wrapped his arms around me again.

Sweat broke over my brow. The beast rose, its Myst overpowered the other two. "Leaving … worse … stay … never leave William again." His words were a broken whisper, blowing hot against my ear. "Promise." Liam's lips nibbled on my ear, making it impossible to think. When I didn't answer, he repeated the words again. "Promise us, princess." I swallowed, but my mouth dried into sand.

"I promise I'll never leave you again," I said knowing they were the words he longed to hear but didn't know if I could keep them. Stroking his hair, I wondered if the beast remembered what the man did not.

"Look at me," Liam whispered, cradling my chin in his hands. "We'll figure this out, starting tomorrow." His lips fell to my forehead, and I frowned. I wanted his lips lost on mine. He chuckled. "If I kissed you now … ah, screw it."

Liam pressed me against the bed, his leg sliding between mine, and he stroked the hair from my eyes. I reached for him, but he grabbed my hands, pinning them above my head. My mouth opened to protest, but Liam's lips swooped down and engulfed me. A surge of lightning struck my skin.

I shuddered as goosebumps erupted and washed over my hot skin. He moaned against me, prying my lips further apart. My legs wrapped around his waist and pressed him into me. Our tongues touched, and my nails dug into his hand, as the pressure built in my stomach. Liam tasted of mint and toasted marshmallows; I couldn't get enough as my body arched, rubbing against him.

My thoughts and old memories ceased. The air thickened, and I couldn't breathe. Ache, sweet need, throbbed beneath my skin. Liam let my hands go, and they fell to his shoulders. I slid them down his hard chest, and to his rippled stomach, memorizing each dip and knotted muscle. When I reached his navel, he pushed back, yellow eyes widened.

"Can't," he panted and closed his eyes.

I swallowed hard and nodded. My eyes stung, and warmth settled over my cheeks. He leaned back onto the pillows and patted his chest. I bit my lip and willed my body to behave. My eyes rolled over his frame before I crawled up beside him, and lowered my head to his chest. Neither of us said a word, and I closed myself off to him and the world.

Liam's thundering heart lulled me with its cocooning rhythm. But the comfort ended there. The nightmares weren't far behind as his light gave way to the darkness of my nightmares. Voices, shouting and screaming, rattled my sensitive eardrums; the heat of battle surrounded me.

My eyes fluttered open as the reverberation ceased. I shuddered in disbelief, scanning my surroundings. Tonight I became what I was born to be, and I wasn't alone. Five more Valkyrie joined me. Two sat on top of winged horses, and three with wings floated mid-air. Male and female alike, we formed a band in the sky as flocks of ravens encased us. On the ground, mages, draugr, and two-natured of all the races banded together. Chivalry, Myst, and Strength ... we came together to triumph, but our enemy wasn't in sight. The golden hay field stretched for miles and lay empty as we stood stoic, waiting ...

We exchanged glances and murmured courageous words. Brows dampened; hearts thundered in my ears. My grip tightened on my sheathed sword hanging from my leather belt. The rumble drew closer, my teeth grinded together in anticipation and maybe even fear. The enemy approached; their taint thickened in the moist Carolinian air. Feet hit the ground and the rough mica burned beneath my bare feet. The surge dulled to an annoyance as my runic talisman blared to life.

My eyes fell to Liam, his orbs baring my soul with ease. "I love you."

"As do I, my darlin'."

Lips joined and parted in a prompt and empty kiss. This wasn't good-bye. We were one, broken when separated. There was no him, no me—only us. Charge and Guardian as it should've been. Liam's thoughts flowed clear into my mind, feeding me strength to stop the ever-looming darkness, and the Phoenix ignited the voided shadows revealing what others refused to recognize.

"See them for what they are," I shouted to my small army. Through me, they witnessed the truth hiding inside the creature's shells. Some gave up on shielding their true, grotesque forms. What they were I did not know.

"Remember what we fight for, hold it close." I pounded my shield to my heart as my blade rose to the sky.

Lightning and thunder crackled in agreement; the Gods were on our side. Today it was Freyr and Thor, tomorrow maybe Hel or Freya, but the Myst was who we truly sought for guidance and victory. My lips pressed down in remembrance. The exact spirit gave birth to those we fought today and the God responsible for their continued existence.

Earth trembled underneath, but I refused to let my fear rise. My sweaty hands quaked as I swallowed a gulp of air. The enemy marched; red and black leather skin covered their misshapen bodies. I recoiled at the visage, as the true demons – the created Valkyrie – of myths approached. Hooves, horns, tails, but no wings were normal for the Dísir of the shattered Hel. Once great men and women turned by the foreboding shadows of their creator –Odin. They were the newest children of the famed God, and they brought the darkness as their companion.

Clouds rolled over the burning noon sky. I spat, gripping my weapons until my knuckles whitened. Left and then right, I glanced; the Fenrirs flanked me, foaming and snapping at the proverbial bit. With a nod, they understood their role, their commitment to serve our purpose. We were of the Myst, and we were all equally its children; just as we all held corruption within our hearts. This wasn't about perfection, and neither was it a struggle for land or country. No, this was about freedom.

"By the light," the blond Valkyrie on my left roared, rising his lightning infused sword to the sky. His electric blue eyes turned to me, lips smirking into a devilish grin. He stepped closer, reaching out a pale hand to my face.

"Don't fret, princess. You were born ready." His British accent, maybe it was his words … Something about him sparked a fire inside my heart, the heat spread through my veins and lifted my spirit into soaring heights. Their war drums hit hard, drawing my attention, and the constant, sickening rhythm caused bile to burn my throat. "Sometimes, you can't turn the other cheek," he said. "No, you must confront and crush what destroys the ones you protect and adore."

The innocent, the human race, the Nine Realms … yes, I nodded. We were the Born Valkyrie, we were the hybrids, the pure bloods, the outcasts of magical society, and we fought without seeking acknowledgement or celebration.

"We are the reapers, the muses, the shamans, and the warriors." My eyes fell to the Fenrir siblings. "That the Nine and Odin wished to control or kill." Shouts resonated, echoing through the folds as I walked among my soldiers. Swords and shields clattered and smashed as we exchanged smiles, nods, and wishes of good cheer.

Clarity and peace settled over my mind. We lined up, baring stoic stances. The fray lay but moments away, and I recalled why this must come to pass. I was the missing piece, but without me, without the Phoenix to shepherd the army, they wouldn't succeed. I was the courage of the human, I was the Myst of the Phoenix; I was also the backbone, the Strength of the powerful two-natured Pooka.

Momma wasn't a human. I blinked as she appeared before me. From the Myst, Lettie Graftfield rose. She flashed a shy smile and shifted into a panther. I nodded and bowed to the real courage. How many faced death and lived to regal its history. She did more than that. Momma gave her life, unknowing if she would live or die so that I would save our people.

Kill me and destroy the greatest weapon the Vanir Gods ever created. Many tried and failed to take my life. I was the connection between these two worlds coexisting as one. Part human and part supernatural blood pumped through my veins. Piss me off and risk my wrath, the wrath of the free. I smirked. Control me; ha, I dared someone, anyone to try. I rose to the sky, my wings beating hard, and joined the Valkyrie.

"Find him," the winds buffering beneath my wings commanded.

The blue-eyed man turned to me. He said, "Find me, Aurie luv."

Warm arms squeezed me tight, awakening me from the odd dream. It was rather fine until the end. My brow creased tight, and I rubbed the sleep from my eyes. What was the Dísir trying to say, and why should I find him? I shifted, trying to find a comfortable position. The strong smell of burning wood and vanilla comforted me as my nose burrowed into Liam's rough, unshaven cheek. The drumming of his heart carried a song to my ears, and I timed my breathing to it.

"Auriel?" His words brushed past my cheek. On instinct, I rubbed my face against his scraggly whiskers.

"Yes?" I whispered, noticing my hand wrapped into his shaggy hair.

"You alright?" he mumbled as I searched his moonlit face.

I forced a smile. "I'm fine."

The last thing I needed was for Liam to worry. Sure, the dream troubled me too. Would Odin amass an army to get me?

He kissed my head. "'Kay, wake me if you need me."

"Uh-huh," I replied, removing my hand from his disheveled hair and suppressing my sigh. Liam grasped my hand, and placed it back, murmuring something that I didn't follow in the harsh tones of Scots Gaelic.

Sleep found me again. The battle was on, though I admitted, I couldn't determine if we were winning or surviving the encounter. My eyes blinked in the shrouding cloud of dust and smoke, threatening to choke the air from my burning lungs. The ground painted red, and the earth laid bare of the summery growth. I narrowed my eyes, scanning for Liam as a mace barreled past my head.

"Where are you?" I whispered, pleading with the wind spirits to convey my message.

"Lay down your weapons," a gruff voice roared over us. The ten-foot devil stepped from the eerie fog. Curled horns jutted from his tattooed crimson head, and yellowed, sharp tusks snapped. He wasn't the devil, not from Christian texts, but he was a sight that sent a shiver rushing down my spine nonetheless. I squinted, noting the lifeless body in his grasp. Silver speckled fur plummeted to the ground. Each piece added an extra beat to my thundering heart.

"Regin," Paulo cried. I hadn't even noticed the draugr before now. All at once, I rejoiced and crumbled. She was my best friend, but it wasn't Liam.

The tears burned my eyes, but I refused to let them fall. Now wasn't the time to mourn my fallen sister. "You will pay for that, demon." Its lips twitched into a smile, and my blood boiled.

"Luv, channel it." The voice of my blue-eyed Valkyrie entered my mind. Our gaze locked, his head cocking to the side as his opponent's strike missed. He rebounded, slicing through his flesh with his blazing blue blade. A sheepish smile followed, sending a flush to my cheeks.

My dream-self stepped into action, cutting down the enemy standing between my new mark and me. Each step became easier as the rage flowed into my blade, engulfing the silver in a white fire. Massive flaming missiles hurled left from my enchanted sword. My rune-etched shield blocked blow after blow on the right as I thundered after the devilish giant.

"Little bird ready to play?" It snorted.

The creature froze, startled by my insanity, or maybe my bravery. My lips pressed together. I tossed my weapon to the ground, and its black pools narrowed with suspicion.

The fighting around us ceased; all eyes fell on us. "Hold," he said to his warriors, and I nodded to mine. This was between us. We circled each other; its veins pulsed and popped from its ugly head. My breath held steady, but I trembled. The evidence shot through my body.

It darted, stabbing right, but I was faster, soaring over his head, and landing behind him. Snickers from my warriors reached my ears, but I fought the smile threatening to spread. I hadn't won yet.

He rebounded, pivoting on his hooves. "What game is this, little one?"

"No game." I opened my palm to reveal the light. "This is your weakness."

It laughed, looking to its minions. "You think I'm afraid of fire?"

They all laughed. My own laughter joined in as I stepped forward. Those beady eyes bore down upon me, daring me to strike. My head cocked to the side, lips curling up as I pulsed my Myst into my palm, willing it to grow with each passing heartbeat.

"Too bad," I sneered and slammed the white fire into its chest. The flame sparked but did little else. *Crap.*

His chest rumbled. "Told you."

The creature grasped my neck, lifting me from the ground. My lungs burned as they struggled for air.

"Teine," my strained voice resonated over the gasping crowd. Lightning exploded from his chest.

Tendrils of energy ignited over the giant's skin, as he staggered back. Grip loosening, I broke loose in time to watch the monster slump to its knees.

"How ..." The demon looked down at its form. The skin cracked open, splitting and splintering into crevices. Light devoured the Darkness.

"Not ... poss ..." No other words left his mouth.

My mission wasn't complete. This Dísir was but one of the many surrounding us now. Even my own stared, mouths agape, as I fluttered to my Guardian's side.

"Reggie lives," Liam channeled. *"Barely, Kiel saved her."*

I nodded and allowed the happiness to penetrate my soul. While some brave souls fell to the demons today, my friends lived to fight the rest of the battle. We survived to fight again.

The crowd parted, revealing my winged warrior. "It's time, luv."

The angel kissed my cheek. His white and grime-covered wings wrapped around my body, pulling me close. I breathed deeply, and I readied myself to face the remaining demons. My eyes closed, and I reached my senses out to the elements. The Gods themselves would hear my plea.

"Do they live, Loki?"

Why would I ask Loki? The Myst rose from the scarred earth. *"You are their judge; you are their jury, Chooser of the Slain."*

My eyes closed, releasing a tear. There was little need to see it, and I knew it glinted gold. *So be it.* I focused on the foes, standing still as statues.

They awaited me, black and red knees shaking, whether it was for death or forgiveness. Loki was right. I was their judge, their jury. Their fear tainted the air; puss and piss infected the earth, leaving putrid scars in its wake. The yellow field dissipated in their wake.

"Beag," I shouted. My tawny wings folded away as I melded my body to the ground. Head flying back, my spine ripped, and a cry shrilled through the silence. Tears flooded my vision as the purity of my humanity suppressed.

My body contorted, taking the form of a massive falcon. I rebirthed with colors of red, blue, purple, orange, and gold. Reflecting the flickering heart of flame, the Phoenix rose.

I was both, yet I was neither, but total control remained mine. My body dove at the fleeing bands of demons. The talons proved lethal, piercing, and burning foes within my clutches. Few stayed, attempting to throw spears and maces, but my feathers shielded my body like armor. The ink-eyed demons ran for their lives; the beast awoke inside. We thirsted for demise, destruction, and to purify their wicked stain from this realm. But power must remain mine; the beast would never stop until the realm burned, and Ragnarok completed.

When the last demon dropped, I descended from the air and shifted back. I shivered in the wake of my nakedness and the carnage that became mine. Liam strolled to my side, his aroma catching my attention. I lofted my discarded sword from the barren field and bent to retrieve my shield. My eyes reflected the molten pools; the beast lingering at the surface. He placed his hand on my shoulder, but said nothing before handing me clothes. I blinked, staring down; I caught sight of my body. Swollen breasts and a well-rounded stomach remained unmarred. My inner dream-self remained shocked, but the dream continued.

"Will we ever have a moment's peace?" I asked him already knowing the answer. *No.* There'd always be evil to rid. Liam retreated as my grinning Valkyrie approached. His lips brushed against mine, hands and wings cradled me. Butterflies and electricity jolted prickled bumps, spreading in a rush down my exposed body.

He broke away. "Don't ever do that again, ducky." My mouth hung open, searching for words to answer. My lips clamped shut; I swallowed hard and nodded. He dressed me, within the privacy of his white wings. "Bloody hell, shifting while pregnant." He shook his head, blond bangs falling into his face. "Dangerous for both of you ... you and our daughter."

"Son," I said, lips turning upward.

His head cocked. "How do you know?"

I shrugged my shoulders as my stomach jerked a spasm. A grin spread across his face, widening with each little kick. His blue eyes closed, and we shared the moment together. Even the fighting ceased to stop long enough to have a family and deep down the fear ate at me. There was much to lose, and I feared for my heart, and for those involved.

"Kiel," Paulo called, and my unconscious-self had a name to stick with his handsome face.

"Probably wants you, princess. You scared the bleedin' daylights out of them." He kissed my nose before flying off.

Lost in this dream and my thoughts, I didn't notice the masked man approaching me from the crowd. I screamed inside, warning myself as he snuck up without a sound. He drew an etched blade from beneath his cloak, stabbing my belly from behind. I stared into the darkness of his eyes; he whispered in a sullen voice. The accent cut as jagged as his knife, "Eun beag, I have failed ye, my friend."

Nickolas withdrew the dagger, bloodied with my life force. My form screamed, falling to the earth. Blood gushed out, running down my thighs, and into the barren hollow left by the demons. I clutched my stomach, no longer sensing the flicker of life, and screamed again. My legs trembled as I stood up; I turned on Nicky. The five elements called forth, as I screamed, unleashing Hel itself, and my fury from my upturned hands. My palm fell, resting upon the Fenrir's chest, and he burned to cindered ash in the inferno of my pain.

chapter
twenty-three

LIAM

After all the commotion, I slept like a baby. Maybe it was due to the woman resting in my arms, but I'd no complaints. A man could get used to it, and I didn't think I'd ever sleep alone again. My dreams were empty, for my heart and soul found the one it sought.

Smack. I opened my eyes to a fist pounding into my stomach. Her head cocked; her jaw dropped and screeched.

"Auriel, Auriel wake up." I jostled the screaming woman. Her arms thrashed at me, scratching and punching me in her sleep. First, she strangled me, now she was bludgeoning me to death.

"Aurie ..." Jamie called to her from the door, and my teeth clenched, shooting a pain through my jaw. Auriel flung her eyes open. They were red rimmed, and smudges of gilded marks lay on her pink cheeks. She cried out a river of golden tears, but why.

Her eyes darted from me to Jamie. She frowned and rolled to the side, taking the sheet with her. I shivered and grabbed a pillow to cover myself.

"Where is my bag? My journal? I need a pen and paper. Now!"

She turned to the bedside table, fumbling and crashing drawers shut. I grasped her arm and attempted to calm her down. Auriel glanced down at my hand.

"Hold a second there darlin'. Why do you need 'em now?" I asked her, trying to get her to focus, before she'd stumbled upon something I'd rather her not find. Every man had a stash of some sort; I was no different.

"To write down her dream," Jamie answered, rolling his eyes, and stepping into my room. He smirked at me, goading, and I'd love to smack the look from his face. Hadn't I told him to stay away? I didn't think he'd make a move on her, but that didn't mean I trusted him either.

I rifled through my desk and pulled out a stack of old journals. They were mine. Auriel retrieved my pencil cup from the nightstand. I liked to draw and kept myself stocked with various charcoals and colored pencils.

"Thanks," she whispered.

Her smile turned sweet and genuine. It reached up into her caramel eyes, which had calmed down. But something changed, and I didn't quite understand it. Auriel eyed me differently.

"How do you feel?" I brushed her hair back from her face, and ignored Jamie's glare attempting to burn a hole in my back. *None of this was for his benefit*, I reminded the beast and myself. He screamed back and fought to rise. Jamie wasn't lying about Nick though the fiend needed more reassurance. The nose tells more than people realize and with enough practice, a lycan or Pooka determined emotions and lies too. But my cousin—on my bastard father's side—had a unique brackish scent. It wasn't offensive, just different, and I'd scented it on my brother and in the house.

Auriel sighed as I stroked her hair. The seeds of love planted long ago, but she stole the roots away. With her back in my life, new ones grew to replace the ones Auriel ripped away all those years ago. Her eyes reconnected with mine, but she didn't answer me. Instead, she flipped the notebook to a clean page and wrote. I watched her, as she scribbled and jotted away. When I thought she was finished, she turned the page and doodled, switching between colors.

I was amazed. Her skill wasn't anywhere near that of mine, but Auriel wasn't half-bad. Yet I bit my tongue, even as the cloaked man on the page jumped out at me. Nick –or me with blue eyes and blond hair – my best friend attacked the woman I assumed was Auriel.

Jamie sat beside her, and he shook his head at the page. I caught the question within his mind, and it mirrored my own. "What would lead such a good man to harm Auriel?" remained the unspoken question. Nick, for all his faults, protected and served well. He believed in honor and the lycan Codex his father created.

chapter twenty-four

AURIEL

Two dreams in one night. Frazzled was an understatement. My hands rubbed the pencil over the smooth surface. There were similarities in each, but the second one left me shaking, and I couldn't stop myself from worrying over the startling truth I foresaw. My eyes widened, and my stomach churned. I was pregnant with another man's child, and my best friend slaughtered said child. He tried killing me too, but I ended him first. Now, I knew better than to march up to Nikolas and start the accusations. For starters, I didn't have all the facts and no future set itself in stone. It'd better change. I glanced to Liam whose forehead scrunched together.

Jamie sat beside me. His hand rested on my shoulder. Liam moved closer, his arm snaking behind my back. I closed my eyes and swallowed.

My hands tossed into the air before slamming down. "Dang, can y'all back off?" *Hello, ever hear about personal space?*

"Sorry," Liam's voice tickled my neck. "It's just ... well ..."

My eyes closed again, deep breaths filled my lungs. My mind searched the nightmarish images. I dropped the pencil as the knife cut into me. He needed to see this, this wasn't a game. His hand nestled into mine, and I let him watch the vision replay. Liam trembled, but I didn't allow him to sever the connection.

"Who's Kiel?" His words were sharp and accusing as I'd feared.

"I don't know." I shrugged, opened my eyes, and dropped his hand. It slapped against my knee, and he didn't attempt to move it, nor did I complain. The warmth spread to my cheeks, and I added, "He wants me to find him."

Jamie snorted, and I glared at him. Eventually, I needed to have a long ass chat with him. He stared at his lap, and his fingers played with a string. Same went for Nick too, but not about the dream. They weren't together; I closed my eyes, trying to figure out how the darkness had infiltrated my old friend.

"How long have you had them?" Liam asked. His hand caressed my knee. The thumb moved in delicious circles, each movement felt like he stroked the butterflies deep into my stomach.

"I have prophetic dreams; sometimes they are more like nightmares." My arms waved as I explained the complex gift of visions and dreams. Liam's eyes sparked with each word, his smile widening into a grin that I'd love to lean in and kiss if we were alone.

"But nothing's set in stone." I reassured him, because unless Liam hurt me, I didn't see myself with anyone but him. As my Guardian, no matter what, we'd always be in each other's lives. Love came naturally through lifelong bonds, and the Guardian Council encouraged it.

He took the journal from me and opened it. "Do you see that?" Liam nodded to Jamie. They were pointing at my poor sketch of Nikolas Fenrir, and I swallowed down my guilt. I hated lies and those who weaved them, yet there I was keeping the truth from them both. Would the Gods forgive me for protecting my friends?

"Yeah … That can't be right," Jamie said, his steely gaze bore into me, brow raising a fraction. Heat rose in my cheeks. His eyes peeled away at my barriers.

"Uh, you want to let me in on your secret?" I lied. Stretching, I bent my body back into the pillows, and Liam moved with me. Jamie's eyes didn't miss a beat as they ran up and down the length of me.

"I know the man in the picture." Jamie's eyes rested on my chest, and I grabbed a pillow to cover myself. He might've had a fling with

Nick, but he'd admitted to his attraction to women. Humans called it bisexual, I didn't care whom he gawked at, as long as it wasn't me.

Liam stood and reached his hand toward me. "I guess that is to be expected."

I allowed him to lift me up, and swayed a bit, but righted myself. The vertigo seemed better today. That, I'd assumed, was an effect of the Guardian bond, and it'd eventually disappear altogether.

"Well yeah seeing as I grew up here and all, but why would a fight come here?" Jamie asked as he stretched out on the bed. "You did too Aurie and so did," he tapped the picture, "that one."

"Guys, it was just a dream." I glanced to the door. No more running. I whipped around and stared Jamie in the eyes. "Why are you here?"

Liam grabbed my arm and leaned down. "He's my brother."

"Well duh, but why's he here ... in your house?" My eyes narrowed as I awaited his answer. Silence. My foot tapped. Jamie smirked and folded his hands behind his head.

I turned to leave the room, but slammed into Liam's chest instead. Stars littered my vision, and he spun me around to face Jamie. Liam's hands fell to my hips. My hands clawed at his forearms. He ignored every attempt I made to free myself of his grasp. My throat dried, and I opened my mouth to protest, but my voice ran away too.

Jamie's smirk disappeared, and his gaze rose to Liam; it darkened, and his lips pressed tight. Liam's rough hands brushed under my shirt and skimmed up my sides. I gasped as my mouth fell open, and my face flushed. His groin connected with my ass, as a heated shiver rushed through my body. It spread over my skin, igniting sparks and threatened to end me. Leaning back, I closed my eyes as a smile spread across my face. *"I knew I could make her smile."*

My grin widened at the sound of Liam's voice inside my mind. His acceptance of me wasn't a dream. "Dude, really?" Jamie's voice snapped my senses back into reality. "Get a room."

"I'm checking her wounds, bro." I peeked at Jamie through my heavy lidded eyes. His face twisted, but his eyes swelled. What lay hidden inside the man was the destruction of lost love. Lycans mated for life, and the same went for their chosen mate. Even with the lies and deceit, I worried about him. "And you're in my room, so git out."

"Liam, I … I'm fine, really." That sounded better than asking Jamie why he was still there torturing himself, instead of finding Nick. I twisted in Liam's arms, but his hold tightened.

"Darlin', I need to see it for myself, now stay still." His rough hands caressed my back, and I'd love nothing more than to fall into them, but his words ate at me. Why didn't he take my word for it? Did he need to do this now, in front of his brother?

"No," I shouted and tugged the shirt down.

"Don't be stupid about this, Auriel—" I shoved him back.

A smile spread over my mouth, but the bile churned. A part of me arose, and my head fell back, laughter screeching, maniacal laughter erupting from my mouth. Hands grabbed the shirt, teeth gritting, as I shredded the fabric. I braced myself, hands pressed against Liam's chest. My skin tore. His eyes grew large. Thought he knew … he said he knew.

"Well … shit," someone said, but stars and salty pools welled up, clouding my vision. Inside, I grew smaller, a speck in the darkness, as a force fought against me. I opposed it, pushing with all my might, but the voice cried out for its freedom.

"I'm not a toy." The raspy rumbles escaped my lips. This side of me I'd tried suppressing. "I won't be a part of this game. You know what … I'm… you can't cage me…"

I clenched through the pain as my wings snapped through their final barrier. They'd always been part of me, and I stretched and fluttered the tawny feathers. My head cocked, waiting for him to speak; he was stunned into silence. I turned to face Jamie's wide eyes, but a twisted grin curled instead. My eyes followed his down my frame. Crap. All I wore was my bra and panties. I scrambled and slipped into a pair of jeans lobbed on an easy chair.

"How …" Liam said, his hand sweeping down. I gasped, and my legs weakened. Thighs clenched together. He repeated the motion, and I gritted my teeth. Heat pooled at my center as he stroked his fingertips across my feathers. I bit my lip and forced my body to turn around. Liam's yellowing eyes greeted me.

I sucked in my breath and blinked. *"I can smell her,"* he said, flashing a wolfish grin. Liam breathed in and lowered his gaze. The heat rushed with it. *"We're doomed. How can I keep my hands off her when she smells delicious?"* My hand found his, and I closed my eyes.

Our Mysts worked as one, connecting us, but I didn't say anything. The love we shared was enough to comfort me. The union reminded me of my parents, but also of my great grandparents. Freyr himself in a vision blessed upon my great grandfather, Sir Thomas the human born. Dark hair and bright eyes, I'd met him once as a small child. I shared this vision with Liam, this memory of the distant past. Queen Morgana of the Unseelie court became his wife and my great grandmother.

Alfheim –the realm of Light Faeries and Elves – was where he lived, forced apart from his ardent love. She brought me through the Bifrost, the bridge that connected the portals to all the realms. My great grandmother carried me there to meet him, although I think she wanted to see him more.

"Grandpa Thomas cannot pass," she had told me then.

"Aurie?" I ignored Jamie.

Together they bore the first royal hybrid, my grandfather Duncan and his twin sister, my great aunt Maeve. No wonder Kiel called me princess; I sort of was one.

"You remember, don't you Aurie?" Jamie asked. A tear slid down my cheek.

"Reòta," I muttered the Gaelic words, as the purple Myst shot from my hand and froze time.

I kneeled, connecting the memory of my heritage and how I came into existence. I was two parts shy of the ultimate hybrid. Draugr and lycan were both missing. My eyes shot between the two brothers. Liam filled one link, and a transformation to draugr fulfilled the other.

Neither painted a future I wanted.

My feet paced the length of the hallway. The men stayed frozen as my hands twisted and turned. If I knew how, I'd unfreeze just Liam. I held little trust for Jamie, and even Nick was right to warn me against trusting him.

I sighed at their predicaments. My friends needed to kiss and make up already. There wasn't much Jamie could do with the information anyway, and they had to solve their own love life. Why'd my parents keep my destiny all hush-hush to begin with? Knowing I'm a Valkyrie didn't allow another supe to determine all my tricks.

"Mair," I whispered, allowing the magic to seep out again. Jamie and Liam both blinked. My hands raised and brown wings snapped open with an audible crack. My eyes slanted. "Yes, they're wings, yes I know they're there, and yes they are real."

"You …"

I rolled my eyes and slapped my hands against my thighs. "Yeah, I froze time too."

"Last night …" Liam's mouth gaped, and I'd flashed a smile before leaving the room.

Even in the hallway, the walls closed in on me, and I attempted putting some distance between us all. We'd had four years of it, but maybe it wasn't enough. The kitchen loomed ahead, and my stomach rumbled a protest. Liam's kitchen and fridge were bare of anything that resembled food. Frozen pizza, frozen Chinese food, frozen, frozen, moldy, chunky… gah. I tossed the rotten food into the trashcan. My teeth clenched, and I fought the urge to gag.

My ass dropped to the ground, and I landed on the hard, cold linoleum. The scent of pine and lemons were still fresh. At least he cleaned now. Both scents reminded me of Momma. My arms wrapped around my legs, and my head rested upon them. I missed her so much and Daddy too.

She'd whip up a feast if she was here, but I'd never have her delicacies again. The thought of not having her Chocolate, Orange, and Whisky Mousse ever again watered my eyes. Everything seemed to these days. Scotch Mist was another favorite of mine, but Momma didn't make it.

Nana made that one.

I swiped a can of cherry crack –Cheerwine soda – from the fridge and cracked it open. More memories of Momma and Daddy resurfaced. She wasn't human any more than I was a unicorn. My eyes closed, recalling her story –lies – of human life and living in New York. Lies, they were all lies, but why? Momma's a freaking Guardian, not mine but my daddy's, since he was a royal fae and a high mage, and she was a pooka too. My head hung and shook as the memories trickled in. A dang giantess hybrid pooka to boot.

As the cold soda slid down my throat, I smiled. Dang I'd missed this stuff. There was still a hole in my heart. Forever it would remain because of Daddy's death and having Momma live didn't lessen the guilt. But coming to Six and Twenty was the right move because it enabled me to find ... Me. I hadn't realized how truly lost I was without my friends.

"This has to be difficult for you, and I'm sorry I didn't tell you," Jamie whispered from the doorway. I shrugged in response. He erred with caution as grey eyes skimmed around the kitchen. If he had told me the truth my first night back, who knew what would've happened. For once, his lies were fully justified, but it didn't excuse the past or his motives.

Jamie's eyes darted down. "So, how long, um ..."

I stared at the can sweating in my hand and said, "Yesterday."

My head leaned against the cupboard, and I sighed. I guess we both lied and kept secrets in the past and present. Could I fault him at all without pointing the blame at myself? No, I'd forgive him. Liam hated that I always did, and I doubted that changed.

"Who all knew about the Valkyrie thing?" I'd need a phonebook to check off all the names of who knew of my so-called secrets. Swirling the can, I looked back on it. Why were they adamant about Jamie and Liam never learning the truth? I didn't see how it would've made a difference, but it wasn't important either.

Jamie sat beside me, and I handed him the can. His brow rose, and he placed it beside him. I shoved his shoulder and watched the smile crack. Good, we were friends still.

"Merric and my family." Nick too, but I left him out. His secret wasn't mine to tell. "Paulo too."

"Aurie?" I watched, as he leaned into me, his smoky eyes smoldering, but I inched away.

His eyes fell to my wings, which nestled against my back. Leaning on them didn't cause pain. Fenrir didn't want me near Jamie, but he was my friend too. Our history ran just as deep. I'd all but forgotten that he too was a Phoenix. Was because the Myst had disappeared but his heart burned with fire.

In a way, it was why we were closer growing up and the same for Nickolas. Phoenixes flocked together. I smiled; we were birds of the same feather.

Jamie's silver power radiated back to me, instead of the fiery brown of his birthright. The air was almost as strong as his fire had once been, yet he didn't use it. Did Jamie know how?

Who stole his Phoenix? Nick asked me about the missing Phoenix, assuming I'd played a cruel joke.

I patted his hand. "I didn't steal your power."

He laughed. "I know that." Jamie coughed. "You're not that evil."

My lip tugged into a half smile. I wasn't exactly an angel, but he was right. I wouldn't steal powers, least of all his. But the question remained, who would?

The wood groaned in the doorway as Liam eased his body against it. Eyes skimmed from bare feet to his full lips. Gods, that wolfish grin could've killed a girl where she sat. Even with my rear planted, and Jamie looming close, all I wanted was to march my weakening knees to his side. A snug t-shirt reading, "House Stark" showed off every delicious ripple; my hands burned to explore. Long, powerful legs hid behind dark denim jeans, molding, and bulging in the right places. His scented soap tingled my nose. That reddish hair, wet and beyond disheveled, fell into his unshaven face. While the gleam in his jade eyes rung out an ancient song that only I heard.

Those massive globes carried a different light now, when he looked at me. My cheeks warmed, and I buried my face into my knees, recalling how he saw me. He acted as if I had the plague. The Liam I left four years ago wouldn't have treated any woman that way. How different was I from the sixteen-year-old girl he had known? Once Liam remembered, would he change his mind again?

"What's the matter?" Liam asked, but Jamie wiped the tear away.

chapter
twenty-five

LIAM

Auriel's light dimmed behind her swollen eyes. I shifted my weight, deciding whether to comfort her, or allow my brother his moment.

Part of me wanted to lift him up and toss him out the front door. It was doubtful that would go over well. She shook her head at my question. Darlin' lied through her teeth; you didn't have to be a mind reader to know when a lady was upset. But I was one, and I read her loud and clear as her mind ventured backwards and relived my stupidity.

My blood ran hot; a tick pulsed through my veins. If she ran, by the Gods and the Myst, I would hunt her to ends of the Nine Realms. Nothing would come between us, not even her magic. After my quick shower, I pulled out a talisman. Etched with protection runes it'd guard against magic. Her Myst shouldn't have worked the first time, but I wasn't leaving anything to fate.

With it secured around my neck, her spell casting days were finished. I'd love her, stand by her side, and protect her, but I refused to forget Auriel again.

There were bigger problems on our hands. Whoever attacked Auriel remained free. I didn't have the slightest clue beyond the Oracle's strange behavior. It was as good of a place to start. They were both strong mages – willed and skilled. Although I was pretty darn sure Aurie froze time, both last night, and she admitted to a little while ago. My hand covered my smile. In the blink of an eye, she went from sitting on the bed without wings to standing with them spread wide.

They were beautiful white feathers that jutted from her back. Even now, I wanted to touch them. No, I wanted her to touch me with them, cradle them around my flesh. My heart raced, dampening my palms from the mere thought. I'd let them finish their moment. My lips pulled at the corners, and I fought the snicker. Not that it was much of one to begin with. Rolling my eyes, I gave her one last glance, before I grabbed my phone to check-in with Dad and Mrs. Graftfield. They'd want to hear about this.

The Oracle made me promise to head over as soon as possible. Her exact words, but she spoke faster than usual. Maybe she wished to tell Auriel whom she was, but I honestly didn't like the idea. For starters, Auriel already knew, and it wasn't like she was jumping at the bit to see her again.

Part of me still wondered if Jamie was right and somehow I'd managed to suppress the truth. Was it coincidence that I gained the power of fire when he lost his? The other half did not understand why anyone would do that to me. I didn't have enemies, at least none that I knew of, but the same wasn't true for Jamie.

Fainauriel Carwen Graftfield. I blinked at the memory and grinned. No, Princess Fainauriel Carwen Graftfield of the Unseelie Court … in Alfheim.

Even if the Phoenix and Valkyrie stripped away, she was royalty among the Fae and to the Gods. Especially Freyr and Freya, the Giant twins, since Auriel's a quarter or more on … her mother's side. My heart raced a little faster. I'd remembered. In my hurry to tell her, I stumbled and tripped rushing down the stairs. "Aurie," I shouted, almost sliding into the kitchen.

Her head jerked up. "Why are you all full of smiles?" She giggled and stood up. I stepped to her and wrapped my arms around her. "Liam?"

The way she fit into my arms mirrored perfection, like a grand design. Last night, my grip tightened at the memory. I kissed the top of her head. Hell, she called my beast to the surface, twice. Such an idiot, I was the realm's biggest moron for treating her like crap when she first arrived. She was mine. I'd make up for it, somehow, I swore to the Gods. Someday I'd atone for my pigheaded stupidity.

"I remembered something, darlin'." She glanced up. Her fiery eyes widened with her smile. "Princess." I kissed her nose. "Fainauriel" I kissed her cheek. "Carwen." I kissed her other cheek, and she chuckled. "Graftfield."

My mouth covered hers, and I drank in her cherry flavored bottom lip. She gasped against me, and I pulled back. Was it too much, too soon? No, Aurie's eyes sparkled, and she leaned toward me, pressing me against the wall. Hungry eyes bore into me. On her tiptoes, she arched up. Her nose brushed mine as she snaked her arms around my neck. When her mouth parted, my hands cupped her face. I bent down and closed the minuscule distance left between us. My tongue rubbed against her, all of her; there was never enough. Hands dropped to her waist and yanked her closer. She grasped my hair and pressed her bra-clad breasts against me.

Jamie coughed, and I ignored him, but Auriel drew away. Our hands touched, and she folded her delicate fingers into mine. I could get used to that. "Me too," she answered my thoughts.

I blinked and squeezed her hand. My heart pounded, not from the connection, but from our kiss. Jamie stared at his feet, and his hand mindlessly crushed the soda can. There was no getting around it. I leaned against the wall and rested a hand over my chest. My brother didn't stand a chance. Her mind reeled, racing as mine did. We were all friends, but her heart belonged to me, right?

"It was always you," she thought. *"Jamie needs to heal. You're wrong about him, you know?"*

My head cocked as her thoughts processed. If it had anything to do with what Jamie told me then it was none of my business. I glanced to my brother; smoky eyes closed as he sighed.

"Darlin', I have to take you to see the Oracle now that you're ... awake." Auriel laughed. I took a deep breath and calmed my thrumming heart.

"Jamie if you'd like to die a painful death you can tag along." He stared at me unblinking. "I don't know what I'm going to do with you yet." My voice lowered. "Of course, you could save everyone a lot of trouble and go home." Jamie nodded and left the room. He wouldn't leave, but it was worth a shot.

She ran up the stairs, arguing the whole time. Auriel tore through her bag, and I grabbed a book down on the Dísir. While not an original, this one was a copy. The druid wrote it long before Odin called out the born and sentenced them to death. It spoke of the white ones and how they held purity above all else. But Aurie's feathers weren't white ... they weren't even swan-like but ... falcon feathers?

I pulled down another book and another and then another. All of them said the same phrases. Valkyries remained pure or retained purity. They had white swan-like wings. I slid the books back onto the bookshelf. Auriel leaned in the doorway.

"Always reading."

I snorted, but she was right, not that it did us any good. My nose burned as she collected her clothing. Some of it had landed on my legs and I picked up the lacey thong. Auriel blushed and grabbed it, but I pulled it out of her reach. "When do I get to see you in this?"

Auriel reached for the thong again, and I dragged her to me. Her long legs straddled my lap, and I ran my finger from her jaw to the swell of her breasts. My cock throbbed and screamed for attention, but I held her. She kissed my nose and ran her hands through my hair. As my hand holding her underwear dropped, she stole them away.

chapter
twenty-six

PAULO

I had poured over the contents of the deserted Graftfield home, searching for clues and the safe that I couldn't recall ever knowing about. Spread before me laid more than I bargained for; I stared at all the photos of my children posed with Auriel. Two emotions ransacked me: relief and worry. My hands trembled, and if I had a beating heart, it would have beat fast. The impossible occurred. A draugr forgot. An immune and immortal draugr fell prey to a mage's spell.

"Come here often, Dad?" Jamie sneezed and strolled into the dust- ridden study. I blinked at the no longer lanky boy, in his place stood an above average sized man.

I swore he'd grown over a foot since I last saw him. He was the spitting image of Merric. Even his eyes held the same menacing gaze as his father. A smile spread over my face. If he hadn't called me dad, I might've taken his head off. Mistaken identity aside, he appeared well enough, and I inclined my head.

"How are you, son?"

"Did you find anything?" he asked, ignoring my question. Our relationship suffered years ago when he left for Charlestown. We'd not spoken over the past few years but his leaving hurt. I'd raised him and then he left. My fists clenched behind my back, and my eyes scanned the study again.

"Not really," I lied and faced him. He remembered. That was what Liam had said. "What can you tell me about all of this?"

"I thought it pretty obvious." Jamie plopped down onto the leather couch, dust billowing and choking him. I turned my back, flipping through the eightieth album for the fiftieth time. The Graftfields took pictures of everything from their family to the trees and flowers to the residents of this town. Every one of us forgot about the smiling girl. Her persona reflected off the photographs. The light and warmth was unmistakable. As Liam said, Auriel wasn't the type of girl someone forgot about. It went beyond her looks or family connection.

The odd eyes haunted me as I flipped through the pages of trees. As each year passed, the fire gave way to a bluish glaze. Jamie peeked over my shoulder. "That's right before she left."

Her eyes blazed an icy deep blue, and the edges rimmed in golden fire. A sword hung from her side, and a shield lay before her kneeling frame. This photo spoke to me; her eyes radiated pain instead of the light. Her grip on the shield yielded white knuckles, and the smile gracing her face appeared fake. "But you didn't forget her." I scratched my chin and studied him from a mirror. Jamie shrugged his shoulders and strode back the couch. He plopped again and stretched his feet over the coffee table. The glass rattled, but he ignored it as he flipped through another photo album.

"Didn't what?" I glanced over my shoulder and raised an eyebrow. "Oh that ... No, the Phoenixes didn't forget." His eyes darkened and glazed over. "And what about Liam?" Jamie motioned for me to sit and picked up a picture frame off the end table. Liam and Auriel attended our school in town. They posed in front of a thick sugar maple sitting to the side of the schoolhouse. The old red building served all the children of Six and Twenty and held twelve classrooms. I used to teach there too, but after Ulf died, I stopped. Losing your best friend ... I couldn't return.

"Nothing I feel matters." He ripped the back from the frame. "He can't forgive me. None of them can."

Jamie turned his head, hiding his watering eyes. Out of all the children I raised, he had it the worst. First, he lost his mother and then his father tossed him away. Internally I sighed; it didn't help when I did it too.

"You've changed," I said. My hand clasped his shoulder and squeezed.

"I grew up." Jamie sighed, slumping backward. "I had to."

"Can you tell me about her, son? Anything ... everything you know about Auriel up until the day she left." Jamie nodded and cleared his throat.

He shifted and leaned his head on the back of the sofa. "Auriel was born on the morning of the Winter Solstice a year after Liam. Her mother was Lettuce, a pooka giant hybrid—of what else I don't know—and her father's a bigger mystery."

"He's a Faerie hybrid," I interjected. The Graftfields were a powerful family, because the human hybrids were neither mortal nor supernatural. They bridged a gap between the two worlds co-existing on the planet. Valentine, my sire, taught me as much. He warned me not to cross them. Draugr didn't fear much of anything so when he warned me, I heeded.

That was the reason I put up with Keelan. Although she wasn't Graftfield by blood, she was the estranged wife of Duncan–the Unseelie Faerie Prince of Alfheim.

Jamie cocked his head. "Keelan's his mother, and she's a mage." I nodded. "She's mated to the Alfheim prince." I gestured for him to continue. He shrugged and glanced at his hands. "Dad you know everything that I do."

"So tell me about Auriel and not her family line. What was she like before?"

He stared at his hands and then glanced to me. "She was sweet and kind most of the time." Jamie sighed. "But more powerful than most. She kept a lot of secrets."

I patted his knee. "I'm sure she had her reasons. How much power?"

"Like Merric and immortal to boot. She'd give him a run for his money." His brows rose as he spoke the words.

The world did not want another Merric. One egotistical hybrid was enough to last me a lifetime. Auriel – I prayed the woman held more sense. Some day that man would cross the wrong supe, and it would probably be me. "But not unkillable?"

"Well that's the thing, Dad. Auriel's not a typical ..." He scratched his head. I didn't like where this was going and wasn't sure I wanted to hear it. My hands folded and unfolded as he searched for the words. He glanced away and back again. Jamie leaned closer, and whispered, "I overhead something last night."

CHAPTER TWENTY-SEVEN

AURIEL

The door closed to Liam's master bathroom. His sigh echoed through the wall, and I touched my heart. Yeah, I'd felt it too, my mind mirrored his. How'd we survive each other let alone anything else the universe flung at us? My hands busied with mundane details like retrieving towels and brushing out my mangled hair. Blood coated the strands and dirt smeared my face. My brush with death shook me, but so much more had happened since then. The memories, Momma being alive... the list continued.

Yet the idea of visiting my grandmother didn't bode well at all. As part of my family, she was immune from the memory spell. The whole reason behind the stupid incantation was to protect Liam, not alter a hundred people. I groaned; Grandma Graftfield gave me the creeps.

We didn't have much in common. Even growing up, we'd clashed. We both harnessed the elements, but the similarities ended there. I hadn't doubted her love for me until I came home to Six and Twenty. While I hadn't recognized her, she knew me, and kept her mouth shut. Why keep me in the dark? Why'd she treat me like dirt? My hand slapped the bathroom counter.

The attack and the memory of the blue ball churned my insides. Grandma's elements were water and air. Together they formed ice. I chewed my lip and studied my reflection. The wound healed, and there wasn't a scar.

"Falbh," I whispered, and the feathers disappeared, folding back into my skin.

The knob creaked as I turned on the water. A hot shower would clear my thoughts. I eased into the hot stream. Liam's expensive shower sprayed me down from all angles. As the water washed over my skin, I experienced a tug in my belly. My pendant warmed hotter than the shower.

"Ouch," I cried out and lost my balance. My head smacked the tile, and I rubbed the spot. Fresh watery blood coated my trembling hand when I drew it away, and I held the Brísingamen away from my skin. Within seconds, Liam scooped me off the shower floor. He cursed himself and shook his head. My cheeks burned as his thick arms tightened against my soaked body.

"Are you alright? What happened?" I nodded my head, as he grabbed a towel from the rack and wrapped it around my body.

"My Algiz went off." Liam scratched his chin, and his eyes darted around. How'd he know about a Valknut and not this? "It's the magical talisman that protects me from danger." I stabbed the charm with my finger and sighed when he shook his head. "When it heats up, it means someone wants to harm me." Liam swallowed audibly as a knock came from the front door.

"Stay up here and get dressed." His eyes widened, and I heard his heart racing. *Or was that mine.* "Don't come down for nothing, even if I call your name." Liam muttered something in Gaelic under his breath and threaded his fingers through his hair. "You stay up here until I return, and I'll lock the door behind me. I have the only key to this door."

I hugged the towel against my body. His widened eyes alarmed me as he turned around. But I nodded, mouth agape, with my words refusing to come. He reached the door and paused, glancing at me. I stepped toward him, but he held his hand up, and shut the door. Shivers ran down my spine. My talisman remained hot, and I layered it on top of my towel, hoping to dull the inferno. I willed my shield to life, pouring reserved power to surround me. The white Myst enveloped me, tickling my skin. I centered myself and concentrated on breathing. Each release of breath manifested more Myst, and I poured it around me.

"Sgàile," I whispered. That was the advantage of being a high mage: invisibility. Not true invisibility, but it was a move to the ethereal state, or essentially becoming a ghost. Mages saved it as a last resort, because it came at a hefty price, and I'd pay for it later, if there was a later.

My ear leaned against the wall, and I strained to hear the muffled voices. My Brísingamen radiated heat but remained tolerable. Whoever was downstairs didn't mean me immediate harm. The thick walls obscured the voices. I couldn't make out the words, but one voice was Liam. The other was a female. Her higher and softer pitch gave her gender away.

Why did anyone in Six and Twenty wish me harm? My trembling hand wiped the sweat away from my brow. I didn't dare breathe as each creak grew closer and louder. My eyes widened. Clothes –my clothing and bag – littered Liam's bed; anyone looking for me would see I was here.

"She was here, but now she's gone," Liam said, followed by the clink of keys, and a female laughing. I growled, as my cheeks grew hot enough to burn the hussy to ashes. The doorknob jingled, and I sucked in a breath. "Odd, I've never had this happen before," Liam said followed by a thump.

"Oh well, I'll have to get that fixed. You're welcome to search the rest of the house."

"That won't be necessary, thank ye fer yer time, William Skyland."

A million scenarios ran through my mind. It was neither the time nor place, but I couldn't shake my possessive growl. Why would I do that? More so, why was I standing here berating myself for it? Liam put himself in danger to hide me, and the notion soured my stomach. That was his job, but I didn't have to like it.

The clock ticked, those big numbers turning over as time passed. He didn't return. Each passing minute ached, and my reserves dipped lower. There wasn't much time before I drained myself. Even the most powerful mage was only as strong as their reservoirs. After that, it was lights out or the long sleep.

My hands shook, and my heart drummed in my chest. What was taking him so long? There were no more voices or sounds as I pressed my ear to the wall. What if they arrested him? I chewed on my lip. Until Liam returned, my tension wouldn't rest. Every muscle and nerve stayed on edge as my counting breaths passed. It wasn't about me; he put himself in danger because of me.

The battle, the prophecy – it was my fight.

An ache ripped through me, and my hand rested over my heart at the thought of never seeing his smile or hearing his deep, velvety voice. The tones soothed me unlike any other. Those rough hands reminded me I was alive, and I was a woman.

My body slid down the wall. After four years apart, I couldn't imagine losing him again. Life and existing didn't matter without him. Sobs caught in my chest. I wanted to reverse time and take it all back: the spell, running off without him, and creating this unbearable rift. All the lies…I'd tell him the truth. Then our future would've changed. I struggled to breathe, and my head dropped to my knees.

I loved him, and I doubted my survival if he were to love another. The thought stabbed me, pricked into my skin, and then sliced it wide open. Frightened child as the smolder of his gaze burned over me. He was my Guardian. He saw through my shield and invisibility. I didn't doubt his position in my life, but there was no denying it now.

The door eased open, and I fought the urge to pounce. A finger flew to his frowning lips, and he shook his head. He walked to the window and stiff hands rubbed over his neck. I followed him and placed a hand on his shoulder. Liam turned his head and kissed my fingers, sending tiny quakes to my core.

"Wardens," he said. "They're searching the town."

He squinted those green eyes, and I tracked his gaze. Below us were supes, more than I'd ever seen. I walked to my bag and rustled around without looking until my hands touched the cold, smooth metal. My spy scope, a gift from my grandfather many years ago. I fumbled with the cap, and it clattered to the hardwood floor. Liam spun around, and I froze. A crooked smile flashed over his face as I bent over to retrieve the lid. I stuck my tongue out and padded back to the window. My hip shoved him over, and he snaked his arm around me. I extended the scope and peered out the end of the venetian blind. At least twenty Wardens. I counted each one, and it was hard to miss them.

They dressed in all black, and all wore the same emblem. Yggdrassil surrounded by the Nine Realms. My eyes rolled. How original, I wondered who came up with that grand design. Liam snickered, and I handed the glass to him, but he tapped the corner of his eyes. Oh right, he had lycan sight.

I closed my eyes and rested my head on his chest. His Myst stabilized me and fed my reserves as it passed between us. Our colored strands melded together. Three souls, three personalities, but were they acting as one? Green, yellow, and blue intertwined around him. My head tilted as I followed the Myst; maybe I misread him all along. Green, I picked it up in my mind and grabbed his arm. I heard him before, and he picked something up from me, but I wanted a clear channel.

"Liam, can you hear me?" I opened my eyes, and his gaze widened. *"I take that as a yes; can you project to me?"* He nodded, grabbed my hand, and interlaced our fingers.

"Wardens from the Nine are searching for you and Jamie. Apparently they read a surge of power, but ..." Liam sighed and dropped my hand.

"He did it on purpose. That's what you're thinking."

Dang that boy! I bit my nails and pondered courses of action. Here, I thought if I gave him a second chance, he'd not use it to screw me over. My fist clenched, but the skin softened. Jamie wasn't strong enough to maintain invisibility. Unless he made an actual phone call then this was ...

No, he wasn't off the hook, but my brow creased with worry. If I were wrong ... One mistake and the Wardens would get him. Did he plan to barter his freedom for me, or was there something else up his sleeve? A small voice in the back of my head screamed. We were wrong to suggest responsibility without proof.

Liam's back tensed, each muscle tightening, before releasing under his shirt. My hand hovered over the span of his shoulder blades, and my head vibrated from his heart. I wanted to comfort him, but was unsure if I should hold him.

Would he want me to touch him, comfort him? Did he like me touching him now? I stood and unraveled myself. A shiver ran over my skin, as the cold sunk in. My hands rubbed over my arms, and I put the glass away.

"Please," Liam said. I wrapped my arms around him and laced my fingers together in the front. My cheek rested on his back, and I breathed him in. I'd never had a smell bring such warmth and comfort to my soul. *"Can you read my thoughts or just project your own."*

"I don't know," I said. He turned around and cupped my face.

Liam's thumb traced my mouth, and I sucked in my breath. *"It'd be nice if you could, darlin'."* He smirked.

"Don't you hate it, though?"

His grin widened, and he shook his tawny head. Leave it to him to joke about it. I gave him a shove, and his hand fell to his heart. My eyes rolled, and I turned back toward the bed, when he grabbed my hand. Liam pulled me into his arms and whispered, "I want you to know what I'm thinking, always. Right now though, I'm torn between hurting Jamie and ripping your towel off."

Liam's rough lips grazed my ear before letting me go. My mouth dropped and so did my gaze. Folded between my breasts and wrapping my body was his towel. Everything happened too fast, and I forgot to put on clothes. My cheeks burned, and I stared at my feet. Liam snickered and faced the window. "See how good I've been?"

The reflection of his eyes met mine; still green but sparking full of mischief. I bit my lip and let the towel fall. The cold air sent a shiver over my body. Liam leaned forward; his strong hands gripped the sides of the window. Thick arms trembled, and his knuckles turned white. *Served him well.* I chewed my lip and glanced toward the bed. The clothes I'd planned on wearing were right there on the end. I strolled to retrieve them and ignored the need welling inside of me.

Strong arms grasped me from behind; I yelped as his fingers dug into my hips. Liam's hand quickly covered my mouth. "Sorry," he rasped.

Hot breath and his dry lips trailed down my neck. I arched into him and rubbed my ass over his crotch. The fire burned inside of me, scorched deeper from the friction. I wanted more.

"Auriel ... Gods help me ..." Liam cupped my breast, rolling the nipple between his fingers, and a throaty moan escaped my parting lips. His other hand slid down my stomach and nestled between my legs, stroking the dewy mound.

I gasped as he palmed the moist flesh. "Liam," I squeaked, swallowing hard as his fingers delved deeper. My breath caught, and the room spun, closing its bare walls in on me.

"Lay down, darling." He nibbled on my ear lobe and pressed his groin against me. "On your back," he added; I nodded unable to form words.

My legs trembled as I climbed on the bed, and a clothed Liam followed. I raised an eyebrow, but I couldn't read him. His nostrils flared, and he chewed on his lip as his yellowing eyes raked over my body.

A blush rose in my cheeks under his intense gaze, and I attempted to cover myself. "Stop that," he growled and grabbed my wrists. "You're too damn seductive ..." Liam's lips consumed mine. The tenderness from last night left, and he replaced it with a raw hunger that stirred my desire further.

Gods, don't let him stop again.

His lips trailed down my neck, and I frowned. When his mouth hovered over my breast, I held my breath. Our gaze met as his tongue darted across the nipple. My hands grasped his head, breath hissing as he teased my other breast. A dangerous grin spread over his mouth, and my brows creased.

"Liam," I said, half warning. His mouth descended licking and kissing my stomach. My hands fisted the sheets as I steadied my breath. When he reached my belly button, I leaned forward to see. His finger slid down my slit. I froze, mouth falling open, and my legs shook. Liam paused, his ragged breath caressing my curls, and his green eyes tinged a brighter yellow. He raised a ruddy brow.

"Do you want me to stop?"

I bit my lip and shook my head. The corner of his mouth curled up, and he moved a tad lower. I dragged in my breath as his lips closed over my bud. A cry ripped through my chest as white spots blinded my eyes. My body vaulted into him, and my hips moved on their own. His finger wiggled deeper, stroking, and caressing me senseless.

"Damn, you taste sweet," he rumbled and increased the suction. I whimpered, gripping the sheets. The fabric tore as the pressure in my belly rose. Still I wanted more and clamped my legs closed.

My mouth opened, and my head rolled from side to side, yet words refused to form. Liam pushed my thighs apart; his intense eyes glared a warning. "Let go," he muttered.

Fingers increased in speed, sliding out of my slick heat as his tongue flicked across my nerves. My belly filled, pooling all my boiling blood until it erupted, squealing as my body rocked and clenched against Liam in alternating waves that left me panting for precious breath. He didn't stop, but slowed his assault as I rode out the currents and aftershocks vaulting through me.

A hand rested over my heart as the beats slowed down, and my eyes half closed. He removed his finger, and I let out a delicious sigh. I didn't know it could be like that. The sweet bliss surrounded me, brushing against my dimpled flesh and ballooning inside my heart. The smallest taste of pleasure left me craving more.

Liam kissed up my body, pausing at the swell of my breasts. The hardness of him pressed against my tender flesh. The warmth and anxiety melded in my stomach as he teased my nipples. But it was more than fear of the legends and tales that stopped me. Yellow eyes flashed up, the beast in complete control, but that was not it either.

My hands curled into his hair, and I stroked through it. No, the problem wasn't any of that. I loved him, all of him including whatever lived inside of him, but I was not a fool. As impossible as it sounded, I knew what love looked like. Jamie wrote it on his sleeve for all to see when he eyed Nick. This ... my eyes stung ... the emotions rolling off Liam were not love, but concern, jealousy, and a crap load of lust.

"You're blocking me again," Liam said, scowling and moving to my side. I shivered as his passion dissipated. His eyes returned to normal, well normal for him. I resisted the urge to curl into myself and forced a smile. He dragged the blanket up from the floor and tossed it over me. I turned to my side, draping an arm over his torso. Liam sighed, clasping a hand over his eyes. "Gods, did you at least enjoy it?"

Duh. "Yes." I chewed my lip. He peeked at me and leaned up on his elbows.

"I've never done that before." *Could've fooled me.* He gulped and reached out a shaky hand. "Do you still have your wings?"

"Yes," I said, shifting closer and resting my head on his heart. I teased my fingertips over his stomach, need building inside of me again. Liam's nostrils flared, and a chuckle escaped his parting lips. "I guess we can rule out mouths." With each stroke, I moved lower until I reached the hem of his shirt. My hand slipped beneath the cotton; he tensed and sucked in a sharp breath. His thick muscles contracted as my palms rolled over the thick-corded muscles. I eased my body on top of him, and his eyes softened. My fingers quaked as they lifted his shirt over his head. Liam's arms encompassed me, and his lips touched mine. I grasped his shoulders and pushed him back, breaking our kiss. He smirked and placed his arms behind his head.

"I like your tattoos." My hand traced the tribal pattern across his chest and down his left arm. Another large one graced his torso, but I didn't recognize the language. Then again, my talents were Scots Gaelic and English. The fluency of the former faltered, but I knew I learned the hard tongue of my ancestors. "What does this one mean?" I asked, tracing the letters.

Liam's head cocked. "I don't recall that one." My brow rose. How'd he forget a tattoo? His lips curved up and spread wide, flashing his teeth. "You're a terrible liar." He snorted and grabbed my head, dragging my mouth to his.

Blue speckles flashed into his green eyes. "You forgot about yours, princess." I shook my head, but he nodded. "Go check yourself if you don't believe me."

I scurried backward and raced into the bathroom. Sure enough, there was a mark on my stomach, identical to his. "What does it mean?" Liam came in and wrapped his arms around me.

"I don't know, darlin'. We can call my dad." My cheeks flushed at the thought of Paulo learning how we got them. "You better get dressed, before I lose my control."

His mouth nibbled on my ear. I turned my head, exposing my neck. Liam made a soft sound and moved his mouth to the sensitive spot, where my neck and shoulder met. "The Wardens left a while ago; we should be safe, for now. I'm going to find Jamie and my dad. Don't leave the house."

I spun around and pinned him to the wall. "Not so fast." My hands fell to his fly, and his heart beat faster. The stiff fabric did little to conceal his desires. I dropped to my knees and scooted his jeans down. My hands ran over Liam's muscular thighs, teasing the insides. More tattoos painted his skin, but I wasn't surprised. I glanced up; his eyes were dark, and his mouth parted. A smile spread over my face. I liked the effect I had on him. My hand trembled as I reached for his boxers. I slipped my fingers beneath the thin cotton, and Liam groaned as they brushed against his semi-erect cock.

He sprung free as my hands grasped the elastic. My eyes widened at the size, although I had nothing to compare it with. I'd read plenty of smut but wasn't one for visual stimulation. My opinion changed as I gazed between his legs. Veins ran over the long thickness growing before my eyes. I took in a breath as I marveled at its beauty. The head peeked from its hood as the salty scent mingled with his campfire notes. Muscular thighs quaked beneath my steady hands.

I grasped the base gently and glided my palm along his length. My eyes locked onto his face as his mouth hissed a breath. I couldn't help the twitching of my lips as I stroked him, increasing the speed and pressure. His hands fondled my hair as his head fell back against the tiled wall.

A bead of moisture leaked from his tip. My nostrils flared, and heat rushed to my stomach. His salty sweetness hit my nose harder and shifted the beast inside. Its tendril scorched my insides as I leaned in; my tongue swirled over the liquid, before sucking the head into my mouth.

"Oh Gods." Liam's hands pulled my hair. "Don't stop," he panted, and I ventured further down his shaft. My speed increased as I adjusted to the velvety smooth heat gliding up and down my tongue. "Baby don't ... Auriel ..." His words trailed as his body tensed under my control. With a shuddering jerk, thick and tangy liquid flowed into my mouth as his cock spasmed between my lips. My mouth refused to relent until he ran dry.

I pulled back and stared at his grinning face. Liam offered his hand, and I accepted it. "You are something else ..." His finger skimmed over my lips. "I ... never mind." He shook his head and kissed my forehead. "I'm going to go."

I swallowed the ache growing in my chest as he stepped away. Granted, he had a beautiful ass, but I didn't want him to leave me alone. He tossed a sheepish grin over his shoulder, and I crossed my arms over my chest.

Liam shrugged and cracked his neck, before crouching to the carpet. I'm technically part pooka, but nothing prepared me for watching him unfold. I cringed, as his skin moved, the bones snapped beneath, and I shut my eyes. The sounds caused me to shudder. Liam stayed calm, nothing more than a grunt left his lips as he transformed into his wolf.

"Look at me." I opened my eyes one at a time. Large green globes stared at me. I knelt to the ground, but he didn't approach. Liam shook his coat, the salt and pepper fur settled back into place. *"I'm going to hunt Jamie down."*

"Don't hurt him," I called out to him, tossing clothing on, but he snarled before turning around. His narrowing eyes stammered my heart, and I backed against the bedroom wall.

"No, I'll kill him," he barked. *"He did this; put you into danger."* I rolled my eyes. I bet they would've come anyway. *"Stay shielded till I return, don't leave, or dare answer the door,"* Liam commanded me, and I blinked. Before I could answer, he padded down the steps. When I followed, he growled, snapping his head around to bare his pearled teeth. *"Stay or I'll make you."*

Tears welled in my eyes. Didn't he understand? I stood at the closed front door for what seemed like an eternity. The swelling ache spread as I clutched my heart. *He didn't feel the pain.* The phrase repeated. Each time another knife slashed through my chest until my soul could take no more. A yawn escaped, and I skulked to the sofa. My eyes fluttered closed within minutes.

chapter
twenty-eight

LIAM

A sigh whooshed out my muzzle, but damn her for trying to follow me. Didn't she realize how real the threat remained … how much it'd hurt to lose her again? I couldn't breathe when around her, but she became my air. Without her, without my darlin' Auriel, I was nothing … I loved her. But I had a job to do and a town to protect. My nose hit the ground. Jamie's citrus scent grew stronger. He'd stayed close, and he wasn't alone.

Old leather and worn books smelled like Dad. With my nose to the ground, the trail grew stronger and led next door to the old Graftfield house. My mouth dropped open as the name registered. Jamie said as much last night. He had not lied to me yet.

Bells and whistles sounded through my brain. Damn, Auriel had cast one hell of a spell. Somehow, I managed to mow the lawn and feed her damn cats without ever recalling her. I couldn't recall ever stepping foot inside of it or even investigating it, but that was what she wanted me to believe. Unlike the other homes, we'd shared a yard and driveway. There were no boundaries between our families. At least there didn't use to be.

The porch mirrored mine, wrapping around the whole house. I laughed to myself as I saw a doggy door. Not the little dinky ones, but the largest I'd ever laid eyes on. Without a hitch, I waltzed right through it and into a tiled foyer. There were low, muffled voices coming from within.

"It's only Liam," Jamie said, but I moved with growing caution. The home lay in a state of disarray, but what caught my eye were all the photographs on the walls, the mantle, and tabletops.

The five of us, Nick had said.

"Auriel's safe?" he asked me, and I nodded my furry head as a smirk spread across his face. My limbs tensed, fur bristled, and ears stood tall.

"Calm yourself, Liam." Paulo flashed red eyes. "I'll give you a moment, but then we must convene council." He stood and brushed the dust from his suit. "Our people will want answers." Paulo stroked his chin. "This wasn't his fault." With a sigh and glance toward me, he walked away.

"Told you I'd find proof," Jamie said tossing an album at my feet. There was not much need for evidence now, but I didn't say anything. I hopped out the way, a yip leaving my mouth. The book opened as a breeze flipped the pages. I glanced over to a photograph of the five of us: Jamie, Nick, Regin, Auriel, and me. It couldn't have been more than five years old. I received the raven tattoo on my arm to honor Odin as a gift from … My mind blanked.

Jamie started at the beginning and turned the pages. Our lives together unfolded. From her birth to her teens, Auriel grew up, and we did too. A growl escaped my muzzle as I tossed my head up. No more lies or half- truths, Auriel needed to explain. I needed to understand why she'd taken it all away.

"Love." Love? That didn't make sense. "Think about it," he said in a hushed whisper. "She broke the Guardian Bond. What emotion is strong enough, baby bro?" He patted my head and motioned toward the couch. "Love is her trigger too, I think."

After last night, I'd wondered what sparked her memory return. The attack became my first guess, but if she'd fallen for me again, maybe there was some logic to my brother's words. His brows furrowed as my mind connected the random fragments.

"No, baby bro." He smiled and shook his head. "You fell in love with her again. She left herself keys in case she had to return." His unspoken words sent a chill down my spine. Auriel Graftfield had never wanted to come home.

"W"hy would the Nine even think we have Auriel?" I bellowed as I traipsed down the stairs in a new pair of jeans, and a repaired t-shirt. I'd ripped it a year ago but refused to throw it away. My lips tugged up, she must have done it while I was gone. It was my favorite, perfect and broken in.

"It's my fault," Jamie said from the floor. His knees hugged tight into his chest. I didn't need to invade his head to find the truth. He wore it for all of us to see.

"You didn't know they'd do this," Auriel said, but her white knuckles betrayed her. Her eyes met mine. "He didn't call them in; Merric sent out a search party after a call from someone else."

Someone else? But who else would have called the Nine?

"The question is how do we keep them away?" Paulo asked, though the answer was we couldn't. We didn't have the means to keep one, my eyes darted to Jamie again, let alone a whole team of Wardens out of Six and Twenty.

"Call Merric and see what he says," Jamie offered but my head shook at the first mention of his bastard father. They wanted Auriel for whatever reason. That notion became clear with a little glance into the Warden's mind.

"I don't want him anywhere near Auriel." Paulo mirrored my thoughts. "The letter Lettie left warned against him."

I raked my hand through my hair and made eye contact with her. She looked ready for blood, and I knelt down next to her. Auriel's fists clenched at her sides, and her jaw set tight. Her eyes swirled with emotion beyond her control as if she were about to erupt.

"What's wrong?" I whispered to her, but she didn't respond. The color flushed out of her cheeks as she stared off in the distance. "Auriel, darlin' you all right?" Her head turned, and her eyes blinked. She talked to someone.

Somehow, I knew it as her face twisted, and her heartbeat changed. I glanced to Jamie, but it wasn't him, although he looked three sheets into the wind. My hand clasped her, intertwining our fingers, but she closed me off. I blew a breath out and clenched my jaw tight.

"We have company; I think it's Nicky and the Oracle."

chapter
twenty-nine

AURIEL

Nickolas and the Oracle waited outside. My stomach soured at the mere thought of her since my memory returned. His arms tugged me closer, and I nuzzled my head into his neck. Jamie stood and fidgeted. Paulo just sat there and watched the three of us.

Liam kissed my temple and rose from the floor. The turmoil of this meeting churned within me and at least I wasn't alone. Suspicions went beyond her silence. The attack never strayed far from my thoughts either.

I'd no proof, not shove-in-your-face concrete proof that my grandmother held a role in my attack. My heart sighed, and my shoulders slumped forward. What motive, if not to kill me, would they have? Plus, she'd know my heritage. The ice had stung like a bitch, and it'd knocked me out, but it wouldn't kill me. No, I clenched my hands. Anyone who wielded ice remained a suspect. Until I figured it out, my returning memory remained a secret. There were gaps still, but the progress chugged along. I hoped Nickolas was pleased and the Gods kept at bay.

The townspeople were in an uproar, and they'd demanded Paulo to fix it. The Nine's infiltration hadn't gone unnoticed since they went door to door. I understood the outrage and felt responsible. Jamie did too, but he wore it as a martyr. Broody and dark came to mind when I thought of my old friend. He hadn't changed much in that aspect.

Jamie's head turned toward the door. Yeah, their bond stood whether he liked it or not. Pain tainted his silvery eyes, and he shifted in his seat. I didn't ask him why he'd done what he'd done all those years ago. Why he would sentence the man he loved to death. To break a lycan bond, shattered the soul. He would have died too.

Liam's hand hovered over the knob, and his back tensed as he turned it.

"Paulo," the Oracle rasped, pushing past Liam and into the foyer in a heave of breathless fury. "I knew we'd find you here." She panted, wrinkles flapping, and my brow rose over her excitement. "You have to do something."

Her eyes connected with mine, and the icy blue orbs sent shards pricking down my spine. We were never close despite living near each other. My mother used to agree with how she made me feel. Second-class and stupid no matter how hard I tried.

I rose up to receive our guests. Well, to greet Nick, but just in case I slipped, I used his covert name. *"Nick, I told Liam."* He kissed my hand.

Warmth flushed my cheeks, and I glanced away, locking onto the cold eyes of Liam. They cut down, slicing through Nick.

"How much did ye tell him, lass?" Nikolas raised an eyebrow and gave me a slight bow. Possessively, Liam's arms wrapped around me and pulled me flush against his frame. A rumble rolled against my back; every muscle froze, and my pulse quickened as his lips grazed my neck.

Nick smirked in response. I gazed around, but only Jamie's watery eyes met mine. Liam had it all wrong, but I'd kept my promises. Not a soul knew what I saw that day on the porch. I felt blessed, watching two of my best friends share an intimate moment. Nick was gay.

"Just about the mind talking thingy." I gasped, as my Guardian's green Myst blended with my red. Together we resembled a Yule tree. *"But I kind of lost my calm and sprouted wings."*

One lip of the Fenrir pulled up into a lopsided grin. *"Sorry I missed it, but ye should tell him everything, eun beag."* His hand fell away. *"No secrets. Secrets get ye in trouble. Give em those memories ye stole away."* It was not that I didn't agree with Nikolas, I did, but I didn't remember the dang spell. *"He wants to murder me, lass. Liam thinks ..."*

Nick's humor resonated through the stilled air. Liam let go. Fenrir's blue eyes squinted, and he lurched forward. I squealed, moving out of the way. Everyone stopped talking, their eyes falling between the three of us. My brow rose, as I plastered against the banister, unknowing what transpired. Nick rolled his eyes and playfully shoved Liam, before sauntering off to the sofa, next to Jamie.

Liam's eyes swam, and he offered his hand. I took it, allowing the flow of our blending to pour over my skin. The heated rush settled in my cheeks as the memory of our morning replayed. His hands dropped to my hips; lips hovered close to my neck, his breathe deep and tickling my reddening flesh.

"Should've told me, darlin'." Liam whispered, "He would've kicked my ass too."

I snickered. Yeah, Nick could have kicked his ass any day of the week. Some secrets weren't mine to tell, not even to him. "I made a promise."

"So he's into guys. Big deal." I wanted to wrap myself in his arms and kiss him. That was the sweet-natured Liam I remembered, sweet and tender, and always doing right by his friends. *"As long as he's not into you."*

I bit my lip. Geesh not everyone was into me or wanted me. Overprotective much? Did he realize what guy Nick loved? *"I have my suspicions."* His hands tightened their hold. *"As long as they're happy."*

But neither Jamie nor Nick appeared happy. Strained and uncomfortable were better words to describe what I saw. Was it because of Paulo and Keelan? Why were they still hiding? Surely their love would have been accepted in a free community.

They loved each other, but was love enough?

My eyes drifted over the town's council, noting how small it was. Paulo, my grandmother, and Nick had represented Six and Twenty. No wonder the Nine bothered their little community whenever they felt like it; there were three members left. The sign said the population sat roughly around one hundred. My eyes drifted to Nick. How many enforcers did the town have?

Paulo cleared his throat before continuing as if two lycans hadn't just scuffled. Liam tightened his grip, and I gasped for air. "I expected backlash, but I didn't expect them to walk right in without warning."

The draugr emotions were off the charts, but unlike the supes and humans, he held stoic in his features. There wasn't a glimmer of unease present in his body language. No wonder they chose him as the leader. Even his voice remained steady but I saw beneath his facade.

"So we strengthen the shield." My grandmother spoke, but my head shook as I leaned against Liam's rigid chest, enjoying the perfection of his body.

"I should turn myself in." Nick's brows scrunched together, and murmurs broke through the room. I winced, realizing I had said the words aloud. The manhunt would not end until they had me. Six and Twenty needed protection from the Nine. My eyes dropped to my hands. I would erase memories again if it helped. The spell eluded me but writing a new one was a possibility.

"No." Liam spun me around; lights danced in my vision. "Not a chance in hell, darlin'," he roared through his tightened jaw. His eyes glowed bright, and I squinted to ease the ache. "Not without me."

But Liam couldn't follow.

"No one's going anywhere," Nick said, pointing at Liam. "Least of all you."

"It has to be me," I protested and stared each one in the eye, ending with the Oracle.

"She'll try to kill you," my grandmother said as her brow creased with worry. Genuine worry, and I blinked. Sometimes I swore she suffered from multiple personalities. "Maeve won't stop until one of you is dead."

The room fell silent as the big secret revealed itself to Liam and Jamie. Neither of them had known about my great aunt's plotting. I said, "I realize the danger, but this has to stop. Show me another way, and I will gladly try."

Liam asked, "Again … kill … what's she talkin' about?"

A sigh tickled my lips. Paulo and Nick exchanged glances. "Have you wondered yet why I'd pack up and leave?" He blinked; No, Liam hadn't thought that far ahead.

"You remember?" asked Paulo, and I shook my head.

"Momma told me why," I lied, and the draugr narrowed his eyes. "She said someone tried to kill me so we ran. Said I erased my memory and all y'alls' to protect y'all from the Nine."

"I won't let you go, not again," Liam whispered. His thumb grazed my chin and forced my gaze. "My job is to protect you; I can't just let you saunter off into the maws of the Nine and a crazed killer."

I turned out of his grip and faced him. "Your job is standing by my side." My hands clenched, but my legs trembled. "You're ... you're acting like I'm a defenseless child when I'm probably the strongest being in this town." My shoulders ached as they hardened and pushed back. Liam crossed his arms over his chest and leaned on the railing. My foot tapped, and my fists balled at my side. "Listen to reason for once. *You* can't go; you can't shadow me forever."

"Right."

"What type of powers?" Grandma asked, but I gave her only a cursory, albeit narrowed, glance. Now wasn't the time to swap secrets.

"I'm not going to let y'all hold me prisoner, while the Nine keeps walking all over this town, threatening everyone I care about."

"Over my dead body," Nick said.

"I'll go with you," Jamie piped up and drew a killer, vein-popping glare from his brother and Nick. Liam would tear him to shreds if I let him.

My eyes threatened to roll. He needed to get over himself already. The Nine, they wouldn't stop till they had me in their greedy grasp.

"Also over my dead body," Nick said, staring into Jamie's eyes. I blinked as both men blushed.

"What part of I don't need a babysitter don't y'all understand?" Jamie winced from my tone. "Y'all've gone mad." I threw my hands up in the air. "Your existence is threatened because of me."

"No, no ... no way I will allow you to go." Liam argued with me. I chewed on my lip. Truly, he could not go. If Sköll caught wind of him, or Nick, the lycan King would kill them both. My hands were coated with enough blood.

"What other choice do I have, Liam?" I sighed. "Aren't y'all listening? I can't ask innocents to keep putting their lives in danger," I pled, but he didn't budge.

His nostrils flared, and his breathing staggered. "Please, someone talk some sense into her." He thrust his arms in the air, accidentally shoving me aside into a lamp, before storming from the room. I was all right, but I couldn't seem to find my voice as my eyes stung.

"Walking into the Nine is a death sentence, isn't that what you always said Dad?" Liam yelled from the kitchen, cabinets and drawers opened and slammed shut. My cheeks warmed, but a shiver ran up my spine. The accident part didn't bother me, but Liam didn't even care.

Before I lost control, I headed for the stairs. Paulo placed a hand on my shoulder, too fast and quiet for me to notice he'd moved. I looked into his concerning eyes.

"Liam's right. It'd be different if your memory returned. All we taught you …" My eyes glanced to Jamie, and he nodded. He'd kept my secret. "But as you are now … We'll find a way to protect you and Jamie too," Paulo said.

I sniffed and wiped the wetness from my cheeks. They'd refused to listen. They needed the protection, not me. For four years, I'd survived their clutches, and I'd give it all up again. My life wasn't worth the price of theirs. I loved them enough to let go even if it meant isolation and heartache. Losing them to the Nine wasn't a risk I was willing to take.

"I'll restore Jamie's Phoenix once I find it," I said.

My brows knitted together. With spells, only the caster typically removed or dispelled, by either choice or death. I motioned for him, and he rose. Why hadn't I noticed it before? Not a spell, at least not in the sense of the Myst, it was Dísir magic and a curse.

"What do you mean?" The Oracle smiled, but it disappeared. Her cold stare cut through Jamie as if he were butter, before shifting back to me.

"I can see the spell—"

"You can see it?" The Oracle's eyes widened. Wrinkled hands trembled, clattering against her walker. What did Grandma hide? I stepped down from the landing and glanced between her and Jamie.

If she didn't hit me with her Myst, then he did. No, the spell would've proven too difficult for him. His essence read low. Any essence we shared manifested as fire.

The same applied to Nick or Liam. At the root of it, Jamie was a Phoenix. Fire – even mine – would've recognized him as one. He shook under my gaze with each step I took. My hand hovered over his shoulder, and I glanced to Nick. Fenrir swallowed hard but waved his hand. I pressed Jamie down and knelt to the side. "Yes, I can see all magic when I form a bond."

I traced my finger over Jamie's bicep. He shivered; the goose-bumps trailed behind my touch. "Each type bears a signature. I can see all three of Liam's Mysts." I leaned closer, calling forth Jamie's Phoenix. His mark of flame rose up into his shoulder, and I drew the path. "Jamie, can you see it too?"

He shook his head and grasped my hand. My Myst pulsed into his palm. I smiled down at him, cocking my head, when he said, *"Just my own. Warden trait to see magic, but you aren't one of them."*

My lip pinched between my teeth. No, I wasn't a Warden, but I descended from a potent line of royal Alfheimians and hybrids. It still wasn't enough. My gaze drifted to Nick; his foot tapped as he eyed his boots. There was more to my power than I recalled. My eyes narrowed, catching his vision. The beast nodded.

"Well this is unexpected." Grandma eyed the door and shifted toward the end of the sofa. Her hands gripped her walker. I waited for her departure, but her mouth opened instead. "What else can you do that isn't normal?"

"Jamie, what do you think?" I cocked my eyebrow and turned to Nickolas. "Nick? How about you, can you see it?"

He stretched, snaking his hand behind Jamie and yawned. "Lycans can smell the Myst."

"Jamie, did she do this to you?" He swallowed hard and gave a slight nod.

"I was afraid of that; I'm sorry." I plopped down on the opposite side and gave him a hug. Why did my friends get hurt because of me? Everyone I cared about was in danger, and it was my fault. When would it end? "I'll start working on a reversal, but it will take time. Hang in there and stick to Paulo in case the Wardens return." I stood up and headed toward the kitchen. "First Liam."

Paulo's brows knitted, and I paused. "Why?" he asked, but I shrugged my shoulders.

He didn't want to know the truth. I loved his sons, my friends, and the whole town. I cared enough for them that I'd find a way to leave. A promise was a promise; I'd fix Jamie, as soon as I figured out how.

He wasn't in the kitchen and the back door lay open. Liam's clothes were in tatters. The breeze whipped them around the porch. I cursed under my breath as his message reached me.

"You promised me too." I reached for the pieces and sighed. Yeah, he had a point there. No matter what I did someone would get hurt.

Weeks passed as I stayed holed up in Liam's house. The only visitors we received were those bearing gifts of food, drink, or blood for Paulo. The debating remained endless; I forced them to understand the Council of the Nine only wanted me. Well so much for the plan, the meeting heads of Six and Twenty ruled against me, and I'd given up for the time being.

Three votes against or four if you had counted Liam's opinion. Jamie agreed with me, but his vote held as much weight as the wind. That left me one option but having a mindreader for a boyfriend fizzled the plan before I tried. While Liam made himself scarce, Jamie and Nick were guarding me twenty-four hours a day.

At least they hadn't felt a need to hide around me. But neither man dared to go against Liam's word. I wished they were the least of my worries. The Oracle, my grandmother, wasn't herself. As the days turned into weeks, she transformed, growing more bold and antsy. The Valkyrie stirred inside of her but was she born or created?

I had not realized it when I'd met her again. It was the Valkyrie, since I amassed the power, and I saw her for what she was. The beady black pools slipped on more than one occasion, but I kept the news to myself. Until I understood more, or what it meant, I didn't wanted to frighten anyone. It was not like I'd just walk up and ask her either.

My eyes rolled in the mirror as I combed my damp hair. "Hey Grams, so you're a Dísir; were you born or created … oh and do you hate me 'cuz I'm your boss?" Yeah I foresaw that going real well.

This marked day twenty-five since my father died, and I staked mental bets around Liam's mood. Already I'd tried everything I knew to catch his eye, but I no longer existed to him. He refused to look at the logistics or maybe he'd forgot. I'd find out if he'd actually say more than morning and goodnight to me.

Sköll –the bastard – fathered him and then lost his dang marbles. Why would I send the man I love to his home? The crazed lycan was our own version of Hitler. Should I wrap a gigantic red bow around his neck too? He imprisoned, enslaved, and massacred his own kind. Heck, the man attempted wiping out Nick's whole family, and he nearly succeeded.

A tear slid down my cheek. Why didn't Liam understand? I sighed and wiped the wetness away. Crying golden tears had its downfall. My shirt was ruined and stained with the glittery marks. I grumbled and tossed it aside. "At this rate I'll need a shopping trip," I mumbled.

"Aurie," Jamie yelled up the stairs. "I'm heading to the store."

Well bless his heart. Dirty mind reader found something useful. If I had to gnaw on another frozen pizza, I'd hurl. But that was about all the conversation Liam and I had this week. "Get some food, real food. No frozen crap."

"Like what?" I jumped at his face reflecting in the mirror.

I covered my chest, clutching a towel to my front. "Jamie get out."

He smirked and turned around. "Seriously, Aurie I've seen boobs before." My eyes narrowed, burning into the reflection. "Asses too."

I grunted and fished around for a top. Yeah, perfect timing to ruin another shirt when I needed it the most. Where the heck was Liam. He'd blow a gasket if he caught Jamie. It wouldn't matter two licks to the wind if he and Nick were an item. I sighed, dragging the tank top over my head.

Black, like my heart and soul.

Jamie left without a word. He didn't skive me out and, if not for Liam, who knew if we would've ended up together. I glanced back to the mirror and shook my head. No, Nick would have mated with him. Loneliness—I hated how the darkness of the emotion had twisted my thoughts.

"*Liam,*" I said, trying for the tenth time to reach him. My stomach ached, and my skin burned when he left. Yep, he ignored me. No kissing, touching … it was as if I didn't exist anymore. My hand clutched my talisman, and my fingers toyed with the chain. "*Screw you too.*"

Jamie came back sooner than I'd expected, and sure enough, he brought me real food. He boasted about a local farm stand that'd been in operation for almost a hundred years. I forced smiles and nodded, as we put the groceries away, but I wasn't in the mood for a chat. My torn and raw lip split open. The blood tinged my mouth, and I spat it down the sink.

I needed to release tension and quick, before I gave myself an abscess or an ulcer. My hand grasped a knife as curses spewed from my mouth. Jamie backed away, placing his hands in the air. Did he think I was going to stab him? I snorted. Like I'd waste physical energy and wield a knife. The blade clattered on the counter, and I dragged various veggies from the fridge. Jamie handed me a cutting board and hightailed it out of there.

"Auriel," Grandmother called to me in the kitchen, as I played sous chef, and released my pent up anger. My cooking skills were laughable, but vegetable soup was in order. She clattered in, pushing her walker. Why'd she need it if she could go all yoda on Jamie's ass?

"If we knew what powers you have in your arsenal then we could devise a better plan." My eyes rolled as I chopped harder. Sirens and bells weren't loud enough to drown out her nagging voice.

Paulo and I decided that, as my grandmother, she should know my abilities. We'd spoken frequently over the weeks, but neither of us knew what to do in regards to her or Liam's mood swings. Wait and watch was in full effect, because suspicions and being Valkyrie weren't reasons to act. Until Grandma either came clean or attacked again, there was nothing. I didn't trust the old woman to watch a pie cooling on my windowsill.

Keelan O'Nally Graftfield wasn't human. Neither was my mother. "Pooka-Pooka," Nick said, reminding my grandmother and tapping my nose. "Hey what'd the counter do to you lil lady?"

I ignored his intrusion and lack of a Scottish accent. Nick Kerr, he'd told me, was born and bred in the South. I laughed when he'd mentioned the last name; I'd used it too.

"Surely, *you know* what she's capable of, Keelan," Paulo said, and I smiled at his emphasis. She'd continued keeping our relationship a secret, and that baffled us too.

'Dae no' tell her, eun beag, yer no' to trust that one," Nikolas warned me, grasping my chin to meet his gaze when I didn't respond.

I bit my lip, wincing at the throbbing pain. A breath forced out of my nose. Nick reminded me too much of Liam that my heart panged against my rib cage. *Gods, why was my Guardian doing this to me?*

"Do you recall the Dísir?" I asked, turning around. He replied with a swift nod, but his crystalline eyes flashed toward the door. Brushing my hands clean, we strolled onto the back porch. "Nikolas, I've dreamt of them. More and more lately." We had spoken about the Dísir before, but before I had not remembered. Before I knew that, I was a Valkyrie and marked as their leader, according to him. The memory gaps made this difficult; part of me was not ready to remember, and it held the process back. Even the thought of it frightened me, but it wasn't why I'd left. What did I know about leading? Would I remember how? My eyes darted around the tree line. We weren't alone. "Is it safe to speak aloud?"

Before he answered, my heart leapt. I breathed in and stared into the trees. Liam roamed out there in the woods. His earthy scent welcomed me all those weeks ago. Now the fire and sap reminded me of what I missed. Instead of standing with me during those meetings, he'd spent the tedious hours free doing his lycan thing.

"Aye lass, we're only speaking of the cruel evil that spreads its talons across Midgard. We'd known their capabilities fer centuries, but tis only recent that they started their eyes upon us." Cracks drew my attention away from Nick's sarcastic words. We both understood a lot about supernaturals. Even the created Dísir weren't all bad. My eyes stayed on the trees, and I held my breath. He was close. My feet started forward. I needed him as I needed air.

"I don't see the gain. The deal was that we stay out of their business, and they keep out of ours. Our dominion was the humans." Or something like that.

He placed a hand on my shoulder and stopped me. My eyes glanced toward Nick. "Aye, but humans daena have abilities or access to magic." His lips pressed down. Yeah I'd forgotten that little tidbit. Born Dísir –high mages, Guardian, norns with a lower case n, and Valkyrie – always bore into the supernatural world. Created, some of them were humans. No one knew why Odin chose to break his own laws. "Think of it like this eun beag, if ye were a Valkyrie and yer job was to corrupt, what would be yer fastest way of doing such a thing?"

I refrained from snorting when he used the demon word, but just in case someone listened, they'd think we held a normal Dísir hate bash.

"Possess the supernaturals and humans, show ourselves, and spread like a plague."

Nick blinked. "That's what they be doing, lass. Darkness spreads." My lip throbbed as I hung onto his words. Did darkness cause him to murder my unborn child in the vision?

"The Nine, Duncan especially—" I winced at the name of my traitorous grandfather. My great aunt and he were the ones who devised the faux sacrifice legend. They'd meant to murder me when I turned eighteen. "—are taking precautions. They're locking them all up or killing them."

The Nine locked up humans ... murdered humans ... My mouth gaped, growing drier by the second.

"So you're saying Charlestown has humans locked up in that prison along with supes and Dísir?" Tears welled in my eyes, and I couldn't bring myself to say the other fate they faced. This wasn't right; the Myst didn't kill humans and neither did we regardless of Odin's meddling. "We have to stop it."

I didn't know how but I knew if someone didn't stop them that they'd never cease. Maybe I couldn't take down a God, but I could take down my family.

Charlestown, South Carolina was the Nine HQ for North America. They chose it because of the large port when they branched into the New World from Europe. He nodded. I whispered, "But not all Dísir want chaos; you do realize they lump us all in with them."

This sort of madness would destroy us all. "Maddening indeed lass, and yes I ken; so does the council but they'd rather ask questions later."

I shook my head, disbelieving the words coming out of his mouth. My family would destroy everything in the universe if they kept breaking the laws. Ragnarok ... the visions ... I tampered my eyes shut as the flashes rocked me. It had already begun. Were we too late?

"There tis also rumor that the realms are sealing off and the Bifrost abandoned to protect what's left."

My eyes widened when he mentioned the rainbow bridge, which wasn't even a bridge. "Alfheim's been sealed for over a millennia." My great grandfather remained the only pureblooded human to step foot in the realm. Apparently, one of the three Norns placed him there. One day he trotted along on his horse, he blinked, and the landscape turned from lush green to snow.

"Aye, tis sealed. Still, those good fer nothin' high elves and fae could help us." Nick shook his fist, and I grabbed it.

My eyes narrowed. "Thomas would never reopen the portals unless Freyr himself commanded it. The dragons and Magda—"

"Nay, and even then I think him blinded. Loki speaks of a new alliance."

I stepped back, dropping his fist. "You would put your loyalty into Loki?"

My pulse increased, and my hand trembled as it lifted up. Loki the Trickster wasn't a God but a nuisance. I shuddered at the memory of his scars. Nick shifted his weight; hyperawareness and remembrance kicking in. We'd had this argument before. My patronage lay with Freyr and Freya–my ancestors. His stayed with Loki, the creator of the lycans, dragons, and sea serpents.

"He's my maker lass." Nikolas' voice held an edge like the pain of a sword. He'd lost almost everything, yet his courage to fight for the greater good remained. The Fenrir clan never ceased to amaze me. If we learned anything from them, it would do us some good to discover their courageous valor. "Even as he stands between me and my mate, I canna turn my cheek."

I pressed him, and my heart sank. Lycans weren't like the werewolves of human lore. One didn't become a lycan from a bite. Instead, they either were born or received the blessing of Loki. The demi-god had refused Jamie's request. He ran a hand over his long face. "Hen's talkin' 'bout becoming draugr again."

I'd dreamt of him as a draugr, and the hilarity of the situation had me toppling over with laughter. Nick wasn't as amused, but I realized the me in that dream never remembered.

"How's your mate aside from that?" Liam strode out of the woods. The wind caught in ruddy strands, whipping terracotta tendrils into his eyes as a tornado of his emotions approached. Jeans hugged his lanky frame forcing my heart to ache and squeeze with every step. Broad, thick shoulders pressed back, straining under his t-shirt. I refused to avert my eyes, and my heart pounded harder. Liam's eyes looked everywhere but me. Invisible—I grew smaller with each passing second. I could've just handed him a knife.

"You know exactly how he is. Yours isn't favoring much better." I suppressed a laugh at how easy he switched between the accents. However, I planned to ask him why he'd kept it from Liam. Neither of them were Sköll, but he did deserve to know whom his father was, and what he'd done to the Fenrir clan. Like Nick, I had not truly blamed Jamie. His family would have died one way or another. I shivered from the wind; Liam's steps slowed. He knew I stared, and he rubbed his arms too.

Nick coughed and nudged my shoulder. I ignored him and trained my eyes on Liam's gait. It would surprise me if he didn't know about his father. He managed to figure out the lycan part. But darkness didn't infect his mind or Nick's mind either.

Both men were trustworthy, dependable, and full of self-sacrificing courage. Okay maybe Liam wasn't so dependable. Still, it was simple enough to say, "oh well, that's a lycan thing," but it wasn't. Not even a Fenrir thing. That was just who they were, and a significant reason why I loved them. Regin too, though she hadn't been around these past weeks. We had been close before Nick took her away before the massacre. I didn't even know if he'd brought her back or where he'd taken her.

Liam's feet creaked on the steps leading up the porch. The two men nodded to each other and did their guy thing. A hug, but men would never call it as such. The gesture warmed me, even if Liam was being a complete ass again. He needed to learn it was all right to disagree, but I had feelings too, and I sensed his. Besides, I'd heeded his commands. My ass didn't run, and to be honest, I could've left. None of them matched my Myst.

Without a word or touch, he strolled inside and left me with Nikolas. The sting was impossible to fight as the tears dribbled down my face. Nick's bear arms engulfed me as he offered comfort. "Ye need to tell him the truth, Auriel."

"That's not it." My body shook, the pain slicing through my heart.

The Phoenix arose, and I slammed the beast down. Scream, punch, I had to do something. "I can't just snap my fingers and have him remember. I sure as heck can't make him talk."

I sniffled and pulled away.

Nick's eyes narrowed, and he crossed his arms over his broad chest. "No," he growled. "Ye both choose no' to and yer hurting the both ye."

The blush burned my cheeks, and I glanced away. I wasn't trying to hide anything from Liam. He shoved me away and kept me there. I'd much rather move past our rift. We're supposed to be a freaking team. I wrapped my arms around myself. Liam was everything I'd always wanted and more, when he wasn't a broody jackass.

Deep inside, even with the spell, my heart knew it belonged to him. If I restored him – if I could – would he hold the same feelings? What if the four years altered something, and he didn't love me anymore? Did he love me now? Doubtful, Liam locked me away in this cage.

"Aye, well …" Nikolas guffawed with gusto, but he'd laughed at me before. My middle finger shot up too. *So glad to amuse him.*

Nick hadn't stopped. My foot tapped, and my jaw clenched at his childish banter. The blood drained from my head. I grasped the railing for support, forcing deep breaths of fresh air to fill my lungs, but the anger spread. It pulsed beneath my skin until the pressure built.

Nick stopped laughing, but he didn't help me either. The back-door slammed, and Liam encased me in his arms. My mind struggled between melting into him and smacking him across the face.

"What the hell did you do?" He was angry, but the distress in his erratic touch and voice overpowered everything else. He pushed my hair aside, tucking it behind my ears. His thumb traced the tearstains, but I couldn't look at him. All the pain I'd endured these past weeks and Liam chose now?

"I did no' do a damned thing to her laddie, eun beag lost control tis all." Nick snickered. "Ah well at least ye ken he still cares, lass." I snorted, and his laughter resumed. "But I swear to Loki, I daena touch her. Just gave her a wee bit of advice."

"Dude, why are you speaking like that?" I blinked, realizing Nick slipped character. My eyes lifted to Liam's face as the shock registered from hearing the thick brogue. *Almost laughable, almost.*

Eyes jumped between the laughing Nicky and the vein popping Liam. The fresh air thickened as the Mysts swirled, not intertwining but repelling. All I wanted for the past days was a little attention, and this was what it took him to give a damn about me? Fists balled. My face and neck ignited. What the heck?

"Because he's from Scotland," I rumbled as the crackle of my wings pierced through my skin and the howling wind. "Crap, another shirt ruined."

"Are you both mad? What if someone sees?" Liam hissed, and I rolled my eyes. Wasn't it my secret to tell?

"Why yes, we're all just a little bit mad here," I countered with my impatient sarcastic tongue. Weeks of pent up emotion waited to jump out of my mouth.

"Be serious ... for once think before you—"

"Before I what, Liam? Think before I act? Tell me something. Do you plan to keep me locked up forever? Hell, the Nine could do that." I shoved a finger in his chest. "What have I accomplished since coming here?" His mouth opened, and I threw my closed hand in his face. "I'll tell you. I've accomplished *nothing* but endless irritation, hurt, and imprisonment since stepping foot into Six and Twenty. One more second and I'm liable to explode. Between the lies and hate, a girl can only take so much before she loses it."

"You ... you ..." Liam's eyes darted around, and he stumbled backward. "Can't blame me for getting hurt ... you're the one who waltzed off into the woods alone."

Was he that dense? Could he not see how he broke my heart by pushing me away?

I blinked, watching his jaw set tight. I wondered if he even loved me, but dang did he even like me? The wind blew through my hair, carrying the thickness of his emotions. Annoyance, I had my answer.

"I'm not talking about that ..." My eyes stung, and I glanced away hoping they would not fall. Just once, I prayed the tears did not fall. The intimacy we'd shared meant nothing. The touching, the kissing, the ... All of it meant the world to me. Obviously, it had meant nothing to him.

My hands fell to my hips, and I gaped at him. His rigid frame towered above me, and his lips pressed thin. Wow. Liam hadn't the slightest inkling how hard and agonizing loving him was for me. Everything I'd sacrificed all those years to save him.

The pain stripped my soul bare. My hands balled up, and my eyes throbbed, struggling to hold myself in check. He didn't even deserve my tears.

I ran away from it all, from him. My legs burned, screaming and pulsing as they moved faster. The forest, dead leaves and fresh growth, burned my nose; the air whipped past my head. Every crack and crunch pushed me to run faster. I could not do this ... I would not ... "Do you hear that; I can't do this!"

Trickling water caused me to shift direction. Without removing my shoes or clothing, I jumped into the water. Icy cold just like my heart needed to be. My teeth chattered, but I didn't allow the sharp sting to stop me as I descended to the dark middle. The water came only to my waist, making it harder.

"Why do you do this to me?" I screamed loud, with all the emotion pushing through my trembling lips. The chirping birds replied their cheery and mournful songs. All the knowledge in the world wasn't enough to make me believe that I could do this without love.

"I'm not like you," I whispered. "Why create me to love if I cannot be loved?" Liam had not loved me. I choked on the thought. There was no future without love. "Why allow me to feel these emotions? Why give me a soul mate at all?"

I sighed into the water as it engulfed my body. Diving to the bank, I laced my arm through the tree roots. The last glance I saw of this realm was the river turning amber with the last tears of the Valkyrie.

chapter thirty

NIKOLAI ULF FENRIR/NICKOLAS KERR

Fainauriel's mind had remained littered with gaps. Otherwise, she would not have asked the same questions again. I sighed; *Loki would have my head.*

My personal life had to wait. I swallowed hard thinking of how Jamie would react. Wrong, I was certain. He failed to understand me most of the time and jumped to his own silly conclusions.

"Ye go after her now, cousin." I reached my hand out and helped him to his feet. He didn't realize it yet, but he was quite stubborn and stupid. The thought had me chuckling. They truly were brothers and idiots when it came to love.

Eun beag wasn't much different. Liam was her protector, Auriel's soul mate, and I stayed the ever-faithful friend sworn by blood oath to guard her. The spark in his eyes showed a longing to follow, and his wolf inched forth. "Why should I?"

The beast wanted to follow, to chase, but the pigheaded man stopped him. "Out of love, ye silly lad. What other reason dae ye need?"

"But she wants to leave me, and she promised she never would. Plus, the books say Valkyries are pure."

I blinked at his whining tone. Had anyone ever told him no? Jamie too for that matter; the Skyland brothers were wee scunners when it came to those they loved. A grin formed and I pressed my lips against it. He sounded so much like Jamie. A bunch of broody bastards looking for reasons to complain, disagree, or fight. My hand covered my mouth, and I watched as Liam braced himself against the railing.

His fear and anxiety stemmed around sex? I bit my lip and shook my head. We weren't human, but the sexual drive was still within us. For the two-natured, it was harder; the beast craved the flesh, the release, and it was difficult to satisfy without a mate.

I laughed as Liam's words spewed forth. "Yer an arse and ye read too damn much like yer brother."

Liam sighed. I'd fought hard against my inner demons this past month, but this wasn't about me and Jamie. We didn't have a wee spat.

The lad ran every time life turned hard. He'd played a small role in killing my clan too, but if he'd come to me instead of fleeing … Loki's wrath aside, my love knew I'd give him the world even if it meant leaving him alone. We moved past that but we weren't above problems. Auriel and Liam needed to talk to each other and work their problems out. "Laddie ye daent deserve her."

His hand rubbed his neck. "I know; I never did, did I?"

I patted his shoulder. No one deserved her love, but she gave it freely. There were secrets about her that she hadn't recalled yet. At least Auriel realized some extent of her power, but not her full potential. I grinned knowing what ran through her veins. "No."

"Why bother then." Liam shrugged. "I can't touch her … can't … "

The wooden railing creaked under the pressure of his hands. I understood his pain all too well. Jamie's sweet face crossed my mind. He strummed my heartstrings with naught but a glance. But I was in the wrong; I'd led him on, kissed, and bedded him as if we were all right. Ignoring his darkness hurt us both.

My lip throbbed as my teeth split the flesh. Lycan design flaws were numerous, and among them included an insatiable desire to fuck. There wasn't a nicer way of saying it, because in the beginning, it was more than enough to drive a maddened lycan into a bloodthirsty frenzy. Over the centuries, we learned to adapt and to love. Some said Odin took pity on our cursed lives. If a lycan found their soul mate, no other woman or man would ever do. Their lives tied together until the day they died.

Five hundred years and the universe gave me Jamie Mc Douglass; I wasn't surprised to learn he descended from Douglas the Black who'd became a lycan after his children were born. He still lived in my homeland.

"There's more to love than sex Liam," I explained. "There's understanding and compromise too." My words burned my ears. I glanced toward the closed door.

Jamie had feared us; he'd allowed the disdain to taint our picturesque world back then. No harm would've befallen him, and I'd have killed anyone who dared to persecute our love. That was why he'd called Merric.

"I know that," he growled; a woman shouted in the distance. Liam's blood drained from his face. My own pulse burned, recognizing Auriel's shrilled voice. Together we ran as the rain pelted from the sky.

Branches snapped beneath our feet and logs appeared in our paths. I prayed to Loki, made promises, and cursed my God all at the same time. No, we would not fail; we would make it on time.

"She has fallen." The wind and rain blinded my vision, but I refused to stop. Mud caked between my toes and I slipped, sliding to my knees. I waved Liam on; he was faster anyway.

My heart thundered, beating against my strained ribcage. *"Jamie."*

"Auriel!" my cousin roared, and I lifted myself from the muddy ground. He wasn't far ahead, and I pushed my legs harder. When we reached the water, she floated face down. Liam dove in without another thought and dragged her to the shore.

"Eun beag ... no ..." Her lips were blue, skin paler than an ethereal, and there wasn't movement in her chest. I prayed again as Liam pressed into her breast, and his lips breathed into her lungs. My hands trembled, and my legs gave way.

'Dae no' take his love away; dae no' take away mine. Take my life instead. My life to spare theirs.'

Loki replied, *"No, Fenrir."*

CHAPTER
THIRTY-ONE

LIAM

Trembling hands fell to her neck, but the only heart beats were Nick's and mine. I pumped her chest again, cursing Auriel under my breath. Liquid stung my eyes as I glanced to him. *You must not give up.* My beast urged me on and so did my friend. Her spirit, I didn't sense it, and the emptiness surrounded me. Wiping the tears from my eyes, I stared down at her lifeless body, clothes stained from the Carolina clay. My thumb smeared dirt over her pale cheeks, before rubbing it across her once pink lips. Oh how I wanted to kiss those lips, taste her, and take her as my own. Every day became a constant struggle not to give in, and I ended up losing her anyway. My eyes burned as they threatened to unleash the agony, slicing through my heart. "I need you."

The words changed nothing; she didn't return. I lifted her wet body and clutched her in my arms. My lips kissed her hair, her forehead, and then her nose. Sniffling, I searched for words to describe what I had lost. "I loved you; I still do. I love you."

"Liam daent stop; ne'er give-up. We canna fail." Nick rushed to my side and seized Auriel from me. He pumped her heart and muttered spells.

My eyes closed; peace and tranquility fell across the forest. *"Don't give up, Liam. Open your eyes."* Flinging them open, I gaped at the ravens perched by Auriel's side. Together they hopped, each landing on my shoulders. My heart raced, and my head swayed from side to side.

"You can heal her."

"No, I don't have the power." Even as the words left my trembling lips, I glanced down at my hands. My fingers glowed greenish blue; my Myst came alive and built within me. My palms ached with an itch crying for release. I shoved Nick aside, grunting as our flesh collided, and he scurried away, eyes widened. My hands pressed upon her chest, but nothing happened. My forehead beaded with sweat as I cursed aloud.

"Focus young one. Patience child." Part of me wanted to wring their feathered necks. With a deep, drawn breath, I cleared my mind of all doubt, all thoughts beyond healing the only woman I'd ever love.

The Myst rose around me, tainting the air with its sea green haze. My hands touched her again; I asked my Myst to surround Auriel, pleading for it to repair her unbeating heart. It spread, enveloping her whole body. The Myst seeped into her skin. Seconds passed by as my heart hammered away like a ticking clock. Nick watched; his body shook, but there were no words.

Auriel coughed, blue-red eyes widening as my pulse skyrocketed even more. I turned her head being careful not to hurt her more as the green liquid cleared from her lungs. The words she spoke, yelled rather, fluttered back into my mind. Realization smacked me, the inferno rising into my cheeks. She meant me; I wounded her heart.

"Thank the Gods, Loki be praised." Nick's eyes and arms lifted to the sky.

"No ..." Auriel replied as she fell limp in my arms. But she breathed, and that stubborn heart thrummed stronger. She could hate me all she wanted, but this —whatever she did – wasn't the answer. I bit my lip and glanced into the trees. Neither was my anger nor ignorance. Every tear, her heart aching ... I ignored it like a fool.

"A bleedin' fool," Nick said, and I turned to him. "She'll forgive ye. Eun beag loves ye too damn much." He grinned wide. "Daent ken why."

I cocked my head and stared at my best friend. "Did I know you too before her spell?" He glanced away and nodded. "Thanks man," I added, and I meant it.

I scooped Auriel up. We fumbled at first, a bit awkward with the wings and the two birds who refused to shoo. Every time I swatted at them, they'd bitten my hand or squawked in my ear. We walked in silence back to the house, but instead of my residence, I brought her home. Her home.

"We depart here old friend, but ye'll hear from me soon." Nick gripped my arm and turned to leave, but stopped short. His eyes darted between the houses. "Remember what I said." He hopped up the steps. "Oh and the whole nonsense daent apply to the born ... But if ye seek absolution, pray to Loki fer guidance."

I nodded and kicked the screen door out of the way. "Hey, uh thanks man." Auriel shivered, but her eyes remained closed. "*I'm telling them yer fleshing out yer problems and to leave ye be.*" I glanced across the lawn and saw Nick entering my house. He flashed another wide grin and waved.

"*Jamie is my biggest concern and the Oracle ... something ...*" Everything that surrounded her was strange. The questions she asked were even more bizarre. Paulo and Jamie kept me in the loop; their concern mirrored my own. None of us penetrated through her defenses though. When you combined it all together, it just didn't add up.

"*Take care of our eun beag; leave Jamie to me. Yer father understands the truth.*" I blinked. He'd fooled me for years. Auriel stirred a bit; her hand grasped my wet t-shirt. I sighed at the warmth rolling from her body. When this was over, and she was safe, I'd sit everyone down and sort this all out. The Oracle, Nick—but I needed to fix us first.

A quick scan of the house informed me we're alone, and I kicked the front door closed. The stairs groaned as I carried her to her room. My eyes fell upon the photographs. Each one made me hug her a bit closer. We reached her bedroom. At least I assumed so from all the girly décor. I chuckled at the poster on her door. A giant unicorn guarded her entrance. White sheets covered all the furniture, and I whipped them off, cradling her with one hand. My mouth dropped when I eyed something familiar. The artwork that lined her walls was hand drawn, and by her headboard rested my handwriting. It's not that I didn't believe it, but this house confirmed our past. My past with her lay next door all those years, and she hadn't destroy it.

A shiver ran down my spine as I took in the whole drawn scene.

The Legend of the Fenrir Wolf ... Poroflr and even Sköll were created that day by the demi-god Loki. As I peeled the layers of wet clothing away, I thought about what Nick said. My mind required distraction from her naked, dimpling flesh, and hard nipples. My tongue ran over my lips, and a strangled groan trapped in my chest.

I left her in her underwear and tucked her under the covers. Her lips were still blue, and her body shook uncontrollably. My hand covered my mouth, fingers stroking my stubble. I hadn't bothered with shaving and liked it. My lips curled. I knew how to raise her body heat. Auriel wouldn't be happy when she woke up. At least I'd enjoy the torture of her soft skin against my flesh. Undressing quickly, the excitement rushed to my head – both of them. The sensation left me breathless, my nostrils flared wider to bring in more of her sweet heat. Even as worry ate away at me, the primal need to touch her rose. My body screamed an overdue notice for attention.

The icy touch of her skin bit into my core as I slid under the covers. On instinct, I wrapped her around me, and pulled her on top, before cocooning us with covers. It proved a bit difficult, getting the blanket around her wings, but I finally managed. We lay there for what felt like an eternity, with her head resting upon my chest, and my swollen cock pinned down in an uncomfortable bend. It was for the best, I told it. It didn't listen.

I wanted to worship every inch of her body, hear her scream my name and come undone in my arms. But we weren't there yet. I loved her; I think she cared for me, and maybe she had even loved me in the past. Until she allowed me to remember, then I wouldn't push the boundaries of our union. She'd referred to me as her boyfriend in her thoughts, but I wanted more.

"I'm sorry that I hurt you, darlin'," I whispered. "I was an ass." Auriel stirred. "Again," I added. Her hips squirmed, making it damn near impossible to think. A lesser man would have snatched them and had his way with her. The temptation built, but damn she'd have my ass.

Auriel ground against me as a groan left her pinked lips. A ragged breath hissed out. Oh Gods, she was killing me, murdering my senses with her body. My breathing grew ragged, cutting the oxygen from my brain. No more fighting her, I didn't want to fight anymore. A moan escaped Auriel's sweet lips. My body ached to explode.

I grasped her hips telling myself I'd make her to stop. Instead, my mind betrayed me as my hands pressed her hard against me. The beast cried out as she opened her eyes, widening in a flash. Her parted lips released a gasp.

"Liam ... I—" I placed my finger over her lips and leaned up, replacing it with my mouth as the blankets pooled around her thighs. My mouth nipped at hers. Auriel curled her hands in my hair and surrounded me with the soft, downy wings. I relented with a sigh and skimmed my lips down her neck and chest.

Her damp bra clung to her creamy flesh; dark nipples jutted through the lavender lace, enticing my mouth with its wonder. I stared into Auriel's eyes as I searched –begged – for permission. She brought my hand to her lips, kissing each tip, before sliding it down to her breast. My fingers dipped inside the lace, squeezing her smooth flesh. Auriel's head lolled back, tossing her damp auburn waves, as small sighs pushed past her lips.

Her curvy hips moved in rhythm with mine as our lips met again. My pace quickened, my need thrumming away within my chest and pulsing against Auriel's body. Hands kneaded her nipples, enticing more moans that threatened us both.

The heat of her pooled between us; the scent of her pleasure was a siren's call to the beast inside. My tempo increased, and my tongue pushed past her parted lips. I expected her to recoil as she'd done before, but her tongue glided in tune with her body. Every inch of her teased and intoxicated, as the heat built deep in my core. Gods, I wasn't even inside of her.

The fever of her voice climbed. "Liam ... more."

I gave her all, pressing myself against her, and gliding my hips faster than before. Our lungs panted and sucked in the desire-thickened air. I leaned back as Auriel spread her wings, pulling her breathless form with me over the edge. We came undone together for the first time.

"I love you," I said to her, and she cried.

chapter thirty-two

AURIEL

Torture came to mind, but he said those words. My lips quivered instead of smiling; eyes leaked instead of shining. Gods, I'd longed for and dreaded this day. The point of no return was upon me, and as I gazed into Liam's eyes, I couldn't say goodbye. Wiping the tears away, I forced my mouth to smile. "I love you too; I always have and for eternity I will."

His arms surrounded me. Heat rolled over my skin. He pulled from around my waist and crushed me into him. My lips parted, eager to drink from Liam's sexy mouth and drink in his flavor. The pangs of desire returned as my thighs squeezed tight against his hard body. We were opposites. My soft body melded against his rocky frame on the tiny twin bed. My eyes blinked, realizing I was home. This was my room.

I pulled away, but Liam's hands brought me back. No, I didn't want him to stop either, but I was home, surrounded by memories of all I'd lost, and everything I once left behind. But I thought I'd lost him too, and here he was; I fell into his embrace. Forget the past, Liam said, and I did. Anything for him, my heart.

"Darlin'," he groaned against my mouth. "Stop." My muscles froze. I scampered to the end of the bed and looked away. "C'mon back here," Liam said. The room closed in, and the air grew thicker. "Auriel." He reached for me, and I flinched away. My brows knitted together; I didn't want to play this game.

I dragged the blanket down and covered myself. "Just go," I said, my lips shaking the words.

Liam stood, and my eyes tracked him like a hawk as he pulled his jeans on. Too perfect and beautiful sculpted like a statue. I'd thought it naught moments before. Soft, I curved and dimpled in comparison. Movies and television shows flashed through my mind. He looked the part of the hero, but I'd never pass for the heroine or damsel in distress. Liam stepped toward the door, leaving his shirt behind. Gods, his jeans slung on those hips like they belonged. I wanted to become those jeans and mold to him like a glove.

He turned around, flashing a wolfish grin. "How are you goin' make me leave and think shit like that?"

"I …" I chewed my cheek, deciding my lips were too sore.

He stepped closer. "Aurie luv, I'm not going anywhere."

"I'm not ready, Liam." My eyes fell to my hands as the lie slipped out. Once he remembered and I knew he wouldn't despise me. A shiver rolled over my skin at the thought, and I lay down. The cold bed didn't warm the emptied depths of my soul.

The floor creaked, and dust particles danced through the light. "Move it," he grumbled, and I gaped at him. *Incredulous man refused to leave.* "You can bet your sweet ass I'm staying."

The twin bed didn't allow me any space without kissing the floor. Before I reminded him of that, Liam had picked me up. I screamed; he chuckled and cradled me like a baby. My eyes were wide as he plopped us down on the protesting bed.

Liam held me, stroking my hair. "I'd never force you darlin', but don't lie to me."

I snorted and played in the thick patch of reddish hair on his chest. The day drained me. The month pulled on every emotion. Everyone depended on me, and the Nine, I had to stop them before anyone else died.

"Talk to me, Auriel."

"Where do I start?"

"Stop blocking me; I can't do my job when you hide from me, darlin'."

His job, right. Fragile and weak, neither of those traits represented me. Heck, I couldn't kill myself, but my eyes opened. No matter what I did or didn't do, there was no running from my destiny. I was the Valkyrie General, the oh-so-mighty leader of the Born, as the Norns weaved. Each passing moment, every new day, I changed. My strength grew, and my Myst increased. I sighed against his chest and glanced toward him. Lies were over and half-truths done.

I retracted the white Myst, lowering the shrouded veil of my mind. My legs straddled him. Liam's eyes widened. "This might hurt," I said and placed my fingers to his damp temples.

My Myst flowed through my tips, connecting with his energy. The memories, the truth flashed forward. Some of it he suspected, and now I confirmed his fears. Leader of the Dísir and that meant immortal. A destiny of war and bloodshed lay before us. If we ignored it, the Nine Realms fell into a sea of fiery ash created by my sorrow.

"Let's get you a pair of combat boots," Liam said, grinning wide. "We can git you some BDUs and guns …"

I cocked my eyebrow. "Seriously, I tell ya the fate of the world rests on my shoulders and ya want to talk wardrobe?"

His hands rubbed up my arms and caressed my shoulders. "You'd be sexy as hell." He sighed and closed his eyes. "Gods woman," he added as his cock swelled beneath me. My eyes darted down his frame and over the stiff outline, straining against his jeans. "You drive me crazy."

I giggled, running my hands over his chest. Yeah he had the same effect over me too. But the pain, the command of my destiny, could I have both? My biggest fears were losing those I loved. Even in the dreams, I searched for Liam first, and then my friends. They were my heart and soul, etched into my supernatural make-up.

"Fainauriel," Liam breathed my name.

My eyes connected with his, tinged with speckles of blue and red. I'd found Jamie's missing Myst, but I wasn't certain how to remove the power without harming Liam in the process. Did he even realize the Myst was there? The fiery essence of his coat flashed in my mind. My lip pulsed as I drew it between my teeth. "What's wrong now?"

I glanced away from his intensified eyes, torn between the flickering fire reflecting in his gaze and the cold grey eyes of Jamie. Both men meant the world to me. All of my friends did because Six and Twenty was a small community. But two fears arose and they both turned my stomach. Liam said my name again, and I blinked.

"Nothing's wrong." A smile forced, fighting against frozen muscles. "I'm just worried is all."

He nodded and swallowed hard. Warm lips caressed my wrinkled forehead. "Jamie did well today. He's showing progress with air."

But the Phoenix fire would change him. The burning cinders raked against the soul and begged for more. There was a valid reason the Phoenix mages were rare. They tended to sign away their own demise, seeking more and more power until they lost control. Was Jamie strong enough to tamper his ambitious nature? Liam stroked my cheek and asked, "Have you found a way to reverse the curse?"

"No," I said as my hands curled into themselves. Why had my grandmother cast the dang spell? "But I know where his Myst went." Our eyes connected again and my heart fluttered as he tilted my chin. "It's inside of you."

Liam rolled from the bed and stampeded down the stairs. The house shook as I fought the dams attempting to burst. *"I didn't know. We need to fix this."* The backdoor slammed, and I choked on a sob. The ache grew with each step he took and slammed into my chest.

Quicker than expected, Liam had returned with clean clothes, announcing that he'd sent Jamie and Nick to buy more. At least I trusted his tastes. Cliché maybe, but the boy dressed well. We were always close, Jamie and I. In many ways, I was closer to him than Liam.

His raw pain and the life he'd lived spoke measures for his strength. But Jamie's weakness was his inability to please every-one. The boy craved acceptance and molded himself into whatever someone wanted. With me though, and Nick, Jamie was free to be Jamie. We never judged each other, at least not until the day he made the phone call.

Some mistakes were hard to forgive even if I understood why. *Love could drive you crazy and lead you to do stupid things.* I sighed as Liam handed me his clothing, but said nothing. My shield remained down, and I opened my thoughts to him. Ruddy brows mashed together as I slipped into his jeans.

The clothes here were too small for my womanly curves. He'd brought me his clothing since I'd ruined my jeans with my dip in the lake. I waited for him to bring it up and the throbbing vein in his jaw alerted me to his struggle.

"You can't die like that but you can sure as Hel scare the shit out of me." Liam's eyes welled but the tears didn't fall. The floor creaked as he knelt by my feet. "I was wrong too, and I'm sorry for being an ass again."

"Has anyone ever told you no?" He shook his head. "That's not going to work, Liam. We have to work together and while we may not agree all the time, we must learn to find a common ground. No more running or blocking. We're a team, and we need to start acting like one."

"What about the others?"

I said, "They're on our team too, but I can't risk their lives."

"Nick won't stay behind, and I doubt Jamie would either. You're like a little sister to both of them, darlin'. You gotta put aside your fears and trust that we have your back."

Compromise became our middle names, and we had not fought again, not even when I brought up rescuing my mom. He'd promised to speak with Paulo and develop a foolproof plan. Until then we bled, sweat, and busted each other up on the training field, of course.

We were not the only ones either. Nick and Jamie, while still in the closet, spent more time together. Inevitable, since they bonded, but I enjoyed witnessing their joy as much as I relished in my own. My eyes scanned the backyard. The four of us started training together, but we worked on magic. Guardian law prevented my spells from harming Liam, so we swapped boyfriends. The brothers pinned against each other, and the Fenrir battled me.

While I'd located Jamie's Phoenix, I had not told anyone else, and had Jamie drawing from his air. Pam —Paulo's faerie assistant came out to help us. She explained even with both elements at his disposal that he'd relied heavily on the fire. The difference laid in the reserves. Non-Dísir magic worked different and required more Myst to cast spells. Each spell required planning and precise execution.

The Fenrir cousins remained in their human forms. After several failed attempts, Jamie and I teamed together. He tapped into my Myst when his reserves depleted, but with a defensive restriction.

"They're in the woods," he whispered, and I shot him a glare. The lycans had excellent hearing and vision in both forms. Leaves crunched, and my eyes whipped toward the sound. My diluted pooka instincts weren't as sharp, but I heard them.

"Close your eyes and concentrate on the Myst." Jamie nodded. I visualized the foggy substance of magic with my eyes open, but I kept pushing him to use other senses. Humans accomplished it all the time. Those without sight tended to have excellent hearing and sense of smell. Why couldn't we do it too?

Birds flew from a tree and dove to my shoulder. I jumped back and clutched my chest. Nicky snickered as the energy pulsed in my hand. A smile crept over my lips, and I tossed it toward where I'd heard him. A dust devil launched him into the air before it reached him. Jamie's eyes remained closed.

My arms surrounded him, and I jumped up and down. He'd done it. Just him, no Phoenix, not tapping into me. Nick wasn't as pleased. A string of Scots Gaelic unleashed from his lips.

"Big furry baby bruise his ego?" Jamie laughed at my mumbled jab. He heard me; I had no doubt about that since Liam laughed as well. I nodded and grabbed his arm.

My Myst blocked out my Guardian. "Again, he hasn't moved."

Jamie wiped the sweat from his head and closed his eyes. I willed the barrier to evaporate and linked to my Guardian again. *"Liam, crack a twig."*

The wind increased, rustling the leaves where the branch snapped. My heart pounded in my ears as I watched him repeat the same spell. He did not mouth the words aloud, but the Myst moved in the same pattern.

Liam lifted into the air, and he screamed as his lanky body flew from the woods to the porch. He landed, kneeling at my feet.

"Nice bro," he said, grinning wide. They exchanged high fives as Nick barreled from the woods. Liam barely jumped out of the way before he tackled Jamie to the ground. Their mouths connected and shared a kiss.

"Whoa."

He scratched his head, squinting from the sun, and glanced at me. "You knew 'bout this too?" I nodded and smiled. "Guess he wasn't lying 'bout not wanting you, darlin'." Liam laughed and picked me up. I squealed, feigning my fright as he spun me around. His red-brown brows wagged. *"Let's give them some room."*

Another week passed, and summer kicked into full force. We trained hard by day, and at night, I worked on my reversal spell. "Move that out," I said to Liam, pointing to the tiny bed. We slept together, as in actually sleeping, but stayed at my house. Everyone else convened at his, including my grandmother. I refused to sleep under the same roof even if she physically couldn't walk up the stairs. There was no change in her behavior or words. Then again, I wasn't forthcoming with my progress. I hadn't recalled anything new, but I'd relearned spells courtesy of Pam.

"Will the princess sleep on the floor?" I rolled my eyes, placing my hands on my hips. His smile cracked, reaching into his eyes as he lofted the mattress out the door. My eyes followed, landing on his perfect butt.

I returned to my spell writing. Something was missing still, but I'd read and reread it a hundred times. Jamie and Pam read over it too. The feeling ate at me, but no matter how many times I stared at it, I knew the spell wasn't complete.

Liam disassembled the frame when he returned, and the diversion grew too hard to ignore. Dang, he did it on purpose, letting his shirt ride up, stretching and flexing his muscles. All those tattoos called to me. I was a sucker for ink. "I can hear you."

His sensual tenor pricked against my skin. The highlight of my day revolved around any time we spent together alone. Whether I kicked his butt training or his embrace encompassed me.

Liam's shoulders tensed, and my face flushed. Hyperawareness settled in as the heat pooled in my center. I closed my eyes but saw the Myst. His smoldering scent burned through my walls. I could pinpoint his location no matter where he hid himself away.

The point of want and crave with desperation attacked. My whimpers begged, pleaded with Liam, to destroy the walls I'd built around myself. The scent burned deeper, the floor creaked with his footsteps. A phone rang, and Liam cursed. Saved by the ring, there was something familiar about that, and I blew my breath out in a steady stream.

His voice carried from the hallway, and I narrowed in on the sound. He'd tell me anyway, and privacy wasn't his reason for leaving. The sexual tension grew impossible to ignore, but somehow we made it through each day.

I chuckled to myself. Tonight that would change. My mind and body were ready for Liam to send my soul soaring to the depths.

"Yeah ... uh-huh ... dude whatever." My eyes opened as Liam stopped in the doorway. A dangerous glint in those green eyes sparked. I licked my lips, trailing my eyes over his tight t-shirt and down to those pesky jeans. He crooked his finger. "Jamie just figure it out. I'm busy."

"Bro keep it in your pants ..." was all I heard before Liam dropped the phone. With a thud, the plastic bounced off the runner rug and clattered. I leaned on my tiptoes and kissed his cheek.

In a hazy blur, Liam lifted me into the air and crushed me against the door. My hands wrapped into his hair and tugged him closer, dragging his thick lips to mine. Our eyes connected; his eyes yellowed and speckled with blue.

"Marry me," he growled. "Become ours," his three Mysts spoke as one. "Fainauriel Graftfield, I've never loved another in all the Nine Realms." Tears blinked from my eyes. He lowered me to the ground, shoving his hand into his pocket. Liam dropped to his knee and held out his trembling fist. "Marry me and stand by my side forever," he said, opening his hand. My mouth dropped. Set in silver, he handed me a topaz ring. The deep blue stone faceted the light; it sparkled and stole my breath. "Well?"

Yes, I wanted to scream, but words refused to leave my dumbfounded mouth. My head nodded, tears splattering on the floor. Liam's eyes widened, a stupid grin falling over half his face. He stole my hand and slipped the ring over my finger. His phone rang again, but Liam ignored it. Warm hands cupped my face and deep green eyes searched my face. "I love you, Liam."

I trembled not out of fear, but at the feelings rolling at me. My eyes glanced to my desk. The question remained when I reversed the spell would he feel the same. How easy I had walked away even if it wasn't simple. Before I remembered, the hardest thing for me was losing my parents. I loved them both, and that was painful, but it wasn't the hardest thing I'd ever overcome. The pain of losing Liam had been so great that I erased him from my memory.

At sixteen years old, I stared him in the eyes and said good-bye. Walking away from Liam then was torture. That was why I'd erased my memories too. I could not bear losing him, and he could not come with us.

I blinked as the memory resurfaced. It was not safe because he was a Fenrir.

"Love you too lil' darlin'. You; the sight, sound, smell … you drive me crazy, luv," he said, rubbing his nose against mine. His hands rested on my hips, and his thumbs rubbed circles over my jeans. I blinked slowly at the words. Every now and then, these quirky Brit sayings slipped from Liam's lips. He'd always been that way but I never understood why. The phone rang for a third time, and he groaned. "I better get that before someone shows up."

The doorbell rang. "Too late."

Liam answered his phone, and I scurried down the stairs for the door. My hand hit the doorknob when he yelled. "Don't open the door." *Too late again.* "There's a breach," he added. His boots clambered down the steps as I stared, gaping at the visitor. Clad in armor, his blue eyes bore into me. "Whoa," Liam said.

"Well now look at you all grown up and lovely," the dark-haired man said smiling. "And you must be William." He walked in, his metal suit rattling.

"Auriel who is that?" Liam whispered as the man shut the door behind him.

I shook my head. "About him …" His eyebrow cocked. Blue eyes swept over the house. "That's Sir Thomas Graftfield, Regent King of the Unseelie Court …" The first Paladin, the man responsible for the Light within me, and my great grandfather.

chapter
thirty-three

LIAM

"Great-grandfather?" He looked my age. I ran my hand through my hair, tugging at the strands. *Well there goes our celebratory plan.* Auriel smacked my arm and widened her eyes.

"Aye," he said in a strange blended accent of Alfheimian and British. "Call me Thomas." His eyes floated over the living room, and I shot a text to Dad, Nick, and Jamie. My phone chirped seconds later, and the front door opened. The Knight smiled and sat on the sofa. Auriel remained in shock, staring at him with wide eyes. "Fainauriel, come sit with me a spell."

Peering around the front door stood Nick. "Looks just like Danny," he whispered.

I blinked, glancing from the photos on the mantle to Thomas. Nick was right. They could've been twins. The same midnight hair and piercing blue eyes, but the elder Graftfield wore a trimmed beard.

Auriel hadn't moved, and I placed a hand on her shoulder. She flinched and glanced at me. My phone buzzed in my pocket, but I ignored it. "How … Why?" she whispered.

A horse whinnied outside. "Achilles," Thomas grumbled. We all jumped back as the black horse walked through the front door. Nick must've left it open. "I told you to stay put you drasted creature."

The animal snorted and tossed its head. I said, "Well then …" but didn't know what to say to the horse prancing in Auriel's foyer.

"Aye …" Nick said, scratching his blond head.

"Sorry children, I didn't mean to intrude." Clink and clatter followed as Thomas approached. "Mori—" He coughed, and his face twisted into a strained grimace. "The Queens are missing."

We exchanged glances. "Queens?" Auriel spoke first. "The Nine."

Thomas extended his hand toward my cousin and paused. "Nick," I offered.

"My apologies young lycan." He nodded, but his lips held tight as he grasped the reigns of his midnight-colored horse. Apologies over what, I had wanted to ask but bit my tongue. "There are two Faerie Queens of Alfheim, the Seelie and the Unseelie. Mori disappeared first, but she'd spent much time on Midgard. I haven't been able to reach her for some time now."

Auriel nodded, reaching toward his face. Her eyes pained, slanting, but not out of anger or distrust. "It's you; my white fire comes from you."

Thomas' black bearded mouth widened. His palm stretched out, and the gauntlet dropped. Yellow-white light poured from his hand. He brushed it against her cheek and touched her hair.

"You are shrouded wee one." Auriel's head cocked, but she said nothing. "Alfheim needs its monarchy; men can't rule the faerie courts, and the dragons grow out of control without them. Can you help us?"

My eyes shot to Nick at the mention of dragons. He shrugged. Auriel stared at her hands. *"Loki brought him. She fights against herself."*

"Yes, I'll try."

He ran the bare hand through her auburn locks. I reminded myself he was her kin, but the beast screamed in my head. My dry mouth swallowed him down.

"You have his hair," he said to her. She blinked, clenching my hand. The heat and slickness of her palm worried me. We'd both had plenty of excitement tonight between the engagement and him.

"Congratulations," he said, offering me his hand. He'd read my thoughts again.

I shook his bare hand, my brow twisting. "How'd you find us?" Thomas smiled at his great granddaughter. "I mean it's not like there's a map here." How'd Auriel ever find Six and Twenty? Nick winked at me.

"Me," she said. "The Nine knows I'm here, don't they? They've always known. The running was all for nothing."

"Aye," Nick answered.

I pulled Aurie toward the sofa. Her body trembled from head to toe. She did not fight me as I guided everyone from the sitting room to the den.

"Blood calls to family. Your light is a beacon, and it calls to the Dísir too," Thomas said.

Auriel held onto one thought, and she projected it loud and clear: This changed everything.

Worry creased her brow. I hoped it didn't change us. We all sat in her living room. She had spent a lot of time the past few weeks cleaning it up and removing the heavy dusty layers. Thomas tied up his horse outside and said he would return. As soon as the front door closed, I pounced.

"What does it change?"

Her eyes closed, and she leaned against me. "My family sits on the Nine Council." I brushed a stray hair behind her ear. "Duncan and Maeve Graftfield are close relatives. Four years ago, when I left, it was because of my great aunt Maeve. She's the one who wanted to sacrifice me."

Tears slid down her cheeks as Sir Thomas clattered back into the living room. The scowl held on his face had not surprised me. Most men didn't like when a woman wept.

"Eun beag, let me explain." Nick did, and I hung on to his spoken words and mental imagery. Her family had meant to murder her, and her great aunt held the one weapon that could end her life. A dagger made of Alfheimian metal, forged by the four winds and blessed by the three norns. The Myst created nothing without also creating a way to destroy.

Had he told my father about this weapon? Nick nodded, and my gut twisted at the thought of anyone harming Auriel. More than that, they held her mother and perhaps the Alfheim royals too. I agreed with her to buy time every day, but the Nine was too strong. We needed an army.

She clung to me, and I stroked her hair. We would have to find a way in and take the risks. Auriel's concern was me but mine had remained her. Getting in wasn't the problem, it was getting out.

"We kept running or at least that was the memory I'd implanted," she said. "I guess I did accomplish keeping my friends safe, but I gave up my freedom and all chance at a normal life." She sniffled and wiped her eyes. "I guess I never will know what normal feels like."

Kids flew through her mind, and I squeezed her tighter. Auriel wanted a family but feared her life too chaotic.

"Mori and I tasted the fugitive life. Before the Great Unseelie War, we ran between the various dwarven manors for years. The twins were just babes then."

"You weren't afraid they'd harm them?"

A wide smile cracked on his stony face. "I was scared shiteless, but we refused to live in the darkness of fear." I shifted, dragging Auriel upright and against my chest. "But I don't recommend it if avoidable."

"What changed?" Auriel asked.

Thomas leaned forward, flipping through a book on the table. In that moment, he appeared older and worn as a knight should have been.

"I lost a daughter in a skirmish. Your great aunt Nia dressed in my armor." A tear rolled from his eye. "The enemy thought her me and struck her down."

I cocked my head as I followed the replay of his memory. The fact he would even let me in baffled me unless he'd meant for me to relive his pain as a warning of what would come. *What having a family in peril times would bring us.* I asked, "Was having a family worth the risk?"

"Nia's unfortunate fate is the one part I would change." His grin returned. "I miss her now even after six hundred years."

Wetness drenched my shirt, and I sniffled too. Apart from Auriel and my mother, I'd never truly lost anyone before. She erased herself to ease the pain, and I was too young to remember my mother.

"That's my fear," she said. "I want a family, but my life …"

"My dear one, do not let fear block your road to happiness." The noisy knight rose from the couch and grasped Auriel's hand. "If you find someone to love, you hold onto them, and cherish your time together. Push forward, explore the boundaries, but do not let the dark world hold you prisoner." Auriel twisted toward him and parted her lips, but Thomas continued, "Fainauriel you are a gift as we all are. Each breath is on borrowed time, and we must chase our dreams and hopes."

I swallowed the lump forming in my throat. "He's right, darlin'. Your fears are real, but it doesn't mean we have to let them stand in our way." Nick nodded. "The same goes for me too. Let's start planning a jailbreak for your momma, and we can search for the Queens. We've trained for weeks now, and I think we're ready." I glanced over at my cousin again. "We might need Jamie on the inside."

Worry creased his brow. "I'll ask him."

"I shall not take more of your time." Thomas glanced to Nick. "Lycan, please show me to your nearest lodgings. The travel drained me."

He cleared his throat, amusement dancing in his blue eyes. "Nick and ye can crash next door."

"Crash?" Thomas repeated the phrase and shook his head.

"Sleep. Besides, the council will want to hear ... Better yet, ol' man, I better take ye to the safest place I ken." Nick turned his head toward the door. There's no way he was staying here. We'd an engagement to celebrate, and I doubted he'd want to have a third wheel with him and Jamie.

"The Oracle can't know he's here," Nick relayed to my head and I nodded, reaching into my pocket for keys. My dad's key came off, and I tossed it to him.

"I'll call Paulo," I said as he caught them mid-air. Nick handed it to Thomas, asking him to hold onto it. His clothing tore free before the Knight could ask why. He barked at him and pranced toward the door. While I doubted this was the first time Thomas saw a lycan, he hadn't been around Nick.

We said our good-byes and when the door closed, Auriel said, "You know he could read your mind, right?"

I grinned. "Good thing my thoughts were mostly pure." She reached up and kissed me, lacing her hands around my neck. I grabbed her butt and lifted her to me. My balance wavered, and we crashed into the door, giggling. "Ready to celebrate Future Mrs. Skyland?"

She murmured, brushing her full lips against mine. "You didn't set the bed up."

My brow lifted. "Who said anything about needing a bed?"

chapter
thirty-four

AURIEL

Liam carried me upstairs, nipping at my sore lips the entire time. Gods I loved my Guardian, and I needed him. Even before the distractions, I wanted this. I wanted nothing more than to think of him and our future. Not the tin man I called great-grandpa or my missing relatives. Not the Nine or my mother either, no, it was my future and me. We crashed through the hallway; he maneuvered blind as I blocked his vision. My hands dropped to his belt, and it dropped along the way. Liam pawed at my shirt, refusing to break the kiss, and drug it over my head. Our hearts hammered, beating in tune as our chests crushed together.

My bare back slammed against the cold wall, and a frame smashed over my head. Liam blinked as the blood trickled into our kiss. A minor cut, I was certain, but he broke away, confusion creasing his face. "I'm fine."

My eyes fell to the floor, and shards lay around his booted feet.

His warm hand massaged my breast, and he nibbled on my lip. "You're more than fine."

Glass crunched beneath his feet as he renewed his steps. The heavy air, coated with blood and arousal, tickled my nose. He crashed into a door, and I yelped as the knob hit my back. My arm twisted behind me, and I grasped at the intrusion until it opened. Darkness surrounded us, and my hand hit the wall, seeking a light. "Bathroom," he said against my lips.

I didn't want my first time in the bathroom. Liam groaned and slid me down. He sighed, leaning his forehead to mine. "Me either." Liam grasped my hands and pulled me closer. "I want you so bad it hurts."

His bulge pressed against me, but he placed my hand over his pounding heart. My body throbbed for him; I ached, my skin burning inside and out because of Liam. "I'll set the new bed up; don't move."

My mouth dropped to protest, but he left the bathroom. We could have used the other two rooms, but I stilled my heart, and took a deep breath. When I'd calmed down, I tiptoed, avoiding the shattered glass, and slipped into my room.

Searching my dresser drawers I sought for anything my younger self had kept that was sexy. I groaned as I came up empty handed. The door slammed downstairs, and I ran to my parents' room. Mom might have something, I thought, and tried not to think of my parents in that way.

Most of their old bedroom lay empty, unlike mine. The drawers were overturned, and the walls were bare. I turned, ready to give up, when I decided to check her closet. Nope, it too was bare of all except a few boxes.

"There you are," Liam said, sneaking up behind me. I jumped, falling against his hard chest. "Luv, we don't—" I turned, silencing him with my mouth. No memory lane tonight, but my lacy bra and thong would have to do. His hand dipped into my back pocket, pressing me against him. "You clothed or not does that."

I removed his hand and shoved it down my pants. Liam's fingers pushed the fabric of my underwear aside, and I shuddered, leaning into his touch. His fingers dipped between the folds. My hands tightened around his neck, needing to feel more of his flesh against mine, but it wasn't enough. I pushed him toward the door, frowning as he removed his hand.

Liam scooped me into his arms and carried me to my room. His old bed sat in front of the windows, but it seemed different in my small room. "I cheated and conjured it."

He plopped me on the bed and kicked off his boots. I crawled to his side, running my hands over his shoulders, and kissed his chest. He sucked in a breath as my head lowered.

Liam's eyes followed my movements, a hissing sigh releasing from his lips. I clawed away at his jeans in a breathless fury. Liam didn't stop me, but he didn't help either as he viewed my cavernous intent.

Freeing the beast proved half the battle as I settled back and stared, drinking in every inch of the man I loved. Gone was the body of the boy I left behind, and before me stood a God with ripples of muscled flesh.

"Yeah, yeah you know you're fucking hot," I said, and felt inadequate under his smoldering gaze. My eyes darted away as the inferno spread over my imperfect body. It settled and ignited into each curve and freckle covering my flesh.

"Come here." His voice was drunk and husky. Liam grasped my arm and pulled me into his warm embrace. "So what are you going to do now?" he asked with a wolfish smile that made my knees tremble.

My skin burned, and my teeth chewed my lip raw. I didn't know what to do. My eyes dropped to the floor. I understood how sex worked; I wasn't that naïve. But why me? Without warning, Liam pushed me onto my back.

His eyes burned yellow-green as his nostrils flared wide. Lowering his head, the heat of his mouth grazed my nipple. The jolt arched my back, but as I reached for him, Liam shied away. My legs grew heavy as the embarrassment spread, until I blazed inside and out. I closed my eyes, terrified and shaking.

Not again, I thought. I'd die if I saw that look on his face. The disgust and hatred Liam held in his eyes that day. My eyes burned in memory; my heart ripped asunder.

"Gods, your mind is broadcasting to the world and ruining my moment." I peeked, refusing to focus on his eyes.

Liam yanked his hand through his hair with a sigh. "What part of I love you didn't you understand, Auriel? That means ..." His mouth kissed the underside of my breast, and a soft moan escaped. His hands shucked my jeans as his tongue teased my nipples. New heat pooled between my dampened thighs as Liam's lips explored my sensitive flesh. "I love it here ..."

His tongue drew a trail down the swell of my stomach; my hands grasped his head wanting and not wanting the torture to continue. "And here ..."

Hands grazed my hips, tearing my panties away. A shiver rushed over my body, narrowing in on my center. I bit my lip and sucked in my breath as Liam delved between my thighs; I saw stars as his tongue flicked at my awaiting bud. My hands tightened, yanking at his hair as the squeal left my mouth. "I even love the way you taste, darlin', and I bet you ..." He tapped his chin and looked to the ceiling. "I bet you ..."

"Oh shut up," I rumbled, dragging Liam by his hair toward my grinning mouth.

"It'd be my pleasure to make you scream instead," he growled between the favoring kisses. "But I've never done this before either, princess, so don't go gettin' your hopes too high."

"Really?" His cheeks reddened, and my heart fluttered. "You waited?"

Liam nodded, his cock slid across my belly as he leaned in for a kiss. "I've waited my whole life just for you," he whispered. "Now stop stalling, darlin'." I giggled, until Liam's throbbing tip hit my slick entrance.

His mouth moved tight against mine, and I drank him up. Inching in, the sensation awakened the beast inside; the Phoenix attempted to rise, but I threw it back. This moment belonged to me. My hips bucked up as he increased the pressure. His legs shook and mine wrapped around his waist, pulling him closer, deeper. I groaned, and his mouth broke away.

"Are you alright, do you want me to stop?" he asked, leaning his dampened forehead against mine. My head tossed from side to side. "Good," he whispered. "'Cuz I don't think I could. You drive me crazy, Aurie luv."

His words caused my body to shudder. Ripples of pleasure rushed over my dimpling skin. He pressed further; we both sucked in our breaths. Tears stung as the stab of a hundred knives cut me from the inside. My teeth clenched, every muscle following as the sensation spread, stretching me with its burn.

"I'm sorry." He kissed my head. "We can stop." Liam's eyes glowed in the darkness, and I reached up to cradle his face. Stroking his cheek, he turned into my hand, nibbling my palm and trying not to move as my body adjusted.

"I'm alright now I—" Before I finished Liam moved inside of me. "— Yes," I murmured as each delicious stroke eased the pain away.

My hips moved to meet each thrust as he panted words into my ear. The hot breath ignited a fire in my core. Each plunge pushed me closer to the lights, blinding my vision, as a tidal wave built beneath my heated skin.

The tangle of our flesh and the salty sweet essence of our joining assaulted my nostrils. His hips twisted, rubbing me just right with each thrust. My insides flooded and pulsed, as a flash of violent colors erupted before my eyes. My muscles clenched hard, massaging Liam with each stroke. A cry erupted from deep within my soul as my body arched, shuddering its release. Our sweaty foreheads came together, as the levees of our love burst at the seams, molding ourselves into one.

"My Gods ..." Liam collapsed onto me, causing another wave of pleasure to flow through me. Words didn't exist as I kissed the top of his head. I might have just damned us all, but it was utterly worth it. "Gives new meaning to seeing fireworks."

The room brightened with our Myst as it ignited and exploded too. "What now Mr. Skyland-Fenrir or is it Fenrir-Skyland?"

"Maybe I'll take your name instead? Mr. Graftfield." I didn't care what name he chose, as long as he stayed mine. My hand pushed his hair aside. There wasn't a future worth saving without him.

We talked into the wee hours of the morning. Nestled against his chest, I allowed the gentle thrum to lull me asleep. By now I should've learned that every ounce of happiness led to the destruction. Tonight proved no different as the whispers of my mind began unfolding into a new nightmare.

"Find me," Kiel said. My eyes scanned around the bloodied battlefield of my dreamscape. We were victorious again, but not without losses. Dirty feathers rained from the sky as the wind whipped the stench of death across my face.

My nose curled. "Ezekiel," I shouted. "How can I find you?"

I walked up a boulder, hefting my worn boots and grimacing at the muscle strain. Peering over the scarred visage, I saw no sign of the winged warrior. A feather floated into my palm, and I stared at it. The tip, tinged in green, meant something.

My eyes fell to my feet, and I glanced down into a cavern. Crumpled near the dark mouth lay the body of a battle battered man. His blond hair matted with blood. My heart pounded, and I jumped down, rushing to his side. I turned the body over, careful not to crush his wings.

"Mom," he said, choking on blood. His mouth opened revealing fangs, and his eyes shone lavender. Confusion crinkled my face. A draugr called me mom. No, the fae couldn't become draugr without burning into ash.

The boy said, "Help me Auriel … find … him. Find Ezekiel."

Tears streamed down my face as I cradled him. I didn't know if I was his mother. What if this was the fate of any child I'd born into the world? My soul shattered, mourning the loss in this dream state because it mattered.

The loss of life mattered whether it was my blood or not.

"Luv," Kiel whispered over the wind. "Free me and save him."

I swallowed, understanding his words. "I'll free you."

Every life depended on me. Their souls depended on the Valkyrie. The least I could do was try, but where did I start first. I was only one person. Find Ezekiel, free my mother, find the Queens, defeat my family … the list grew endless. Whom did I help first? Could I help them all before we ran out of time?

I gasped for breath when I awoke. The sun blared through the window, and the clock flashed noon. Liam stood in the doorway, hair dripping and stark naked. His green eyes blazed, and his love-filled emotions rolled over my body.

"Mornin'," I said, forcing a smile. Those thick lips tightened. He strode into the room, feet stomping, and leaned over me. My heart fluttered, and my throat swallowed audibly.

His hand shook as he reached for my face. "Who is Kiel?" My mouth dropped, but what did I tell him. "You shouted his name in my ear and wouldn't wake up. I shook you for ten minutes." *Crap*. "Damn right darlin'."

I raised my fingers to his temples. "Can I show you?" Liam nodded, closing his eyes. He grimaced when our Mysts connected, and his teeth ground. A tear slid from his eye as the dying child replayed in both our minds.

I wiped it away, severing the connection. "Sweetie, I'm sorry," he said as his face softened. "I'm a lycan; we're jealous." Minty breath blew out, and I managed a small smile. "So you have to find him?"

My hand roamed through his wet hair. "Among other things. My house arrest needs to end, Liam I can't help anyone from here."

"I know." He winced. "But you can't leave me behind."

My arms pulled him onto me, and my lips brushed his. "You cannot go to the Nine. Your father will kill you if he finds out you're alive."

He scoffed and glanced away. "And they'll burn you at the stake or whatever the hell they planned."

"Maybe, maybe not, everything changed last night." I sighed. Just when I thought I had everything figured out ... "They know I'm here. Grandpa and Aunt Maeve can track me."

His head rested on my chest, and he kissed my breasts. "They sent Wardens—"

"Didn't find me. That's curious isn't it?" He mumbled his response, encircling my nipple with his warm tongue. "You're distracting me."

He batted his lashes. "Want me to stop?" *No.* His teeth grazed my nipple, and I arched into his naked body.

"No, but I need a shower." Liam raked his teeth over my other nipple, and I squealed. "Join me."

His grin spread. It didn't matter he'd finished his bathing. We stumbled under the spray, and for a split second, I missed his shower. All those fancy heads beating their hot streams over my achy muscles were nothing compared to a hot lycan's hands. I leaned against the cold tile and lifted my leg onto the shower seat. Liam entered me without resistance, but the soreness remained.

My breath sucked in as his arms wrapped around me, and dragged my back to his chest. His lips dropped to my ear, whispering his love as my body adjusted. The scent of wet wood burned my nose; it overpowered, but laced with wet dog. Liam chuckled at my thoughts and mentioned dousing himself with cologne. I leaned away, mocking disgust as a throaty moan left his lips. My body bent forward, and my hands rested on the seat. He moaned louder as I wiggled my ass against him.

Slowly he rocked forward, thrusting in time with my hips. My head hung as my back arched to meet him. Nails scratched the tile as I sunk my teeth into my lip. The screen door slammed downstairs, followed by footsteps on the stairs, but they stopped before descending. Voices called for us below, but with Liam mid thrust, I didn't want to deal with anything –or anyone – right now. Liam slowed his strokes. My whimpers slipped into soft moans as he claimed me from behind. Liam's hand worked over my clit, building the pressure in my belly, but I couldn't release with visitors below.

"Shh, it's only Paulo and Reggie," Liam answered my concerns. My eyes widened, and I turned my head. Was that supposed to relieve me? His head dropped to my ear. "Take a rain check?"

What the heck was that supposed to mean? His speed increased, and his nails dug into my hips. I gasped, clawing at the shower wall. "Yes." Liam bit into my shoulder. Copper tainted the air as his teeth broke the skin. My teeth gritted, relishing in the combined pain and increasing pleasure. "Harder," I panted, thrusting my ass backward. My insides tightened as my head flung into the wall. I shattered, screaming and scraping at the tile.

"Mine," Liam whispered, slamming into me and holding my hips steady as he erupted. "You … are … mine." My eyes flickered to the ring, and I smiled. Yeah, I was his. I'd find Kiel to save the child, but Liam was it for me, and now I bared his mark to prove it.

He pulled back, and I turned in his arms. I blinked as dizziness swept over me. Gods, he was gorgeous. His fingers danced over my shoulder, and I followed his movements. His bite didn't heal, and I didn't care. Like most myths, the werewolf bite was false. It took a lot more to become a lycan, including Loki's blessing and a reason. I was already immortal.

Our visitors knocked on the bathroom door. Regin giggled as Paulo cleared his throat. My cheeks flamed even as the now icy water rolled over me. "You both get clothed … properly," Paulo said.

Liam coughed, covering up his laughter. "Sure Dad, see y'all soon."

"I trust you will not delay us long, kids."

I worked hard stifling my giggles as Liam's mouth found mine. The tang of my blood tainted his lips. His dripping hair brushed down into my eyes, and I raked it back. The heat of him encompassed me, and I didn't want to leave.

"I love you," he said.

"We should go ... before we don't." Liam's wolfish smile returned. Was he trying to rewrite the definition of humping like rabbits? "Something like that," he whispered in my ear.

My eyes darted around the bathroom floor. "Where are my clothes?"

"Shh." Liam smiled, leaning over and grabbing my clothes from the floor. I reached for them, but he drew his hand back. "Wait you can't wear those." He smirked and dropped them under the spray.

My hands fell to my hips. "William Donovan Skyland."

"Two can play that game, darlin'." My eyes narrowed, and Liam laughed at me. "Okay babe, I'll be good."

He shut the water off and wrung out my clothes before casting a spell. I watched as his Myst danced in the air. The fascinating part was he didn't use the fire at all, unless he shifted. When he cast spells, Liam dug into his earth Myst.

"You really don't know." My eyes widened. I'd hinted to him about the fire but hadn't told him more.

He crooked his brow. "What don't I know?"

I explained everything I noticed from the shifting to the triple nature. But I didn't see the fire then, and now it made sense. Liam tapped into the Phoenix when shifted as a lycan, and I'd rarely seen him in that form.

He handed my clothes over, and we dressed. "So you're saying someone took his Phoenix and put it inside me without me knowing?"

Rusty brows creased, but the worry rolled off him. We had a similar conversation the other day, but he ran out before I could explain my theory. "Why'd anyone do that?"

I shrugged. "I think I can fix it, unless—"

Liam spat, "I don't want it."

"But can we trust Jamie with it?" He had froze them both. Granted, he'd tried running away, and they'd attacked him first. Plus, he'd started learning how to call on the air. I'd hate to see his progress dissipate. Liam glanced to me, studying my mind and, I was certain, my thoughts.

"I trust him even though every time I do it bites me in the ass." He smirked, leaning in to kiss me, but I wasn't thrilled. Without knowing who threw the ice, who was to say we weren't giving him more ammo to use against us. We lacked evidence against him and my grandmother, but at least they weren't working together. I didn't want to empower Jamie and have him hurt Nick, Liam, me, or anyone we cared about.

"Darlin', the only way to hurt me is to leave me." He grasped my chin. "Promise me you'll stay with me … forever." Liam's nose rubbed against mine, and I searched his soul for the truth in his words. He loved me as I was. Liam wasn't chasing that silly girl who thought she had to die because of some misconstrued prophecy.

"I promise you, William Donovan Fenrir-Skyland that I will never leave your side unless Freya herself commands it upon my death." I placed my hand over his heart, which was an act of oath Nick taught me. "Swear upon that which you cherish above all else," Fenrir had said.

"I promise, Fainauriel Graftfield that I will never, ever leave your side unless Loki commands it upon my death." Liam's lips kissed mine as his hand rested on my thundering heart. "No man, woman, supernatural … etcetera shall ever come before you in my life, for you are my world, and the light that illuminates it."

In the eyes of our patron Gods, I was his, and he was mine.

"Now stop fretting over Jamie, my wife." Liam lifted me into his arms and showered my neck with kisses. I giggled, squirming under his attacks. But as we stepped through the threshold, a nagging sensation overwhelmed me, striking through my shield.

I glanced around, seeking out the source, but we were alone. My eyes skittered to Liam's smiling face, and the black pools bore through to my soul. I bit my lip and willed the Myst to calm my trembling hands. How long had Liam been possessed by another Dísir?

chapter
thirty-five

JAMIE

My hands rubbed down my face, as my breath blew out in a hiss. I should've taken her down after she fled the city; I should've done my damn job. Damn my emotions and my conscious for not taking Auriel into the Nine like my mission required. Playing nice didn't get me anywhere but hurt, confused, and discarded. Just like Dad.

Nick, I snorted. I grew tired of his games, of his existence and hold over my heart. Back and forth, hot and cold ... understanding the beast had proved impossible. The door slammed behind me, as I stepped onto Liam's back porch. After this week, I was at a loss of what to think. He'd kissed me. Nick tackled me in front of my brother and the whole world to see. Everything I'd worked for hung by a thread, and the Oracle wouldn't think twice about throwing my sorry ass to the dogs. She'd hated me long before Auriel had fled, and I didn't understand why.

We all loved Auriel. My hand smacked the railing, and the sting radiated through my palm. Why'd the Oracle single me out? Whether I wanted it or not, I was Nicky's until one of us died because then the other would die too. I sighed and leaned over the railing. The sun beat down on my neck, and I relished the burn of the springtime heat. The thickness of the air grasped and suffocated, snuffing out my light. But life had still coursed through my vein; I should've known better than to think Nick had died in the massacre. A dream for a normal life, I surmised and grilled the notion into my head.

"We aren't normal," the Oracle spoke behind me. I hadn't heard the scuffle of her walker. "Careful boy, you're sounding like my granddaughter."

Aurie used to daydream about human life. It didn't make sense why she envied them growing up, but understanding her destiny shed new light on her dark world. Shadows surrounded us. The blocks built high and wide, and it wasn't fair to put it all on her shoulders. Nick and I agreed even if we didn't speak about her future.

"I never thought I'd see a day where I agreed with a Mc Douglass," Keelan said in a rather warm and inviting voice, for her. Every hair managed to stand on alert. She placed a bottle, not just any bottle, down on the railing. My lips licked and eyes widened at the liquid golden fortune of the Graftfield line. Twenty-year-old scotch called, demanding I sample its secrets.

"I'd hardly call it an agreement," I replied and lifted the bottle to my trembling lips. The pungent scent flared my nostrils, burning my eyes like fresh smoke; the amber drug swirled in the bottle like liquid fire. I took a swig from the bottle, and the smoky, heather-honeyed smolder slid down my itching throat, soothing my shaky hands. Gods – I'd missed this – cheap shitty crap didn't light a candle to Graftfield scotch whiskey. Danny wouldn't miss it, seeing as he was six feet under.

I flinched at my thoughts. Danny deserved better; he was a better man than I'd ever become. The unconditional love he held for his daughter spoke as such proof. I couldn't muster even a smidgen for my soul mate. Nicky deserved better too, but he was stuck with my sorry worthless ass.

"We're known for our scotch. Now that ain't no firewater. Sir Thomas brought it." I nodded, deducting another sip from the fancy bottle. If only the scotch would block out her annoying voice then I could relish in the contrast of flavors dancing on my tongue.

I faced her, leaning my back against the railing. My legs crossed, and I met her wrinkled gaze. "What do you want, Keelan?"

She had torn my world apart, piece by piece, until nothing but my shell remained. The fact Keelan approached me meant one thing: the crone was desperate. The Oracle stuck me between rocks though. I couldn't call to Liam or Nick without alerting her too. She would block it or knock me out again.

"I want to call a truce." *Ha, not going to happen.* But the pesky voice in my head told me to hear her out.

"Uh-huh." My eyes rolled, and I brushed invisible lint from my t-shirt.

"And what would that entail?" I sampled another sip and enjoyed the inferno pulsing through my veins. Where was Nick when I needed him? He had promised to keep her away from me. The biggest hurdle we tried to jump but failed was coming out. How'd he save me from the backlash when he wasn't around? I wiped the bottle over my sweaty forehead.

She glanced toward the back door. The knob moved and then stopped.

"Merric and my husband want Auriel in Charlestown. Duncan says she isn't safe here anymore."

My eyes narrowed and squinted down at the Oracle. Had she forgotten whom I worked for? The freaking Nine Council remained the true danger. Besides, Auriel had surrounded herself with two Fenrir lycans, a draugr, and the first Paladin ever created to boot. Did the Nine fear King Thomas? *I sure as hell did.* The man sweated power, and his touch scorched my skin, not to mention the power Aurie held. I choked on the expensive scotch, and the witch pounded on my back. "Good luck with that."

"Jamie, I'm a very patient woman, as you should know by now. If we can't bring the horse to the water then perhaps we can bring the water to Charlestown." I wondered how true that was. Did she actually think herself capable of capturing a two hundred and forty pound, six-foot-seven lycan-Mage Guardian hybrid? *The only way she'd go to the Nine without a fight.* Her mother was prisoner and apparently her grandmother too, but she wasn't jumping at the bit to rescue either of them.

The thought stirred my stomach and the bile rose. It would have to be Liam. Hell, she'd not go to those lengths for Nick, Regin, or even me. My brow rose as I thought, *give me some of what she's drinking.* "With your help, I can succeed."

My eyes fell to the grass. I did not want her to succeed. Aurie belonged here until she figured out her own messy life. Nicky all but burned the notion into my brain. But the dark side stayed intrigued and the voice grew louder.

"And what exactly do I get for helping you?"

"Your Phoenix back, recognition for helping to save the world." Her eyes narrowed, and she elbowed my ribs. "And anything else you want, eh-eh."

I chuckled and glanced to my feet. What I wanted ... Did I want freedom from Nick's bond? I swallowed hard and stared at my feet. Did I desire open acceptance of our relationship? My eyes closed, and I zoned in on my beating heart. *"Maybe it's time to let it go,"* the wind whispered.

What did the wind mean, let go of his control or of my fears? The wind didn't reply. The back door swung open. Auriel stepped out, her face twisted into a scowl. She wrapped her arms around her body and ran to me with widening eyes that darted between her grandmother and me.

"Jamie, I need to speak with you ... alone." I clasped her shoulder and led her away. Keelan didn't say anything, nor did she smile. Her head nodded, slow and knowing.

"What's the matter?"

"I think Liam—" My hand flew up on its own accord. Whatever happened between them wasn't my business. I didn't want to know about my brother, and I'm sure he didn't want to hear about my bedroom adventures.

"You made your choice." My body shook, as she said each word, and the awareness finally settled in. Darkness snapped inside. Lights flashed, blinding my vision, and I fell to the ground. The tendrils shoved into my eyes and ears. I saw nothing but inky oceans and the muffled sounds of its crashing waves.

"Choice?" Auburn brows rose and fell.

My hands reached out, and I sought anything solid. "What's happening to me?"

Auriel cried, "Jamie ..." but her words cut into the rushing static.

Nick appeared on the shore. "Ye ne'er loved me." I crawled closer; his voice rumbled, as my blood ran hot. "Everything we had meant naught to ye."

Tears glistened in his eyes. Nicky's lips quivered ever so slight, but my liquid courage screamed through my veins. As I turned to leave, he whispered, "Let it go."

"No," I screamed. The words stopped my heart, and my hand flew to it. Not loved, but love. If I faced him now, I'd never leave. My body betrayed me, knees growing weaker. Digging deep, under each level of pain, hidden under all the imperfections and the lies, I found my words.

"Of course I love you."

He stared down at his rough upturned palms. "No, ye daenna love me and maybe I daena love ye either." His legs stepped backward into the dark waves, and he disappeared. There were no words, as the hot iron of the words sliced through my soul.

"Let it go ..."

My hands clutched at my stomach. It churned, growing uneasy with each breath. The air turned stale, and my mouth filled with cardboard. My shoulders heaved, and the muscles in my back screamed in protest. I couldn't let him go. How do you give up on your heart and soul? No, I would fix it.

Gods, I would save us even if it meant destroying me.

"Jamie." Auriel's words were the lightest of breezes. "Don't do this. He's your love. You love him."

The heat of her body grew closer, as if she were the rising sun. "I'm sorry. I'm sorry ..." That phrase I had whispered repeatedly throughout my life. It did not stop me from ruining everything my tainted hands touched.

Everyone I loved suffered. The white light burned through the shrouded dark recesses of my mind. I gazed into her smoldering eyes laced with concern. Her head cocked to the side, exposing her neck, and her puffy lips tugged into a shy smile. Liam marked her, but instead of celebrating, here she was saving my worthless ass again.

"I'm sorry too," Auriel said, as I reached for her hands. The surge of her beneath my flesh ignited a fury. Let go. "This is going to hurt, sweetie." She grasped my head in her hands, but nothing happened. "I see it; I swear I do ... teine ... thior ... tearnaich ..."

Fire, grab, let go …

Auriel chanted the words, as her flames ignited the curse tied into me. The wall grew with each pulse of the Myst. A scream erupted from my throat, as the pain sliced through me, but she refused to let go.

"Hurts, please, please," I begged, standing up and pulling away. My knees weakened, body wobbling on gelatinous legs. Wetness blinked, rolling and sizzling upon my cheeks, as she burned me alive.

"Be strong, Jamie." Her nails dug, searing my flesh. "This is all my fault, let me fix it, Gods, give me the strength," she prayed aloud. My body shook, and I lost my balance. On unsteady legs, we dropped as one to our knees, but Auriel did not stop, her onslaught continued.

"Almost … don't give up on me yet, Jamie." My eyes shut tight, jaw tensing against the pain. "Never give up," she whispered the last part, and my eyes opened wide. Crystal unblinking blue eyes stared back at me. Gods she was as beautiful as an angel; Aurie was an angel, a valkyrie angel.

"I can't … Aurie …" My chest seized; I struggled to breathe. The darkness battled hard against her, and I feared she wasn't powerful enough. No one held the power to save my tarnished soul.

"Nicky, I need you. Brother, Auriel needs you." I sent out the thought, hoping to the Gods that they came.

chapter
thirty-six

PAULO

The explosion rocked the house, pictures rattled and crashed from the walls, and the scent of burning flesh tickled my sensitive nose as I ran outside. The chaotic source sat at the end of the winding driveway. In the street, Auriel held Jamie's head in her hands. A wall of yellow-orange inferno encircled them. People from the town pointed shaky fingers and witnessed the event with widened eyes. Whether she was harming my eldest son, I didn't know.

"Auriel let him go," I cried out to her, but she didn't stop. She didn't glance up or shake her head. The heat blistered my skin when I stepped closer. I winced; the beading bubbles formed and exploded over my flesh.

"Keelan." My strangled voice called for the Oracle, but she wasn't on the street. "Where is she? Where is the Oracle?"

The only responses I received were shrugs, as more citizens watched on. Reggie approached; her scent alone I picked out of the crowd. Peaches, leather, and ice were not enough to calm the combined storms attacking from opposite directions.

"Nicky says we have to let her do this," Regin whispered in my ear. I turned toward her; our cheeks brushed. Blue eyes blinked and quickly glanced away. "Auriel will save him and restore his Phoenix. He also mentioned darkness."

My eyes widened at the term. As a human, I knew of one God. Everything else held a death sentence in Spain. Reborn into this existence and over five hundred years of this life taught me much more. Theology aside, the Myst –the source of all supernatural – created Darkness, as it created Light. Channeled by the Gods, it created new races, but it was the Fae and their cousins who learned its secrets, and spread it to the four corners of the universe. Much of modern religion found its roots within the Myst and Odin.

Regin's heart rate soared and fingers wrapped and twirled her blond hair. Heat radiated from her arm as it dangled dangerously close. *Gods but Poroflr would rise from the dead for even thinking about his daughter.*

"Even to defeat the Darkness …" My hand fell to my mouth as Jamie pled and drew my attention. Tears streamed down his soot-covered face. "I won't sacrifice my son."

Reggie gulped, but my eyes refused to budge from the scene. A cry ripped through the crackle of the flame; Auriel sprouted massive brown wings, shining with the sheen of white fire. Valkyrie; few understood the power they possessed before they crossed over. I wiped the ash from my face. Humans would've called them Angels.

Their magic purified any wickedness, but few realized their real purpose, or the two warring sides. They guarded the Nine Realms, created to serve and protect the Gods, but they answered to the Myst before all others.

"Dad what's –" Liam's eyes scanned the street, and he ran through the flames, grasping both Auriel and Jamie.

Auriel shouted, "No" and screamed, "Nickolas." The Fenrir appeared from nowhere and joined in the circle.

Soft fingertips brushed my hand. "The Phoenix protects them," Reggie said with awe as the flames built higher, blocking the vision. We were at the mercy of Fainauriel Graftfield, and I was outright powerless to stop her, as she wielded the fiery Myst. My mouth dropped at the realization. I, a draugr, was not immune to her Myst.

I'd met Valkyrie before with their cold black eyes. Auriel's eyes were golden. From the steam rose a man. Regin asked, "What is that?"

"No, it can't be," someone else murmured as my eyes widened.

But it was, and Aurie was wrong. That wasn't darkness. A man, the spirit, the ethereal… a Dísir rose from the inferno like a shining beacon of gold. I blinked, as the crowd gasped. The naked man solidified as his feet touched the earth.

"I have no clue, te amo."

chapter
thirty-seven

AURIEL

"Gu bràth gam fìor, dìleas gràdh liubhair pòg dìleas rùn!" My words cracked like lightening through the thundering sky. Smearing my sweaty brow, I drew strength from within and the Gods themselves. The words tumbled me into a vision of the past:

The wind blew against the window, and rattled the frame with its words. It shattered. A young woman, a younger me, with fiery, unruly hair stood in its alcove. The rain poured around me, adding to the sorrow that reflected in my eyes.

"Gu bràth gam fìor, dìleas gràdh liubhair pòg dìleas rùn," I whispered in a voice that echoed my own in the present. As the Gaelic phrase left my lips, a crimson Myst flowed from my fingertips, as I invoked the Phoenix. Whether my current actions repeated this process, I didn't know. I saw the past alone, as the words left my lips.

My eyes fell to Jamie. My mind and body became one, as I clutched his head in my hands. His eyes widened, as the flames slowly died. My lip curled up into a smile.

"It worked ... It *actually* worked." The blood rushed from my head; my body swayed, and I struggled to keep my eyes open. At least I succeeded, but I required a good rest and recharge.

"Auriel, are you alright?" Jamie asked, as my eyes fluttered closed. Feet shuffled, gasps, and more noise came closer. The fading energy closed in on me.

"What is that? Where did it come from?" Their murmuring voices reached my ears. "Dísir!" someone shouted, but I lacked the strength to turn my head.

My mouth opened wide into a yawn. "Need rest." I crumbled to the asphalt, before the words left my mouth. Hands caressed my face; they were too soft to belong to Liam or Nick. Everything dulled, touch, smell, even my shield went kaput like the inferno.

"Get your hands off her," Jamie said, and I tried to open my eyes. The arms, too warm and comforting, held me tighter.

"Mate, I'll give you three seconds to—"

"Eun beag, what did ye do to him?" My eyes flashed open. Everyone stared. Their gaze jumped between my Guardian and me, and I followed it.

My jaw dropped. "Ezekiel," I mouthed starring into his cold blue eyes. "No …" I smacked him, until he'd put me down. Dreams aside, he was not my enemy, but it gave him no right to manhandle me. My eyes narrowed on him.

"What did you do?" Kiel shrugged, and I turned to my Guardian. His eyes were wide but unmoving. "Liam, wake up. Gràdh dùisg!"

My lips connected with his, but it did not change his frozen state. The power within me had drained

"Auriel–" Paulo said but stopped and scratched his head. "What happened?"

My face twisted, as I walked around his solid body. My eyes raked up and down but found nothing. I glanced to Kiel who shot from Liam's body. His eyes burned through me, following each movement. There were questions, but nothing mattered more to me than fixing Liam.

"What happened?" Paulo repeated again and grabbed my arm. Dizziness washed over me, and I shook the lightheadedness aside and focused. My brow rose, as I stared at his pale hand clasping my arm. *That's what I wanted to know.* Nothing I said or cast would have frozen Liam. I scratched and shook my head, ignoring Paulo and Nick. My eyes fell to the naked Kiel and raked over his flesh. He didn't even try to hide himself.

The Myst, the answer lay in the magic. My eyes closed, noting Liam had two signatures now. The missing link ... Where there was once Liam, now there were two: Liam and Ezekiel. Was he trapped inside all along and reaching out through the dreams? His brow cocked in response to my unvoiced question.

"You can hear me," I said. He nodded. Just peachy and here I'd just gotten used to Liam and Nick knowing my thoughts. Could I hear Kiel? He shook his head and smirked.

"I didn't do this," I said, biting my bottom lip and refusing to look at anyone. My hands trembled, as my skeletons rattled. It didn't matter what they thought.

"Yes ducky, you did," Kiel whispered, grasping my shoulders. His British accent made him sound like a pompous ass. No, that wasn't a fair assessment at all. We stared each other down, and I fought to keep my eyes north of his equator.

"I did not." My teeth gritted. His hand reached to brush my cheek, and I turned away.

Jamie called his brother's name. He received the same response, which was absolutely nothing. Nick tried too, and I fought the urge to roll my eyes. As his charge, he'd respond to me if he could. At least I hoped for as much, but maybe we were all wrong.

"Plan B then." Paulo stomped away. Inky hair blowing in the stiff breeze. I tilted my head and attempted to place my hands on my hips but the energy to move faltered.

Jamie answered the question before I asked it. "Plan B ... Oh, this is bad. He's putting us on lockdown."

"Where's my grandma?" He shrugged, shoving his hands in his pockets. "You're a terrible liar," I muttered under my breath.

He couldn't hear me, only Nick and Kiel did, but they were too busy sizing each other up. I was too busy trying to fix my husband and didn't care if Fenrir ripped the Valkyrie to shreds. Someone needed to pay, and I needed a nap before I finally confronted Keelan Graftfield.

We stood in Liam's room, where Nickolas was kind enough to tote my frozen husband. Paulo insisted we all stay under one roof since the accident, everyone except Sir Thomas. We had kept him concealed, fearing the Nine would capture him too. I was terrible and had not visited him either. My hands covered my face, and I fought the tears as I sat on the mattress. No matter what I did or did not do, everyone in my life found themselves burned, frozen, or dead.

As the hours passed, Kiel sat with me but sat on the arm of the chair. Nothing changed with Liam as his wide, green eyes stared. My lip quivered; eyes had long past cried out. No matter which way I twisted this situation the blame rested on my shoulders. Worse ... the pull ... was gone.

If I had not casted the spell ... if I hadn't left him four years ago. Ezekiel shifted to the edge on the bed. Fingers reached for me, but I scooted away. Whatever the future held for us it was not now. I was Liam's, and he was mine. Better or worse and frozen fell under worse. Broken bond was worse too.

"You're wrong, princess." I raised my hand, preparing to hit him when he grabbed my wrist. "I'll say this once, so you best listen missy." His eyes searched my face, as I trembled under his grasp. "I was Liam, and Liam was me. We can survive apart. If you're his—" Ezekiel's eyes drifted to my Guardian, "—you are mine too."

My stomach churned at the thought, and the bile scorched my throat. I shoved Kiel aside and ran for the bathroom. My chest heaved, heart thundering and breaking all at once. *Why?* I didn't want this. *Gods, did you hear me?* After rinsing my mouth and splashing water on my face, I left the bathroom. My eyes connected with a worried Ezekiel; I tried making sense of his words. Tried figuring out who and why too but to no avail. Dísir but was he born or created? Could someone knock mine out too?

"It was inevitable, poppet." I blinked and wrapped my arms, hugging myself tight. Exhaustion warred within and battled against pity, doubt, and angst.

"The Oracle came by; she wishes to speak with you," Paulo said with void of emotion from the hallway. I leaned on the doorframe to the bathroom and rubbed my arms. He did not need to voice his emotion. His anger and resentment vibrated thicker than fog. The fault rested upon my shoulders. I had brought chaos to his peaceful town again and assaulted one son while freezing the other.

Yeah, I didn't like me either.

"I'll be right down," I whispered, and he turned to leave. With everything that went down, I'd forgotten about his memory too. Although I doubted he wanted me casting spells on him. "Paulo, do you remember me yet?"

He cleared his throat. "Yes, child after your display in the road my memory returned." His eyes shifted to Liam and then to Kiel.

I winced at his statement. "I didn't come back to do this; I'm sorry, Paulo." His brown eyes softened. "I'm in love with Liam."

He nodded, as Kiel cleared his throat. I blew out my breath and glanced to my feet. When did my life spiral out of control? I'd bitten off far more than I could chew.

My head dropped, and Paulo walked to me. His cold arms drew me to his chest. "Your dad – he'd be proud." My eyes stung at his mention. "I love my boys, you know that, but I was wrong to judge you." He sighed, and I tried not to wipe snot on him. "You can't help what happened."

I couldn't help what I was either.

Paulo stepped away, and I wiped my eyes. "I made him remember." My body shook. It wasn't the whole truth. Liam wanted the memories, but he did not press me. I'd feared he'd change his mind and rush the process. "I cast the memory spell in the first place too."

His head cocked. "How long?" His frail body tensed, as those brown eyes turned red. "Damnit girl how long have you remembered? Did Liam know?"

I flinched as he lunged for me. Before I could step back, Ezekiel jumped in front of me. Paulo curled his lip in disgust.

"Don't you bloody threaten her," Kiel said, and I stepped back. The power radiating off him almost equaled mine. Almost. His hand touched my shoulder.

Paulo laughed, revealing his extended fangs. "Your presence is a threat … demon."

My heart pounded as their emotions raged. I shrilled, "Over a month. Liam and Jamie know." I tried to ease the growing tension.

Paulo stepped toward Kiel and bared his fangs again. The two circled each other, as my heart rate skyrocketed. Liam would know what to do or … *"Nick, I need you!"* But he didn't respond.

"You could've trusted me." Paulo swung at Kiel, and I swallowed the rising bile again. "It'd make running this community easier, but it is lies upon half-truths. Does she know? Or was that a game too?" His finger pointed downstairs, and Ezekiel rushed Paulo, tackling him to the ground.

I froze, trembling as they fought. Punches flew and words jumbled. They moved too fast, and I didn't know who was who. The rage tainted the room in a heavy red Myst. My lungs struggled to breathe, and I lacked the energy to create a shield. Knees slammed into the hardwood floor, and the sting radiated into my bones.

"Stop it! Gods … no more, I can't take this." Friends hurting friends, family betraying family … it ended now. My eyes widened, and I shook my head so fast it hurt.

"It's her isn't it?" Paulo asked himself and backed away from him. Ezekiel spat blood on the floor.

I replied, "Larger than my grandmother." I stared at my hands, folding and unfolding them, and trying to figure out how to say this cryptic-like. "All signs point to it, but why not hurt me now?"

Everyone had to realize my weakness: Guardianless and running on empty. The knife wasn't the only weapon that destroyed me. Paulo cracked his neck and released tension, as I awaited a reply. All he gave me was a long sigh, before he descended the stairs.

"Emotional pain is deadly." I turned to follow Paulo, but Kiel reached for me. He held my gaze hostage. "Imagine spending twenty some years trapped in another body." His hands cradled my face, and his finger smoothed over the skin. "It's inevitable that Liam would fall in love with you, as he protected me. Just like it was foreseeable that I'd become smitten beyond reason with you." I opened my mouth to speak, but his finger slid down to cover my lips. A spark exploded. "It was unavoidable that you'd love him instead of me."

The sob caught in my throat. I backed away, but my eyes remained on his. The dreams ... the reality ... which was the right path? My lip trembled, dropping on its own. I took another step and shook my head.

What Kiel said made no sense. Which one was the Guardian? His eyes shifted to Liam. That was who I loved, whom I was supposed to love. I had to save him. Nothing could stand in my way, because without him, I was nothing.

"Aurie?" I raced for the door but paused in the entryway.

No. My eyes stung, but not from his words. Somehow, even though I wanted to scream and call him a liar, he was right. As impossible as it seemed, Kiel and Liam were at one time the same person, and now they weren't.

"Wait," Kiel said. "Bloody hell, I won't press you, ducky." As the words left his lips, a veil lifted and exposed his pain. My head tilted into a nod, my eyes watering and burning. I hurried down the stairs, before the sobs overtook me; the floodgates unleashed within. The truth shattered inside of me as I clutched the banister. Each piece sliced through my heart and soul.

My knuckles whitened, as the wood gave underneath my grasp. It broke free, as I released a scream. My heart thundered, and I opened my mouth again to release the pressure. My eyes widened as Paulo approached, and my hands filled with fire. The Oracle waited by the front door, but I pushed past her. Air ... breathe ... I bypassed the porch just in time for my wings to snap free. My knees crumpled to the earth, and my arms opened wide. I tossed my head back and cried out again.

"Too much, too soon ..." their whispers reached my ears, and I agreed. My eyes closed, leaking the tears I'd held. "Why? Why do I always screw up?"

A buffet of air danced over my skin. There was no need to open my eyes. I sensed his magic like my own. Water not fire.

Elation – wasn't that what most people felt when they'd found the one? Why was I filling with sorrow and ache? If I'd left well enough alone, but I didn't understand.

The ground shuddered beneath my legs, and I peeked up at Kiel. *"Gods, so beautiful."* His lips curled into a smile, as he crouched down and stroked my face. My vision flashed back to the dream, and his wings wrapping around my body, and then to the child. "This wasn't my intention, luv. I ne'er meant to hurt you."

His hands reached for mine, and our fingers entwined. My skin hummed, and our essences combined, flowing in perfect symmetry in and out of my body. His lips fell to my forehead, increasing the connection. A burn spread over my cheeks, and I struggled to breathe under the thrum of his power refilling and touching down to the depth of my blackened soul.

Cold drops of rain pelted us from above. Neither of us moved. I didn't want Kiel to let go, and I fought not to touch my lips to his. A growl rose in my chest, and it urged me to claim him. My hands moved to his shirt, grasping the cotton, and dragging him closer. His lips slid down to kiss my nose before pulling away.

His blue eyes darkened. "Shield yourself," he said before flying away. I blinked and touched my fingers to my lips. My head tilted, as understanding connected within my mind. I'd channeled and acted on his emotions not my own.

My breath blew my hair from my eyes, and I lifted my palms. He'd leant me his Myst. The electric blue essence rolled over my aching skin. I glanced at the skyline, searching for signs of his white wings. Emptiness, not even a fluffy cloud to trick my eyes, lay before me.

"Fainauriel ..." the Oracle called my name, but my knees sank deeper into the muddy lawn. The water pelted harder, sheeting and stinging my skin. His emotions poured from the heaven-filled blue sky. The acid of his pain melted my flesh. "Listen to him."

I glanced over my shoulder toward the porch. She rested against her walker under the protection of the overhang. A smile plastered over her face, and for the first time I sensed that it was genuine. My head shook, as I recalled his words. Shield ... yes. I pulled his Myst into me, until it paled into a sky blue, and built the protection around my body.

Grandma lifted me up into an embrace, but my muscles stiffened. Her touch burned like venom. My stomach churned recalling the same chilling smile right when she released her icy Myst by the stream. It had to be her.

"I tried to stop it, child. We love you, but it wasn't enough." Her words rocked my mind, and I shook my head. Who was we, and what did we try to stop? Grandma shushed me, as her body swayed. "I'm sorry, so sorry."

I bit my lip; the wrongness didn't fit. "Let go," I said. "Grandma let go." She sniffled, and I leaned away; her eyes leaked. The streams reflected the sunless rays of light but ran clear. My hands gripped her shoulders. "Please just tell me what's goin' on."

She shook her head. "Auriel, these are for you."

I stared at her wrinkled hands holding a box that wasn't there before. My fingers grazed hers, and I lowered my shield, as a shock rippled through me. I swallowed hard and seized the box. "Why?"

Grandma sighed and closed her eyes. "To save you the pain, but I couldn't change it. We won't stop trying."

My mouth dropped, and I stared at her. "Why is everyone so dang cryptic," I said. "I realize my life ain't simple, but this crap doesn't help."

My cheeks blazed at my outburst, but it was the truth. Pain twisted on her aged features. "I shouldn't have come home."

I brushed past her and Paulo, who I hadn't noticed. I tossed the box on the bench inside the foyer and slammed the door behind me. The steps disappeared beneath my feet as I tackled them two at a time. No change in Liam but I couldn't help the churning guilt eating at my insides. Those guilty emotions were mine, and I stared at my tapping fingers. No lies, we'd promised each other, and I'd keep it.

"So ... I don't know how to explain this," I began, but choked on the words. "I can't deny that he's you as much as you are him." I shook my head at how wrong it managed to sound. "Gods, come back to me Liam. We can get through this together, but I can't do it alone."

My hand stroked his face, but it wasn't the same. Too cold and stiff, his skin didn't have the right amount of energy. My lips touched his, but there was nothing there. The sensation, that intense pull I felt throughout my entire body was gone. Was Kiel right? Was he the part of Liam that drew me in? Now he's gone too. Did everyone abandon me in the end?

Paulo knocked on the door even though it was open. He couldn't hide his emotions any better than I could. His weary eyes met mine. "I … I don't know what to say."

He'd heard my words, and I glanced to him. Kiel was his son too; a piece of Liam hidden somehow within the same body. The draugr attacked him when he rose to my defense. I laughed inside; chivalry wasn't dead, but Liam would've done the same. My brow scrunched at the strange thought. Was it him all along? I wouldn't know until I fixed my Guardian.

"That makes two of us," I said not looking away. Fear wasn't an emotion I felt with the elder draugr. Hard to fear a man who saved two young children and raised them as his own. Jamie and Liam weren't the first, and I doubted they'd be his last. He was a big softy for a so-called bloodthirsty killer.

"Lycans are on patrol, and Jamie went out to grocery shop before I lock us down." Paulo jingled his keys and tossed them to me. I caught them one handed and followed him downstairs. "I'm going to take the Oracle home. Don't answer the door and stay upstairs with Liam." His eyes widened, and his finger pointed. "Lock yourself in and trust your talisman."

A deep breath filled my lungs; my eyes darted around the foyer, as it released. It was quiet, too quiet. Nothing but the rain and my pounding heart resonated in my ears. The smell changed too and with my senses finally returning to normal, Liam's new scent penetrated my nose. I walked up the stairs with the box in tow. Unease settled over me with the gift from grandma.

Her words replayed in my mind. Everyone treated Kiel like the enemy, but they were wrong. I sighed and entered his room, glancing around, noting every element of Liam's new life. Curiosity got the better of me, and I continued through his home and left his bedroom.

My first stop was Liam's childhood bedroom. I flicked on the light and gasped in amazement at his room. It was just as I remembered it when I left. Sketches littered Liam's desk by the doorway. He always made my drawings look like kindergarten scribbles, and I chuckled.

Stepping in, my body twirled around, searching for signs of me. We'd known each other since my birth. Mom said the moment he saw me, "a cooing little bairn that boy was," I mocked, recalling her description of his eyes burning green. At only a year old, he'd become the youngest Guardian. Anytime I was in danger, she said, he waited until I was safe. Of course as we grew older he developed other ways to rescue me. Tears stung my eyes, recalling Mom's stories. I would save her just as soon as I figured out how to fix Liam. She came next now that Kiel had found me, and after mom, the Queens. He played a role in this, in my future. How convenient that the Nine would put them together.

I wanted Thomas with me ... I didn't know him well, other than the stories Daddy shared. But I knew who he was the moment I opened my front door. How many grown men ran around in full suits of armor? Not that though, he looked just like my daddy.

I continued to explore the second floor. My hands clutched the box the Oracle gave me as I made it to the end of the hallway and the final door. Jamie's room and more memories rested behind it. My hand fell to the oak door, and I hesitated even though I knew he wasn't home.

I'd spent more time in these rooms than my own. We were inseparable for so long. Friends, connected from birth. But it was always the five of us in here. Weird that I'd witnessed a future with him. His bond to Nick ... Love wasn't supposed to be easy. I sighed, as my head rested against the door. Sometimes it was like we ripped ourselves apart just to put the pieces back together. But it didn't solve the problem. Like a bandage, it only covered the surface. In my dreams, that was the lesson. My soul belonged to someone else, two someones, but at least I'd have a choice.

The door creaked as I opened it. My eyes squinted from the bright light, as his signature scent faded, giving way to old leather and paper. I walked to Jamie's bookcase, where the aroma grew stronger. Magical texts, written in different languages, lined the shelves. Of course, I wasn't surprised; Jamie was always the smart one.

If Liam basked in chaos, Jamie emitted harmony. At least that was how it used to be. His world stayed neat and organized, although his style of dress begged to differ. The boy made wrinkled clothes and bed head look good. He wanted harmony, but like me, disorder filled Nick's world.

I craved chaos. The last four years, I lived in a prison of my own making. Was that what I did now by staying here? I'd have lied to myself if I argued otherwise. Sure, I wanted what most girls did. A husband, courtesy of the lycan bond, children, world peace ... but something lacked from this perfect world. The holes in my heart refused to refill.

"What are you doing in here?" I jumped at the sound of Jamie's voice. The box flew through the air. The mismatched paper sheets and envelopes landed all around the floor. My mouth opened to speak, but only a squeak released. My hand rested on my pounding heart. Turning around, he grinned wide, arms crossed, and his lava eyes swam. I resisted the urge to beat him senseless.

"Come here." He crooked his fingers, and my brow rose. Letting out a huff, he closed the distance. Jamie's arms wrapped around me, and my heart rate settled.

"Thanks," I said, pulling away to grab the letters.

"Sorry, I didn't mean to scare you. " Liar, yes he did. Jamie bent down to help. "What's with all the letters?"

"I'll get them." I shooed him away, as my hands scurried about the mess.

"Grandma gave them to me."

"How much do you really know about her?" His arms dropped, slapping against his dark jeans. The floorboards creaked, as he stepped back. I turned to see his brows knitted tight, and his lips twisted into a frown. The look on his face cut at me, as he made to leave. What did I say? I bit my lip to keep it from quivering. The frostiness of his tone hurt, but I didn't know why. Why was it suddenly my fault?

If he knew something, why didn't he come out and say it? My head shook. Stupid Skylands and their inability to own the heck up. My eyes rolled at his bizarre behavior, and I stole a cleansing breath to ease my rattled nerves. Weirdo ... I glanced at the stack in my hands. Two letters remained in the box, and I pulled one out and opened it:

"Dear Mom,
We arrived in Delaware today, but we're unsure how long we'll stay. Auriel seems to be adjusting well, but she cries for Liam in her sleep and constantly asks about her friends too. I

really think she's still in love with him. This was her decision. Are you sure we did the right thing? We did everything she asked us to do. Only she has the power to undo it. Auriel wrote it, right down to the key to unlock it.

Lettie's at her wit's end. We don't understand the key she left us either. I wish she'd just been born normal. This feels more like a curse.

Love,

Danny"

Outside lightning cracked and rolling thunder followed. Storms did not bother me, but this one pounded my heart into bits, as it slammed against my chest. The reaction of my mind wasn't much different. I stared out the window. The rain pelted against the glass pane leaving behind teardrop spots. The sound did nothing to soothe the fray inside my soul. Each pang echoed; my flesh shivered. It called to me, as my eyes fell down to the lawn before spanning out to the street.

A strange man stood in the road and looked up at me. A raven perched on his shoulder, and he wore rags for clothes. I blinked, and he disappeared. Shadows, yes, my mind played tricks on me.

"Knowing and remembering are two different things. They never taught you how to harness all sides of you, child."

I stared out the window. *"Kiel, is that you?"*

Part of me wished to see the man again, just to prove that I wasn't crazy. The other part wished to flee, but I needed to know more. I couldn't control what I was, or what I'd become.

"Remember first, and all shall reveal itself, my child." The voice sent a chill down my spine.

"But I did remember," I said back, placing my palms on the glass.

The whisper reminded me of the wind, yet it was not. The trees didn't sway. The man reappeared, standing on the grass below the window. At least on the second floor I was safe. My trembling hands rattled against the glass.

I didn't recognize him through the endless downpour and rolling fog. The glimpses I caught came when lightning illuminated the sky.

"Jamie," I called out. My widening eyes never left the spot where I last saw the man. "Jamie!"

"What is it, Aurie?" I cringed at the disdain evident in his voice. He was probably rolling his eyes too. Jackass needed to get over himself or whatever PMS crap he'd allowed to overthrow his sense. I pointed, tapping on the window, as the reflection of his eyes widened. Jamie breezed past and pushed me aside. "He's speaking to me."

"Who? Auriel, there isn't anyone there." I shook my head and looked again. As the sky lit up, the man was gone. He snorted, and Jamie gave me an icy look before leaving the room.

There was someone, there had to be. A body rush hit me and wobbled me from head to toe. Even as the hairs stood up on my neck, I refused to glance out the window again, as my heart thundered. My arms crossed over my chest, and I rubbed my arms. He was just too afraid that I was right.

I picked up the letter, and I tucked it in the box. Another glance around the room yielded nothing, and I headed for the door. As I hit the switch, lightning struck close by, and the man's reflection manifested in the window.

The stranger … he was in the house. His lips curled into a grim smile, and a scream erupted from deep within, but as I opened my mouth, no sound escaped. I shouted for Jamie, Nick, Regin, and both Kiel and Liam, but only a gurgle came out. As his hand touched my shoulder, I passed out.

"Fainauriel," a masculine voice called my name, as the scent of coriander and cinnamon assaulted my nose. My eyes blinked. A small room enclosed upon me, and as I glanced around, I saw the walls were unfinished and peaked into a steeple. Hardness jabbed into my back, and my hands smoothed over the glossy surface.

"Ah yes, there we go." Hands clapped. "She awakens." My eyes burned, as smoke filled the room, hiding his face. But I'd met him before. Fingers snapped, and the smoke changed direction. The gangly, black-haired man spoke. *Loki.* Was I back in Asgard? "No my child, we are still on Midgard."

He gave a slight bow, as I tried to sit up. Stars and spots formed in my vision, and a cold cloth smoothed over my forehead. Bony hands pressed me back down.

"Why am I here?" Loki smiled, and I recoiled from the gesture. His teeth were yellow and jagged. The burns and scars covering his neck and face didn't help matters either, as his hood fell back.

Freya's voice flittered into the stuffy room. *"To understand."* I attempted to sit up again, but he wagged his finger. *"To learn."* I blinked.

"Her spirit is here," Loki whispered, pressing his hand over my breast. I trembled under the intrusion of his touch. "Your heart commands the Phoenix." He patted above my heart and then leaned away. His fingers tapped together and thin lips pursed "You've created a problem, Fainauriel. You weren't supposed to free Ezekiel."

"Okay," I squeaked, voice shaking in time with the rest of my body. Two birds circled above me, before landing on his wide shoulders. My eyes widened, recognizing the avian twins as Hungin and Munin. "But I did."

"Don't fear death, Valkyrie, for it doesn't fear you," Loki said, smiling again and ignoring my admission. "She will choose your side." My face twisted, brows scrunching together. What in the Gods' name was he talking about? "All for the better; I should've done it before. After all he does love you."

My eyes closed. No, this was a dreadful dream. More confusion, as if I didn't have enough endless questions and riddles in my life. I pinched myself, and the demi-god chuckled. Nope, so much for wishful thinking.

Wherever there was, I was there in the flesh.

"Stop scaring her, and let's get down to the point." Freya's voice bellowed through my head, as if it was Thor's thunder, and I opened my eyes. She still wasn't here. Loki gave me a tight smile and nodded.

"Your flesh may have been born into the world of mankind, but you aren't as the others perceive you to be," Loki began, and I wanted to smack him. My fingers twitched, and I placed them on my thighs. "Your magic stems from beyond their reach, and this is why your Nine covets it." His brow rose. "Why some of the Gods want you dead." I bit my lip as he spoke and noted the radiating soreness. "Before you were born, the norns foresaw my destruction of the realms. They charged an elf with interfering, you know her." My head cocked; palms grew sweaty. Yes, I knew whom he spoke of; all of Alfheim knew her.

Morgana the scarred princess rose above all and defeated an evil queen. She freed the Unseelie court from chaos and revoked the laws banning love.

"She succeeded in saving Midgard to an extent, and so the Gods forgot about the warnings and went about their boring little lives." He leaned closer, blue eyes widening as his pale skin grew translucent, and whispered, "But *I* did not forget."

I bolted back and drew my knees into my chest. The room closed in as Loki tossed his head backward and released a spine chilling cackle. "Who are you?"

"Any questions, dear?" Freya interjected as my eyes shot toward the roof.

Yeah about a million and one. Her reddish Myst enveloped me and seeped into my pores. Breaths rasped and I clutched and clawed at my chest. The heat of her love pulsated through the room, but I refused the distraction my matron created. A censer rattled on the windowsill as a blackbird pecked at the metal. Loki's words repeated within my mind, as did Nick's frequent visits to the demi-god.

Odin lied and scorned the races. The words we learned in school, human and supernatural alike. What if those words had been wrong? A putrid breath pushed past my tightened jaw as the darkness retreated from my body. The blackened Myst absorbed into Loki's outstretched palm. For all he had done wrong to my kind, I did not hate the all-knowing God or Loki. Hatred for my family and what they had done was all I knew.

"Indeed." I forced a smile and watched his drumming fingers.

Freya appeared in a flash of pink light, and I shielded my eyes. "Odin's demons are your foes though, and he will amass an army to defeat you."

"You're brighter than he realizes." Loki rose from the rickety chair, one I hadn't seen in years. We were in my attic.

I lifted my gaze to Freya's soft blue eyes. "Why would anyone want to kill me?"

She smiled and reached a hand to my face. "The Aesir stands where the Myst wants nothing," her gaze flickered to Loki, "supernatural or human, we are all powerful because of the Myst not because of Gods or Goddesses as we'd have you all believe."

I swallowed hard and digested her words. She was a Goddess. "In my dreams, I fight demons. They're large, disfigured, and frightening."

"I want to tell you a secret, young one." Loki placed his hand on my shoulder. I inhaled a sharp breath, but I didn't recoil. "There is no good, and there is no evil. Just darkness and light, but inside of us all, it exists. It's up to each of us to choose a path."

"Isn't that what you removed?" Loki shrugged

"And the Dísir?"

Loki laughed. "You are *my* army."

My mouth fell open in mock surprise. Loki rose, and his features rippled beneath like tossing a pebble into a still lake. No scars, no age, not even time had touched him. I blinked and shook my head. "Yes, Odin coined the name demon to spread fear and hatred of my creations he couldn't control. Then he recreated the Valkyrie, but he did not possess the same love or devotion as Freya. At some point, arguably by the draugr, those tales passed to the humans." Loki turned to her and kissed her hand.

"Our children are born," she said. "Odin's are trapped souls from his cache." Trapped was Ezekiel, he said as much, but he had wings. Where mine were tawny, his were white. "He entraps my children and steals their spirits. When Liam was born, he blended the two."

My eyes narrowed on the bird pecking on the small window. The sky lay beyond it, blue and bright. I gritted my teeth, as I recalled all the lies and hate spewed over the Dísir. The tales of the old religions, the uprising of the demons, angered my smoking hands. Because of a selfish God, I'd no future beyond the windows of my prison. Whether it be an actual cell within the Nine or the walls of my own mind. Freedom was a luxury not afforded to my kind and any who chose to follow.

"I am Legion." I sighed and chewed the inside of my cheek.

"Four years ago, you discovered the truth." Loki paced, shuffling his feet over the boards. "I'm not certain why it took so long, not even when Nickolas spoke to you." He blew out a breath. "My child was your key, but he failed to unlock your mind."

The whispers and guidance, that first night in Liam's house, Nick pressed upon me the importance. Six weeks later and the Gods intervened, as he said they would if I failed.

My brow scrunched, as I flashed back to the spell, and the letters. "There were three." Nick was one of three.

Silence settled over the room. "What about Kiel?" They exchanged worried glances, and my chest ached.

"Tell her," Freya said. Her hands fell to his broad shoulders, and he glanced up at her, smiling. "She deserves to know."

Loki swallowed hard and stared at his feet. "Kiel was the soul of Liam." My eyes burned, as the words registered. Soul mate. "Now he lives separate, taking on the form he once held before Odin had captured him." *What had I done?* Hot liquid spilled from my eyes. "Don't cry my dear. You freed them both."

He didn't understand. My eyes closed. What I felt with Liam disappeared when I released Kiel. Before I left, for sixteen years there was no one but him. When separated there was no one until him. The spell I'd cast ripped forever out from under our eyes. Twice I'd broken him.

My fists curled. No, I'd fight it. I couldn't toss in the towel just because of a little slip. We were stronger than that. Kiel would understand, and if he cared for me, he'd stand down. I lifted my gaze and sniffled. The positive energy poured into my heart; the light filled the void.

An explosion of colors streamed in through the glass. The Myst stole my breath, as the rainbow of colors convened inside his body. The concentration of color outshined Freya, yet they called him the demi-god. "No, my child." I blinked; Loki's hands steeped and flattened, and his face lit up into a creepy grin.

My chest heaved and coughed for air. "*You* ... are the Myst ..."

The Myst curled like tendrils of smoke and brushed against my skin. It eased the ache of my soul.

"Liam didn't know." Freya shook her head, oblivious to the silent conversation. "It's hard to notice when it's all you know." Then why was Ezekiel important?

Would the child die in the future if I didn't pick him? I winced and glanced away. My hand covered my pounding heart; could I live with that decision?

"I wouldn't fret about it now, Fainauriel." Freya leaned down and kissed my forehead. "None of it will matter unless you can prove your worth to the Myst."

Her eyes flickered to Loki. Ah, so she did know.

I sat up. "Wait how am I—"

His bushy brow rose. "Bring down the Nine and prove that you can stand up to them. Start with Charlestown. But be prepared; there are allies, powerful allies within the depths," Loki said. "Push aside what the Nine believes. Your heart will be your judge and jury even to those you otherwise call enemy."

"My mother's there. Are the Queens there too? What do I look for?"

How could I do this? I wasn't strong enough, and even with all the training, I still struggled with control. Freya grinned, her eyes shining.

"My child." She stroked my hair. "You are because the Myst made it so. But if you fail, it will rewrite the world again." My eyes widened.

"I don't mean to be rude." My eyes darted between them both. "Why exactly do you care?" My eyebrows rose, before furrowing. "And how are you on Midgard? I thought the Gods couldn't walk here."

The deity stared down at her pale hands. "I stand before you not as a Goddess, Fainauriel, but as a Valkyrie." Her pale robe ripped, falling to the ground, as her wings sprang free. "I'm yours to command when the time arrives." She bowed, and my cheeks enflamed.

"So ..." My breath hissed through my teeth, as the tension in my head built. "You're telling me that you're no longer a Goddess. Liam's soul is split —oh and he's frozen by the way —I have to take down the Nine, save some of them, and then what?"

"Prepare for war," Loki said with cold eyes. "Prepare to take down the Nine fully and then we march on Asgard."

I laughed, crumpling over myself. How absurd. My head shook, and I fell backward onto the hard wooden surface. March on Asgard? *Maybe when pigs fly*. "Pigs can fly, my dear, and so can cats," Freya said with a wink.

"You expect me to take on Asgard too?" My breath hissed through my teeth. "Y'all are insane. All of this is crazy. I think I liked it better when people wanted to sacrifice me." I ripped my hand through my hair, ignoring the pain as it stuck. "You can't be serious."

Her smoldering gaze conveyed her dead seriousness. "If you fail, all Nine realms fail too. If you succeed, the Myst allows Midgard to stand until it destroys itself."

"What happens to the other realms? To Alfheim?" My family and the last clutch of Dragons lived there. Freyr lived there; surely, Freya would want to save her brother.

"It will cease along with whatever life remains." No, there had to be a way to save them too. If I accepted this fate, as ludicrous as it was, I wouldn't do it half-assed.

"I want them all," I said, starring Loki –the Myst –or whatever I was supposed to call him, dead in the eyes. "Save them all, not one."

Loki didn't blink and leaned forward. "You dare—"

"Yeah, I do," I said, gritting my teeth and straightening my back.

He raised his brow and stroked his smooth chin. A sly grin spread over his hawk-like face. Oh, crap. His hands folded and unfolded as the smile grew.

"If you fail … Fainauriel if you refuse this mission then the world will burn to a cindered ash. My child, let's finish this. I have a gift for you, dear, and I'm afraid you don't have a choice."

"Loki, it is time," Freya said as Loki's hands pushed me down again. His grip tightened, as pain seared into my shoulders, blisters forming on my bare skin, and a disturbing grin remained on his face.

"What the … let me go … ow … Loki stop it, no—" Tears spilled over; I screamed.

"Muna," he said, gritting teeth as the pressure increased and spread into my head. White light flashed and blinded me, as searing pain wracked through my skull. The last sounds I recalled were my voice screeching and glass crashing.

chapter thirty-eight

LIAM

The words left her lips, and I could do nothing. The Myst enveloped every part of me and tore through my defenses. Even the beast subdued. Oh, anger didn't come to mind with Auriel. My head stirred, and the bitterness of my tongue boiled into laughter. No, that was too easy for her. Fuming, raging, and foaming at the mouth to rip her apart into a million shreds. That was what she did to my heart.

Awaking to no trace of Auriel didn't bode well with the monster, who screamed for revenge. She promised. My fists tightened, and I resisted the urge to add more holes to my walls. Jamie offered little help, though he did a splendid job of berating himself. We stood in his room. My eyes scanned for minuscule signs as he retold the story of the previous evening. He hadn't believed her. Damn, I didn't believe half of what he relayed, but his words were honest.

A Dísir had lived inside me; he fled, but not before touching my wife. My hand touched my heart. I felt no physical pain, and the notion soured my stomach. Auriel accused me before, in her thoughts. Since the day she arrived, my soul cried whenever we were apart. Nothing, but reddened rage filled the void.

"Do you think Kiel stole her?"

Jamie snorted and shook his head. "You've seen what she can do."

Truer words there or however the saying went. But she had weaknesses. My shoulders slumped, and I leaned over his desk. A shoebox rested on top. I sighed, blowing the breath out of my mouth. Letters piled inside and one laid open on top.

"Momma,

Thanks for the advice. It took time for the spell to fully manifest. We falsely implanted the memories, as you suggested. If anything happens to us she'll return to you. We hope to come back someday when she is older and ready to fulfill her destiny. We miss you and love you, Momma.

Love, Danny"

There was more deception than I realized. I folded the letter and picked another, but the more I read, the more my head pounded. How much of our mess was Auriel, and how much was Keelan's doing? The memories that returned to me, they screamed treachery of an enormous magnitude. I had had Jamie's essence; he was emptied before but had she refilled him? Auriel wouldn't do that; her style involved enormous amounts of pain. My brow creased as the memory unfolded. She'd already left when the Phoenix became mine. I recalled us both at school, and we kissed. She acted strange all day, and then it was like she didn't exist, but without any pain. My eyes closed as the realization hit. Auriel erased herself from me because she loved me.

It left Keelan as the remaining benefactor. No one else held the power she had or the malevolent behavior I'd not noticed before. Why did the Oracle do this to me? Why steal Jamie's Myst and insert it in me? It was not like I ever used the power. Even Auriel noticed that. Besides, I had my own. "I've asked that question for years, brother." Jamie responded to my thoughts. How did he remember and push past Auriel's spells?

"You may have had my magic, but my blood still bled that of the Phoenix. Nick too or didn't he tell you?" Jamie sighed, tossing a baseball in the air. "I never stopped trying to find her." He rose, walking until our noses almost touched. His eyes blazed golden.

My mouth fell open as I remembered the boulder. "You used to love her." I didn't bother looking at him. I knew he did, even now, he loved her, but he wasn't in love with her. "Now you love Nick?"

He gulped, and his scent changed to a sour, salty note. Jamie ... my heart went out to him, but I'd love my brother no matter whom he loved. "It's complicated."

I shook my head. Love shouldn't be complicated. "Dad know yet?"

"No." I flinched from his tone. "Don't you dare tell anyone," he snapped. I faced him and met his fiery gaze. My hands came up as he stood up. "Not a damned soul."

"Dude whatever. You know I'm not judging, right? Y'all looked happy."

They did too, and it was all that mattered to Auriel and me. He stepped to me and stood there, gawking at me.

"I need to find her," I said, ignoring the dull ache left in my head.

"Why she's still your woman?" Jamie frowned. "Well she did kiss him and used plenty of tongue."

His words sank in. "She did what?" the words trembled.

"Oh don't worry, little bro; we caught him for you." His mouth twisted into a grin, and his eyes darkened. A summoned energy ball made of fire hit me square in the chest. Stumbling back, my eyes widened before the lights faded out.

CHAPTER
THIRTY-NINE

AURIEL

My new surroundings startled me as I awakened. Again I found myself somewhere else than where I conked out. Home welcomed me with its cool, empty bed. No Liam. I shot from the covers and moved faster than usual. What did Loki do to me? My blood pumped hard, but I felt invigorated ... as if I could ... take on the world. I glanced to the clock, and it read six o'clock. The sun would set soon, but that couldn't be right. Night fell when Loki took me. How much time did I lose? My chest ached, and my hand covered my heart. No ... *"Liam?"* No reply came, although I wasn't surprised.

"Nikolas where are you?" Without another delay, I sought the Fenrir and raced next door. He didn't respond, and dread ate at my soul. *"Ezekiel?"* I asked again. *"Jamie?"* Again, I received no reply, and panic set in. *"Nikolas ... Fenrir!"* As a last result, I called out to Nick again.

"Aye, eun beag ye have need of me?" he replied when I reached Liam's front door. Locked, how I left it. My fist dented the door, but no one came and my key was inside.

"Yes, Nick, the boys aren't responding. But I have news."

"Eun beag, Liam's frozen." I'd figured as much since he didn't respond, but why wasn't Jamie opening the door or answering my

calls? I pinched the bridge of my nose. The lockdown … unless Paulo had cancelled it?

"No, Paulo initiated it this morning. I'll be there soon."

He had not returned last night as the draugr said he would. What had delayed him and where the heck was Jamie? Nick stayed away because he delegated the patrol and hid my great grandfather. I paced the front lawn, the stiff grass crunching beneath my feet, wishing for a cell phone. Technology irked me, it was too easy to track, and I knew the Nine held an extensive reach. Or so they told us. How much of that had been a lie too? Why would my parents have insisted I hate the Dísir when I was one?

As I awaited Nick's arrival, I sent my Myst out in a blanket of pallid haze to determine what pinged back inside the house. Nothing. My head cocked. *That wasn't right.* I sent the fog further, encompassing all of Six and Twenty in a wave of my power. Nothing I recognized returned. Jamie and Liam were gone. My knuckles cracked; I released the tension building within my bones and jumped at the crunching sounds flooding out my thundering heart.

"Dang Loki, what'd you give me?" The energy equated to ten cups of coffee and the urge to run surged through my veins. My heart rate had changed too and it beat faster. Already sharp senses had altered too, and they were already above par compared to most supernaturals.

Loki replied, *"Your birthright, Fainauriel."*

I wiggled off the crawling sensation of his echoing words screeching though my ears. Birthright my ass, he did something to me, and I aimed to figure it out. But there remained more pressing matters than Loki's tricks.

How did Jamie and Liam get outside the shield if Paulo put everyone on lockdown? I stared up to the second floor and blinked, my hand clutching my chest.

A smile spread across my face, as the proper words flashed in my mind. I ran home for my spyglass. Not just any old spyglass, but one constructed in Alfheim, the contraption possessed old Elven magic. The Unseelie Queen had tinkered as a child, designing and creating items with her hands. The love she poured into the items would later manifest as her hidden Myst. A gift from my great grandmother and one of many I'd forgotten about.

"Té-eigin feuch," I whispered, holding the tube to my eye. My vision changed, and my stomach flipped from the motion. It zoomed in on Alastrine, the Nine US HQ in Charlestown, SC. Before me lay a twenty-story building nestled by the Atlantic Ocean. A wrought iron gate surrounded the perimeter, which fooled the humans. I pressed past the illusion the Myst had wished me to see, to believe, and I dug deeper to uncover the truth in the reflected lie.

I pictured Merric, the proverbial wizard behind the curtain. Tall and lean, with dark hair and Jamie's cold grey eyes, so much like his son in looks and personality, Merric had coveted power under the disguise of revenge and lover's vengeance. Why he had allied himself with my great aunt was beyond me, since she sat upon the throne he wished to destroy. As the Elven representative on the Nine Council, I would have thought them natural enemies. She sat on the same council that had condemned his wife to death. What had blinded him from the truth?

Narrowing in on Merric proved simple. Too easy but I had to take what I could get without any leads. Mage, mage, and draugr blended into three strands of grey. After connecting to him, I found the facade of the HQ dissipated like a rolling mist. In its place lay the secret world of Charlestown, SC complete with its magical prisons and miles of housing for those who lived under their control.

Further, I pressed past the iron walls; I saw him with my mother. Strawberry blond hair covered her face. Tendrils marred with clumps of dirt and blood. I gasped, and my hands clenched. Her once broad shoulders slumped forward, as he talked to her, but she didn't move. Momma sat bound and shackled with iron rope.

"Auriel." Nikolas wrapped his arms around me and spun me around, disturbing the spell. His grin widened, but mine faltered into a scowl.

"Nikolas," I hissed. "I was in the middle of something."

"Sorry lass." He rubbed the back of his neck. "I 'ave a surprise for ye." He motioned over to the trees. Out stepped his lanky sister and I blinked, not recognizing her at first. "I had her on town watch while I was ... occupied with you."

"Reggie," I squealed, jumping up and down.

The same waitress from my first night back, the one who I'd sworn had used magic stood before me with her arms spread wide.

I watched as her blue eyes lit up in amusement, but it didn't take long until I swept her into a bear sized hug.

"I had charms made tis a pity ye hadn't queried 'er."

"I thought you were lost forever," she said, her eyes glistening. Unlike her brother, Reggie grew up right here in South Carolina. Dang, she had changed from the scrawny girl I once knew into a beautiful woman. My heart swelled, eying the Fenrir siblings. Regin wrapped her blond hair into a ponytail and grinned wide. Good to be back, surrounded by my best friends. I wished the circumstances were different and that we could have all been there in that moment as we had once been in better times.

"Where's Lannie, is she well?" Nick frowned at the mention of his oldest sister, and next in line for the lycan throne.

Reggie answered for Nikolas. "We don't know." My lips tugged down. Gods, I thought I warned them soon enough. Only three known survivors ... three out of hundreds of first generation Fenrirs. What kind of madness were we facing?

"I checked for the lads before coming," Nick said and placed a hand on my shoulder. His face long, the frown etching new lines on his unshaven face. The clothes he'd worn also showed wrinkles and his sloppy-neat composure was bordering on well, sloppy. "The Oracle tis also gone, yer grams left in a wee tizzy."

"Do you have a key?" I asked, pointing to Liam's front door. Nick smirked and strolled to the door. I assumed that was a yes, until he lifted his leg and kicked the door down with one swift movement. I gaped at him, but he shrugged and waltzed right in. "I could've done that."

He poked his head back out, grinning. "Nonsense, I 'ave to help the big, bad Valkyrie somehow, lass."

I ran into Liam's house, barreling right up the stairs. The chill reached me before I made the last step. Dissipating, the pale blue tendrils of the Myst remained. Faint lines of the fire loomed too. Underneath it all ... *Air*. "Ice and fire."

"Could it be from the freezing spell, lass?" I swallowed and nodded. Not the air, but the fire and water made sense. If Kiel cast anything as I did, but there wasn't a way to know for sure. The Air and those grey remnants weighed on my soul. My teeth gnawed into my bottom lip, and I couldn't let it go.

"Why take Jamie?"

My brow creased as my own words sank in. We'd all banked on their hatred for one another. My hand flew to my chest; heart throbbing, as my brow dampened. I brought the spyglass to my eye again and concentrated on Liam. At first, I had not found his three-natured signature, but his Myst had altered. If I remembered, what Freya and Loki said about the Dísir…the white light? No, he had blue, green, and … red.

We followed the Myst trail that I saw. Green belonged to Liam. No, I saw it all along, but I didn't remove it on purpose. That was not my plan, well, not for that day. Jamie – fixing Jamie remained my purpose. The darkness surrounded him, and it smothered his mind. Like the two natured beast, it sought for control. But like a plague, it eats at the heart and soul. Eventually, it led to pure chaos of the mind, body, and soul. If not controlled than those inflicted would have spread the disease to those around them. I glanced toward Nick; his palm brushed over Jamie's bed, and pain filled the ancient man's eyes.

Mind opened , and I saw it now in the room. The underlying blues of Liam's residual Myst were gone. Taking a deep breath, I noted that his campfire smell wasn't the same either. Everything was wrong.

"Jamie can't wield ice, but then again there are many mages here that can." Water mages were common. *"Wrong child,"* Loki said.

"There was a struggle here." I pointed to the torn carpet and ignored the voice. My eyes stung, but I swallowed them down.

"The sea—" I plugged my fingers in my ears and sang la, la, la over and over again to block out Loki's voice. I loathed shared minds. Maker or not, a girl needed to think. Besides, Nick needed to focus and not realize his mate went cuckoo again. I'd kept that part of the darkness from him.

I sighed and leaned against the bookcase. This was exactly why I ran away four years ago. I didn't want those I loved getting hurt because of me, yet it didn't matter. What did Grandma say? She tried, but it didn't matter.

The Nine killed my father, captured Momma, and now had Liam. They held the Queens too. Somehow, I just knew they held them all.

Nick placed a hand on my shoulder. "Do ye think Jamie helped?"

My fists clenched as I forced air through my nose. "They hate each other, but it wouldn't surprise me if he helped her." My fists clenched again, my nails biting into my palms.

He sank into the bed and leaned forward. "I never meant to lead him on, but ..." Nick blinked his red-rimmed eyes. "Murdered my family, but I cannot not love him, eun beag. I forgave him." He dropped back on the bed, and the springs groaned under his massive frame.

Nick's thoughts ransacked me. In Jamie's eyes, he had a chance to get away. In my eyes, Jamie Mc Douglas remained a coward, who ran away when crap got hard. Maybe I was the pot calling the kettle black, but at least I tried saving those I loved from pain.

"He would've run anyway," Nick said as Regin sat beside him. She wrapped her arms around him and drew his head to her shoulder. Nick sniffled as I increased my shield, pulsing my Myst and blocking him. I hated blocking my friends but I had to keep my head. "He doesn't love me."

My lip twitched. "Jamie does." Nick shook his head. My hands rested on my hips, and I towered over him and Regin as she mouthed a warning. "He's torn and scared, but he loves you Nikolas Fenrir. Time for those big girl panties and a lot of forgiveness because everything that stupid boy does is for you." He stormed out of the room before I'd even finished.

Reggie said, "I warned you."

"When ye mate, ye'll understand why I forgave him, Reggie."

"How do you put up with that?" I paused in the hallway, remembering before the Gods summoned me. The box of letters lay on the desk, and I grabbed one off the top. The weight and feel made my pulse slow.

"Lycans aren't like you." Regin sighed. "When our mates ignore us or hurt us it's a thousand times worse." My brow rose as I glanced at her. *Were we talking about her or Nick?* Because Nicky had more patience and heart than anyone I'd ever met. I shook the thought away and concentrated on the letter. If Regin wanted girl talk, she'd spill her secrets.

Looking at the letter, I noticed one addressed to me. Useful or not, they were written by Momma and Dad. My brows pinched, and my heart sank. I thought I had lost it in Virginia at the skanky hotel:

"Dear Auriel,

We thought we were doing what's best for you. If you're reading this, then we were either captured or dead. Don't come after us no matter what.

You are the greatest gift the Myst ever granted, and your father and I hold no regrets. Go to Six and Twenty and find Liam. He's your Guardian, your protector. Never forget your strength and faith.

Always follow your heart and let it guide you.

We will always love you,

Momma and Daddy

"Fat chance," I said, walking into the living room. Nick shot me a puzzling glance. "Get my grandfather, and we'll find Paulo. I know where they've taken Liam."

"Eun beag, what about the Dísir?" *Kiel* ... "Can he help?" I shook my head. He had left me after ripping out a piece of my soul and refused my calls. But something told me our paths would cross again. My eyes narrowed toward the window as the sun descended behind the trees. *Soon.*

chapter fourty

PAULO

For five hundred years, I had lived through phenomenon and downright evil of unimaginable measures. None of those events compared to the demi-goddess fluttering before me with her falcon-like tawny wings. Even under the moonlight, she had shimmered all my anger and irritation aside.

"Auriel, are you alright?" I asked with concern as she waltzed into my living room from the open balcony like a rustling breeze. Crossbreed, abomination the Nine called her once. I begged to differ, but I'd always held a soft spot for the unwanted, damned, and twisted creations of the Nine. Damned and unwanted by my mother during the Grand Inquisition because my father was Jewish. Like those here, I too was a half-breed. Half Catholic and half Jewish, but I saw persecution for a crime I held no control over, and the result turned me into a slave.

"I'm peachy-keen." She grinned but the smile faded, revealing coldness. Her voice held steady, and she faced me. The pain in her eyes answered more than her words. Gone were the swirling molten pools of golden fire. Crystalline eyes of the palest blue peeked out at me from her moonlit weary lids. The irises lined in glittery gold.

"The boys are not. They're gone."

I crossed my arms, rubbing my biceps. "What do you mean?" *I've only been gone for a little over an hour.*

She paced the length of my living room and twisted her hands. "It's been over a day since you left me, Paulo. Grandma left too."

Did she read my thoughts? Auriel nodded. A shiver rushed from head to toe, and I could not recall the last time human emotions took over my stoic control. Jamie had warned me about this too, but Keelan never led Six and Twenty astray. At least with nothing we could have proved. I eased into my leather chair and gripped the armrests. The woman even left her husband behind to help me build this town.

"Her house is empty, and every belonging vanished into thin air." Auriel sighed and shook her head. "She fled."

Bitterness pooled in my mouth. I was not immune. The memories still knitted together, reconnecting, and made my hands tremble.

They had known our every move. Auriel nodded ... Was she ... she nodded again. My brow rose, but she didn't elaborate. What was going on here? Draugr should have been immune. Auriel shook her head and knelt to my side.

"I told you so."

It didn't add up. Why not hand over Auriel when the Wardens came? I rose from the chair and loosened my tie. Pam and her stupid dress code ... I hated suits. "What do you have in mind?"

"It's a trap, but one I can't ignore." She stepped to me and hugged her arms around me. My body stiffened at her warmth and enticing scent. I reminded myself that this was my son's woman as her breasts pressed into my chest, and her breath skimmed my neck.

"I need your help Paulo," she whispered. I swallowed hard and almost choked from the human reaction as tears stung my eyes. "You know the Nine and their weaknesses."

"Anything, you know it." Auriel dropped her arms and smiled. Her eyes creased, spilling golden tears down her pale cheeks.

"You know how to get in without detection." I couldn't refuse, not when my children were in the devil's den. Her head cocked to the side. "Nick says they're ready."

I nodded. "Give me five minutes."

Time to prepare for battle. My eyes narrowed as I caught my reflection. One we were bound to lose. Getting in was the easy part, we'd have to fight our way out. Donning my leather pants, black t-shirt, leather vest, and biker boots gave me plenty of hiding places for my arsenal of weapons. Tonight I chose my silver knives and the Katana swords forged from Alfheim iron and dipped in silver. Unsheathing them, I marveled at the etched runes covering the blade.

"It's been a long time, old friend." I smirked; there was no such thing as too many weapons. Running my finger over the blade, my blood dripped onto the silver coating. Supernaturals preferred metal weapons to more advanced weaponry, but I tucked a few revolvers into holsters too. I pulled my hair back. The last reminder I held onto of my previous life aside from some clothing. Dry lips tugged up, and my eyes opened, blazing crimson red.

"Paulo, we're ready." Auriel called from downstairs. The crisp beat of her tawny wings sent a breeze up the stairs, carrying their scents. Just the five of us; I sighed inward. It was not impossible, but this wouldn't be easy. I glanced around one last time before descending the stairs.

"Well, well, Paulo Skyland, how dashing." Reggie winked at me. If I could have blushed, my cheeks would have reddened for sure, but I felt the heat rise. Instead, I allowed the smile to spread. She did not recoil as I expected. Most supes were not used to the fangs and crimson eyes, but nothing seemed to bother the lycan. Modesty didn't bother Regin either as her clothing hit the floor, and I spun around. Bones cracked and crunched and no matter how many times I have heard the sounds, the chills chased up my spine.

"Thomas," I said, extending my hand to the common clothed Knight and attempting to alter my attention. Well, more common perhaps, because he still wore armor, but changed from the metal suit to one made of … my eyes widened … blackened dragon scales. I read about the armor in books but had never seen the thick, diamond scales before now. Hooked to his belt rested two swords. My brows lifted, and he smiled. *Impressive.*

"Remind me ne'er to get on yer bad side." Nickolas laughed, dressed in his typical attire, and brought me back to reality, but I didn't see Auriel. A chirping sound drew my attention as a tawny falcon landed on his shoulder. Regin barked, and I glanced over at the large wolf wagging her tail. Even as a wolf ... No, I could not allow myself to think of such matters and glanced away. Nick grinned wide as a finger stroked the bird's head. "Eun beag is ready."

Seeing Auriel in her form, I'd recalled the safe, the one I couldn't find or remember before. The second floor had an office, and a large picture of Freya and Freyr. Lettie stored Freya's feathered cloak, among other gifts and artifacts for Auriel to use. The cloak allowed her to cross the Nine Realms without the need of a portal or invoking the Phoenix.

A mysterious man, with an eye patch, gave it to her on her tenth birthday along with a battered tome written in Scottish Gaelic that held her entire lineage; Elven, Ice and Fire Jotunn, and human combined. On her twelfth, he returned with a Brísingamen marked with an Algiz. It had belonged to a retired Valkyrie now in the service of the Gods.

"Let us do this then," I said, and Nickolas laughed. I couldn't help it if I messed up their slang, but you think I'd learn after five hundred years like he did.

CHAPTER FOURTY-ONE

LIAM

Charlestown, SC

I paced the brick room as my palms sweated, and my heart raced. There wasn't any escape. I'd tried all the windows and the door. To make matters worse, my brain had struggled processing thoughts when memories of Auriel ransacked my emotions.

Stolen kisses, holding hands, laughter … she had taken all the joy from my life. Four years of waiting and existing without her, never knowing I had once had her. A rough palm dragged over my face. Nick had known too. I kicked the chair. He and Jamie both knew all along and never told me.

Hurry up and wait for my fate while he'd stood on the sidelines ridiculing me. My fists balled at my sides as I stared around the walls of my cell. A sigh tickled my chest as my head dipped. None of it mattered anymore. Sköll lived here, and how long before he came after me to finish the job he'd begun. I plopped in the chair by the desk centered in the room.

Sentenced me to death as a newborn baby—my file said as much. Paulo had kept the information from me fearing that knowing would hurt me. I rested my head on my fist. As far as I was concerned, my father was Paulo, and I loved him as much. He made me the man I was, not the asshole who had created me.

Those who loved me, raised me, they were whom I cherished; Auriel, even Jamie, and of course Nick and Regin too. I blinked and laughed out of desperation. There were better memories to recall than my bastard father. "Gods how could you allow me to forget at all?"

I chewed my lip. Why did they let Auriel cast that damn spell, let that monster rape my mother ... and Danny, they had allowed someone to murder Aurie's father. I stood and paced. No reply came, and I wondered, for the first time, how much control the Gods had. My fist hit the concrete wall and bits littered to the ground. I'd rather have forgotten being the bastard son of a murderous lunatic.

My legs gave way, and I slumped to the hard floor. Leaning back, I let my eyes flutter closed. Nothing in life was worth this punishment. I sighed. The last time I saw Auriel, before she returned, we were kids and leaving school. I waited ... the Oracle made me wait ... she always knew she'd return. How did Keelan know unless she was in on the plan? My fists clenched again. I let Auriel down; I should have demanded more from Mrs. Graftfield.

"Quiet Liam." A female penetrated my mind, but I did not recognize the voice. I opened my eyes, and sat up, but remained alone. Who else knew I was here?

"Who are you?" I telepathed back.

No response.

A soft knock rapped at the door before it creaked open. A man entered, dressed in a black security uniform. He carried a steaming tray, which wafted the scent of meat; he placed it on the small table near the barred window. Before he departed, he cleared his throat and bowed. My eyebrow rose without effort. Why would anyone submit to a prisoner?

I stared at the silver dish, trying to decide whether I trusted the food. A whoosh at the door drew my attention. A piece of folded paper lay on the floor. Hastily, I picked it up:

> "Dear Liam,
> The stars spoke before either of you were born. You are a Guardian born of an ancient bloodline. Auriel is a hybrid, born

for greatness. She alone bridged the gap between our worlds, but she can't do it without your help. Her grandfather and I could only protect her for so long. We knew it was only a matter of time before they found her. I've already lost my son, Liam. I can't lose Auriel too.

The elves and fae remain at war over her existence. We believed the uprooted Unseelie Court fueled the rift with lies, but we couldn't prove their source. Maeve had a dream; we didn't doubt it then. She said Auriel would die and save the world. We all assumed Maeve's words were true until Auriel came forth with her own visions.

Merric, blinded by hate, refused to believe her. Her death starts Ragnarok. We chose to put our faith in Auriel and sent them away. We've managed to fend off searches until recently, without revealing our deception to the council. The young Warden, who questioned you, was my husband's guardian in disguise. He even arranged for her to stay behind, to watch over Six and Twenty in order to appease the council. He loves Auriel that much and risks himself every day.

There is much to tell you, so much I wanted to clarify, and no more time. I write to you now because I know I've wronged you.

My only hope is that you'll believe me. I tried to make you stronger, hoping she'd complete the memory spell once they were settled, but I was too late. Auriel had cast it before they left, on you and herself. I was immune, like Jamie. She never cared for me, and while it hurt, it was for the best. The pain I've caused, I can't take it away.

The Nine is lost to us. We're taking Aurie home when she arrives. I'll need your help; she won't want to leave. It's time to end this feud once and for all.

The council is determined, but we will hold them off for as long as we can. It's up to you to convince her to use the Bifrost and travel to Alfheim. Sir Thomas is waiting for you both.

Sincerely,

Keelan Graftfield

I scoffed at her twisted words. No, he wasn't waiting in the Bifrost. No, the Warden hadn't stayed behind. The King waited on

Midgard. My Gods was anyone sane in this world? I pinched the bridge of my nose as the words settled. The letter made no sense. Okay, so it sort of did, but a war between the fae and the elves? They were hardly a different race. Elves were just fae without wings.

Travel the Bifrost? Take Auriel to Alfheim? Nope. Was I supposed to propel her over my shoulder and pound on my chest? "Me Tarzan. You Jane." My laughter bubbled out. I tried controlling her, and it exploded in my face.

"Liam," Auriel's voice rocked me out of my silent reverie. My heart raced; she was close. It still felt like we were a thousand miles away from one another. *"We'll be there soon, hang on. I love you."*

I'd no choice but to listen to her. Even though I wanted to scream, "Stay away." But the words refused to form, as my knees buckled beneath me. She loved me. The ache, as if a part of me were missing, settled inside. Our hearts bared so much pain; how much more before they blackened and died. Scars and bruises littered mine. Pieces scattered through time that she alone could mend. Auriel, I forgave her, always. Yet again, she saved me. Wasn't I supposed to protect her?

No. She'd reminded too. My job revolved around her, true, but I was to remain at her side. We were a team, equals. Our bond promised nothing else. At least it would if she would stop breaking it.

chapter fourty-two

AURIEL

As we approached the Nine's eastern headquarters, and home of the beloved council, I sensed Liam the strongest. Elation should've been the first emotion coursing through my veins, but where there should've been lightness, heaviness settled in over my avian body.

I thought they'd keep the brothers together ... unless Jamie was involved. Gods, I wanted to be mistaken for the Fenrir's sake. For the sake of my friendship, but this wouldn't mark the first time he'd turned on us to benefit himself.

My form suffocated me as Nick relayed his agreeing thoughts. "No, eun beag, tis daena feel right."

I swallowed the realization, the truth. One of our own turned on us.

Nick understood though. Feelings would wait. There was no other choice but to move forward with our plans. A time and place for everything, we couldn't afford the bitterness creeping in.

We skirted the shield's edge. The pinpricks of Nick's soul fell through the gaps of my shield. I nudged him mentally, sending out what little warmth I mustered. One wrong move and the Wardens would descend upon us. Right now, Paulo stayed confident—we'd keep the element of surprise. But I wasn't a soldier, not like the draugr and not like my grandfather the Paladin Knight.

"They're expecting me," I said, closing my eyes. Leave it to me to state the obvious but I grasped at the straws of my own sanity. *"But not as I am and not with the help."*

The thought comforted me even if I shrieked and trembled with fear on the inside. My little talons landed on Paulo's shoulder. I'd asked him to lead the way since he knew the layout of the HQ. We decided that if I saw any illusion I'd bite him twice, three times if I wanted him to stop, and chirp if I sensed immediate danger. Thomas did the same from the rear, minus the chirping and pecking. Laughable, but they didn't expect it.

The council awaited my arrival, and Paulo mumbled about increased activity. His whispers were light enough to reach my ears. Regin's tall ears twitched, and her furred head turned toward the draugr. My vision darkened and flashed back to the dream where I thought she died. Losing Jamie to the darkness in his heart was the same. It sliced through me, but his actions changed nothing.

Nikolas stayed in his humanoid form to translate my other thoughts. He'd shift within seconds if needed, but he wasn't helpless in his human form. The Phoenix remained strong in his heart, unlike his mate. I'd known his father, but the wisdom, honor, and love inside his heart was his own. The Fenrir clan –created by Loki from his original son theFenris wolf – bridged the same gaps as I did.

Few understood the delicate balance between man and beast. The fragile state it left the mind easily gave way to both darkness and light. Control and a strong heart were required, and few possessed it. Loki approved those who sought the lycan gift instead of allowing their existence to spread over Midgard. My bird brows rose. *It's a good plan if you think about it.*

There were thousands of questions rattling through my mind. Each passing breath brought new ones as we moved through the silent night. I held no answers and relied upon the blind faith of my former Goddess.

Walls built around my heart and soul, though they would not sway the outcome of our mission. My eyes darted between my friends. They risked way more than they let on coming here. If

Sköll caught them, he would not hesitate to take the Fenrir siblings out. He did not blink when he murdered his own brother, yet one would die, and the vision never revealed who. Neither of them was replaceable, but all signs pointed toward Nick.

"*The road to freedom remains blurred,*" Freya said. "*But they shall not fall tonight.*" I nodded my feathered head in agreement and cleared my mind.

Perched on Paulo's shoulder, we tiptoed the outer perimeter. The evening gave little cover with the large moon shining overhead. "*After all these years, they still have holes in their defense,*" he thought.

I'd always wondered how the council and guards remained unaware. This wasn't the first time Paulo broke in, and I doubted it would be his last dance. The Nine was aware of his actions, but for whatever reason they allowed his freedom runs to continue. Maybe they didn't realize how he did it, or they knew where he lived. I would not pretend to understand half of what the Nine Council allowed or disallowed. A branch broke in the distance, and we halted, bodies tensing one by one.

The same went for my family; I saw nothing of their actions doing anyone good.

Regin's snout lifted to the air, and Nick followed her motions. My tiny heart hammered enough to shake my body. Paulo shook his head and thought, "*Raccoon.*"

One by one, each muscle relaxed, and Great-Grandfather drew out a long breathy sigh. Calling him Great-Grandfather felt odd because of his youthful appearance, but I doubted he'd take kindly to me using his given name to his face. King Reagent also seemed wrong even though both names were quicker off the tongue.

Neither were important, but the more I thought about the mundane problems, the more relaxed I became. The more relaxed I became, the more I focused.

Waves crashed, breaking across the shore. This hole lay near an abandoned park located north of the headquarters. Graffiti and spray painted names lined the short stone wall surrounding the metal graveyard. I closed my eyes, picturing small children laughing and enjoying the splendor of youth.

The life I led even then afforded me little pleasures. The joy and love I'd once had came from those around me. My eyes shifted to the guard station, and the split in the chain link fence that lined this section of the compound. Wrought iron made more sense, but I'd take anything working to our advantage. But the Nine's goal wasn't keeping people out.

The façade and intricate spell work kept humans from stumbling upon our secret world.

"Inside is naught our problem." The thick magical shield of melded Myst meant nothing. Its design differed from Six and Twenty. The goal turned a complete one eighty as I sampled the construction. My vision narrowed, and the realization battered my insides. "Aye, my dear, it keeps them in and humans out. Is naught good for anything else."

Paulo threw his hand up alerting a halt and placed a finger over his lips. Two fingers pointed toward a large circular tower with connecting bridges to the building wing. I flew into a nearby palmetto tree for a closer look. The leaves blew in the hot humid breeze and ran through my ruffled feathers.

A Warden stepped from his booth and lit a cigarette. I wanted to ram the cancer stick down his throat. The nose curling nicotine cloud made me sneeze as it overpowered the salty sea air. The guard narrowed his eyes, but shrugged and turned around. Four sets of breaths exhaled at once. Thank goodness, bird sneezes attracted little attention. We awaited the guard change. We'd have a two-minute window to enter the building and elude any interior patrols before finding Momma, Liam, and hopefully the missing Alfheimian Queens.

The time to act fell upon us. Paulo tapped Nick on the shoulder and pointed toward the moving guard descending the stairs. He nodded and closed his eyes, communicating with his sister. I'd offered to cast a spell for total mind blending, but she'd declined. I flew from my lofty perch into the open door. We gained entry into the prison, where Paulo once worked.

If not for his thoughts, my mind would reflect those around me. It felt too easy seeing as each of us had a history within these walls, some of it lived and breathed. A constant reminder loomed in the air of where we came from, and the lengths our blood went to in the name of the Gods.

I sensed everyone at once as we eased through the shield. Emotions rolled over me like a tidal wave, and the hatred, love, fear, and worry collided with my tiny-feathered body. It ripped and shredded at my façade, threatening to destroy me. Momma, Liam, Jamie, and one more I hadn't expected—Ezekiel.

"Stay with Auriel," Nick said to Paulo, contradicting the plan. The flash of rage in his eyes made him move back. He sensed Jamie too, and his cold eyes gave him away. His emotions conflicted; as he stepped in the direction I'd sensed his mate, he halted. When he faced us, there was no hiding the agony rippling over his timeless face. Paulo nodded his head; none of us understood the lengths a mated lycan went for love. Not even Regin, as far as I knew she hadn't mated yet. His boots sounded in the distance, and each thump rattled my heart. My eyes drifted between the pulling sensations.

We were now lost sheep walking into a pit of starving lions. The draugr sniffed the air, and I cocked my head. "Liam is in the eastern corridor, and your mother is in the south," Paulo whispered to me.

I envied his sense of smell as it still managed to outshine mine. What I would give to smell Liam's woodsy scent as he wrapped me into his arms and told me he loved me. The reality painted differently, and I'd be a fool-headed woman to ignore all sides of my new life. Kiel, his draw overpowered me. The part of Liam I loved, maybe always loved. My head shook. The piece created as my true half. I'd felt him etch into my soul before he flew away, and I sensed him even now as if he had become a part of me.

The dreams of my future, the future we'd share if I chose him haunted me. The images sent a chill through me as I recalled my best friend stabbing my womb. All of that love came with a hefty price. Splitting him from Liam helped the older child, right? Liam was still my husband—soul mate or not – I loved him too. For sixteen years and six weeks, we were together. As my Guardian, we survived as a team.

"Liam first," Thomas ordered, and a grim smile spread over Paulo's lips. The draugr disagreed, but he kept his thoughts to a minimum.

Without a word, I flew from Paulo's shoulder. Quicker and easier to hide, it made no sense to stay. Besides, I'd see danger before they did courtesy of my predatory vision. Once in flight, I promptly saw

I wasn't alone. Hungin and Munin joined me in my aerial search. How many creatures of the Myst turned on Odin and his followers?

"Who said they belong to Odin?" Loki laughed, and my flight staggered for a moment.

I righted myself and narrowed in on the draw of Liam. My senses muddied the closer we were. We soared from room to room, squeezing through the bars. Each cell held a prisoner, but not the ones I sought. Their startled looks and hopelessness ate through my shields. If I could, I'd release them all. Perhaps I would. If for any reason, a final lesson to the Nine. Never pen or reject what you refused to understand. Embrace it, nurture it, and love us instead. That was what Momma and Daddy did for me, and I'd never forget it.

CHAPTER
FOURTY-THREE

JAMIE

The council of the Nine was an incredible sight. Many of the members lived and served since the founding, which predated draugr, hybrids, and even the resurrection of humanity from the great flood. The power and wisdom radiated to my core when in their presence. It humbled me now as their gazes studied and scrutinized me.

My eyes remained on my surroundings. Merric said not to look at them unless addressed. I stared at the marble floor beneath my heavy feet, skirting my eyes over the raised balcony where the Council of Nine sat in their lofty chairs.

Nick ... he left me no choice but to side with the Oracle. This was the only way we could be together, but the steep price required more forgiveness. My reward for delivering Fainauriel would seal our fate for eternity. Merric promised to change me and avoid the disappointment when Loki rejected me. I risked a glance upward as my eyes followed the strange smoke rising in the air.

Prince Duncan's lavender eyes burned through me. "Where is Fainauriel?"

The heat rose to my cheeks. I glanced away, but his wings fluttered his descent. We came nose to nose. Sweat beaded on my forehead despite the cold air conditioning of the chamber. His short auburn hair and pale skin did nothing to soften his unaged features. Frozen like Aurie … Hard to believe he was her grandfather when he appeared younger than I did. His lips pressed tight, and his hands reached for me. I stepped away, recalling the burning pain from Aurie's white Myst. Duncan's lips twitched, and amusement danced in his eyes.

"I expect her soon," my father replied, with a steadiness I envied. Staring down again, my legs and hands both trembled.

The Faerie Prince snapped, "I asked Jamie." With his words, my head flew up. I gulped, twisting my fingers. He looked … relieved. My brows rose, as the hardened lines around his eyes faded. Nick and Aurie were wrong about him, but why'd his wife create this charade?

"She … I …" I could not form the words and scratched my head. He didn't want her here?

"Oh now, Duncan, stop badgering the poor lad." Princess Maeve spoke. Her silvery blue eyes sparkled even in the lowest light. Both born in Alfheim: The realm of the light faeries. There was nothing light about her midnight hair or the cruel soul within her svelte body.

"I'm more interested in dis other one ye captured. Ye claim he is lycan?" I nodded to Sköll but resisted eye contact.

Any person who slaughtered his own family —without valid reason – wasn't one I'd call a friend. If I'd had the slightest inkling of what he'd planned, I never would have turned on Nick and his family. Gods, I was such an asshole. What was I even doing here? Oh right, Nicky told me to get on the inside, but now what? My eyes darted toward the exits. We were all in danger.

"Ye still are." Duncan's eyes widened at the same time as mine. Was there a blood Graftfield who could not read minds? *"When he sounds the alarm, find me."*

I bit the inside of my cheek as his words sunk in. "Why are we even convening? Mages don't care about two natured politics," Malinda, the representative for mages, piped up. I'd agree with her in most cases, but Liam was more than two-natured. I thought the council already knew, but as I glanced at my father, I saw his head shake.

My eyes flashed to Duncan, and I pled silently. If he loved his granddaughter, he'd allow no harm to come to Liam. As a Phoenix, he had to understand the Guardian bond. She broke the bond once, and they'd barely survived. I gulped realizing the thin ice I had stumbled upon in this strange twist of family dysfunction.

"Regardless of yer opinion, I wish to see this lycan," Sköll growled at Malinda, and he crossed his massive arms. Larger than Nick's, the shirt he wore strained to maintain his size. His lip quivered up and bared his teeth.

"No," Duncan snapped, but his eyes were on me. "There isn't time for your ... games."

Someone banged a gavel, and my gaze fell back into to his. He grasped my arm. *"Shut up before you get us all killed."* The faerie prince patted my cheek and tilted his head. Duncan's eyes widened, and my heart rate soared.

"She is here now," he whispered, before flying from the room.

I ran after him, not realizing how fast he flew. The rest of council followed albeit none of them appeared concerned when I glanced back. Only Merric kept up with me and ruined my plan to slip away.

"Do you wish us to sound the alarm brother?" Maeve asked, but the faerie ignored her. My heart pounded as we approached the cell I'd tossed Liam into after we arrived.

"It's empty," Merric whispered to me as Duncan screamed, "Activate the TBM and alert all Wardens." The Transmitting Broadcast Monitor was an elaborate alarm and detecting device. Those of us who trained within the Nine withstood the brain-numbing siren. "Even the trainees ... find her damn it, find my granddaughter!"

My lips twisted. Had I read him wrong after all? Sirens and Wardens ... Duncan was pulling out all the stops. Aurie held more power than I'd ever witnessed, but could she withstand the alarm and the guard? Merric cocked his head toward me, but I ignored him. I picked up a stray brown feather from the floor. Twirling it around in my fingers, I understood that I'd never known who or what Auriel was, let alone what she was capable of but did they know?

"We need to go, Jamie." Merric grabbed my arm and tugged. "I know where she's headed next." My arm tore free; I wanted Nick, not Aurie. "C'mon boy."

chapter
fourty-four

LIAM

The door had slammed against the wall, sending a cloud of dust into the air. Three birds surrounded me, but I recognized the two ravens. Two lycans, two ravens, a Knight, a draugr, and a single falcon made for a fascinating rescue party. My brow rose, and I chuckled. This sounded like the beginning of a bad joke.

Thomas' mouth tugged up into a smile. "Let's go son, we've still got to make it to Lettie," Paulo whispered and lifted me up to my feet.

"Where's Aur—" A screeching sound filled the prison. The brown bird landed on my shoulder and pecked at my neck. Paulo shushed the falcon and waved us on. It flew away, joining the other birds at the head. Thomas spoke fast in hushed tones, informing me of Freya's cloak of feathers as we made our way into the main corridor. I stole glances at the brown bird gliding up ahead, swooping up and down.

"Is it you?" I asked, picturing her sweet, smiling face as I remembered each curve of her visage. My hand rubbed over my face as I attempted to read her mind. She kept herself locked down and pushed back at my attempts.

My anger from before had dissipated. Emptiness grew in my heart and soul. I'd thought forgiveness was enough to fix us. Each passing second she seemed farther away, but the primal need to pursue her had disappeared. The Guardian bond remained, and I cared for Auriel, but those extraordinary, mind-numbing feelings were gone.

"Get yourselves out," Jamie said as he rounded the corner. Before I responded, eardrum-blowing sirens ripped through the silence. The Myst ceased my legs, and my hands flew up and covered my ears. Dizziness and the ability to think halted. Howls, yips, and shrieks followed, growing louder with each passing second.

One by one, we fell to our knees as the Wardens surrounded us. All of us save Dad and Aurie, both of which still stood.

"Where'd ye think yer going?" a tall, young blue-eyed Warden asked over the noise. I blinked; how were they unaffected?

"Wherever we want to son," Paulo hissed, blue strobe lights reflected off his drawn fangs. The Wardens eyed each other before stepping backward. Their magic wouldn't stop or restrain a draugr.

"Ye will ne'er make it out alive," he growled back as a loud popping noise drew my attention. Red Myst swirled in the hallway as the shrilled war cry of the Valkyrie silenced the alarm. My veins surged with newfound courage. Her brown falcon wings spread out wide; they blocked the hallway as Auriel knelt to the marble floor. A feathered cloak lay between her bare shoulders.

She glanced up; her new gold-rimmed icy stare seared over the Wardens and matched the twitch of her clenched jaw. My little darlin' was royally pissed, and my grin widened.

"How dare you threaten us?" Her voice resonated from the heart as she rose to her feet. My eyes soaked up the scene, scanning right down to the black combat boots, echoing her steps. Beautiful and fearsome as always but my heart did not beat faster. Her eyes crossed to me, and she nodded. The veil dropped, and her thoughts rang clear. "*There are different kinds of love*," her thoughts said. "*Ours has changed, or maybe this was temporary. Either way, I still love you, Liam.*"

I replied, "*You're still my friend no matter what happens.*" She nodded again. "*I will always love you.*"

Thomas handed her a sword. Her memories relayed its artistry. The razor sharp blade forged and etched, with the runes of her family and in the dwarven lands Alfheim. Silver and iron laced and melded together. Both were capable of killing supernaturals. Aurie slid it into her sheath hanging from her jeans. Thomas handed over a shield, and it featured the same protective runes etched over the surface.

"Ye are no threat to us, witch." Laughter bubbled up as Auriel drew upon her power. The heat washed over me as she dragged it from all around her. She raised an eyebrow, daring them to move closer. After tonight, history would change. That particular thought ran through her mind.

"You talk too much." Sweat beaded on their foreheads. They tried subduing her, but their ability faltered. She sauntered around the enclosed circle, remaining out of their grasp.

Auriel unsheathed her weapon, and her smile widened. The Wardens exchanged furrowed glances, and their thoughts relayed what their bodies hid.

A rune-etched sword rose to the sky. "Teine beag."

The collected Myst unleashed, combining with her Phoenix, and poured into the blade. Flickering white fire coated the surface. The wardens paced and watched. Nimble hands and fingers trembled. My own heart beat waiting for a taste of the action. She aimed for the chatty one who seemed to be their leader; her white fire streamed off the blade, hitting him squarely in the chest.

Our team held steady as he screamed in agony. The Warden tore his clothing from his body and tried to shift. Patches of fur ignited as they sprouted, and the harsh odor turned my stomach. The flame spread quicker than he could react, burning him to silvery ash. I blinked and swung my gaze between Auriel and the dead Warden.

Regin and Paulo stepped away from her. I grasped her hand. She was stuck with me till the end even if she burned a Warden with the flick of her wrist. "Whoa there darlin'."

Auriel squeezed my hand and let go. She held control; her molten eyes cooled and retracted to a crystalline blue. "Anyone else want to stop me?"

Her eyes narrowed, and I scanned the hallway waiting for anyone to make a move, ready to shift if needed. She couldn't take all the glory. The darkness inside of me wanted her to burn them all. My hatred for the Nine ran bone deep as I sensed the ones responsible for it all; my life, my anguish, and my anger. The Council. My eyes scanned over each one until I connected with a set of ice blue eyes. Fenrir. Father. Sköll.

He nodded, knowing. Yes, he knew what I was. His bastard half-breed son lived. "Get hi—"

"Shut it, Sköll." Merric shoved him, and I blinked. Sköll snarled, grumbling words that weren't understandable in any language. How could a man hate me that much without ever knowing me?

I stepped out, but Nick's hand grasped my arm, and he yanked me back. Where'd he even come from? Auriel saw too and jumped in front of me. "Are you mad?" Her wide eyes seemed to say, and the same echoed in Nickolas' eyes.

"Cousin, tis a death wish. Ye isn't strong enough." Even as the words left his mouth, Sköll's eyes connected with mine again. His lip lifted, and his snarls reached my ears.

Whether he cared about Nick or Regin's lives was lost on me, but not his hostility toward me. No, that preceded everything. "Only Lannie, wherever she tis, canna defeat him."

chapter
fourty-five

AURIEL

"That's enough, *Fainauriel.*" I turned away from Liam and came face to face with my grandfather. Thomas Duncan Graftfield, Jr. and the crowned Prince of the Alfheimian Unseelie Court. I cringed as he used my Faerie name. There wasn't an ounce of remorse left in my body, but there remained plenty of molten fury. Regardless of his motives, everyone needed to butt out of my life and stop trying to protect me from my destiny.

"I say when it's enough, Duncan," I snapped, red blinding my vision as if an atomic bomb exploded a bloody mass into the sky. My hand flew out, and I pressed the blade to his chest; it took every ounce not to run him threw.

My teeth gritted and head throbbed as I spoke to him. "You lost that right. Kidnapping my mother and murdering my father sealed that fate."

"Duncan," Thomas interjected. "Where is your mother?"

He ignored him. *"You think I'd slay my own blood?"* His hands fell to his hips. *"I've done nothing but protect you since you were but a wee bairn."*

My hands trembled, threatening to drop my sword. Tears stung, threatening to fall as the weight of the lies, deceit, everything I'd ever known, unfolded. He told the truth. Thomas nodded and confirmed my fears. I hated him more for it than thinking he wanted me dead.

"Let us go, let them all go," I whispered, stretching my shielded arm in the direction of the others. He shook his head, and I backed off.

"Have it your way then." My blade lifted.

"Auriel stop," Thomas said. I shook my head and sniffled. The man in front of me was the enemy regardless of his innocence. Because of him I had to hide. *"That's your darkness."*

"Auriel you didn't listen …" Jamie drew my attention His words trailed as Nick's hand wrapped around his throat.

"Run, get my momma," I relayed to the Liam. He grabbed Paulo and darted away. The remaining Wardens didn't dare follow. "Call off your dogs, grandpa."

The clicking of heels grew louder, and the crowd parted. A tall woman with silky black hair walked through the council. The hundred or so years were kind to her youthful features, but I recognized the darkness tainting her soul. It tainted mine too. She tapped a small dagger against her palm.

"You remember the seax?" Maeve's brow arched, and a sly smile touched her lips. My chin lifted. Thomas stepped in front of me and Nick dropped Jamie to join him. The Knight hissed, "Maeve what's the meaning of this?"

"Father," she said. "What … are you doing here?" The voice cut through me like a thousand daggers. The one in her hand disappeared behind her back. My heart raced, and my legs wobbled, but I found the strength to stand. The voice … My great aunt killed my father. I peeked through the small gap left by Thomas and the massive Nick. She dropped the knife, but picked it up, and tucked it into her burgundy robe.

"Where is your mother? I will not ask you again," Thomas roared, and Duncan trembled.

My eyes widened as I caught sight of the family runes. Maeve had the sacrificial knife. *"Run, luv."* Ezekiel. The room spun as Maeve pressed against my mental barriers. My shaking hand grasped Nick's shirt, and I held firm.

"Breathe, eun beag." Maeve straightened her clothes and faced Duncan. My makeshift guards shifted closer, concealing my body.

They knew I was there, but the barrier protected me from her weapon. Calm, cool, and too collected for a woman caught off guard. She thought I hadn't recognized her.

Duncan whispered, "Take the Council to safety." Her eyes connected with mine, and I shivered under the gaze. Was it always her? Did she attack my parents and murder her nephew?

The Council argued, and Sköll voiced his objections the loudest, but my great-aunt led him away. He'd wanted the Fenrirs taken into custody. Her whispers reached my ears, and the promises soured my stomach. We'd fail and not make it out alive, according to her. My thoughts flashed back to Regin's body clasped in the devil's hands.

Maeve glanced at me once more, and I forced a smile. This was far from over, and I'd make sure she paid for her sins. Over my dead body would I let them take my friends. The large door at the end of the hallway slammed closed, and my protectors stepped aside.

That left Duncan, Jamie, Merric, and the Wardens. "Grandpa, let us go," I repeated and gripped the hilt of my sword. Two Phoenixes, a draugr hybrid, and the supercharged two natured warriors. Grandpa's Guardian hid nearby; I sensed the chains in his Myst. Not all Guardians developed romantic relationships with their charges. He loved my grandmother even as she aged, and he remained the same. It'd be quite sweet and romantic if she hadn't tried to kill me and lied to me.

His eyes met mine. "It's not that easy."

"Duncan," Thomas warned.

Jamie crossed the invisible line, and I drew the blade to his neck. Merric moved faster than I expected and pinned Nick against a cell door. My eyes narrowed, recalling every time he'd stabbed me in the back. His chin dropped, and he pressed against the sharp edge. I wanted to forgive him and trust him … both him and my grandfather.

"Hurt him and you hurt your son." The ache in Jamie's eyes tore into my soul. He'd not told his father about the lycan bond. Nick choked, but he'd shake the draugr if needed.

Regin defended her brother, growling and snapping at the draugr's heels. Merric released my friend, but I held the blade tight against Jamie's throat.

Fenrir grasped my shoulder and whispered, "Fer me." Nick adds, "All of this was out of love."

I dropped the sword from his neck and stepped back. Nick embraced him as Merric shouted. My breath sucked in, as their love and passion rolled over my shield. Nick dipped his head and kissed Jamie. My heart fluttered as two of my friends shared their intimate moment.

"Shut your mouth," I snapped at Merric. No wonder his wife had an affair. The draugr rounded on me, but I turned out of his sneak attack. Grandpa engaged and pinned me against the wall as chaos filled the hallway.

It happened faster than a knife fight in a phone booth. Even as I struggled with the psychic and physical assaults of Duncan, they didn't dare move. Not a step toward me. Regin and Thomas were another story, they surrounded them, and I kicked and screamed to break through. Reggie snarled, fighting against their attempts like a true Fenrir. Thomas sliced through the Wardens. He too was immune to them. The lycan bit and tore, kicked and swiped, but she wouldn't last long if I didn't do something soon. Even a Fenrir was susceptible to a Warden.

"Kiel ... you need him," Jamie said. Merric turned on his son and Nick shifted, lunging for the draugr throat. "The oracle captured him." That was why I sensed him.

I heaved Duncan off, but he slammed me against the opposite wall. A blade drew out of thin air, and I spat on the ground. My hand tightened around my hilt, and I summoned my shield, which had fallen from my grip along the way. A fireball flew by, striking down one of the Wardens attacking Regin. They kept coming. As soon as we took one down, more arrived. I eyed Merric, and my mouth dropped. Did he switch sides?

"I don't want to fight you," grandpa said, frowning and speaking in my mind. "We've arranged passage to Alfheim for you and Liam. You must go."

I blinked, as his blade connected with my shield. The impact vibrated and rattled my voice. "My fight is here." I flinched as he struck again. "This is my destiny, Gramps."

"Where's Nana?" I deflected his next attack. Duncan's mind quieted. Whether it was understanding or a ploy, I didn't know. My faith in him lay broken in two like my heart, split between two men.

But could I take my grandfather down? My blood flowed through his veins and vice versa. My jaw clenched as I pressed against him. Inner strength and the Myst weren't enough. Grandpa knew it too; I lacked the prowess of a cold-blooded killer. He turned the fight again and pinned me against the wall. The force threatened to crack my wings. My heart hammered against my rib cage as my eyes scanned for any escape.

"Have faith, luv. Have confidence in yourself, and those who stand against the wickedness of our realms. Invoke the Phoenix." Ezekiel reached out to me, and the light bulb I called a brain flickered on.

"Eun teine." I managed through my gritted teeth as white flame spread over my body. Duncan shrieked, falling to the ground, patting the fire out. Grandpa was a Phoenix, but our patron's power coursed through my veins. Loki's laughter echoed through the hallway. My breath came in bursts as it caught. That was what he did to me.

Duncan scrambled across the hall with ever widening eyes. Freya's ability existed inside of me. This was my new destiny; this was my prophecy. I clutched my shielded fist to my chest. The white fire flickered over my skin before it extinguished and left my skin sweaty.

"I warned you; I warned them all." My voice altered, sounding less like me, and taking on a Norwegian accent. I blinked and shook my head. He stared at me and then down the hall.

He glanced back. "Go." A smile formed over his lips, as he held his healing arm. "No matter what I've done or do, Fainauriel, I love you, and I'm proud of the woman you've become. I'll do what I can and distract the council."

"Fosgail." I tossed my hands to the heavens as my red Myst released again.

The cell doors clicked. A wispy fog filled the hallway, lending cover, but it wasn't mine. That'd keep the Nine Council and Wardens busy for hours. I glanced to Reggie and shouted over the chaos. Blood covered her coat and spilled over the marble floor. I ducked and spun on a Warden.

She pounced, ripping her throat, and came to my side, dragging and shaking the Warden's battered body. On the inside, I chuckled while I dusted off my hands, smearing the grime on my ripped jeans. Jamie's citrus scent burned my nose as I walked away. Regin growled at him.

"Aurie please …" he gasped, but my steps increased. One noble deed didn't eliminate the betrayal. His love for Nick … no. What if I'd been too late, and Sköll had claimed Liam's life? Was the power or whatever his prize worth more than his brother? I shuddered at the thought. The notion ate at me, the bile rising.

"Talk and walk, I don't have time for your groveling," I snapped at him. His treachery penetrated deeper than any before. His actions put all our lives at risk. He put those I loved in harm's way. How could I ignore that?

Follow your heart … My heart screamed forgiveness.

"I can … explain. Nick …" He grabbed my shoulder, and I tossed him off. "Your grandmother promised …" My eyes rolled, but I bit my tongue. I bet she promised him Nick. "I never wanted anyone to get hurt. Nick said to do it."

I whipped around and pinned him to the wall by the throat. "What are you babbling about?" Eyes bulged as Jamie struggled, clawing at my hand under my newfound strength. He was bigger than I was, but I didn't let that detail stop me.

"Sköll," he said with a rough and raspy tone.

"Eun beag … Let him go, Fainauriel." I let him drop. Nick seldom used my name unless he meant serious business.

"What about him?" But I already knew.

"He suspects Liam is a Fenrir."

My eyes narrowed. No, he held something back. "Liam *is* a Fenrir. He's *his* son. Dang, I thought everyone knew that." Everyone but Sköll because the King thought him dead, or at least he did before Jamie waltzed him in here.

Jamie nodded, and I had half the mind to freeze him in place, and then smash him to the four winds. The danger … Liam could have been harmed.

Nick placed his hand on my shoulder, and I stumbled out of his grasp. He made me madder than a wet hen. If anything happened to the Fenrirs, I'd come back and tear every appendage from his mate's body. Then I'd throw his cunning, immoral, stealing, sorry ass straight to the depths of Hel. I huffed and blew out my breath. No, that was too good for him. Maybe I'd send him to Svartalfheim, to the dark elves ever-burning realm where my great-great grandmother ruled in the chaos she loved. After all Jamie wanted to live forever. The idea curved my lips.

The burning rage clouded my thoughts, and I stalked away. The sounds of his feet pitter-pattered behind me, and my head shook. Dang, neither of them took the hint.

"Someone told Sköll." His voice trembled, giving my thoughts pause. "I swear to the Gods that I didn't turn them in. I might be an idiot, but I didn't come here to kill anyone." *Pfft, yeah right.* "Aurie, I'd never do anything to hurt you or Nicky. Hurting Liam accomplishes that."

His fate rested in Nick's hands. My name might've been chooser of the slain, but his words rang true. He did not rat out his brother or Nick and Regin.

"Fine." I glanced to Fenrir. "We need a way out of here." I placed the hood of my cloak on the top of my head and transformed into a falcon flying away from Pandora's Box. Not that she ever existed in the first place.

"I meant the Valkyrie ..." Jamie scratched his head. "Didn't you know she took him too?"

chapter
fourty-six

JAMIE

Nick grasped my hand and squeezed. He'd forgiven me on some level and publically accepted me as his mate. Not over the kidnapping but my past problems. This was his idea after all. Years in the shadows ended, and my chest lightened. The world and its weight freed from my broad shoulders. The path before us filled with hills, but I held faith for once.

My father stepped forward. "Find Morgana," Merric whispered. His reaction shocked me, not the yelling or initial response, but the acceptance of my choice. For the first time, I saw him as a father. "I'm going after Maeve." I blinked as he reached for Nick's hand and shook it.

Merric darted down the hall, and I watched until he'd disappeared. *Did that just happen?* Nicky pulled me closer and kissed the top of my head. "Aye, let's get out of here before—" A prisoner lunged at me screaming about revenge. Nick grabbed his shoulder and pushed him into a cell. My hand ran over my face, and I eyed the open cells. Anarchy – damn it some of those prisoners deserved cells.

Nick shot me a sidelong glance. "I know I look just like him." He fought the smirk curling his lips. "This way," I said and pushed, shoving convicts with my shoulder, toward the higher security wing.

These prisoners hadn't committed crimes, but their power or abilities had outweighed the risk. Most held no control and it turned my stomach. Was this what they held in store for Aurie and Liam?

"Duncan would've locked 'er up, not Maeve."

I groaned. Her room stood empty. "But there can't be no rules." The words blended through my clenched teeth as my eyes swept into the other empty cells we passed.

"Morgana," I called for her but should've known better. She hid herself on Midgard or tried to, but she was the last of her kind and a royal.

We turned back and retraced our steps, double-checking each cell. Druids manifested all five elements in their Myst: water, earth, air, fire, and spirit. Light was another name for the spirit. For many, they became a legend. Rumors circulated; Morgana once sat on the council, even created the original union, but they removed her for an act of treason.

Up ahead a tall hooded figure outstretched her arms. "Morgana," I shouted and pressed my way through the crowd. In her hands, she gripped a large wooden staff with a rounded moonstone at its tip. Her palm lifted and tossed me back with a shockwave of pure elemental Myst. The colors blinded me as they flashed and knocked the wind from my lungs. I toppled right into Nicky, and he grunted as we hit the stone floor.

"Well, well, Jamie Mc Douglass. It's been years since you've visited little old me." Morgana spoke with her blend of English and Alfheimian accent. As she lifted her head, I saw the calculated coldness behind her glowing lavender eyes. She hadn't aged at all from when I was a child.

Swallowing my unease, I managed a nod. "We need your help." Her head cocked to the side as she contemplated me. When she glided toward me, I still didn't have an answer. "Please … Thomas is here."

Morgana lived because of her heritage. An Alfhemian Elf kept their immortality on Midgard. A given with her lavender jewel-toned eyes, exceptional height, and pointed ears. *Pure blooded.* Paulo and Merric often left me with her during my mother's incarceration. That didn't make us friends, made apparent by the rainbow flame bouncing in her free hand.

"He's here looking for you," I squeaked. The druidess' lips tugged up. "She needs—"

Nick cut me off and approached the druidess. He held his palms open. "Yer Grace," he said with a slight bow. "Ye knew my father, Porofolr." The Myst extinguished in her palm.

"Nickolas?" Her eyes softened, and I got to my feet. The Myst drew into my palms and formed a shield. With the Phoenix returned after Auriel's spell, I held half a chance of absorbing or deflecting part of her spells. Morgana removed her dark hood. Black hair tumbled to her shoulders in a silken wave and violet eyes blazed to life, rounding out her cherub face.

"Jamie, get away from her," someone yelled after me. I spun and came nose to nose with a green-eyed woman. Sweat beaded on my forehead, and my heart pounded in my ears. They killed her. We watched them execute her. The violent gory scene played over and over in my head. The Nine went as far as to record it.

My mouth dropped open, and Nicky dragged me away from the woman. "Tis a farce." I blinked as she disappeared before my eyes. He pulled me into an empty room and sat me down. Morgana guarded the entrance. "Hen, talk to me."

"He's pale. We'll carry him." I heard their words, and my eyes darted between them, but none formed on my tongue. Why'd my momma's spirit visit me? Nicky had gathered me into his arms before I objected and left the cell.

"Eastern sector is where we'll find Lettie." Wait what about the other Queen? Twice he had to duck to avoid the blows. Wardens and prisoners blurred together, and there wasn't a way to distinguish who was who.

"Merric follows; do you wish me to take care of him?" Her eyebrow raised, but I shook my head. "My cousin is not prisoner here."

"We are here ..." Nick's words trailed off as he slid me down. Blood and burnt flesh made up the room. I gagged and retched from the scent. Auriel killed the guards; she killed anyone she didn't know. Their blood painted the walls with an eerie warning. I shuddered and wondered how close she'd been to ending my life. *"Verra close, hen. I'll speak with her and set the record straight."*

"Thomas," the druidess cried, stepping into the room. His blue eyes smiled as he stepped to her. True love, I had no doubts about it. It reminded me of the look I saw on Nick's face when he'd chosen me.

"Mori," he breathed her name, as his arms lifted her up, and spun the druidess around. "I love you ... missed you."

Stolen moments such as those kept love alive. Nick's memory kept me alive after I'd thought he'd died. His lips grazed my temple.

"Tha gaol agam ort-fhèin.," he whispered, answering the looming question I'd carried for weeks. Had Nick loved me as I loved him? "Always. Stop worrying yer pretty head."

I chuckled and ran a hand over my scruffy face. My skin hadn't seen a razor in days. Nick pulled me into the hallway and slammed me against the wall. My heart raced as a low growl vibrated in his chest. He blinked, and ice blue eyes swam with molten lava.

"Nicky." I pointed to an empty cell. The hallway left us exposed and a warden or his uncle could sneak up on us. A quick glance and we chuckled, barreling through the closed cell. His fingers laced into mine, and he dipped his head. Our lips hovered, and the heat of him poured over my body. My skin ached, and my lips parted, begging for a kiss.

If Morgana and Thomas could share a moment then so could we. Nick lifted me into his arms, and my legs wrapped around his waist. His cock pressed against me, and I groaned, curling my hands into his t-shirt and dragging him closer. Our noses touched, and a gasp erupted at the contact. Nicky waited though, and I didn't understand why. His hands cupped my face as his fingers stroked my stubble. I grinned wider with each tender movement he made.

"Ye're killing me." He snorted. My arms laced around his neck as he teased me. I rested my head against the wall and sighed. He smelled of sweat and nature; I wanted him to smell like me.

Dire times we'd lived through but all I wanted was a kiss. Long and hard ... toe curling ... Like an I-wouldn't-survive-without-you ... kiss. *Gods, just make him kiss me already.*

My hands moved to his face, and I leaned forward. Nick didn't pull away as I planted my mouth on his. My skin ignited; it seared straight into my core and tugged my insides. His grip tightened, and his massive body crushed me harder against the wall. I nipped at his pink lips until they opened. Hands grasped his hair and yanked him closer as his tongue dipped into my mouth. From my head down to my toes, my body tingled. Nick ground his body against mine. My chest ached, but I wanted him more than air.

Someone cleared their throat, but I refused to release him. Nick stayed close, his hands gripping my shoulders tight.

A foot tapped, and I pushed the sound away.

"I get that y'all are in love, but I need Nick's nose," Aurie said. I chuckled, and he pulled back. My lips followed, and I stole another peck.

His eyes remained on me, and a grin spread over his sweet face. Nick caressed my cheek, and I turned to kiss his rough palm.

He said, *"Èisd ri gaoth nam beann gus an traogh na h-uisgeachan, cuspair."* My feet slid to the floor.

"You too." I nodded; I'd wait and stay safe until the danger had passed. My eyes refused to watch him walk away even if they weren't leaving yet.

I whispered, "Tha gaol agam ort."

"Always," he thought and winked. How long did we have?

"Jamison git your ass in here," Liam bellowed from the room next door, and I shook my head, smiling because Nikolas Fenrir loved me. Not because of our bond, but because he loved me as I was.

chapter
fourty-seven

AURIEL

"Nana," I whispered to my great grandmother. "What of Selene and the others?"

"There isn't time to explain. I must open the Bifrost now." Few supernaturals traveled the Bifrost because the Nine forbid it. Those who attempted it went to straight to the big house.

"I can't go ..." I glanced at the door. "Nick, I need you."

Liam grasped my hand, but I shook my head. His grip tightened, and I cupped his face. *Not now*, I begged, but my pleas went ignored. "I have to find him."

"The hybrid's her fiancé," Thomas whispered to Nana.

"Husband," Liam grumbled and glared at his feet.

"Husband?" Jamie asked, and my face heated to a boiling. "When did you—"

"Lycan bond," he said, meeting my gaze. I bit my lip, and the rush of blood splashed over my tongue. He sat, kicking his legs out wide. Jamie winced, and I raised my eyebrow, but he said nothing. I'd ask Nick about it. Liam gazed at me; yellowed eyes blazed as the lycan's fists clenched and released. His soul tore, and so had mine.

Kiel remained the missing link and a piece of the man I once loved. He had to let me go. "Git then."

I stepped toward the door and quickly jumped aside. Merric rushed in behind him, dragging two prisoners. I stifled a snicker, pausing at the door.

Jamie asked, "Dad, what are you doing here?"

"I'm coming with you." Merric punched the inmate, and a scowl formed on my face. He caught me and smoothed his suit. "He'll live."

Jamie's eyes brightened, and I glanced to Nick. Fenrir shrugged and cocked his head toward the door. Right, we were on a time crunch. But the change in the draugr intrigued me. We'd assumed he'd abandoned Jamie. Father and son who had always had their differences. Perhaps the journey would heal their rift and change his destiny.

"As am I," Maeve said, and I turned to face the murderess.

Thomas moved in front of me, shoving me backwards into the brick wall. I shook the stars from my head. "Just bloody grand and all that rubbish."

My fists clenched, and I eyed her for weapons. Her hands were empty. Her nose shot into the air. "The rest of the council departed. Duncan even managed to get Sköll to leave."

Liar. Crap that didn't help our chances. "I'll go alone." Their caroling of no's vibrated my skull. Maeve moved away, and I marched past without a word. "Stay Liam."

The Wardens worked quicker than I'd expected. I raced through the almost empty hallways. Few fought anymore and many others lay upon the floor wounded, but few were dead. My hands rubbed my arms. Search for the lost souls they'd said, but I didn't understand what I looked for. Did the Valkyrie and Dísir look like me?

My head shook, and I turned back to the Myst.

"Come back … what did you do to me?" Liam asked in my head, but I tossed him out. Guardian or not, he needed to stay put. Sköll skulked this place, and it wasn't his destiny to take down his father. I halted as I sensed a draw. My body lurched forward, following the pull.

Up ahead I saw my grandfather fighting with a prisoner. Their Myst flung back and forth. I slid into another hallway, to avoid him as he pressed the prisoner closer to my position. My eyes peeked around the corner and widened as they came nearer. A thought occurred to me as I watched the scene unfold. Grandpa was older than dirt, but it was somewhat daunting to watch him fight in hand-to-hand combat.

I saw it firsthand, but the Myst was entirely different. The dark-haired girl pressed him and hurled blackened missiles. Her gaze met mine, and her eyes flashed black.

"Dísir," I whispered. She cocked her head and acknowledged me. "Let her go." I stepped out from my protective corner and pulled my blade.

The small girl pulled in the Myst. I shook my head. No, she didn't understand. My heart ached as I leapt in front of my grandfather and ran my blade through her neck. Hot blood splattered in my face, and I spat it out.

My fingers shook, and my sword clattered to the ground. What had I done? I faced my grandfather. She would've killed him. I did what I had to. *"Chooser of the slain."* Loki laughed in my head, and I tossed him out.

"We are too late." His violet eyes dropped to my feet. "I tried to stop it." My mouth dropped, and I closed it. What did he try to stop? No one stopped the Norns once they'd weaved a path. I learned that the hard way. He shook his head and turned the corner, heading opposite of my friends.

My head cocked, staring at the space for a moment. All the dots clicked together bit by bit. I dropped my gaze back to the small girl. Her blood congealed under my feet. I'd killed one of Odin's Valkyries. Kiel and my grandmother were his, and my destiny demanded I slaughter them too. I knelt down to close her eyes and retrieved Thomas' sword. Well we'd see about that. My hands and knees sank into the blood. Killing for the sake of killing, I shook my head at the thought. This young girl didn't deserve life; Grandpa defended himself, but everyone deserved the chance of redemption.

"Very good," Loki said, appearing near a large oak door. "Hatred is a powerful emotion, but love and forgiveness defeat it. You've passed your first test."

My mouth dropped open, and I glared at him. "This was a test?" I hissed a breath and strode toward him, my fist gripping my sword. He wanted hatred; well I'd show it to him. This life ... my destiny. I drew my sword from its sheath. Blood stained the hefty blade.

"You can't kill me, dear."

I swung the weapon, and it sliced through his body. Particles of Myst dissipated and scattered. His laughter echoed off the walls. But seconds later, Loki stood before me unharmed. My hands trembled, and my eyes darted around.

"You … you're not Loki."

He smiled. "I thought we'd established that." He chuckled as amusement filled his eyes. My cheeks flared, and the temperature rose. The demi-god fought to maintain his laughter. I growled and forced air through my nose. His finger crooked, and I glanced behind me. What did he want now?

"I don't understand," I said. Loki glided forward and clutched my free hand. I flinched, recalling the last time he touched me. Those words haunted me. Another misdeed ruined lives; I tore apart my own heart and soul. Loki guided me through the hallways and my heart thrummed. Each passing moment brought me closer to my soul, but farther from Liam.

We weaved in and out of hidden passages. Instinct or fear forced most I encountered to run away. Loki stopped and placed a hand over my heart. "It's close; can you feel it here."

The draw, yes I felt it, but I hadn't wanted to believe. The choice wasn't mine, and it never was. Nick and Jamie they didn't have a say in their bond either, but their future brightened. I envied them.

The demi-god cocked his head. "You have a choice, but every option holds consequence." I'd loved Liam blindly from birth, and I still did. The bonds and strands of our friendship wouldn't come undone overnight. But I knew nothing else aside from him. Kiel remained a piece of him even if he had his own body now. "Just like you have the choice to walk away." I turned and closed my eyes. My leg lifted and with it shards of proverbial glass embedded into my heart. Images flashed of the future. A child, a real family, and more than I'd ever hoped for. Together we'd save the young man who called me mom.

"No, there is no choice." In the room before me was the man who would give me the future of my dreams. The other led to the nightmares.

Layers of magic surrounded the chamber, and it sparked as I reached for the handle. I snared my hand away and stared down at the welt forming on my hand. It healed, but the magical burn remained. The spell felt familiar; ice trapped his door.

"I've already tried that, Aurie luv." Kiel called from the inside with his thick English accent.

"Ezekiel," I whispered. My heart hammered and filled. I hated it.

"Bloody hell it tis you, ducky. Thought I was going mad." I turned to ask Loki how to free him, but he'd left.

I transformed into a falcon, using Freya's cloak, and squeezed through the bars at the top of the door. On the inside the cell was small, the smallest I'd seen. There wasn't a bed, not even a window but a small table held green crystals and stones; another layer of magic held him. My eyes glanced to the floor, and I saw larger jagged, green glowing rocks holding Kiel in place. Etched on them were Odin's runes.

"Be a dear and move those emeralds."

He faced away from the door. How did he know I entered the cell? The pieces were heavy, solid gemstone, and I transformed back in order to lift them. Physically, I couldn't lift them and call on the Myst. When the final piece moved away, the magic evaporated.

"There all done," I said, dusting my hands off and staring at the back of his unkempt blond head. Far better than staring at his cute ass or tattooed back. He'd an impressive fallen angel with full wing span covering his corded muscles, and my hands itched to trace the lines.

Kiel faced me. My eyes widened as his electric blue eyes raked over me and stole my breath away. My chest ached, and the sound of my heart echoed in my ears. He cocked his head and smirked. "You remembered me, princess."

A few days passed, nothing more, why would I forget him? I swallowed hard, willing my lungs to breathe. In his presence, my mouth dried, and my legs weakened. As he stepped forward, I had stumbled backward, clattering into a table, before hitting the floor.

"Breathe luv," he said.

I trembled as his hands lowered to lift me up. It wasn't fear alone that caused my body to shake. The power rolled off him; it pulsed and caressed my skin. He held equal power to me ... Who was this man? Kiel's lip tugged up into a half smile. "You're my rescue party then? They send a bleedin' mutt." He ran his hand through his hair and over his face.

"Bloody hell, well aren't I special." The caressing energy slapped across my face. My mouth opened to speak, but I had nothing to say. Staring at his hand, he snapped his fingers. My eyes narrowed in on his thumb, and I resisted the urge to break it. "Well what you waiting for? I'm not the only one, y'know?"

His eyes rolled, and I fought another urge to slap him. What did they do to him? This wasn't the Kiel I met days ago. No, he cared and treated me well enough. Granted he left me too. My eyes fell away; I didn't know him at all.

After playing stone face for a few moments, I stood on my own. Faith, have faith, and conviction his once sweet voice told me before. Now when he opened his mouth, I prayed he shut his trap. Kiel snorted, reading my thoughts.

Good, I hoped he choked on them.

He led the way after showing me how to undo the spell. Whoever had done this had been sloppy and left the spell work behind but some of the words were unfamiliar. "Who cast it?"

I rubbed my arms and assumed the worst. "Your lovely grandmother."

Yeah, no shock there. She'd stolen Jamie's Myst and messed with Liam, forcing him to wait for me. I blinked; Grandma managed to thwart most of my plans. How much damage had she accomplished? Nick and Regin hid their identities from her; she concocted the plan to kidnap Liam and Kiel too. Grandma attacked me in the forest. My feet slowed down, but he said nothing. She lied to everyone.

My head ached, and it swam, sprinting for freedom. I glanced to him and bit my lip. His expression softened, and he reached for me. The sweet and salty scent enveloped me with his heat as Kiel held me. Tears refused to fall though the realization equaled a million bees stinging my skin.

"She can't kill you." Instead, she'd made my life a living hell and hurt me the one way she could. Grandma went after those I loved and held in my heart. I assumed she shared the same information with Aunt Maeve.

So much for normal. Kiel chuckled, and its warmth vibrated my ear. I blinked realizing my head rested on his bare chest and pulled away. The grip on my arms tightened, and I gazed upon his face. Blue eyes warmed, and those lips turned up into a smile. My skin heated under his stare. His head bent as if he meant to kiss me.

"No," I said after a few moments. "Let's go."

"Right, on we go then. Don't want to keep Liam waiting." He turned on his heels, shoved his hands in his pockets, and stomped down the hall. I followed but said nothing. There was nothing to say. Kiel needed to understand and not jump into this half-cocked. I didn't want to think about any of this. As it were, I was a stuck duck in a dry pond.

Finding the next Valkyrie proved far easier with Kiel leading the way. All belonged to Odin but seemed harmless. He was the only one separated; the rest grouped together in a large community cellblock. My brow lifted, and I wondered why. He offered me no explanation. Heck, Kiel hadn't bothered turning around.

"My name is Fainauriel, I was sent to save you and mean y'all no harm." ... *blah blah blah*. I let my wings span out and dipped with my body as I knelt before each Valkyrie.

They stared, eyes darkening into black pools. My mouth dropped, and I glanced to Ezekiel. For a split second, something crossed his face. But I blinked, and it faded away.

"Yep, it's the truth chaps and gals. Let's get a move on it, shall we?"

My pulse thundered the hot blood through my veins, and I blew out my uneasy breath. I faced Ezekiel, who smiled sheepishly and shrugged his wide shoulders. I yanked on his arm and pulled him aside. Eyes narrowing, my finger jabbed into his chest. "What is wrong with you?"

"Peachy luv," he said, reaching out to me, but I stepped aside. He moved with me, pinning me against the wall. My breath stayed steady, but my heart leapt from my chest. "Every moment with you drives me mad." Kiel brushed his lips over my ear. "They should lock me up in Bedlam and throw away the key."

"I ... I ..."

His lips tickled my jaw, and I gasped for breath. My hands glued to the wall. Palms down and fingers primed to the stone surface. If not, I'd touch him. All bets were off, and there was no going back. "Careful ducky, twenty-two years trapped away does things to a chap."

"We will follow." I peeked around him; the other six nodded in unison. Two others mumbled their yeses. Kiel turned, his hands staying on either side of my head. My eyes watched his tense jaw soften.

"Right then." His hand snaked around my back and pulled me against him. One at a time, they spread their smaller wings, which allowed them to hover and fly. "With me Aurie luv, can't afford any more dallying." I scoffed at him, and he rolled his eyes. "Stand on my feet and put your wings away."

I did as he said, but Kiel's amused smile burned my ears. His head flung backward as his wings snapped out. They were as large as mine. "Wrap your arms around my neck."

We stood nose to nose, and I forced my eyes elsewhere. The intensity of his gaze made me forget I was angry or annoyed. He'd helped in his own way. "I've a grand idea for repayment."

"Get out of my head."

I breathed him in as he moved my head to his shoulder. Gods he smelled good enough to eat. Salt and sweet caramel, with a touch of musky man tickled my pooka senses. Kiel chuckled, his calm heart beating in rhythm with his wings.

"Here we go, ducky."

The wind whipped past my face with all nine wings beating. His arm snaked around my waist, grazing my hip and rubbing circles over my tank top. Butterflies, or as Nana would say the bumbles, danced in my stomach and over my skin. I swallowed them away, reminding myself whose arms surrounded me.

We swooped into the cell where my mother stayed, and I met the glare of Liam from across the room. I didn't need to be an empath. Everyone could see his reddened face and clenched fists.

"About time," he grumbled, but his warm arms picked me up, and his lips dropped to mine. My arms reached around his neck, and I leaned into him. His green eyes glowed, and I gasped in surprise. My mouth opened, and for a moment, no one else existed. No one else existed because I might as well have been kissing the air. Gone, all of it, and I didn't want to believe it was possible.

"We're ready," Nana announced. Liam cursed as I stepped to her side.

While any supernatural held the ability to survive the Bifrost, only a few possessed the power to forge a new door. Druids were one of those races and the rest were the Gods and Goddesses. The majority of druids didn't dare try such a feat since the Nine outlawed them. The punishment far outweighed the risk. But if she had this type of power, how'd they ever lock her up in the first place? She provided no answers, but I wasn't surprised. Riddles and questions became my life, and I realized quickly that none of it mattered. Nothing changed me.

Even though I left and collected Odin's Dísir, more supes filed into the cell seeking refuge. We'd crammed in the cell like sardines and the temperature rose. The air grew thicker, and the smell turned my empty stomach.

"Auriel first," Liam and Ezekiel said together. I snorted and blinked at the men.

How dare they give me orders. "No, I go last." My eyes slanted. Liam burned daggers through me as his hands gripped my arms.

Keeping my voice soft and steady, I explained. "I have the power to hold the portal open, and it won't drain me as easily. Besides, I can enter the Bifrost without Nana "

"I'm not leaving you alone. You don't get your way this time." Liam scowled and turned his head. "You promised me." Ignoring him, I made a path to Momma and embraced her. I hated good-byes.

"You stay safe, Aurie." She sniffled in my ear, and I bit back my own tears. "You come back to me in one piece." She grasped Paulo's hand.

I whispered to Nana, "Where does this go, you know, just in case something happens?" My voice stayed low.

"She used to live near a community of shifters and lycans called Old Growth." Her voice lowered to a hushed whisper. "Your mother was born there, but she left when they passed a no hybrid ordinance."

Momma never told me much about her childhood or her side of the family. She descended from the frost giants. *Loki* ... my hand flew to my mouth.

"Well bless my heart," I mumbled. Her brow rose, and I bit the inside of my cheek. I waved her off and asked, "Then why go there?"

"There's another portal there for starters and deep in the forest, miles past their lands is an abandoned campground, with fresh water and access to caves." I nodded; I couldn't argue her logic. We needed food, water, and shelter. Mages conjured some of it, but if this turned long term, it risked draining the mages. "You have two and half Fenrirs with you; they'll not mind us too much, and they do not like the Nine."

"You and you," I pointed to Merric and my sneering aunt. Her silver-blue eyes narrowed as she sauntered past me, but I tilted my chin up.

"She won't dare interfere with Thomas around. He'll find the seax."

Nana gave my shoulder a squeeze, and motioned for Liam to take over before resting in the chair. I leaned in and gave him a peck on the cheek. He didn't smile, and it nipped at my heart. There was so much raw emotion rolling off him that I didn't know if I should cry or kill someone. At least I held solace in knowing I wasn't alone. We were both more confused than that poor chameleon in a bag of Skittles.

"Take him, I don't want you alone."

I cocked my head. Why would I do that? My eyes caught Ezekiel's gaze. I didn't want to be alone with him; I didn't trust myself with him. "How about Nick?" I asked and scanned the room for my friend. "Hey where'd he go?"

Nana asked, "Who's next?"

I peeked my head into the hallway, searching for him or Regin, but saw Wardens approaching instead.

"We can't take them all," Liam said, reading my thoughts.

His arms wrapped around me, and his chin rested upon my head. I gripped my sword, which hung at my side, and took a deep breath. Each echoing step beat in time with my pounding heart.

"Can you increase the portal, mate? We've got company," Ezekiel asked. My body stiffened at the sound of his voice; the realization that his arms were around me, and his chin rested on my head hit me as the words vibrated along my spine. Gods, I'd thought ... my hand flew to my mouth.

"Can we?" Jamie asked; I thought he went through already. Did the Fenrirs go too? He shook his head, and the worry creased over his face.

I whispered, "I won't leave Nick and Regin behind."

Kiel sighed. "Wouldn't dream of it, luv."

My eyes glanced to him and then out into the corridor. I counted one ... two ... five ... twenty. Twenty Wardens and our draugr were both gone. Dang it, I didn't want to kill another soul tonight. Sweat beaded on my forehead as I strode out. Dang, I'd have thought they'd have air conditioning here.

"Teine," I whispered, willing the Myst into my blade as I dragged it free. Liam stepped to my left and disrobed. By the will of the

Gods, I kept my eyes from watching. Husband or not, his body rocked. Kiel came to my right, summoning a sword pulsing with a silver-blue sheen Myst. I blinked even though I'd watched him in my dreams. Heavy boot steps came from behind, and I risked a glance.

Thomas nodded and drew his dual white-fiery blades. "Could use a good battle."

"They'll stay together and act fast. Fend off the Wardens. Give 'em more time." I nodded my head toward the door.

Liam nodded as his jeans hit the floor. His bones crunched, and I grimaced at the sound. "Wait for them to attack luv," Kiel said; I shot him an eye-rolling look as Liam snarled.

"Stop," I said when they were twenty feet away. "Let us pass and I'll spare your lives." They exchanged glances, and the majority turned around, but five remained. "News travels fast," I mumbled under my breath.

"Can we leave with you, Princess?" They bowed, and my cheeks warmed.

Liam growled, and Great-Grandpa grunted. I cringed and said, "Don't call me that."

Kiel snickered. "What do you think, *princess*? Trust them?" I shoved him. Titles meant little when the leader was an immortal elf.

"If y'all are lying, I can tell." They exchanged glances again, and I retracted my shield. "So can the King."

Thomas sheathed his blades and frowned. "Come forward, please, one at a time."

A woman who appeared my age inched forward. Her large brown eyes made my heart smile. I was happy for any light in this suffocating darkness. "Liam read her mind while I process her emotions." He snorted his disapproval. "Do it."

"Please, give us your hands. Time isn't on our side," Thomas said. I smiled, and she extended her shaking hand.

Kiel placed his blade against her neck. "What's your name Warden?"

"Fauna." It suited her; a heart of gold, but her body trembled. I'd tremble too if he held a sword at my neck. She didn't back down though, and courage surged through her veins underneath her fear.

"She's just a kid." I swallowed and embraced her. Every muscle tensed and then relaxed. Her Myst stayed strong and uncorrupted.

Kiel placed his hand on my shoulder and tugged. I released her and stood by his side.

He grasped my hand and kissed the knuckles. By the time we'd finished with the Wardens, few remained back in the cell. Nana and Jamie almost drained themselves, both sweated and appeared extremely faint. I offered to recharge them, but they both had refused.

"You've gotta stop offering yourself up, darlin'," Liam said, palming his neck. "Except to me." He smirked, and I shoved him playfully. His arm snaked around my waist. "We'll figure this out." My eyes stung at the thought of figuring anything out. He wiped the tear as it fell. "You hush now; I'm not going nowhere."

I sniffled and turned to Ezekiel. "You could help too."

He'd all but blended in with the wall. It'd be just as easy for him to recharge Jamie and Nana. My breath blew out in a steady stream, and I pushed my personal crap aside. I didn't have to decide today or even tomorrow. Liam was right. We'd figure this mess out. Until then we all needed to work together.

"Oh, I am." His lips tugged into a grin. My eyes rolled, and I turned my back. "You're still missing two lycans."

My body froze up as the blood rushed from my head. Crap, I'd forgotten. Where were Nick and Regin? Turning around, we came nose to nose. Well, sort of, Kiel had a few inches on me, but not by too much. "What do you know about it?"

His blue eyes narrowed. "I know they're still missing, ducky."

He licked his lip, and I pushed him. "Don't call me that and don't even think about it mister."

"What's going on?" Liam and Jamie said in unison. My Guardian's eyes darted between us, but Kiel crossed his arms, and leaned back against the wall.

"Nick and Reggie are missing," Ezekiel and I said in harmony. Jamie ran for the door, but I blocked it off. I tilted my head and grasped his shoulders. "He'll kill me if anything happened to you."

He shoved me, but I didn't budge. Liam grabbed him and tossed his brother back. My eyes narrowed as the plan formed. "Don't make me cast a spell on your ass."

chapter fourty-eight

LIAM

My knuckles cracked, releasing the weight of her rampaging thoughts. If she thought I'd let her stay behind, she was crazy. I refused to let her sacrifice herself. The Gods entrusted me with her life, and as her Guardian, I would do my damned job.

"I can feel him," Jamie whispered. My eyes closed at his unvoiced comment. Nick was in trouble. With all the voices, I'd not heard his call.

Auriel strolled back from the hallway with the Dísir man. Her face flushed, and her eyes burned. She did not like her new Valkyrie friend, and it would almost be comical, except I didn't like him either. The way he watched Auriel burned my blood and vision red. My eyes narrowed as our eyes met. I didn't like how he talked to her either, with his haughty accent and pet names. A complicated force shifted between us, and she'd felt it too. I loved her, and even though those intense feelings had evaporated, the bond remained.

She was mine. The beast ignored the man. How did love disappear, and what did it all mean? "More important matters, Liam. I love you. Remember that always."

"I'll find them." Morgana offered, but Auriel grasped her hand.

"I will; I can call to him." Her voice shook, and her worries mirrored my own as her forehead wrinkled. If Sköll captured them, there remained the bitter truth; he wanted us all dead. I moved toward the door, but before I made it, Auriel decided for all of us.

"Cuileag." The word had rolled off her tongue before my body tumbled back into the portal, separating me from the only one I'd ever loved.

Despite the trials we faced, I wanted her to find happiness. I didn't even have the opportunity to tell her. Auriel deserved that much. No matter the state of my mind, the beast, or the spells cast, forever united us. Not even the Gods, the Realms, or the Myst separated our souls. Wherever she landed, I'd find Auriel because I was her Guardian.

We spiraled through time and space. I'd read about the Bifrost, but this marked my first trip. My ass landed hard, and my brother tumbled on top of me. Thomas and Mori cursed up a colorful storm.

I blinked and stared at the hallway. No, not at all what I'd expected. "Where's Kiel?" she asked, and I glanced around but did not see him.

Jamie rose; tears filled his fiery eyes. "I still feel him."

His bond survived the portal and crossed the realms. My hand fell to my heart, but there was no pain. Maybe I'd been wrong.

"Watch—" Kiel barreled through an open door and knocked me down.

I shook the stars from my eyes as he mumbled, "Sorry mate that drop's a bleedin' pain in the arse." I scurried to my feet. My hand reached for him and squeezed his shoulder. Mori rushed over, and her eyes darted between us. I'd rather crack the life from his neck, but it wouldn't solve our shared problem.

"Do you sense her?" He blinked, and I shook his shoulder. Kiel's eyes trailed down to my hand, and a smirk tugged on his lips. "Answer me," I growled.

Mori said my name in a warning tone, but I ignored her. "She's well enough." He patted his heart and stepped from my grip. Kiel turned toward Jamie. "Nick and Regin too. I believe we'll see everyone soon."

Thomas asked, "Who are you?"

He spun around and bowed. "Ezekiel Drake, at your service."

CHAPTER
FOURTY-NINE

AURIEL

It sickened my stomach. They'd left me with no other choice, because Liam and Kiel would've stuck around. I forced them into the Bifrost. Two wolves missing and I saw no need to add to the number. The tear ran down my cheek, and I left it alone. "Get it together."

I stared at the walls of the cell. This served as my momma's home for the last six weeks. The stone walls and bars her only comfort. My family imprisoned her like Nana. I touched my heart; they're the monsters. The cell door shut as the familiar tug of grandpa's Myst laced through the corridors. My hand rested on my hilt, and I summoned my shield. Odd that Maeve claimed they all left. My boots skidded and slid over the tile as I followed the trails. Nick didn't answer my calls, and it quickened my steps; I called out for him and Regin too.

I didn't understand it. They'd stayed right behind me, when I found my momma. By the time I came back with the Dísir, he'd left. "Nickolas …"

My steps slowed as I approached an intersection. The place resembled a giant maze, and I followed it by the Myst alone. A howl in the distance froze me as my hand dragged the sword from its sheath.

"What are you waiting for?" Loki whispered in my ear. I forced a breath out of my nose. My hands became sweaty, and the scent of blood curled my nose. A commotion in the distance and a pain-filled howl pierced my eardrums. Voices shouted, and glass crashed. I willed my legs to move faster.

My heart pounded as I slipped into the room. The council chambers, I assumed from the quick glance. The room was too large for a cell, and the wraparound podium held empty chairs.

"Grandma."

"Get back," grandpa shouted as the Oracle faced me. Her eyes pooled into black globes, and she held a silver dagger in her hand. I breathed a sigh, noting the triple moon etched on the blade. She didn't wield my knife, but she'd held onto the one type of weapon that could've killed a Fenrir.

In the opposite corner, three large wolves fought. Sköll had them cornered. The smaller two bled, but Sköll appeared unharmed. Their blood pooled on the marble floor, and deep gashes slashed along their legs.

Together they weren't strong enough to take down their uncle. Both were purebred, but the following generations lacked the ability. Nick's Phoenix gave no advantage either.

"*Eun beag, no.*" His words echoed in my head. It was why they sought Lannie. While not technically blood related to the siblings, their father Porofolr raised her. Rumors said she was responsible for his darkness, but I cared little for gossip.

"No, indeed."

Grandma lunged, but she had moved too slow. I dodged her attack and rushed the wolf. Nick shouted in my head again, but I ignored him. No, I couldn't kill him, but he couldn't kill me either. My family sure as heck wasn't helping, and I'd be damned if Sköll thought I'd just sit there. My hand grasped the coarse furry scruff of the larger animal and tossed him to the side. If he were heavy, then I hadn't felt the weight. I turned and rushed him again, tossing my shoulder into his body.

I roared, "Enough." Sköll sunk to the floor, growling and foaming from the mouth. My hands smoked as I drew in the Myst. I reached toward him, and he snapped. If I touched him and sought his darkness, I might've saved him and the remaining Fenrir clan.

"Behind you," someone shouted, and I twisted just in time to evade my grandmother's dagger. My fist clenched around my sword, and I pulled it from my sheath.

The Oracle summoned a ball of blue Myst and hurled it at my head. I dodged it as my eyes flashed back to the night on the boulder. There lay my proof. My eyes slanted, and I brought the teetering blade to her wrinkled neck. "It was you."

She laughed, and I pressed the blade into her jowls. Grandpa stepped in front of her, and I froze, recalling his help tonight and the words—good and bad. "Don't—" His words cut off as the room filled with Myst, and the lights dimmed under the thick fog. I blinked, my eyes burning from the magic.

"Are you alright?" I asked Nickolas, but he didn't answer. With my blade pointed out, I swung it back and forth and stalked through the haze, willing it to disperse. All three seemed to have disappeared under my grandfather's spell.

The sound of whining led the way. My feet shuffled until I reached a soft object. Dropping down, I pulled the animal's muzzle into my lap and stroked the wet, matted fur. Tears stung my eyes and poured over. If it was Regin or Nick, I didn't know, but neither lycan was replaceable in my heart.

"Should we tell her?" I heard a feminine voice whisper, and a snicker of laughter followed. My hand waved, hoping the Myst would dwindle. When it did, out stepped both my friends. My jaw dropped in disbelief, and I glanced over to my lap, where not a Fenrir lay dying, but a bearskin rug. "Dang it," I said half-laughing and tossed the skin aside. "I'll get you back." I poked Nickolas in the stomach, before throwing my arms around Regin. "And you too missy."

"Aye, lass, but let's leave this miserable place first." His eyes turned toward the door. "Everyone get out? Jamie?"

I nodded and told them about the spell. Nick hugged me, and no explanation applied. Unlike him, I required more time to forgive our dear friend, and it'd take even longer to trust him again. Jamie put too many lives in danger, and while it served a greater purpose, coming into the Nine, we were lucky. One day in the future that luck failed if my dreams were correct. In the future, my friends died … everyone died.

"Y'all will need to explain how you ended up here," I scolded. I allowed the Myst to fill me to the core and drew strength from Freya's spirit. Folkvang remained the safest place for my wounded warriors to recuperate and for me to get the answers I sought.

I grasped their hands in mine. "Drochaid," I said, recalling Nana using the word. My Myst retracted and solidified before my eyes. Unlike her portal, I created a door. The hinges creaked open on their own.

Nick raised an eyebrow, and Regin made a squealing noise. She never cared for magic.

"Lassies first." I snorted, and he opened his mouth. The opening gateway cut off their response. We landed on the Bifrost as a flash of light blinded me. I shielded my eyes and fell back, falling to my rear with a thud. The light dimmed and a golden boar snorted; a large man, with long red hair held the reigns and smiled. My mouth dropped, but words refused to form.

"My apologies, Princess Fainauriel, but your chariot awaits," he said in a thick Norwegian accent. I glanced between him and the beast. He appeared familiar, but it wasn't possible. "Your friends are also most welcome."

"The Faerie King," Nick said in a whisper. He and Regin landed in a similar fashion. "The God Freyr. He's yer kin." My eyes widened, as the God of Light inched the chariot closer and reached out his hand. I stared at it.

Thoughts of Freya's hall and lands deserted me. I wanted to find my family and friends. But most of all my heart ached. And as I closed my eyes, only the darkness of my actions came to mind.

"Where to my child?"

It hit me like a ton of bricks. Lightening cracked through my pounding head. They were wrong. All of them dead as a doornail wrong. My posse and little ole me would save the realms, but I was not Legion. Long before my time the Phoenix spoke of him, when Stonehenge seemingly appeared from nowhere. "It was inevitable," he'd said, and he was righter than rain during a summer drought.

Humans knew his story although Odin painted him as the devil. I destroyed my life to free him, and we'd need each other to right the world. He was Legion – the fallen one. Odin created him to serve the Aesir.

The Myst, Norns—or who knew what connected our souls. I said, "Take me to Legion."

The End

Coming Soon

The Chosen: Imortal Tempests - Summer 2015 (excerpt available after the acknowledgements)

Altered (Beyond the Brothel Walls #2) - Spring 2015

Sign up at www.raezryans.com for news about upcoming titles and other exciting offers.

About the Author

R ae Z. Ryans is a member of the RWA and RWA Fantasy, Futuristic, and Paranormal chapter. She currently resides in Alabama with her family. Published since the age of fourteen, Rae enjoys writing romantic, erotic, fantasy/paranormal stories and poetry. Her name pays homage to her brothers: Specialist Ryan D. Rexon and Zachary U. Berthot.

She is currently working on Beyond the Brothel Walls #2: Altered. This post-apocalyptic paranormal romance is emotionally driven, dark fantasy.

Also available on Amazon and other major retailers,
Constricted: Beyond the Brothel Walls
Chivalry and Malevolence: Alfheim Book One

www.raezryans.com
www.facebook.com/raezryans

Acknowledgements

I would like to thank Aimee Lavalle for her constant critiques and guidance. She's never afraid to tell me when something doesn't work or my point is unclear. This book wouldn't be what it is today without you.

Diayll Sales for her constant nagging that I write and put myself out there. You're my bestie even though we've never met. One day I hope to read my name in one of your books. Put the Xbox down and pick up that pen already!

Bethany we met on Facebook through a game and who would have ever thought we'd click. Sometimes I swear we're twins. Your feedback and guidance has helped in so many ways, and I hope you continue enjoying the stories I write.

Jessi Gibson for throwing awesome release day parties and making me not feel like a total spazz for freaking out. Seriously, she writes some wonderful romance and is an inspiration.

Mark without you my British and Scottish characters would have read flat. Your humor and advice has shaped Ezekiel, Thomas, and Nickolas in this book, and of course Veric in Beyond the Brothel Walls.

Jenny your guidance and superb editing made this dream a reality. I know my crazy words and names might've driven you a little mad, but I kept you on your toes, and you taught me so much. I look forward to more projects in the future.

My family … thank you for putting up with me. Years ago I started on this long journey, and I wouldn't have made it without y'all.

Lastly, I'd like to thank my fans. While these stories are entertainment, I hope you fall in love with my characters as much as I have.

THE

chosen

IMMORTAL TEMPESTS

COMING SUMMER 2015

ChApter
ONe

Immortal Rule Eleven:
You will respect my laws as you would respect your King, your maker, and the realm of Midgard. Those failing to abide by my laws forfeit their afterlife, and with it, the lives of any children they have sired.

Corentin de Hauteville

King of the Draugr
Paris, France

"*Your days are numbered.*" I shoved the note into my jacket pocket and glanced at the human corpse. *Merde.* His face lay contorted and his blood puddled, staining my Persian rug. He arrived naught, but an hour ago, but already I read those four words a thousand times over, and just one conclusion drew: war. I tore it out again, and my fist tightened around it. The paper crumpled, sweaty from my dampening palms. Part of me wanted to destroy it and pretend it did not exist, but the other part heeded that I give the threat my undivided attention. If I died, they all died. Every draugr and I also assumed hybrid draugr too, would crumple to the earth.

"Felix, ready my belongings." My hand rubbed against the rough side of my chin as I awaited my second child to appear. Upkeep for a draugr was simple even if the modern children preferred the term vampire. I was a bit old fashioned. While we altered our appearance and cut our hair, they did not come back once we changed them. After thousands of years, I could not bear to part with my short beard.

There was not much to pack. Long ago, I gave up on material possessions and a public life. As an eternal King, I walked away and sought peace. All of my children enforced my laws, played liaison to the magical world and ran my beloved Alliance of Draugr.

Everything in life was replaceable, everything except me. I smirked in remembrance of my curse. The Myst —my mother- said those words when I attempted to end my miserable existence.

"And the human, sire?" My head leaned against the glass of my penthouse suite. The tug in my gut stood as a warning; things were shifting in the realm of Midgard. Could we keep escaping this? The Council of the Nine's future remained uncertain, torn asunder, and its members scattering to the four winds.

"Dispose of him," I said, raking my shaking hand through my dark hair. My eyes blinked as I caught my reflection. Few survived the maddening chaos of time and those were the strongest of my line. If they knew their fate lay with me, would they become stronger?

I shook my head as it dropped, and pushed my body from the window. My eyes lifted as I gazed out into the city I called home. The tall iron construction, once considered an eyesore, always raised my spirits. The Eiffel Tower, the wonderment and allure were not lost upon me, but I longed for someone to share it with.

"Dame Blanche." *White Ones.* Pieces of me, it desired the heart-thundering heat of battle as if it were 975 again. *Valkyrie, Phoenix, and Guardians. Dísir —the keepers of the Nine Realms.* My lips curled into a wide smile. *Come for me,* I dared them. *Corentin awaited them with the entire draugr race at my disposal.* I chuckled at the thought and glanced back at a solemn Felix. *Come for me fools and witness the hurricane, I shall cause.* "Blood will rain from the skies." Secrets or no secrets, I would unleash Hel itself on the world before I allowed anyone to take me down.

My eyes narrowed as I knelt, studying the human corpse for more clues before I lifted him to the incinerator. It came to me then like a light bulb or flashing beacon. The source vibrated against my skin, burning as it rubbed the surface. *Something came to me.* The heaviness lay in the air, and it smelled of ocean waves.

"How did it come to this?"

I glanced at the corpse again, and Felix joined me. His blue eyes stared out in utter disbelief at my carnage. Blood stained the courier's neck where my fangs punctured his skin. My eyes stung the longer I soaked in his grotesque presence, and I forced myself to look away. Fueled with bitterness and angst, I broke my vows —my laws.

Immortal Rule One: No killing humans unless necessary to maintain the secrets of the Myst.

My jaw set tighter, and I closed my eyes. By nature, I was a killer, but it did not stop me from trying to end that fate. As Loki's bastard son, perhaps it was inevitable I would murder again –laws or not.

"Sire all is ready," Felix said, and I open my eyes as he flicked invisible ebony hairs from his suit jacket. The sound of his nails scratching against the surface sent a chill down my spine. Felix did not smile as often as I liked. He did not need to shadow me as if he were my valet, but he did, and I grew lazy for it. "Except the body. I called in a crew."

I gave a curt nod and stood, rocking on my heels, before rolling up the rug. Felix raised an eyebrow but did not stop me. I needed to do this, and I would find his family and offer restitution. Cold hearted at times, but I owned up to my mistakes.

My eyes gazed out the window again as the rain fell, blanketing the early evening Parisian air with its tears. A reflection of my soul, each drop represented a piece, a year … nay decades and centuries. The fluttering sounds deafened my ears, and my head leaned against the cool glass. Felix's eyes widened as he raced to my side. "Sire?"

A light shined through my darkness and froze me. It spiraled through me as she twirled in the rain. Dark hair plastered against her rouge-kissed skin. The curve of her dainty frame, delicate yet strong, swayed to invisible beats. Her hands reached out to her sides, and her mouth opened wide into a charming smile that took my breath away. In front of my hotel, the woman danced in the rain, and the thought made my lips curl higher. A bark of laughter escaped, and I blinked as the picture disappeared. Visions were not impossible for me, a gift from mother, but they did not intrigue me like this before. Who was the dark haired beauty and where could I find her?

If I held a beating heart, it would thunder for her. Raw ache dragged across my body, settling into my core, and triggering the memory of a chestnut horse, painted in my brother's blood. I shook it away as Felix asked, "Sire shall we depart?"

"No," I said turning around to face him, but not before, I caught my yellowing hazel eyes. Felix stood stoic, dark blue eyes unmoving.

"Very well sire." He did not leave. Not a huge surprise as he tended to shadow my every step. But Felix was not one to overstep his bounds. When he spoke, he made sure it was worth his breath.

My finger tapped on my chin, teeth grinding as I contemplated the message. The dark haired woman pushed through instead. She was naught, but a distraction meant to ebb the flow of my life. Yet I could not step away from the window. My eyes sought for any signs of her.

I laughed and shook my head. "Felix, have my visions ever proven wrong?"

"No sire."

My brows rose. "I had a new one this afternoon." Another chuckle unleashed. "Nothing to say?"

"No sire."

"You are no fun." Felix rolled his eyes, and I smiled inward. "Not so hard is it?"

"Oui," Elise said, entering the living room. "He has no humor, sire."

I sighed and ignored the childish banter I'd started. The streets below crowded and music thrummed from my club next door, pulling me into a trance. My eyes narrowed, as a flutter of dark hair disappeared under the awning. Damn those windows; damn my eyes. The answer was here; the answer was in Paris. The dancing woman was here. The surge over power and magic overwhelmed and burned. I pinched the bridge of my nose and shook my head. *She was the assassin.*

My teeth mashed together as I pressed past a stunned Felix. Fists balling at my sides, I stopped. My hand trembled as it hovered over the doorknob. Humanity would not suffer anymore. The draugr fell with me. If the assassin succeeded, I was unsure if it was a bad thing.

My head tilted ... yes ... no. *I was not ready to die, at least not today.* A smile tugged my lips higher, wider they splayed as the woman's likeness passed through my mind again. My belly ached, bubbling up the maddening laughter as my head tossed from side to side. I turned to face my children; their eyes reddened and rimmed with emotions that begged me to stay. "I take my leave."

"Corentin ... sire—" Elise's eyes darted around, but they wouldn't dare defy my order.

"Elise." Felix warned and took a step toward her. My hand flew up to halt him. He knew good and well that I did not enjoy their sibling rivalries before or after their change.

"This is *my* hotel." My hands spread up and wide. "There are cameras everywhere. Go to the booth if you must." Supernaturals weren't the most honest types. She nodded and swallowed hard, but her eyes hinted the concern she did not dare voice. *Rumor spreads like wildfire.* I chewed my lip and stopped when the tang of blood hit my tongue. My hands delved into my pockets as I took them both in. I had unnerved them, yes, but this note was my burden to bear. If I perished, we all died, but the likelihood of that happening remained slim. I refused to become their hostage. As it was, I had barely a life to live.

"I'll be at the bar." Before they could react, I turned on my heel and left my suite.

Sign up at www.raezryans.com to get more info,

excerpts, and realease dates.

www.ingramcontent.com/pod-product-compliance
Lightning Source LLC
Chambersburg PA
CBHW060219030726
47499CB00004B/1116